For
Mom, Dad, and Bill

"WITTY, HIGHLY INTRICATE BIG-CITY POLICE THRILLER ... KEEPS YOU GUESSING ... HARD TO PUT DOWN."

—*USA Today*

In an atmosphere that crackles with authenticity, from the lofts of Little Italy to the Queens headquarters of a Jamaican drug posse, a web of murder and graft links the Mob, the world of pro basketball, and some of the behind-the-scenes power brokers of New York law enforcement. Manhattan prosecutors Butch Karp and Marlene Ciampi are on the case, working free-lance. Butch goes undercover, playing cat-and-mouse with the killers, using all his mean street smarts and hard-won wisdom in the often perverse ways of the New York City judicial system. And the very pregnant Marlene takes center stage, refusing to let a few labor pains stop her from following some dangerous leads. But a pair of hitmen intend to stop her by doing what they do best. In this exciting, lightning-paced, suspenseful novel, Butch and Marlene show their mettle in the down-and-dirty world of cops and criminals.

MATERIAL WITNESS

"Compelling intrigue, action, and dialogue."
—*Kirkus Reviews*

"Robert K. Tanenbaum knows how to plot and pace, writes dialogue that snaps, creates stories that need to be told.... What more can you ask in a thriller?"

—Jonathan Kellerman

Material Witness

Robert K. Tanenbaum

A SIGNET BOOK

SIGNET
Published by the Penguin Group
Penguin Books USA Inc., 375 Hudson Street,
New York, New York 10014, U.S.A.
Penguin Books Ltd, 27 Wrights Lane,
London W8 5TZ, England
Penguin Books Australia Ltd, Ringwood,
Victoria, Australia
Penguin Books Canada Ltd, 10 Alcorn Avenue,
Toronto, Ontario, Canada M4V 3B2
Penguin Books (N.Z.) Ltd, 182–190 Wairau Road,
Auckland 10, New Zealand

Penguin Books Ltd, Registered Offices:
Harmondsworth, Middlesex, England

Published by Signet, an imprint of Dutton Signet, a division of Penguin Books
USA Inc. Previously published in a Dutton edition

First Signet Printing, August, 1994
10 9 8 7 6 5 4 3 2 1

Copyright © Robert K. Tanenbaum, 1993
All rights reserved

 REGISTERED TRADEMARK—MARCA REGISTRADA

Printed in the United States of America

PUBLISHER'S NOTE
This is a work of fiction. Names, characters, places, and incidents either are the
products of the author's imagination or are used fictitiously, and any resemblance
to actual persons, living or dead, events, or locales is entirely coincidental.

Acknowledgments

To my partner and collaborator, Michael Gruber, whose genius flows throughout this book and who is primarily responsible for this manuscript;

To my basketball coaches in high school and college, Paul Ryan and Rene Herrarias, who painstakingly taught me the fundamentals of the game and gave me the chance to play;

To Detroit Pistons coach Ron Rothstein, who kept me apprised of the realities of the N.B.A.;

To Donald Sterling, who permitted me to practice with the Los Angeles Clippers.

CHAPTER

one

The dying man in the white Cadillac moaned and said a name that the driver didn't catch. He was not in any case interested, although he was mildly surprised that the man was still alive. The driver peered through the swishing wipers, looking for a good place, trying to control his irritability. He thought he was too old to be driving around with corpses; it was something he had done a good deal of in his youth, and he believed that he had more or less put away childish things.

The driver had planned at first to dump the car and the body in a parking lot at Kennedy, or alternatively, to drive down some mean street in south Jamaica and leave it. The problem was that the guy wouldn't die, and the driver had a long-standing objection to shooting people where there was even the slightest chance of a witness. In this way he had survived nearly all of his contemporaries. He was fifty-four, in good shape, and at the top of his profession.

When he saw the small, darkened shopping center looming through the light rain, he made a quick decision, pulling off Jamaica Avenue into the parking lot, signaling carefully as he did so. A second car, an anonymous blue Chevrolet sedan, entered the lot behind him. The Cadillac led the Chevrolet around to the back of the long commercial building. Both cars shut off their engines and their lights.

The driver of the Cadillac switched off the dome light and left the vehicle. He was a medium-sized, stocky man of vaguely Mediterranean appearance, a look accentuated by his deep tan. His most remarkable feature was his mouth, which was large, floppy and bent down, like that of a flounder. In this mouth was clenched the stump of a thick cigar. He wore horn-rimmed glasses and his pepper-and-salt hair was conventionally cut. Against the chill rain he had put on an unfashionable little waterproof tan cap, and as he stood waiting for the other driver to emerge, he hugged a tan raincoat around his body. It was not really adequate for the weather, but he owned no winter clothes anymore. Although he had been raised in New York, all his business interests were now in warm climates, and he intended to keep it that way. He wore old, thin pigskin gloves, as he always did when working, even in a warm climate.

The other man was younger—in his mid-twenties—and shorter, despite the lifts in his small, pointed tan loafers. He wore black gloves and was dressed more suitably than his partner in a thigh-length leather coat. Despite the November cold, however, he had the top two buttons of this coat open, revealing a sprout of dense hair at the V of his patterned silk shirt, amid which nestled a set of heavy gold links. Visible among these were a cross, a St. Christopher medal and a charm in the shape of a hand making a rude gesture with the middle finger, all in gold.

Above this mass of metal was a jowly dark face that bore a thin, down-hooking nose and a sensual, petulant mouth. The eyebrows were heavy and touching each other, and the eyes were small and too close together. It was a face made to sneer.

The younger man approached the Cadillac. "So, Carmine—what're we doin'? Where the fuck is this place?"

The older man said, "He gets off here." He pointed over at the end of the lot, where a big semi-tractor, a red Toyota and an old panel truck were parked, and added, "Go over and make sure nobody's in those."

"What the fuck, Carmine! They're empty. It's fuckin' one in the morning. You think they're making deliveries?"

The older man suppressed a sigh. "Just do it, Joey, huh? Just once, *do* something I ask you to do, without a song and dance, OK?"

Joey muttered something and stalked off across the gleaming asphalt. He glanced cursorily through the front windows of all three vehicles—he had to climb the step on the semi to do so—and then trudged back to the cars.

"Like I said, nothin'."

Carmine nodded. "You thought, but now you know." He gave a last look around the full circle of his vision. It was a good spot for a spot picked at random. The back of the shopping center gave onto a straggling high hedge shielding a cyclone fence, beyond which was the blank rear concrete wall of a tire store. There was no view of the streets on either side.

"OK, let's move him to the driver's side," said Carmine.

Joey was about to complain about this too, but stifled his remark. Guy wanted to be an old lady, let him. The two of them dragged the dying man out of the passenger seat and wrestled him behind the wheel.

Joey was panting from the exertion. "Now can I do him, Carmine?" he asked irritably.

"Yeah, go ahead—no, from the passenger side, not through the window."

Joey grunted, pulled a large automatic pistol out of his waistband and stomped around the front of the Cadillac. He leaned in through the open door and fired two shots into the temple of the man in the driver's seat. The sound echoed off the concrete walls, and the interior of the car lit up like a little stage. Joey put the gun away and slammed the car door.

"I do that right, Carmine? You got any comments on that?"

Carmine looked at his cigar, which had gone out in the light, misty rain, and without further comment entered the Chevrolet. Joey got in and they drove back to Jamaica Avenue and several streets east on it in silence. Then Carmine pulled the car over under a street lamp.

"What now?" asked Joey.

"Map. I want to see what's the quickest way to La Guardia."

He studied the map for a moment, then folded it neatly and put it away in the glove. But as he made his instinctive glance at the rearview mirror, he checked and cursed.

"What?" said Joey.

"Look out the back, Joey. What do you see?"

Joey looked, and saw a semi-tractor pulling out of the parking lot they had just left. "What the fuck! Carmine, I swear to God I looked in the fuckin' truck—it was empty."

"It wasn't empty enough. They got a place behind the cab where the guy sleeps. Did you check that? No, what am I, crazy? Why am I asking?" He gunned the car into a wide U-turn and shot off west in pursuit of the tractor.

"Maybe . . . shit, maybe he didn't see nothin'," said Joey.

Carmine did not consider this comment worthy of reply.

Patrolman William Winofski, of the 105th precinct, cruising his radio motor patrol car down Braddock Road in Queens Village in the calm center of the graveyard shift, was entirely justified in expecting that nothing would trouble his working life. Cops love Queens. The City's largest borough sprawls toward the rising sun from the broken and troubled lands of Brooklyn, a boundless inhabited steppe, until it merges with the uttermost and mysterious East, Long Island. Cops love Queens because it is calm: in its vastness occur each month fewer crimes of violence than take place in a single Harlem or Bedford-Stuyvesant precinct. Cops love Queens so much that they park their families there; more NYPD officers live in Queens than in any other borough. Easy living and easy policing—on the leafy streets of Queens the only gunshot to be heard from one year to the next is from a cop committing discreet suicide in his finished basement. It was, additionally, a Tuesday night, just after Thanksgiving, chilly and raining: good cop weather. Even down south in the 103rd, in Jamaica, Queens's own excuse for a high-crime area, things would be quiet.

That was fine with Winofski. He realized how good he had it compared to others on the Job. The 105th was one of the City's quietest, a long, narrow strip making up most of the border with Nassau County, so far east that nomadic Mongols could often be glimpsed on the horizon. His major worry in life came not from the guns of malefactors but from the current plight of the City itself. It was 197_, and the town was broke.

Winofski had only three years in; he would be one of the first to go if the promised cutbacks actually hit the NYPD. He had already glanced at a post office recruiting bulletin. The benefits were better, and carrying mail would be exciting compared to patrolling the 105th in the wee hours.

Winofski looked at his watch: nearly 4:00 and halfway through his shift. He would cruise through the little shopping mall at Jamaica Avenue near Springfield Boulevard, check the back to insure that nobody was doing any unauthorized Christmas shopping, and then run west on Jamaica to one of the few all-night restaurants supported by the quiet, early-to-bed neighborhoods of the 105th precinct.

The parking lot of the mall was black and shiny and empty of cars. He swung the RMP around the stores to the service area and drove slowly down the narrow alley. As expected, the corrugated iron delivery doors were shut and intact, and the back door to the buildings were at least closed. Everything was as it should be, except for the white Cadillac Coupe de Ville parked in the middle of the service alley. The car registered but dimly on Winofski's mind. He was not anxious to get out in the rain to check it out.

But when he came around the other side of the mall, instead of pulling out onto the avenue, he swung around for another pass, one that brought him closer to the white Caddy. The car was new and clean, glistening in the rain, its windows giving back the gleam of the alley's fire lights. As he passed it, he slowed. Winofski was raw and lazy, but he was still enough of a cop to sense in the fact of a luxury car parked in the back of a deserted parking lot, glowing like a beached whale, that air of indefinable wrongness that the police learn to associate with crime.

He backed up and studied the car for a minute. The

interior was invisible because of the reflections. He took down the license and called it in for a stolen-car check. The car looked intact and undamaged—still, joy-riding teens were the likely cause, at least in this precinct.

The check came back negative. The car was registered to a M. C. Simmons, at a Forest Hills address. Winofski figured some housewife had lost her keys just before the mall closed and hadn't wanted to pay a locksmith overtime. Her car would keep until tomorrow, and if anything went wrong, she had zero deductible.

The rain was heavier now and very cold. Winofski cursed softly and pulled the collar of his black slicker up as he scuttled over to the driver's side of the Cadillac. He snapped on his six-cell flashlight.

The left rear window was punctured and crazed and stained red. There was a human face pressed against the glass of the driver's window. The face was dark, sucking up the beam of the flash, but the single eye that was showing bulged hideously and gleamed like a cue ball in a spotlight. Winofski's heart jumped; he touched his gun and looked inanely about, although there was no one awake within a half mile of him. He then peered more closely at the window, moving the flash around to illuminate different planes of the man's face. Winofski's experience with violence was limited, but he knew what a bullet hole looked like and that a man who had two of them in his head was likely to be a victim of homicide.

Winfoski was not a particularly ambitious policeman, nor did he consider himself clever. As a result, he did not touch the car, or drag the body out, to see if it was really dead, or go through its pockets, or investigate the glove compartment or the trunk. He did, in fact, none of the things that patrolmen occasionally do

when they find dead bodies in cars, but instead—now
in a mild daze—fell back upon his excellent police
academy training and did it by the book. He (1) secured the crime scene. No problem there. And (2) he
called it in. And (3) he waited for the arrival of a sergeant and a homicide detective.

The sergeant was there in eight minutes. The ambulance from the New York Medical Examiner and the
man from Queens Homicide both arrived about five
minutes later. The sergeant was grumpy and appeared
to blame Winofski for getting him out on a night like
this. The man from the M.E. was quick, casual, and ex-
hibited the cheerful and vocal cynicism of his kind.
The homicide detective was old, tired and quiet,
dressed in a gray plastic raincoat buttoned up to the
neck and a shabby tan canvas rain hat. His name was
Harry Bello. Winofski thought he was the oldest serving officer he had ever seen; he looked like Winofski's
grandfather, who was seventy-five. In fact, Bello was
fifty-six, but with a lot of hard miles.

Unlike Winofski, Harry Bello had, of course, seen a
lot of bodies, most of them killed violently. He looked
at the dead face pressed against the window, then at
Winofski, with eyes that seemed to the young patrolman to be only slightly more lively than those of the
victim.

"You touch anything?" he asked.

Winofski said he hadn't. The sergeant agreed. Then
Bello asked what time he had found the car.

"A little before four," answered Winofski. Bello
grunted and turned away. The van for the Crime Scene
Unit arrived, and the crime-scene detectives rolled out
and began taking photos, stringing yellow plastic tape
and looking for clues. One of them was singing "It's
Beginning to Look a Lot Like Christmas."

After checking with the CSUs, the M.E. opened the door of the car, and the man's head and upper body slumped out of the car. The two holes in the man's right temple showed matte black against the shiny brown of the skin, and the exit wound showed the usual soufflé of hair, bone, blood and brain tissue bulging out of the skull like a mushroom. With the head down, this began to ooze and elongate in a manner that brought sour gases into Winofski's young throat.

The M.E. said, "I'm gonna take a chance and pronounce this guy dead at the scene." Then he and his assistant rolled up a gurney with a body bag lying open on it, and began to heave the corpse out of the car. It took a while.

When the body was lying flat on the gurney, Bello stepped forward slowly and looked at it. The man was dressed in a loose suede car coat over a turtleneck jersey that had once been bright yellow, but which was now thick with dark blood. He had dark slacks on and suede loafers. The belt of the car coat hung down almost to the ground. Bello picked it up and tossed it onto the body. It had a dark, oily stain at its end. Bello reached into the corpse's back pocket and drew out a wallet.

"Jesus, he's a big motherfucker," said the M.E.'s assistant. The man was so tall that the body bag would not zip up all the way.

"You think he's with the pros?" the M.E. asked. The others all looked thoughtful. The equation was simple: black man, height of a giant, expensive car.

There was no money in the wallet. It contained, however, several credit cards and a driver's license in the name of Marion Simmons.

"It's Marion Simmons," said Bello in a flat voice.

"No shit!" said the M.E.

"Ay-ay-ay!" said the ambulance assistant.

"Marion Simmons?" said one crime-lab guy, a Lebanese who didn't follow pro basketball.

Winofski, who did, simply gaped at the enormity of it all, and mentally kicked himself for not having recognized the name when he made the stolen-car check.

The other crime-lab guy didn't respond at all, since he was buried in the well of the backseat, where he had just found another ejected case of a 9mm pistol cartridge. There was one on the front seat too. He placed it in a plastic bag and crawled backward out of the car.

When he stood up, the M.E. called out, "Hey, Ernie! You know who this is? It's Marion Simmons."

Ernie said, "Who, the stiff? Jesus!"

All the men paused for a moment in silence, watching the rain bead up on the body bag. With the exception of the Lebanese immigrant crime-scene tech, each had seen Simmons alive, and not just alive, but radiating the fierce energy of the professional athlete in the first flush of youthful prowess. That he was now mere meat shocked even these professionally unshockable men.

Then Bello coughed heavily and asked Ernie for a plastic bag to put the wallet in, and Ernie showed Bello the 9mm cases, and the Lebanese began to dust the interior of the car for prints, and Winofski remembered that he was supposed to call for a tow from the police pound for the Cadillac and walked back to his RMP, and the M.E. said, "Shit, I'm freezing out here. Let's get this thing on ice, Julio."

Bello went back and sat in his car with the door open and lit another cigarette from the butt of one in his mouth. He was trying for cancer, but no luck yet. He thought about taking a hit from the flat pint of CC he kept in the plastic briefcase lying on the seat. But no, he hadn't actually ever drunk at a crime scene yet: before, yes; after, God, yes, but not actually at. That was one rule. Another was, he was not going to bite his gun. He was not going to end up in a body bag with the M.E. cracking jokes by way of a send-off.

Stupid, but there it was. The rules and habits formed over twenty-five years on the Job were rooted deeper than even his despair.

"Hey, Harry, check this out."

It was the crime-scene tech, Ernie, and he was holding up a large plastic bag containing another plastic bag full of white powder.

"It was in the glove," said Ernie. "Must be eight hundred grams."

"Toot?"

"You betcha. Good shit too. Commercial grade. My tongue is still numb. Now we know how he could jump like that. Coupla hits of this and *I* could get fuckin' rebounds off of Kareem. Jesus, what a thing, though! Kid was averaging, what? twenty-five, twenty-seven points a game the last six games, getting triple doubles too. The Hustlers are fucked." Bello was unresponsive; Ernie paused and said, "You a fan?"

Bello shook his head. In fact, he watched a good deal of basketball. It was basketball season, the City was a basketball town, and Bello spent most of his off-duty hours staring at whatever the TV threw up at him, and drinking, until either the station signed off or he did. Necessarily, some of what he watched was New York Hustlers games, so he had seen the thing on the gurney leaping through the air and doing the other skillful contortions characteristic of NBA stars. But he had not envied Simmons his skill as he now envied the athlete's current state.

Ernie saw that he was not going to generate a conversation about the Hustlers' prospects without their star power forward and drifted back to his van. Bello stared out the window for a few minutes. There were half a dozen things he should be doing now: minutely inspecting the car, getting the feel of the scene, making sure the crime-scene guys hadn't missed anything, scanning the neighborhood, insuring the integrity of the chain of evidence. He should have found the shells and the dope. He should be on the horn now, trying to establish what Simmons had been doing during the last evening of his life.

Homicide—at least the kind that cops called a mystery, like this one here—was like an hourglass: the sand started running at the victim's last heartbeat, and after that you had twenty-four hours to figure out whodunit. After that the odds that you would ever find the killer went down precipitously. Bello wasn't jumping on this case because his jumping days were over and because he was fairly sure that it was not going to be his case. Not once the brass found out who the victim was.

He looked up. Winofski was standing there, dripping and looking ill at ease. He said, "Um, they said to hold everything just like it is." Winofski had never been the first officer on a homicide before, and since he had learned about Simmons he had been filled with both apprehension and excitement. People would be buying him beers for the rest of his life on this one. He was worried about Bello, though. The homicide DT was supposed to own the crime scene after the first officer, but this guy didn't look like he owned his raincoat.

"Do you need, like, any help?" Winofski offered.

Bello looked at him. His eyes were like lumps of burnt coal. He shook his head.

Sirens sounded in the distance. Winofski looked startled and became even more nervous when, after a few minutes, they could see flashing red and blue lights as what appeared to be a motorcade swung into the alley. Shortly thereafter, there were three more cars parked at different angles around the crime scene with a large white van from one of the TV stations disgorging cameras and mike booms and a blow-dried reporter.

The suits were out in some force, looking remarkably spiffy for men who had been dragged from bed in the deep of the night to observe the loading of a body bag into an M.E. bus. There were five of them: a preppy blonde from the Deputy Police Commissioner for Public Affairs; the Chief of Patrol, Queens, in full uniform; the Chief Inspector in charge of Queens Homicide; a man from the Queens D.A. named Thelmann, and Detective Lieutenant Brian McKelway, who was Harry Bello's watch commander.

These, with their associated drivers and the TV crew, made a considerable crowd as they wandered around shaking hands with one another and observing the scene, so that the citizens of the City might know, when they saw this scene for eight seconds on the news, that justice was being served, and that the murder of one of the most famous people in the City was not being casually ignored.

They were also there to begin an operation known to members of the NYPD as a slick. In the Vietnam War, a slick was a medical evacuation by helicopter—a rescue. In the NYPD the term had come to mean a gathering of suits at the scene of a politically important crime in order to pre-establish credit and protect against blame. If the murder of Marion Simmons resulted in an arrest and conviction, they would share in the credit. Were they not there at the very beginning, expressing confidence and professionalism before the cold white glare? Exerting leadership right on TV? If the result was failure, surely it was the fault of incompetence in the lower ranks, and one of the main functions of a slick was to choose a fall guy.

As the brass milled around, getting wet and waiting for the TV to set up, Lieutenant McKelway wisely headed straight for Harry Bello, as being the only person likely to know anything. Bello had been only six months on McKelway's watch, and the lieutenant was not pleased that this particular case had fallen, in the luck of the draw, to the man he considered least likely to succeed in solving it.

He led Bello by an arm away from the crowd and the lights.

"What you got, Harry?"

Bello looked at his lieutenant blankly. McKelway was a medium-sized, scowling man with short red hair and freckles. Bello didn't know whether he was impatient and irritable with everyone or just with him, nor did he much care.

"I got a dead basketball player," he responded in a dull voice. "Took two in the head at close range. A nine. We got the casings. And the car's full of dope."

"Dope! Oh, Christ!" said McKelway. He glanced nervously over to where the suits were conversing. McKelway was a hard-charger, twenty-three years younger than Bello, bound and determined to make captain by fifty, and pinched by the fate that had placed him in one of the relatively unmurderous precincts of Queens. This Simmons thing was a case that could get him to Manhattan, where juicy cases dropped from the trees every day, or to Brooklyn. Brooklyn was where Bello had made his own spectacular reputation.

He turned back to the older man, and wondered yet again whether this feeble boozer was really the legendary Bello of Bed-Stuy. McKelway realized that they had parked Bello with him as at a rest home, but he had also thought that the magic of the name might have added some luster to his group. But in this he had been disappointed. Bello did not tell cop stories; he was not free with tricks of the trade; he did not respond to the good-natured jibes that passed for social interaction in the squad room. He was quiet and punctual, but passive as a rib roast and about as useful in a homicide investigation.

Nevertheless, he was the responding officer of record on this mess, and would have to be handled, forthwith.

"Ah, Harry—this case—you're gonna need some help with it, right?"

Bello looked at him noncommittally. He might have been watching a late movie.

"So I thought I'd call in Fence and Morgan to, ah, do the field work and just support the case. We'll get together tomorrow when we're all fresh and decide how to play it, OK?"

Bello nodded.

"OK, good. Now on this mess here—me and the chief inspector'll handle the questions. You just stand by in case we need you. And for chrissake, don't say anything to anybody, especially about the dope."

McKelway walked back to his lords and masters. Bello stood at the edge of the crowd, the rain dripping down his hat, trying to fix in his mind why he didn't just hand in his shield. He remembered. It was to avoid having to spend seven, rather than just two, days a week sitting in front of the TV getting drunk. On nice days he sat in Doris's garden, out back, watching the weeds take over. He wasn't sure he could take it fulltime, not with a gun in the house.

Two more TV vans had arrived, and another couple of cars containing police officers. Bello saw Darryl Fence and his partner, Chick Morgan, get out of their unmarked and confer briefly with McKelway. Fence and Morgan were hot this year. Bello didn't blame McKelway for steering Simmons to them. He had been

a hot detective too, once, him and Sturdevant. He
shook his head violently. A silly thing, but he always
did it when the image from the hallway on Lewis Avenue came into his mind.

It was down to a couple of times a week now. It
would pop into his head, a scene lasting little over a
minute that turned his whole life into shit. The booze
helped. Maybe it would kill enough brain cells after a
while, maybe the very cells that stored the memory: he
didn't know, but he was willing to try.

A sudden actinic glare told that the suits were on
TV. They spoke into the mike booms, poking at their
faces like the greedy mouths of nestling birds. Nobody
asked Bello's opinion. He spoke briefly with the crime-
scene people, collected his evidence, got back into his
car and drove away.

The next day was a regular day off. He stayed drunk
most of the morning. In the late afternoon he made
himself a ham sandwich and staggered out into the
backyard. Wet leaves from the big sycamore lay in
dark piles on what used to be flower beds. In the yard
next to his, he could see through the low chain-link
fence that his neighbor was out wrapping his fig trees
in burlap. All over the City, men of Italian extraction
were doing, or had done, this homely task so that they
could cheat nature and grow figs in a climate hostile to
their cultivation. Bello had a fig tree too, but it wasn't
wrapped.

His neighbor waved to him, and Bello waved weakly
back and then got up and went into the house. The
neighbor was the kind of man who liked to chat across
the fence, and today he didn't want to talk to the guy.
The neighbor was a retired cop, shot in the line of duty.
He had his three-quarter pension, a wife, a large and
noisy family, his fucking fig trees, and . . . What else?
His . . . Bello's mind couldn't formalize the concept

of honor, but the loss of it had strangled his heart. He could think only that his neighbor hadn't let a partner of twenty years get killed in a stinking hallway in Bed-Stuy. Bello sat in front of the TV and watched nothing in particular until he fell asleep.

His next shift was a swing, and he arrived promptly at four at the homicide squad room in the 105th, a building on Hillside Avenue, not far from the Queens County courthouse. There was a note on his desk that McKelway wanted to see him. He knew what it was about. He took out his notebook and sat down at the old Royal and carefully typed out his notes from the Simmons killing. He put them, together with the DD5 situation report, in a case jacket. Bello was a rapid and accurate typist. He could even type drunk. He had typed up all the reports when he and Jimmy Sturdevant . . . he shook his head from side to side like a housewife trying to shake a spider from a rag mop. Then he picked up the large manila envelope that held the evidence bags from the crime scene and went to see McKelway.

He knocked on the door and went in and mutely placed the stuff on the lieutenant's desk. He said, "This is all of it. I don't have the autopsy yet."

McKelway looked surprised. "What's all this?" he asked.

"The stuff on Simmons. I figured you wanted it for Fence and Morgan."

McKelway leaned back in his swivel chair and gave Bello a look that even in his fogged state struck him as very peculiar—appraising, contemptuous, but with a tinge of something close to fear.

"No, Harry," said McKelway slowly. "What I wanted to say was that it's your case. All yours."

CHAPTER

two

Far from Queens that day, on the isle of Manhattan, on the tenth floor of the Criminal Courts Building at 100 Centre Street, Roger Karp, called Butch by his few friends and "that big son of a bitch" by his more numerous enemies, sat at the prosecution table and watched the jury in *People* v. *Dodd* file back into the courtroom and take their seats in the box.

Ramon Dodd, twenty-three, street name "Baggy," was watching too from his seat at the defense table, flanked by his glum Legal Aid Society lawyer. The Legal Aid lawyer was glum because this had been a shitbag trial, which he never would have got into if his client had shown any sense, and taken his advice and pleaded guilty.

Of course, if Ramon Dodd had had any sense, he would also have not shot dead his local drug dealer at six o'clock on a spring evening in front of a street full of people, after a loud and noisy argument. If he had had any sense, then, having done it, he would have ditched his pistol, or at least stashed it with somebody other than his girlfriend.

But Ramon Dodd's life had been but a twenty-two-year prelude to his current state, devoid of sense from its beginning to the present moment. Even now, as his doom approached, he glanced vaguely around the courtroom as if its proceedings had nothing to do with anything he had actually done. He was a typical professional low-level New York street criminal—that is, a mildly retarded black man with a ten-minute attention span and the foresight of a trout.

Asked to decide between (a) a long career of moving heavy objects around for intermittent minimum wage and (b) a brief life on the streets, where he might hold as much as a thousand dollars in cash in his hands (this had happened to him twice), Dodd had had no trouble choosing the latter course. Given the clearance rate for the kind of crimes Dodd was capable of, it was not entirely an irrational decision.

This trial was his eleventh appearance in court on the present indictment, a number not unusual for a New York County felony. The Legal Aid lawyer appointed to his case knew that delay favored the defendant. Witnesses might forget, might die, might get sick of the whole thing and not show up. Evidence might get lost. The prosecution might relent or slip up in some way.

In this case, delay had not worked for the defendant. Karp did not relent and he had not yet made an important slip in twelve years of practice as an assistant D.A. And he wanted Dodd, who had already killed two people that Karp knew about. He had done his first murder at age sixteen, had received a juvi sentence and served four years in kiddie jail. Starting fresh, as the law requires, he had lost no time in killing again, this time his sister's boyfriend. He had copped to manslaughter and served twenty-seven months.

With this as background, Dodd might have been justified in thinking that killing people was but a minor irritant to society. Like most petty criminals in New

York, he had an understanding of the real constraints of the system that would have done credit to a full professor at the John Jay College of Criminal Justice.

The jury trial, for example. Dodd understood that every accused felon was entitled by law to a trial like the one he had just had. But with New York County racking up one hundred thousand felonies a year, this was clearly impossible, and the well-known institution of plea bargaining blossomed forth. It was a kind of ameliorative magic: robbery became larceny; burglary became trespass; attempted murder became simple assault; and murder became manslaughter. The law accepted conviction on a lesser crime than the one that was actually committed in order to avoid a complete breakdown of the system; it preferred corruption to strangulation.

Corruption it was, for what had started as an expedient became a virtue, almost the only virtue. The skills of the trial lawyer, which had been prized above all else in the New York D.A.'s office, had fallen into disuse, while the ability to make convenient deals was praised, not least by Sanford L. Bloom, the district attorney, who was not, and never had been, a trial lawyer.

Still, murder was an exception, even now. Under the laws of New York state, if you were judged guilty of murder you had to serve a minimum of fifteen years in prison. For other crimes you were subject to the max-out rule, which said that you couldn't serve more than two-thirds of your maximum sentence. Thus, if you could beat your murder rap down to manslaughter, and pulled a two-to-ten sentence, you couldn't serve more than about six years, and you might serve a good deal less: a lot better than a sure fifteen plus.

Of course, whether they would let you cop or not depended, oddly enough, on whom you killed. Not all

lives in New York state are worth the same. If the life
you take is a policeman's, or a jailor's in the line of
duty, then it is murder one, and you are in serious trouble indeed. Aside from those privileged lives, murder
in the Empire State is only murder two. If you're looking to cop a first-degree manslaughter plea on murder
two, first try to kill only those close to your own age
and socioeconomic and ethnic background, and second, try to do it as spontaneously as you can manage,
and without endangering others.

Dodd had scored high on the first criterion, since his
victim was a black street criminal, but rather worse on
the second, since he had told at least four individuals
that he was gonna off that motherfucker Bennie D.,
giving approximate time, place and method, and exhibiting the .38 Smith with which he had eventually done
the deed.

Dodd was mildly surprised when they didn't offer
him man one. Because if they didn't let you cop to a
lesser, of course, they had to take you to trial on the
top count of the indictment, and a murder trial took not
only skill and confidence, but also balls, because if you
lost the trial, the defendant would be free. He wouldn't
be shuffling off to Attica even on a reduced charge; instead this guy that you had painted during the trial as
the soul of depravity would be out on the street,
thumbing his nose at you, and the whole world would
know it. But Dodd had not, of course, counted on
Karp.

It was not that Karp had never offered a reduced
plea. It was a necessity. But he was not in the least
afraid of trials. He loved trials.

And, having read over Ramon Dodd's yellow sheet,
he had decided that killing three people in a relatively
short span of time pointed to a social dysfunction so
severe as to require at least fifteen years of the sort of

kind and usual punishment they dish out in the state penitentiary. So Karp had offered nothing but a guilty plea to the top count, murder two. Dodd had refused, and so here they all were.

The jury was seated now, and the clerk of the court asked the foreman if the jury had come to a verdict. The foreman, an erect elderly gent, stood and answered that it had.

"On the charge of murder in the second degree, how do you find: guilty or not guilty?" asked the clerk.

Karp's stomach tightened involuntarily. A thousand hours of work and six months were about to be distilled into a single word. He looked over at Dodd, who was licking his lips nervously. Perhaps he was now thinking that he should have taken the plea. If he was actually convicted, he had nothing to go on, no other angle to play. He would have to *pay for his crime,* not something that had previously been an issue to him.

The foreman cleared his throat and said, "Guilty." The courtroom murmured in that special way that courtrooms do when a verdict is announced and which, if you are a lawyer on the right side of a verdict, is sweeter than the impassioned cheering of thousands. The jury was polled. They all said "guilty" too. The judge set a date for sentencing, thanked the jury, uttered a short homily to the effect that crime did not pay, and banged his gavel.

Men came to take Ramon Dodd away. If he survived his time in prison, when he next breathed free air he would be considerably older than Karp was now.

Karp did not watch Ramon Dodd's translation from person into statistic. He gathered up his notes and transcripts into the manila folders where they belonged and shoved them into the hinged cardboard box—the literal "case"—in which he kept all his personal file records for each trial.

Then he rose from the table. Karp was a very tall, well-built man, in height a little over six feet five inches, and rangy, with broad shoulders, long arms and extremely large, bony hands. The features of his face were large too. The nose was broad and long, and had been broken and reset with a bump in it. The mouth was wide with a hint of sensuality. Under a heavy, bony brow, above high cheekbones, sat the most remarkable feature of Karp's face, his odd, slanted gray eyes. Narrow but at the same time extraordinarily wide, they had small yellow flecks in them: the eyes of a not entirely domesticated animal.

Karp moved up the aisle of the courtroom with his characteristic lope, the loose-limbed stride of a natural athlete. Which he was.

As he walked through the hallways of the Criminal Courts Building, he received in passing the accolades of other assistant district attorneys—respectful and nearly awestruck in the case of the younger ones, flippant from friends, envious or grudging from others.

Karp had some good friends among the other A.D.A.s, but he was not generally a well-liked man. He combined impatience and an almost brutal frankness with very high standards of performance, never the foundation for settled popularity. And those who came to the New York D.A.'s office with strong ambitions quickly found out that being nice to Karp was not the way to the heart of District Attorney Bloom. Rather the opposite, in fact.

Karp entered his office, on the sixth floor of the building. He was at this time the bureau chief of the Criminal Courts Bureau, which was responsible for misdemeanors and a mixed set of the less egregious felonies. Within this homely operation Karp, remarkably, ran what amounted to a homicide bureau.

There had once been a genuine homicide bureau,

founded by Bloom's predecessor, the legendary D.A.
Francis P. Garrahy, and staffed with the best prosecutors in the world, of whom Karp had briefly been one.
But the bureau had been dissolved. Murder, the reason-
ing went, was just another felony, and there already
was a Felony Bureau.

But Karp understood that murder was different, and
through a series of manipulations and pressures, playing subtly on Bloom's enmity (for Bloom could not
imagine that anyone could actually relish the political
danger inherent in a major trial for murder, and lived
for the day when Karp would ruin himself), he had arranged things so that he and a group of lawyers that he
would supervise and train would be responsible for a
substantial number of murder trials.

Karp waved to Connie Trask, the bureau secretary,
seated at her big desk in the center of the bureau's
outer office, and received a gold-rimmed toothy smile
in return.

"The good guys win again," she said.

"Every time, lady, every time," replied Karp.

"Don't forget four o'clock for you-know-what," said
Trask.

"You-know . . . ? Oh, yeah. Christ, I almost forgot!"

"Your ass if you did, boss," said Trask caustically,
"and *he* wants to see you at a quarter to five."

The male pronoun used with the particular inflection
Trask put on it, and in the present context, could have
referred to only one person, the district attorney.

"What does he want now?" asked Karp sulkily.

"Probably wants to congratulate you and give you a
raise," said Trask, in a tone so slyly parodistic of a
brown-nosing employee that Karp laughed aloud.

Trask was a treasure, a handsome black grandmother
in her late forties, a representative of the class of minor
civil servants, often women, without whom grass

would grow in the streets of the cities of the Western World. She forgot nothing and took shit from no one, and ran the administrative end of the bureau with such merciless skill that Karp had enough time to do trials—not a typical occupation for the average bureau chief.

Still smiling, Karp walked through the outer office and into his private one. He hung up the coat of his blue pin-stripe, picked up the case file for *Dodd* and walked over to the row of five glass-front bookcases lined up along one wall. In these Karp kept a personal file for the murder cases he had handled. Each had four shelves and each shelf held just five case files. Karp slipped Dodd into the last remaining slot on the top shelf of the last bookcase. He would have to write a note to Connie to order him another one. There was plenty of room along the long wall under the window.

He sat down behind his desk and considered the rows of cases. A simple multiplication popped into his mind, and he realized with a faint shock that he had just finished his hundredth murder case. And, although he did not think of it at the time, every one of them had been a conviction.

A couple of hours later the outer office of the Criminal Courts Bureau was packed with people giggling and trying to be quiet under the continual shushing of Connie Trask. The ceiling of the office was decorated with balloons and crepe paper, and a long folding table had been covered with a cloth and drinks and snack food.

Karp felt the first stirrings of the unease that the prospect of a party always brought on. He did not like either the taste of alcohol or its famous effects on the brain, which in his case were instantaneous and devastating. Nor did he enjoy the familiarity that drink engendered in others. But, although he would not go out of his way to attend one, in the course of his management of the bureau many parties had been placed in his way. There was some sort of celebration nearly every week: a birthday, an anniversary, a holiday.

The secretaries and clerks seemed to think that the last few hours of the day, especially on, as now, a Friday, were not strictly the Empire State's to dispose of. In this Karp meekly deferred to Connie Trask's opinion that since much of what they did was bureaucratic make-work in any case, the diversion of work time for partying was more than made up by improvements in morale. And it was true that he had no cause to complain of the office staff on those occasions when heroic effort was required.

Karp's role in this particular party was special, as he was by way of being the author of the feast. The party was in honor of the (temporary) departure of Marlene Ciampi, an A.D.A. who had become Karp's wife that past summer and was now spectacularly pregnant. Karp and Marlene had, of course, cohabited for many months before the wedding, an open secret from one end of Centre Street to the other, and the baby was both unplanned (the result of a statistically improbable failure of a birth-control apparatus) and most welcome.

"Here she is—shussh!" said someone in a stage whisper. The door opened and in stepped Marlene Ciampi. "Surprise!" shouted the company, and Marlene, who was no more surprised than the Democratic party is when it elects a mayor of New York, mimed the most profound astonishment, as was expected.

As always, Karp's spirits lifted at the sight of her; he was besotted by love as he could never be by alcohol. In late pregnancy she radiated a glow that could be felt across the room, and her marvelous tawny skin seemed to shine. She wore a maxi-skirt of a shimmering gray material and a white maternity blouse under which she seemed to be concealing a basketball.

Karp did not have much experience of pregnancy, having been the youngest of three brothers in a particularly isolated family, but he had been amazed at the matter-of-fact way in which his pregnant bride had dealt with this momentous change. It had something to do with her own position as the middle child in a family of six, and that family but one of a vast interrelated tribe of Italians, several of whom were bearing children at any one time.

Marlene, after some initial and typical sickness—which she, confounded by her clever but treacherous IUD—had not even recognized as being what it was, had not flagged an instant at work. She was, in fact, more energetic than usual, since she had taken up the task of establishing a new, though tiny, bureau devoted to the prosecution of rape and other crimes of sexual violence, which had become her chief interest.

He waved to her and she circulated through the crowd until she was smiling up at him.

"Drunk again, I see," said Marlene.

Karp swished his plastic cup, which contained an inch of white wine and the rest 7-Up.

"I can't keep away from it since you corrupted me."

"Yes, and unlucky me, I've lost my taste for it, just when I need it to drown the boredom. Tab for another month. I'm getting hog fat anyway."

Marlene was, in fact, thinner than when Karp had first met her, four years ago. Then she had possessed the spectacular beauty of a magazine model: finely sculpted cheekbones, a firm little chin, a straight, long nose with a charming dip, and a broad, high forehead, all dressed in that miraculous skin. Her eyes were glossy black and heavily lashed.

Karp had by now grown used to the odd way she

held her head when in close conversation, cocked to the right so that a wing of thick, shiny black hair fell over the right side of her face. Her right eye was glass. She was also missing most of the two smallest fingers from her left hand, both losses the result of having been blown up by a bomb meant for Karp himself. The scarring had been repaired by surgery of colossal expense, worth every penny in Karp's opinion, but she would never again possess the flawless beauty that she had once had. Instead there was something that Karp found even more breathtaking, a spare and almost feral loveliness, like a falcon's.

"Nice crowd," said Karp.

"Yes, I'm popular," said Marlene. "It's my deodorant. I heard Raney and Balducci are supposed to show up."

"You heard? It was supposed to be a surprise."

"Hey, am I a trained investigator or what?" she replied, and then looked long at the throng. "I'm going to miss this place," she said sadly. "Just when things were really rolling."

"You'll be back. Luisa will watch your little empire."

Luisa Beckett was a tiny dynamo of a criminal prosecutor who had been recruited from the Brooklyn D.A. to second Marlene in the new sex-crimes unit. "Yeah, the Bureau-ette will be fine. What bothers me is the kid. Six weeks off and then I leave her with some Guatemalan. I know, I know, we've been over this, but it still sucks."

"What, you're afraid when he's twenty-one, he'll say, 'Mom, I don't want to go to college. I'd like to pick coffee'?"

"Very funny, but one-liners are not what she's looking for," said Marlene with a flash of irritation. "Sympathy and sincere concern is the ticket."

"Sorry," said Karp automatically, and assumed the distracted blank look he wore when he was about to be lectured.

Marlene caught it and changed the subject. "By the way, congrats on Dodd, my hero."

"Yeah, yet another dumb, skinny black kid in the can," said Karp, bitterness touching his voice. "The grinder turns again."

"They're not all like that."

"No, but most. Speaking of which, I figured out today that Dodd was my one-hundredth win. How do you like that?"

"It's only what I expect," said Marlene complacently. "Why do you think I sucked the genes out of your young body? Shouldn't we celebrate?"

"Yeah, we could throw a party in the Tombs," said Karp.

"Good idea. What do you want for a present?"

"I don't know," said Karp. "There should be a list of the appropriate gifts for each round number, like for wedding anniversaries." Karp mimicked the plummy voice of an etiquette mistress: "Fifty is the vase of sewage sludge. Seventy-five, a selection of matched dog turds, and finally, one hundred, the most discriminating go for used Kleenex."

"Hey, Butch, you hear about Simmons?" said a voice behind them.

Karp turned to regard a squat man of about forty-odd, wearing the opened vest of a three-piece suit and a smudgy white-on-white shirt with its tie yanked down four inches. His face had the wise, monkeyish ugliness of the revered Yogi Berra, whom he resembled in physiognomy, in ancestry, and, to an unfortunately much lesser extent, in baseball talent. He was an A.D.A. and his name was Raymond Guma.

"Yeah, I caught it on the news, Goom," replied Karp. "Hell of a thing."

"A guy I know in Queens says it was a drug hit," said Guma. "His car was full of it."

"A drug hit? Simmons was pushing drugs? What, steroids?"

"No, toot. A ton of prime flake, apparently."

Karp gave him a disbelieving look. "Goom, the guy makes—made—a million and a half bucks a year. He'd have to work full-time selling dope out of his car to clear that much. And who is he selling to? The fans? Kids in schoolyards? The guy was six-ten, for crissakes."

Guma shrugged. "Hey, it's Queens anyway. What the fuck do they know? Meanwhile, the Hustlers are gonna be dead without him."

"There's other guys on the team," said Karp.

"Yeah, but they can't fly like Marion," said Guma.

"Who can't fly?"

This question was asked by Roland Hrcany, as he came up behind them, beer in hand. Hrcany was taller than Guma, but looked even less like a typical lawyer. His fine white blond hair was neck-length, and his body was almost grotesquely overdeveloped. His pale eyes and square-cut lumpy face was rescued from an appearance of brutality only by his engaging, if bad-toothed, smile. He was a ferociously aggressive prosecuting attorney and looked it.

"Simmons could fly," said Karp. "We were speculating on the Hustlers' chances without him."

"Yeah, hell of a thing," said Hrcany. "I figure they'll move James into power forward."

Guma said, "James is no Simmons, one, besides which he's hurt. If they were smart, they'd convert Blanding from a center to a power forward . . ."

"Blanding can't shoot for shit," Hrcany retorted.

"He doesn't have to *shoot,* Roland," said Guma impatiently. "What he has to do is catch the fuckin' basketball and *put* it in the basket. He's seven fuckin' one, for chrissake!"

"That ain't the game, Guma," began Hrcany, at which point Marlene said, "Uh, guys, excuse me, sports talk generates the deadly rays of boredom which are dangerous for the development of the foetal brain."

"Marlene, what the hell," said Guma. "If it's a chick it won't matter, and if it's a guy, Karp'll teach it to shoot hoops and it still won't matter."

Marlene gave him the finger in a friendly way and scooted, to the extent that she could still scoot, into the crowd.

The three men talked about the Hustlers and about basketball in general, the kind of impassioned and knowledgeable talk that constitutes ninety percent of the off-job conversation of the majority of American men. Karp was conscious, as he always was, of the deference they paid to his opinions. This was not because he was their boss, but because he had been at one time one of the best high school basketball players in the country, two years high school All-American with his picture in *Sports Illustrated,* on three all-state teams, the state championship, full scholarship to Cal, where he had burned up the PAC-10 in his sophomore year.

Then, in the second game of his junior year he had been submarined under the boards. There was a massive pile-up and a 250-pound forward had dropped his full weight across Karp's left knee as he was struggling to rise. Everything had torn loose, and Butch Karp had instantly become one of the might-have-beens that litter the back alleys of big-time basketball.

Through a monumental act of will, Karp had refocused his competitive energy on the law. An indifferent student in high school, he had applied himself in college and later in law school and had won himself a place in what had then been the best prosecutorial staff in the nation.

But his injury created a kind of pain that was not merely physical. (The literal injury now represented little more than a twinge in cold weather and the need to watch himself during exercise.) For most of his young life, the jock world had supported and encouraged him, sheltering him from loneliness.

But as soon as it became clear that he would not be able to play during his college years, that world had dropped him without a thought. His coach at Cal, a surrogate father, who had invited Karp to his home, who had listened to his problems and shared his confidences, became a stranger. The friends, the girls, the hangers-on, vanished as well.

Karp had been devastated. Lost and miserable, he had drifted into his hasty first marriage. Recovering, he had discovered in the heady competition of the courtroom some of what sports at the highest level had once supplied, and enough camaraderie from similar men. There were an unusual number of almost-great athletes in the New York D.A.'s office. Guma had been good enough for tryouts with the Yankees. Hrcany had won letters in both wrestling and football.

Yet in his heart, Karp believed he was different, that had it not been for the accident he could have gone all the way, and become another Bill Bradley or Pete Maravich.

"I know Nadleman," Karp said. The conversation had come around to the Hustlers' coach.

"Yeah?" said Guma.

"Uh-huh. Not well. He was playing his last year for UCLA when I started with Cal. I played against him a couple times."

"No kidding! Any good?"

"He was all right. An OK college point guard. Not that athletic."

"No you, you mean," said Hrcany.

Karp smiled tightly and shrugged. He never talked about his life in basketball. He never wanted to hear coming out of his mouth the pathetic reminiscences of a has-been. This was unusual, he knew. Everybody in the Criminal Courts Building had heard about Guma's afternoon with the Yankees and how he had talked with Phil Rizzuto and Mantle.

But Karp had cut basketball out of his life with a thoroughness that amazed his friends. Karp knew it was mere petulance, a childish attempt at revenge on the sport: if he couldn't play in the big time, he wasn't going to participate at all, not as a fan, not as an amateur player or coach, not even—beyond the dictates of cordiality—as a water-cooler guru. When he saw basketball on TV by accident, or passed a playground with a lively game, the pain was undeniable; that it was also ridiculous did not make it less so.

Several other men had joined the conversation about the Hustlers and basketball, and Karp was able to slip away. He went over to Marlene.

"I got to go," he said. "Bloom called a meeting at a quarter to five."

"On a Friday?" said Marlene in tones of outrage.

"He's a busy man," said Karp, who, though he deferred to no man in his contempt for the exiguous Bloom, had lately come to believe that a perfect and chill correctness was the only appropriate response. This he did not in any hope that Bloom would reciprocate, but because he had always felt a vague uneasiness at participating in the casual and profane deprecation of the D.A. that took place in his bureau. The man was, after all, the district attorney, and Karp was in his chain of command.

He kissed Marlene good-bye and assured her that he would see to her cartons of personal gear. Then he left and took the elevator to the twelfth floor.

As he ascended, he prepared himself by assiduously thinking good of Bloom. The man was undoubtedly a fine politician. He knew every source of power in the state and was well in with nearly all of them, from the unions to the governor's staff. He was a shrewd conniver for budgets, and in this he compared favorably with the late Francis Garrahy. Garrahy had believed that working for the New York D.A.'s office was in itself so great an honor as to render any other reward superfluous. Thus his minions had labored (and happily, for the most part) in cramped, dirty quarters at derisory rates of pay.

This situation Bloom had improved, as he had the office's record keeping and other details of administration, for he was at heart an administrator, as Garrahy had at heart been a prosecuting attorney. He was also skilled in public relations, so that the office had kept much of the reputation (if not the abilities) it had built up in the Garrahy years. That was all Karp could think of by the time the elevator stopped.

Karp emerged in the D.A.'s reception area, which was decorated in corporate modern: teak furniture, upholstered in shades of leather, a patterned gray carpet, abstract paintings, and a young and lovely receptionist who took his name and told him to sit. Although it was the stroke of the appointed time, Karp knew he was in for a wait at least of fifteen minutes. He read the new *Sports Illustrated.* Another plus: Bloom kept all his office magazines up to date.

Called in at last to Bloom's office, Karp was surprised to see another man seated in one of Bloom's maroon leather side chairs. Karp recognized him as Kevin McHugh, the director of Bloom's public affairs office.

Karp was gestured into another chair, and Bloom gave him one of his patent toothy false smiles and took up some minutes with jocose small talk. Bloom had the perfect teeth and the perfect, slightly tanned skin of the extremely wealthy. He had large, moist muddy eyes, a full mouth and a thin, prominent nose. His hair was light brown and carefully razor-cut. He was near fifty but looked younger, like the anchorman on a suburban TV station.

"So this is Mrs. Karp's last day on the job," said Bloom. "I trust her unit won't suffer from it."

After taking a brief moment to figure out who "Mrs. Karp" was, Karp said, "Luisa Beckett's in charge while Ms. Ciampi's out."

"That little colored girl?"

"She's a fine attorney," Karp said flatly, amusing himself by imagining what the feminist typhoon that was Luisa Beckett would have done at hearing herself so described.

Bloom grunted noncommittally and said, "I've asked Kevin to sit in here because I'm concerned with this damned Chelsea Ripper case."

Karp glanced over at McHugh, a slight, genial man with a fringe of reddish hair decorating either side of a bald head. He wore thick tortoiseshell glasses and an owlish expression.

"The Phelps case," said Karp. "But public affairs . . . ?"

"Yes," said Bloom. "It's a big case. There's national press involved. The whole thing has to be very carefully managed. And on top of that . . . Kevin, you tell him."

McHugh said, "The *New York Times Magazine* is

doing a cover story on the office. We've been trying for this for months, and they finally rolled."

Karp slipped into the usual pose of polite incomprehension he affected when publicity was the issue. "I don't understand. What does that have to do with the Phelps case?"

Bloom looked at him in disbelieving pity. "What does it have to do ... ? Christ, Butch, I said *national* press. We have to put this bastard away. What I want to know is, are we going to?"

Karp said, "Well, I could get my files up here if you want to discuss the legal situation in detail."

"No, no, we don't need the details," said Bloom impatiently. "Just the payoff. We got to try this case and win it. Now, what I'm concerned with is this insanity business, the what-d'y-call-it—"

"The competency hearing," Karp said helpfully.

"Yeah, the competency hearing. Are we going to have trouble with that?"

"Well, that's up to the docs in Bellevue. If they declare him fit to stand trial, he will. If not, there's not much we can do about it. It's not like we think he's malingering."

"What do you mean?" asked Bloom.

"I mean he may well be a genuine nut. Look, the guy broke into three apartments that we know about and murdered and mutilated four women. He kept souvenirs too, which was how they caught him. The smell, I mean. So there's no question about guilt right now, but only whether he's capable of assisting at his own trial. Then, at trial, he could also plead insanity, and then the docs can argue about whether he knew what he did when he did it and that it was wrong."

Bloom looked at him peculiarly and smiled. "There's no way we could, say, sway their opinion? Or overturn it?"

Karp looked at him blankly. Bloom knew that Karp had, in fact, once overturned an insanity determination by a Bellevue panel, although in that case the doctor had fudged procedure and lied about it under oath, and in that case the defendant had been a cold-blooded killer who knew exactly what he was doing and didn't care that it was wrong.

"Maybe we should wait for the competency decision before we think about that," said Karp in as equable a fashion as he could manage.

Bloom stared at him, as if expecting some further reaction, and then said, "Yes. Well. I'm sure it will work out. I'm counting on you, Butch." This with another flash of teeth.

"Thank you," said Karp. "Is that it?"

Bloom signaled that it was indeed it by turning away and talking to McHugh about another subject. Karp got up and left, his leaving unremarked.

"What a pain in the ass!" exclaimed the younger of Marion Simmons's two murderers as the two men watched the second day of television coverage of their handiwork. They were sitting in one bedroom of a small two-bedroom furnished apartment in Manhattan, Joey lying in bed and Carmine occupying a vinyl armchair. "Shit, that blow must've been worth fifty large, maybe seventy-five. And it was right there. Fuck!"

Carmine looked at his companion bleakly. It had been too much to hope that Joey would see what a blessing the discovery of the drug cache had been for the two of them. "Joey, it's the best thing that could've happened."

"What're you talkin' about?" said Joey, his exiguous forehead knotted in puzzlement.

"They found dope, which means they're gonna be looking at that angle—the cops, I mean. That means they'll stay out of our business, which is good because, like this situation here is unusual because, when you whack somebody, the smart thing is to clear out of town, which we can't do, because of that little problem we got."

"What, the truck driver? So we whack him too; so what?"

"No, listen to me, Joey. Try to think it through. Whacking a guy is not just you go up and stick a piece in his face and bang-bang. Not if you want to keep healthy." He saw the boredom creeping into the other man's face, but persevered. He had been told to show the kid the ropes, and he had never done less than his best at anything. "It's like craftsmanship, Joey. There's a right way and a wrong way. OK, we seen the wrong way, the last couple things we did. Now we're gonna try the right way, which is we think it all through *before* we do the guy. Now, we checked the guy out— what do we know about him?"

"What's to know? He's an asshole, drives a truck."

"Yeah, right, Joey. He works for Korvette's out of a yard in Jamaica. He goes to a warehouse in Jersey City, picks up a trailer of appliances, TVs, and drops them off at different stores in the city and out on the island. Then he takes his tractor back to Jamaica, gets in his car and goes home to Hempstead. Anything pop up at you?"

"Yeah, you wanna write his life story before we hit him," said Joey in a tone of affected weariness.

"No, Joey," said Carmine patiently, "I mean what's he doing in an alley in Queens in the middle of the night?"

"Sleeping? Jerking off? The fuck I know!"

Carmine ignored this and continued, "OK, there's also a red Toyota and a panel truck in the lot. So I check, and the truck belongs to a plumbing supply in the shopping center, but nobody heard of the Toyota there. So the story is . . . hey, you following me, here?"

Joey had turned back to the TV, where a more interesting story was obviously being played out. Carmine walked over and snapped the TV off. Joey stared up at him in sullen irritation.

"The story, Joey, is that he had somebody in the back of the truck with him."

"He did? Like a chick, you mean?"

Carmine forced an encouraging smile. "Yeah! Very good. He was meeting a girlfriend. She drove her little red car there and they went into the back. So that means the girlfriend saw it all too."

Joey brightened. "So we gotta whack out the honey."

"Yeah, but first we gotta find out who she is, which means we got to have a talk with what's-his-name, Stanley Malinski. OK, let's talk about the setup. The first thing is, you got to boost a car . . ."

Carmine kept talking for some time, the details of how they were going to lift and question and kill the truck driver, and more boring crap about protecting the deal and how they couldn't use any local talent because nobody was supposed to learn that they were even in town before the deal was ready to go. Joey listened with half an ear. Whacking out a chick was what his mind was on, and the fringe benefits that would accrue to him personally when that went down.

CHAPTER

three

The good thing about dying in Queens is that it's a short drive to the cemetery. The borough boasts necropolises rivaling those of Thebes in population, if not sculptural grandeur, and has long been the ultimate destination for New Yorkers, many of whom, having sworn throughout life that they would not be caught dead there, eventually are.

The funeral of Marion Simmons, three days after the murder, was well attended, perhaps three hundred people in all, in a cortege of over a hundred vehicles, moving across Queens from a church in Jamaica to the cemetery in Woodside. The day obliged by coming on dark and chill, with a thin, intermittent rain.

There were any number of sporting celebrities at the graveside: the entire Hustlers team was there, gigantic and somber, like a grove of rain-washed poplars, and the other NBA teams had all sent representatives. There were families and friends beneath dripping umbrellas, a group of the merely curious, and an assortment of funeral buffs and sports fans and politicians. The press was out in force: on the access road overlooking the gravesite three TV vans were parked, and long-snouted cameras probed for the most affecting three-second spot.

Leading the mourners, flanked by Simmons's mother and sister, was Bernie Nadleman, the Hustlers' coach, a tall, thin, pleasantly horse-faced man, looking grim and drawn. Behind the coach walked a shorter, stouter man in his late fifties, in a fedora and black cashmere coat, whose lugubrious expression could not entirely hide his air of pugnacious self-importance. This was Howard Chaney, the owner of the Hustlers, whose major investment, boxed in mahogany, they were now preparing to lower beneath the earth.

The police were represented too, but more lightly than might have been expected for a murder of such magnitude. Besides the security detail, the photographers, and a few suits from Police Plaza, there was only one detective present, and he was drunk.

Harry Bello, in his tacky plastic raincoat and tan cap, swayed gently among the mourners. Just this once he had broken his resolve never to get loaded before going on the job. It was because of the cemetery. It reminded him of what had happened in the hallway on Lewis Avenue. And what had happened to his wife. Impossible to endure anywhere near straight up.

Still, he was there because the detectives in charge are supposed to attend the funerals of murder victims, and Bello was willing to at least go through the motions. There was always the chance that the murderer would come screaming through the crowd and throw himself or herself on the coffin in a paroxysm of remorse, or that the detective present would spot someone in the throng—someone, say, covered in dried blood, grinning and rubbing their hands in glee as the corpse was planted.

Bello's dull eyes roved over the crowd, less from interest than from habit. They settled naturally on the intimate group around the actual grave: the mother, the sister, the coach, the team owner. Dimly he recalled seeing Chaney on television, angrily denying that Simmons had ever used dope. He had sounded as if he believed it. Bello wondered who had leaked the story. It could have been anybody from the police commissioner on down to the crime-lab technicians, for which reason every good detective kept a little bit of evidence private.

When Bello had been a good detective, when he had been with Jim Sturdevant, he had done the same. He shook himself to chase the memory away, but try as he might, he could not scrape from his mind the instincts and experience of over twenty years. There was something wrong with the group around the grave. Simmons had been unmarried, but there should have been a weeping young woman in the crowd. There was always a girlfriend. It was inconceivable that a man as attractive and wealthy as Marion Simmons had no romantic interest. That was one thing missing.

And there was something else. Bello had read the autopsy report. The two bullets to the brain were the immediate cause of death, but Simmons had been shot a third time. The pathologist had found another bullet wound in the chest—a mortal wound, although Simmons had remained alive until the shots to the head finally killed him. The third bullet had passed completely through Simmons's body, and the evidence of clotting suggested that the shot to the chest had been fired more than an hour before the victim had died.

Bello stumbled back to his car. He had done his duty. There were no obvious murderers at the scene. He had no real hope of solving this one. The three days since the killing might as well have been three years. Nor did he really care.

He drove home to his tree-lined street in Corona,

kicked irritably at the wet leaves clogging his unraked walk, and worked for the rest of the day on improving his drunk. It took a good deal of drinking to make him forget, for a while, that although Simmons had been shot three times, only two shell cases had been found in the car.

Karp came awake all at once on the Saturday after the party, stiff and sweating, and with an oppressive feeling of having mislaid something important. It was a few minutes past five and still quite dark. He rolled over, closer to the heat of his wife, and sought sleep again, but failed.

He got out of bed, threw off the faded sweatshirt in which he slept and walked naked down the ladder that led to the sleeping platform. Karp and Marlene lived in a single room on Crosby Street in lower Manhattan, a room that was thirty-three feet wide and a hundred feet long. It was divided at odd intervals by partitions anchored on one wall and extending two-thirds of the way into the room, so that the loft was like a series of stage sets. Every surface was painted white, and the furnishings were a combination of junk-shop bohemia and the castoffs of a respectable Italian household, melded amusingly by Marlene's lively imagination.

Karp stopped by the tiny closet that had served the employees of the former tenant (an electroplating concern) as a toilet, and then trudged down the length of the loft. He passed the kitchen and dining zone, the bathroom (containing the bathing pool that Marlene had converted from a huge rubber electroplating tank), the parlor zone, with its Tiffany lamp hanging under the skylight and its battered red velvet whorehouse sofa, and came at last to the gym.

This was a large, dusty area between the parlor and the small office that Marlene kept for herself beneath the windows at the far end of the loft. Lined with dusty cartons and crates containing the relics and memorabilia of both partners, it also housed their exercise equipment: Marlene's speed bag and body bag, hanging from hooks, a set of rough shelves holding bats, gloves, balls, shoes, and similar impedimenta, and Karp's rowing machine.

This was an elderly affair that Karp had picked up on Canal Street. It was made of dark, sweat-stained wood and blackened metal. He slipped on a pair of sweatpants, sat down in its seat and began to heave on the oars. He had been doing this nearly every morning for the past ten years, a simple, mindless, constant exercise that burned off energy without putting excessive pressure on his bad knee. After the first five minutes, this particular morning, he noticed something different, an uneasiness, a restlessness, a feeling of constraint. His body wanted something else.

That last meeting with Bloom insinuated itself into his mind. It was not just the nastiness and degradation of it, but the sense that it represented the pattern of his life, from now into the indefinite future. Bloom would not get any better. He had made a try for the governorship and failed. He would be the district attorney for all eternity. And Karp would work for him for the rest of his working life, which, as his family responsibilities grew and he became more dependent on his salary, would grow steadily worse. His defiance of Bloom would grow ever more veiled, then fade away in exhaustion and despair. He would become, at last, another empty suit.

It was not to be borne. Karp stopped rowing. Suddenly the machine had become too much a symbol of his present state: endlessly rowing a vessel nailed to the ground. He stood upright, his stomach knotted. His eyes fell on a large cardboard carton. A pale glow had begun to fill the loft through the skylight, and something golden shone within the box. He reached in and pulled out a trophy, something from his high school days. He pulled out another and another, setting them, dusty and tarnished, on the shelf: state championships, all-state high school player of the year, most valuable player awards, awards from shooting competitions. Under the trophies were T-shirts from the basketball camps he had worked at, summer leagues he had played in, a Cal warm-up suit and his old high school uniform.

And at the very bottom of the carton was a deflated basketball and a rusty air pump. The ball was a prize too, the game ball from when they had won the state championship in his senior year. Karp sat on the floor, stuck the needle in and began pushing the plunger. The ball took shape under his hands, slowly swelling, giving off that sweet rubbery smell that gonged up through his nose, shaking loose memories.

The ball got hard. Karp stood up and bounced it once, twice. It made the right, well-remembered sound on the wooden floor. Karp put the ball in an old gym bag, and picked up an elaborate knee brace made of canvas and stainless steel. He hefted its weight, frowned and bounced lightly on his bad left leg.

Then he tossed the brace aside and, rolling up his sweatpants, applied a heavy Ace bandage to the problem joint. A T-shirt with the logo of a local pizza joint on it, a hooded sweatshirt, his old Converse high-top sneakers and a light nylon jacket completed his outfit. He grabbed the gym bag and walked softly toward the door of the loft.

Not softly enough for Marlene, who spoke from her warm nest in the sleeping loft. "You going out?"

"Yeah."

"Jesus, it's quarter to six," she said after checking

the bedside clock. "Nothing'll be open." Karp usually ran out on weekend mornings to pick up the papers and a breakfast treat from the local ethnic richness: bagels, Italian pastries, dim sum.

Karp said, "Umm, I'm going to shoot some hoops before I go to the store."

Sounds of Marlene struggling upright in bed. "What!"

He opened the door. "It's OK. I'll take it easy."

"Whatever you say," she said sleepily. "We'll have adjoining rooms in the hospital."

The playground to which Karp traveled is located at West 4th Street and Sixth Avenue. It is a famous place for weekend pickup games, with a rep that, while not quite as daunting as that of Rucker Memorial at 155th and Eighth in Harlem, is still plenty tough. Kareem played on this court, and the lanes in front of the baskets are known in Greenwich Village as Death Valley.

The park was locked, of course, but its chain-link fence, like that of virtually every playground in the City, had been neatly detached from one of its supporting posts and rolled back to form a triangular entryway. Karp entered this, took out his basketball, walked to a foul line, and shot.

The ball went through neatly, just grazing the rim. Karp trotted forward, picked up the ball, shot a right-handed lay-up, caught the ball as it went through, did the same on the other side, and then, for the next hour, without a break, ran through his whole spectacular repertoire of shots from every corner of the half court, getting up to fifty-two in a row at one point.

The sun was well up now, filling the playground with smoky yellow light, and a dozen or so other players were on the other two half courts, taking shots or chatting. Karp had felt their eyes on him the last fifteen minutes. He sat down by the fence, mopped his face with a towel and pulled off his sweatshirt, letting the cool autumn air dry his sweat.

A game of three-on-three organized itself, in the traditional and mysterious fashion common to pickup games. Karp found himself playing on the same side as a large coffee-colored professorial type with a pointed spade beard and thick glasses on an elastic band, and a stocky, aggressive, balding Irishman wearing a Holy Cross T-shirt. Their opponents were two curly-haired Italians and a very tall black kid with expensive high-tops and a red wool hat.

They played hard, basic, in-your-face playground ball. The Irish guy was an aggressive rebounder who could pass and move, the professor played the classic big forward, dunking with elan, while Karp stayed outside, sinking hooks and jumpers with monotonous regularity. He discovered to his delight that he could do all the stuff he used to do—behind the back passes, between the legs dribbling, convincing pump fakes and the rest of the playground razzle-dazzle—and that it still gave him the same pure and innocent pleasure.

Since the rule at West 4th was winners out—that is, the team that got the last basket took the ball out for the next play—Karp's team made short work of its opponent, winning 21–4—in-your-face ball indeed.

The next team of challengers was far tougher: two obvious Big East alumni who had played together many times before and had worked their give-and-go to a high pitch, plus a spidery black teenager wearing knee-length socks and cutoffs, who spent much of his court time floating a yard or two in the air. These forced Karp's team to six successive game points, at which stage the Holy Cross guy was brick red and staggering, before Karp ended it with an impossible left-handed hook jumper from twenty feet.

"Nice run, Pizza," said the professor to Karp. "You're not from around here, are you?"

"I've been away," said Karp. They were setting up for another game, but Karp begged off, packed up and walked south on Sixth Avenue. He was light-headed from hunger, and with an all-enveloping joy, as if he had found a long-lost brother or child. At an appetizer store he bought a dozen bagels and lox and cream cheese, and walked all the way back to SoHo, tearing with his teeth at one of the bagels as he walked.

Marlene noticed the change in him the second he came through the door. "What happened? You look like you just got laid."

He put down the bagels and said, embracing her, "I got a couple of offers, but I decided to save it all for you."

"Fat and pregnant as I am?"

"I'll dredge you in flour and dive for the wet spot," said Karp, dragging her, not unwillingly, toward the red velvet couch that the couple favored for their frequent quickies.

Sighs and the creaking of the venerable springs. Then, just as Marlene was uttering the string of shrill calls that signaled both her partner, and most of the other residents of Crosby Street, that she was, despite her odd shape, still capable of Getting Her Rocks Off, a vast cacophony of noise burst upon the couple, freezing their bodies and bringing forth many a strangled curse.

One of the disadvantages of the couple's loft, and the reason Marlene had been able to obtain it so cheaply, was the presence of a squat black motor, about the size of a refrigerator laid on end, that occupied its own wire cage near the door. This machine, which bore a dusty brass plate stating that it had been manufactured by Thos. Edison & Co., was connected by a wide leather belt to a great spoked wheel. The wheel, when turned, operated the industrial lift that serviced the metal-working firms who still occupied the second and third floor of the building, and the sculptor who had the floor below Marlene's loft.

This machine invariably started up on Saturday morning, as the tenants secured their weekly deliveries relatively free of the congested traffic typical of downtown Manhattan. It rattled and stank of ozone in normal operation, but worse, it could not keep its belt on, throwing it off regularly with a clattering noise out of the earliest Industrial Revolution. This mishap caused the instant ringing, at shattering volume, of an emergency bell, a device with a gong as wide as a soup plate, mounted over the motor itself. This morning, as usual, the ringing was followed by clumping steps on the stairs and a cheerful pounding on the steel door.

Marlene having fled to the bathroom, Karp yanked on his sweatpants and opened the door, to find two Puerto Rican youths grinning at him. The foremost said, as if it were news to Karp, "The machine broke, man. I hope we din interrupt nothing."

Karp grunted and let them in to shut off the bell and fix the machine, which they did with many a wandering look at the appurtenances of the weird people nutty enough to live in a factory, focusing special interest (evinced by many a Spanish exclamation) at Marlene's lacy underthings, scattered in full view.

"We have to get out of here," Karp said when the workmen were gone, and the lift was groaning and clanking as smoothly as it ever did.

"Why?" said Marlene.

"Why! Give me an hour and I'll make a list. It's five floors up and no elevator. It's dirty. It's got metal dust in the floor that'll never come up. It's got rats. It's non-stop truck traffic during the day and the only park within two miles is full of used spikes and junkies nodding off. Not to mention that goddamn machine. It's no place to raise a kid."

Marlene's eye narrowed and her jaw tightened, and as she was wearing her black eye patch, this gave her expression a piratical fierceness.

"I like it here. And it's getting more civilized. The factories are moving out, and artists and regular people are moving in. This loft is worth a fortune too. The other day Dagmar the transvestite offered me twenty-five K for the key."

"Good for Dagmar," replied Karp sourly. "Let her . . . let *him* live here. With that kind of money, plus what I have, we could get a real house."

"What, in the burbs? Like Donna Reed? Uh-uh, baby, not this kid. You married a city girl."

"OK, we could get a co-op. Or an apartment in a good building."

"Butch, we pay $250 a month here, and I got a five-year lease with three more years to run. The owner lives in Florida and his son-in-law owns the wholesale rug place on the first floor. They forgot about us. You realize what a deal that is? You really want to move from all this space to three little boxes on the West Side, which is about all we could afford even if we're both working?"

Karp sighed. This was not the first time they had gone through this. He was a skilled professional disputant, but so was Marlene, and she was, he knew, passionately attached to this odd dwelling place. She had lived in it for years before meeting Karp. It represented hours of grungy work: cleaning, painting, framing, plumbing and re-wiring, most of which she had done herself or with the help of friends and relatives. She was as attached to it as any Chinese peasant to his ancestral paddy.

And beyond that, in realms of illogic through which he feared to penetrate, the loft represented an emotional anchor for his wife. Karp was not a man who vibrated with sensitivity, but his instincts had been honed by long association with the less than tightly wrapped segment of the population. At the best of times, Marlene walked a fine edge. The shining coin of her, that he loved wholeheartedly—her fine spirit, her brilliance and passion—had on its obverse something that frightened him out of his wits. When feeling constrained, or dependent, or blocked in some purpose, she might descend into a black, heedless intensity, at which times, Karp believed, there was nothing she would not do, unto the destruction of self and anyone in the way.

She wanted what she wanted—him, baby, glory, home, career, to nurse and to yank foul bastards off the streets and into jail, using any means at hand. Given her present state of enforced unemployment, he thought it unwise to press the point about moving.

He said, "OK, whatever. See how you feel when the kid comes."

She smiled at him and said, "It'll be fine. Both my parents grew up four blocks from here and it didn't hurt them." She looked at his painful effort to appear cheerful, and her smile took on a wilder aspect. "As I was doing before we were so rudely interrupted ..."

On the following Monday, Karp rose and went to work alone, leaving Marlene luxuriating in bed, declaring that she intended to remain in her peignoir until noon, eating bonbons and reading trashy novels. Karp walked to work, as he did every morning, as he had when he had lived a good deal farther north in Greenwich Village; he liked to walk and he was convinced that constant walking had improved his bad knee. The loft was ten minutes on foot from the Criminal Courts Building, and Karp had to admit that, as much as he disliked the place as a venue for family raising, you could not beat the location.

Karp was now doing what millions of other New Yorkers do on the way to work, reading the *Daily News,* although few habitually do so while walking full tilt down a crowded street. His remarkable peripheral vision (one of his great advantages as a ball player) prevented excessive collisions, while his huge size and profuse apologies when one did occur avoided any unpleasantry on the street.

He read the crime news first, of course. The *News* has always had a keen interest in mayhem, and Karp had no less, for such news was both a preview of what he had to look forward to and a kind of review of the performance of his office. Nothing interesting had happened the previous night in Manhattan, or at least not anything sufficiently bizarre or gory to make print. He did note with passing curiosity that the murder of Marion Simmons had quite disappeared for the press, except for the ritual deprecation of the ill effects of drugs on athletes.

At the office, Karp moved briskly to his tasks. After nearly ten years it was second nature to him. First in importance was the manning of the whole system—the calendar courts, where justice of a sort was ground out wholesale, the arraignments, the four perpetually running grand juries, the complaint room, through which the police turned over the products of their daily zeal, and the medical hearings, at which it was decided whether the accused were mentally fit to answer for their purported crimes. All of these had to be supplied with a warm body representing the People of the State of New York, failing which the system could never reach that desired judicial orgasm known as clearance.

Karp could arrange the warm bodies, but there was no way that he could supervise what they were doing. He could pick the best of the people who were crazy enough to want to work in the D.A.'s office, train them to his impossible standards, and selectively sample their work by reviewing indictments and other case paperwork or by dropping in at various courtrooms unannounced.

On a very select number of cases, where the crime was particularly heinous, or where it involved a defendant who Karp thought had been getting away with murder (sometimes literally) too long, he would take charge of it himself, with a junior assistant district attorney at heel, to handle the details and to learn how the thing was done.

Karp cursed under his breath and slapped the indictment he was reviewing down on his desk. It was flawed, and in a particularly stupid and careless way. He pulled up a yellow pad and wrote out a set of scathing comments in his bold, wandering hand, clipped it to the indictment and tossed it in a wire basket. After a few minutes he sighed, retrieved the document, and rolled up his note into a neat ball. Karp's wastepaper basket stood not by his desk but on top of the farthest of his five low bookcases. He gently lofted the balled-up note into the air. Two points.

The action reminded him briefly of that weekend's pickup game, and he smiled to himself as he wrote a simple "see me" on the errant indictment and threw it again onto the proper pile.

He stood and stretched, and bounced his weight on his bad knee, feeling the stiffness and the perpetual low ache. The little game had pleased him more than he could well express. Its cleanness, energy and brisk closure acted as an antidote to the eternal semi-nightmare of his working life. He pondered once more on the odd fault of character that had led him to deny himself this simple pleasure for so long.

This pondering had just started to go deep when it was cut short by the phone: Connie Trask telling him to go to Bloom's staff meeting. Cursing, he assembled some yellow pages of notes, together with various report forms, slipped into his blue pin-striped suit jacket, and headed upstairs.

His fellow bureau chiefs were assembling in the D.A.'s large anteroom when Karp arrived. They were all Bloom appointees and he had little to say to them beyond the conventionalities. Not one was a serious trial lawyer. On their part, they treated Karp with varying degrees of chill, covered in some cases by a bluff and unsolicited heartiness. Karp sat in a corner of a sofa and pretended to be busy with his notes.

The appointed hour came and went, and went some more. Inquiries at the receptionist yielded the knowledge that Mr. District Attorney was with the Press. Everyone but Karp seemed to think it a perfectly adequate excuse. Several bureau chiefs picked up spare phones and began conducting their business from the anteroom. Others settled down to a comfortable chat. It was obvious that none of them had to be in court.

Forty-five minutes past the hour, the receptionist's phone buzzed, their call to enter the conference room. At that moment the door to Bloom's inner office opened and two people came out. One was a short oriental man lugging a leather bag, a long tubular case, and a motor-drive Nikon. The other was the tallest woman Karp had ever seen.

The chiefs had all surged forward, Karp bringing up the rear, but they all froze momentarily to view this phenomenon. Karp, who was good at estimating height, judged that she was six-one and a bit. She was striking rather than strictly beautiful, with bold features—a large nose, a long, full mouth, pale eyes brought out by heavy black outlining—all topped by a frizzy mop of red-brown hair that added six inches to her apparent height. She had a black leather trenchcoat slung over her shoulders, on top of a gray pants suit that accentuated her endless legs.

As she moved past the press of men in the narrow gap between the receptionist's desk and the anteroom furniture, her eyes lit on Karp and she gave him a long, appraising look.

"How's the weather up there?" she asked, deadpan. She had a husky voice, deeper than contralto.

"Stop slouching," Karp shot back, and was rewarded with a peal of astonished, booming laughter.

"Who was that?" he asked the receptionist when the tall woman had gone.

She grinned. "Her name is"—giggle—"Ariadne Stupenagel. She's from the *Times.*"

Karp recalled the long-sought magazine article. "Oh, yeah," he said. "It must have been an interesting interview. She looks hard to fool."

The receptionist rolled her eyes and giggled again, and Karp walked toward his meeting.

"What did you do today?" asked Karp of the bride that evening.

"Watched the soaps," said Marlene. "Worked my fingers to the bone scrubbing and cooking and cleaning. Made some calls about child care. Had lunch with Larry and Stu downstairs. Talked to my mom. Got some calls. It's a full life. What about you?"

Karp was at the table shelling peas, nearly his only culinary skill. Marlene was poking with a wooden spoon at a large pot of steaming mussels, whose garlicky and wine-heavy scent filled the loft. Karp thought he could get to like this.

"The usual Monday. Bloom nagged me about Phelps, and I had to tell him that there was a good chance that the asshole was headed for Matteawan. Phelps, not Bloom. And then I came home to my beautiful wife and a delish dinn, prepared with love and made of strange substances, all probable aphrodisiacs."

Marlene said, "He's so glad I'm not a career girl anymore, he's squirming in his chair. But enjoy it while it lasts, my love; it will be brief."

"I intend to," said Karp, tossing his peas into a pot of bubbling water. "And speaking of career girls, I met a strange one today. She was interviewing Bloom for the *Times*. Tallest woman I ever saw. Had a funny name too . . . Stu something."

"Ariadne Stupenagel," said Marlene.

"How did you know?"

"She was one of my calls today. Stupe and I go way back. She was my freshman roomie at Smith, and we ran with the same crowd until she left."

"What, she went for the full basketball scholarship at Holy Cross?"

"No, she was asked to leave. Too hot for Northampton by a long way."

"Drugs?"

"To be sure, but just for starters. Sex was her downfall. She was very naughty and not very discreet about it. And as you probably noticed, she's hard to miss," said Marlene as she served out the meal. She sat down and poured a short glass of wine for both of them. "Very naughty indeed," she said, smiling.

"Worse than you?"

Marlene sputtered. "My dear! I may have let fall a few scandalous hints from my dear dead college days, but believe me, Ariadne made me look like Anne of Green Gables. Item: she kept a Honduran busboy in the closet of her room practically all sophomore year.

He was about four-nine, and as she told anybody who would listen, his tool was a significant percentage of his total length. Item: she literally fucked a man to death once. A French professor with more years than sense, defending the honor of his nation. That's what got her canned. I saw the drained corpse. Her farewell party was the event of the century. The dorm bought her a plaque."

"Terrific," said Karp. "But what's she like?"

"Fun," said Marlene, considering. "Not someone you would want to bare your soul to, but basically a good egg. No malice at all; honest, if she remembers; give you anything she owns; take anything you own; a whim of steel. And of course, the body itself lets her get away with a lot."

"What did she do after?"

"Oh, I think she picked up a degree in some big state diploma factory, and took off for South America. She stringered for a couple of papers. Lived with the *Times* guy in Buenos Aires for a while. She was in Chile during the coup, apparently fucking her way through the inner circles of both the commies and the Pinochet people. No, that's catty. She's really a terrific journalist, ovaries of solid brass. They kicked her out, but not before she'd filed some incredible stories. Anyway, she was in Miami for a couple of years, and now she free-lances here in the city."

"You kept in touch?"

"Not really. Occasional calls and cards, and the old girl grapevine. But she called me today on that piece she's doing about the D.A. I'm going to have lunch with her tomorrow at an elegant *boîte*, her treat, get as drunk as I can in my delicate condition, and, she imagines, feed her the real dirt on the office."

Karp took a drink of wine, gagging slightly as he almost always did, but getting it down. "I hope that's just a figure of speech."

"Don't you wish! But really, this is deep background—no names. And I'm damned if that schmuck is going to come on like Mr. District Attorney." She grinned. "But what I'm really going to do is boast on you."

"Oh? What will you say?"

"Oh, I'll rave about your great track record, your famous exploits. She'll be eating her liver with envy, and I'll love every minute of it."

In his heart, Stanley Malinski thought that death was an excessive punishment for an occasional piece of strange in the back of his Peterbilt, but he had been expecting it momentarily for three days. They had been unpleasant days. From the simple self-told lie that the killers had never seen him, he had gone on to fantasies of flight—name changing, hiding in Brazil—to drunken stupor, to fits of incoherent rage, and finally to his current dull sense of despair. It had never occurred to him to involve the police. It had not occurred to him to struggle when the two guys had picked him up in the truck yard.

Thus, his surprise, when he found himself sitting in the passenger seat of his own car on a dark industrial street near Kennedy, with the older of the two hoods behind the wheel and the little one in the backseat, was simply that he was still alive, that the older guy was questioning him politely, that he could still feel the tingle of hope.

"OK, Stanley, the main thing here is, we got to tie up all the strings," said Carmine. "We need to talk to anybody who saw stuff they wasn't supposed to see, and make sure they forget what they saw. Like we're talking to you. We don't want any trouble, just a little conversation and then we're out of here. You follow me?"

"Yeah, sure," said Malinski, trying as hard as he could to project sincerity into the flat, dark eyes of the other man. "Hey, I told you I never told nobody, I swear to God...."

"I believe you, Stanley," said Carmine. "But we still got to talk to the girl."

Malinski could not keep from jumping a little at that and swallowing hard. "The girl?"

"Yeah, Stanley, the girl who was in the truck with you. The one who drives the red Toyota."

Malinski, to his credit, had not mentioned the woman and now made a feeble effort to protect her. "Oh, just somebody I picked up in a bar. Honest, I don't think she even looked out the—"

"What bar, Stanley?"

"Um, the Danny Boy, on Bell." It was a very feeble effort.

"What's her name?"

"Hey, she's just somebody who hangs around ... um, Francine, I swear to God she never told me her last name."

Carmine didn't know whether he believed the man or not, but he did not have time, nor was the situation right, for him to exercise his considerable skill in extracting information. In any case, he thought the man was not lying in what he did relate.

"OK, that's it—one more question, Stanley. You ain't left-handed, are you?"

"No. Why?"

Carmine got out of the car, and Joey put a cheap .32 revolver to Malinski's right temple and fired. He then placed the gun in the dead man's twitching fingers and left the car himself.

The two men then walked silently to their own

Chevrolet, which they had previously stashed at the murder site, having used a stolen car to pick up their victim. Carmine thought it had gone pretty well. Malinski's wife would report odd behavior prior to the event; the gun was a cheap street shooter that anyone could pick up anywhere. It would pass as a suicide, and would have no connection whatever to Simmons. Carmine was thankful that Joey had remembered to keep his mouth shut during the questioning of the driver, to distinguish right from left, and to refrain from taking a second shot. It could work out after all, provided they got the woman.

CHAPTER
four

"On this Phelps thing," said Karp. He paused and tapped on his desk with a pencil. "You should have no problem finishing it off yourself."

"Myself?" asked the man on the other side of the desk, amazed. His name was Peter Schick. He was a loose-jointed, tall, red-haired man, and very nearly the youngest and least experienced member of Karp's staff. For the four months he had worked for the D.A. he had done nothing more than legal research for the senior people, stand in at calendar courts when someone was away, and such legal broom work as answering *coram nobis* petitions from the incarcerated wanting to be let out.

Karp shot him a look. "Yeah, there's nothing to it. The guy's a cinch for Matteawan. They're decorating his room right now. Just make sure he's run through the medical hearing, process the paperwork, and he's gone."

"What if he's not crazy?"

"Oh, in that case you'll let me know. Unless you want to prosecute the Chelsea Ripper by yourself. Fame, fortune, the plaudits of a grateful city . . . ?"

"No, thanks," Schick replied with a nervous laugh. "I can barely find my way to the men's room as it is. OK, that's Phelps. What's next?"

Karp consulted the list he had prepared for the weekly meetings he held with each of his junior staff, and scratched the Phelps item off. "OK, next: what about the dismissal on Paxton?"

Schick looked puzzled. "Yeah, that's gone. Last Tuesday. They got a confession from the other guy."

"So Paxton's out of jail?"

Schick shrugged. "I guess so. I could call the Legal Aid—"

"No, don't guess," said Karp. "Know! Every person in custody is your responsibility until he walks out the door. Not Legal Aid's, yours. And don't trust the paperwork. Call. Know where the body is. If you don't, one day it's going to show up in an embarrassing place—inside when it's supposed to be outside, or vice versa."

Schick nodded, flustered, and made a note. Karp moved on to the next case, sympathizing, regretting once again how little time there was to bring young attorneys along in some way other than sink or swim.

Ten minutes later, Schick having left fuller than he had been of legal procedure, tactics and caveats, Karp turned again to his morning's paperwork. He had forgotten something, something to do with Phelps. It was some detail he ought to have discussed with Schick. It didn't rise to the surface, which was annoying because Karp prided himself on never slipping where procedure was concerned, although he habitually forgot birthdays and once had shown up for work on the Fourth of July.

It was because it was the Phelps case, he concluded, dismissing the thought at last. Bloom was riding him on it, unreasonably, needling him, as if it were his fault that the man was a maniac and thus incompetent, as if

Karp could weave some legal magic so that Bloom could go on TV and tell the public that the dastard had got his deserts. But in fact there was nothing to be done; even Schick could handle it.

The phone buzzed. Connie Trask said, "There's a Ms. Stupenagel and a Mr. Ube here to see you."

"Oh, shit!" said Karp.

"Want me to get rid of them?"

"No, I just forgot I agreed to see them. Send 'em in."

Karp had agreed to the interview mainly to please Marlene, who had built Karp up shamelessly during her lunch with her old friend. Nevertheless, he was ever wary of the press.

Stupenagel was wearing black silk pantaloons tucked into soft leather boots, a red T-shirt with a sequined design on it and her black leather trenchcoat. She looked like she had learned to dress for success at the court of Ming the Merciless.

They made small talk while the photographer scooted around the office, crouching, bobbing, standing on chairs and taking what seemed like dozens of pictures of Karp. Karp remembered not to pick his nose or yawn.

The photographer exchanged a look with the reporter, excused himself and left.

"I thought we could talk more easily alone," Stupenagel said.

"I have no secrets," said Karp with a bland smile.

"Ha-hah!" Her laugh was full-throated and hearty. "I doubt that. Your wife tells me some very interesting stories. I think your career has the makings of a fantastic article."

Karp said, "Wives tend to boast, and Marlene has a vivid imagination. It's not all that interesting since Perry Mason retired."

"Oh? What about the Israelis kidnapping you? What about being shot by Cuban terrorists? What about the psychopath who faked being incompetent so he could cover up the fact that he was a mass murderer? Not too dull there, hey?"

"Um, let's roll back a minute. I thought this article was going to feature the district attorney and the office generally. I thought all you wanted from me was just some general background on how the office works."

"Originally, yeah. But I spent two hours with Mr. Bloom, and all I got was a lot of numbers and bureaucratese. There's no flesh there, dig? And I like my work to have flesh, glistening with sweat and pulsing with blood." Her eyes glittered as she stared at him.

"That's very colorful language, Ms. Stupenagel—"

"Please, it's Ari, since we're former roommates-in-law. And you're Butch, right?"

"Right. Well, as I say . . . Ari: colorful language, I can see where you're a writer and all, but really, the incidents you mention make up a very small part of a D.A.'s career. Most of it is very dull."

She nodded once and flashed the kind of smile one puts on after hearing a significant departure from the strict truth, and said, "Fine. Bore me."

"Hmm?"

"Bore me," she repeated. "I want to know what it's like. Tell me how the office works on a day-to-day level: what the people do, what they love, what they hate, what they fear. I didn't get any of that from Bloom, because, if you want my opinion, he didn't know. I suspect you do. Am I right?"

Karp signaled agreement.

"And I get the sense that you and the D.A. don't see eye to eye on a lot of things."

"The usual trivial professional differences of opinion."

"In fact, I heard you've caught him with his hand in a particularly dirty cookie jar, and not just once."

"I can't imagine where you could have heard that," said Karp, deadpan.

"Imagine that I heard it from those ruby lips you know so well." She gave him a smile, along with a burst of pheromones and body language that promised much, and which would have been reasonably effective on Karp were it not for Marlene and what she had told him about La Stupenagel, and the understanding that this was as much part of Stupenagel's professional equipment as her steno pad.

Karp sighed. "Ari, let's stop for a second. What you're trying to do, *I* do for a living too. Getting information out of people who don't want to give it to me is mainly what this job is about, in the preliminary stages. Q. and A. it's called, and the difference is that the guy *wants* to talk to me, because he wants to convince me that he didn't do it, one, or his buddy didn't do it, two, or, three, his buddy did do it instead of him.

"And the other difference is that when *I* write something down, I got an audience of twelve people, and if they all believe me, it's not just a matter of somebody seeing something they don't like in the *Times*. It means somebody's going upstate to get fucked in the ass every day for fifteen years. I just mention that so you know I know how to get information out of people who *really* don't want to tell me the truth. I'll stipulate that you do too, so let's stop fooling around."

She laughed aloud again. "That's great! I can use all that. So what do you want to do?"

Somewhat taken aback, Karp replied, "I'm glad to talk about my perceptions of the job and my career, within limits. I set the limits. You don't pump me. I don't care to talk about the D.A. personally or office policy. Also, this is it for the bureau. I don't want you talking to anybody else besides me—"

"I can't promise that."

"In that case, I'll see you in court, as we say around here," Karp said flatly. They locked eyes and flared nostrils for a long moment, and then Stupenagel grinned.

"OK, deal. Can we get some coffee? I'm dropping."

Karp got up and went out and came back in five minutes with two coffees, during which time the reporter had read, upside down, all the papers showing on his desk. That he got his own coffee impressed her enough that she was vaguely guilty about this for about seven seconds.

"So," said Karp. "What do you want to know?"

Evening, a week later, and Karp was down at the end of the loft bouncing his basketball, moving on sneakered feet, dribbling around his neck and between his legs, recovering the fine moves. He wondered why it had never occurred to him that the wooden-floored loft with its great empty spaces was a perfect practice room for basketball. The ceilings were high enough too. He could set up a basket. . . .

Marlene called him to dinner, and for an instant he experienced a flash of intense and unbearable memory: his mother calling him for the same reason as dusk closed in on the suburban driveway where every day after school he would shoot and rebound and dribble and shoot again, hour after dreaming hour. "Just a minute, Ma." Another ten shots, another call, another excuse, until, sighing, she would come out of the house and take the ball from his hands.

Karp walked down to the kitchen zone. "Watch this," he said. Marlene turned from the stove and watched as Karp performed an elaborate fake involving separate motions of his head, torso and legs and the whipping of the basketball around his body with blinding speed.

Marlene rolled her eyes. "Very impressive. Where did you learn that?"

"It's a variation of something Meadowlark Lemon used to do on the Globetrotters. It's a two-man fake for when you're double-teamed and need to pass to the open man. I didn't think I could still do it."

"Well, now you know and your heart can rest. And it was smart of you to keep this particular aspect of your behavior veiled during our courtship."

"Basketball is my life," said Karp primly.

"It will be your death too if I have to put up with that *k-dunk, k-dunk, k-dunk* for the next thirty years. What started this anyway?"

"Hey, what can I tell you? You married a jock. I suppressed it since law school because of my knee and missing the pros, and it just popped out again." He smiled wonderingly. "It gives me a lot of pleasure. And I don't get much from the job anymore, so . . ." He looked at her and twisted his face into a goatish leer. "And not enough sex."

"Get away from me, you maniac," she cried. "No, really, this is all ready. Sit down."

He sat. "What is it?"

"It's Chinese food," ladling it out of a wok. "Beef and snow peas with oyster sauce."

"You ordered take-out?"

"No, I made it, dear, with my own tiny, worn hands. Is it good?"

"It's great," he said, amazed, and looked at her as if at a second Madame Curie. "I didn't know you could make Chinese food in a house."

"Few people can, which is why the Chinese are so

poor. I mean eating in restaurants all the time, with the tips and the baby sitters, I can see—"

"OK, I get it. I bet Ariadne Stupenagel can't make Chinese food."

Marlene sniffed. "I should say not. Is she still dogging your footsteps?"

"Yeah, but today was the last day. She's apparently sucked me dry," he said between mouthfuls.

"I trust that's a figure of speech."

"I won't dignify that with a reply," he said. "But she certainly cut a swath through the office. Guma is in love. 'Cunt to the eyes,' as he put it."

"Charming. So what do you make of my old roomie?"

Karp sat back and considered. "She's quite a character. Smart as a whip, and sneaky. I told her I didn't want her talking to the other people in the bureau, but I know she was doing it anyway. She spent a whole night in the complaint room; Guma got her in. She's a great interviewer. She pisses you off, but you can't help liking her. On the other hand, I wouldn't trust her as far as I could throw her. She reminds me of you a little—"

"Thank you very much!"

"Oh, didn't mean about trusting. I mean she's cocky, fearless, moves right in and does the job. Like that. What I don't much like is the naked ambition. And the way she uses sex like a blowtorch. You don't do that. I don't think she keeps anything ... private. A little scary, if you know what I mean."

Marlene nodded. "I do, I do. At lunch last week she was a little hincty about me being pregnant, mocking, like I was letting down the girls' team. Still, I did like seeing her. She was one of those people in your life that you always wonder what became of them. When is the article coming out, or didn't she know?"

"This Sunday, as a matter of fact."

"So soon?"

"Yeah, she said they had to kill the story that they were going to have as the feature, the cover story, and she jumped in and said she could have it ready, so they went for it."

"Wow, a cover story! You think you'll be in it a lot?"

Karp laughed. "I don't know. Maybe. But Bloom staring up from the cover is going to put a crimp in my Sunday. Maybe I'll go right to the crossword."

But in fact, when Karp that Sunday picked up the *Times* at his usual stop, a Chinese candy store on Mott, the face that stared up at him in full color from the front page of the magazine section was not Bloom's but his own.

Karp felt sweat break out on his face, and his knees went wobbly. Irrationally, as if from some obscure guilt, he looked up to see if anyone was watching him. The proprietor was, flashing a gold-toothed smile, nodding behind the counter, giggling with his wife in Cantonese. "You famous now," he observed.

Karp paid and left the place in a rush, sticking the paper under his arm and reading the magazine section as he walked through the streets of Chinatown. It was worse on the inside: Ariadne Stupenagel had based the entire piece on Karp and his career: the hundred straight wins, the spectacular and dangerous cases, his ideas and ideals. The title of the article was: "Karp for the Prosecution: One Man's Fight Against Crime in New York."

Back at the loft, Karp paced the floor muttering while Marlene read avidly and rapidly through the article.

"This is great," she said. "According to Stupe,

you're 'rough-hewn, towering, Lincolnesque, with piercing gray eyes.' "

"It's a disaster," he wailed.

"Why do you say that? It's all true, as far as I can make out, and she doesn't particularly dwell on your fights with Bloom. In fact, she hardly mentions him."

"That's just the point. He's going to go bananas over it."

Marlene looked at him strangely. "Since when do you give a shit what Bloom thinks?"

"I don't! It's just that . . . it'll look like I was whoring after p.r. like he does all the time. And he'll be able to be slimy and sarcastic about it, and everybody will nod and grin, like, yeah, we knew Karp was just another glory hound. Like that. And people, scumbags that I don't even know, will be sidling up to me with 'Great story, Butch,' and I'll have to grin back. And what I'm trying to teach the staff about being cool with the press, not to have the press influence cases, that'll all go out the window. It'll seem like total hypocrisy."

"That's all in your head," Marlene said breezily. "You have this whole thing about getting credit for what you do. God, didn't you have your picture in the paper a lot when you played ball?"

"Yeah, but that was different," said Karp, knowing it but not really being able to say why.

"I don't see how. You deserve some recognition, for chrissake! Like my dad always says, 'Whosoever tooteth not his own horn, the same shall not be tooted.' Besides, fame is fleeting." She waved the magazine section. "This will be wrapping garbage in a couple of days, and a week after that nobody will remember it."

"Yeah, well, anyway, it's not going to be a fun couple of days," he said gloomily.

Nor was it. Karp's staff was, of course, joyful and

mocking by turns for a week, which Karp could not stifle without appearing boorish. The secretaries framed the magazine cover and hung it in the outer office. Guma made enlarged Xerox copies of the face from the cover portrait, and when Karp walked into his regular staff meeting, every attendee was wearing one as a mask and spouting quotes from the article, amid unseemly glee.

Bloom, at his staff meeting, was snidely cutting, but in a new way, as if *he* now had something dirty on Karp, as if he had walked in and found Karp in bed with his own mistress, as if they were fuck-buddies now. Karp found this more distasteful by far than Bloom's usual naked enmity.

Karp's cup of woe spilled over when a sleazebag pimp in high heels and a floor-length leopard coat stopped him in the hallway and asked for his autograph on the magazine cover. He was extremely rude to this person at some length, and afterward stalked head down with a brow of thunder back to his office, slamming the door so that the glass rattled, at which moment his secretary put through the call that was to prove the most remarkable of the damned article's sequelae.

It was Bernie Nadleman, the coach of the New York Hustlers. He began to introduce himself, but Karp, still feeling ornery, cut him off abruptly. "I know who you are, Bernie. What can I do for you?"

"Well, that article in the *Times* . . . I heard you were working in the city when I got here, but I never realized you were such a superstar. And I thought I'd make contact again."

This was lame and both of them knew it. Bernie Nadleman was three years older than Karp, and their only contact had been about fourteen minutes of court time total in a single Pac-10 season, plus a short, unmemorable conversation at a dinner thrown by sports-writers. Nadleman wanted something. Karp waited for it, and after a few moments of desultory conversation about the NBA season, it came.

"Well, look, Butch, the thing of it is, I could use some help on this Simmons thing."

"What sort of help?"

"I don't know—just find out what's going on. Put a bug up somebody's ass. I can't get a straight answer from the cops here."

"Have you talked to the Queens D.A.?"

"Yes, but I get nothing but stalling and horseshit. That's why I'm calling you. I figured it was better if I had an in."

"Well, I'm not much of an in with the Queens D.A. It's a completely separate operation. We're all in the same business, but there's usually not much need for cooperation once somebody takes jurisdiction. It's like different basketball teams."

Nadleman gave a sour laugh. "As bad as that, hey?"

"Worse. But what's the problem anyway?"

"The problem is nobody's doing shit on the case. They're still hooked on this crazy idea that Marion was selling dope. I get the feeling they're not exactly putting the full press on the case. They got one detective on it—one! And the asshole doesn't even return my calls.

"The league is going crazy too. Every time one of my guys takes a leak there's a schmuck in a lab coat hanging around with a little bottle. It's fucking killing the team."

"I presume you don't believe Marion was involved with dope?" Karp asked.

"Shit, no, he wasn't involved with dope. He was the cleanest kid I ever worked with. Didn't smoke, didn't drink, didn't chase pussy: the kid *lived* for basketball.

Anybody offered him cocaine, he would've cold-cocked them."

Karp, who was familiar with the degree of self-delusion practiced by basketball coaches about the strangely configured beings on whom their personal fortunes depended, said nothing to this, but simply grunted and replied, "OK, Bernie, what I'll do is I'll make a couple of calls over to Queens, see what I can find out, and get back to you."

Nadleman thanked him effusively and offered two passes to the Hustlers' game with the Sixers on Friday. Karp accepted gladly. He hadn't been to a pro game in years.

Dutifully, Karp made the calls. Quite aside from the favor to Nadleman, he was himself curious about the unlikely association between an NBA pro and a big bag of coke. He called a Queens D.A. bureau chief he knew slightly, who was not in, and then called Shelly Nowacki, who had worked in the Manhattan D.A. during Karp's early years. Nowacki was generous with what he had, but he didn't have much.

"Funny thing," Nowacki said ruminatively. "You would think, a big star like that, they would put the max on it, but no. Nobody here is pushing the cops, and the cops, what I hear is that they gave the case to some rummy. It's the dope angle, is what I think."

"What angle is that, Shelly?"

"Well, you know, the kid gets into dope, he figures he could sell some, at least make his jones, somebody finds out, and blam. This ain't the South Bronx here, but we got a pretty heavy set of Jamaicans down in St. Albans. Colombians too. If it was Colombians, we're lucky they didn't do the whole team. So—some prick zapped him and got away clean, and unless a snitch rolls out and says, 'I hear Lefty had a hard-on for Simmons,' we're at square one. That's how the cops figure anyway; and anyway, they're not going to particularly bust hump for a coke fiend. As you know."

"As I know," said Karp. "Are we so sure he was a coke fiend? What did the autopsy say?"

"This I don't have on me. You could check with the DT in charge. But figure: who the fuck is going to leave fifty K worth of prime nose candy on the corpse to give a mistaken impression?"

"Who indeed?" said Karp. "So what's this guy's name?"

"What guy?"

"The DT. The rummy."

"Oh, him," said Nowacki. "Name's Bello. Harry."

Karp wrote it down. "Who's his partner? Anybody else on the case?"

"Nope, far's I know. He's solo. Like I said, low priority."

"OK, thanks, Shelly. This is good. And would you let me know if anything breaks?"

"Yeah," said Nowacki. "But don't hold your breath."

The Danny Boy Bar on Bell Boulevard in Bayside, Queens, on a Monday afternoon served perhaps half a dozen serious drinkers at tables and a couple at the bar, not at all like the wild scene on a weekend night. The blinds had been pulled down lest the light of day disturb the concentration of the patrons on their shots and drafts, and wan shafts of sunlight provided the appropriate film noir effect.

The day bartender was not busy and had plenty of time to chat with the big stranger at the bar.

"It must pick up at night," said the stranger.

"Yeah, we get a nice crowd, especially Friday, Saturday."

"Does Francine still come by?" the stranger asked.

The bartender smiled broadly and lifted his eyes. "Hey, old Francine! You know Francine?"

"A while back. I ain't seen her in a couple three years. She still a redhead?"

"Fuck, no—a brunette. You're sure we're talking about the same Francine?"

"I guess," said the stranger, sipping his beer. "I know she used to hang out here. A piece of ass."

The bartender laughed again. "Yeah, that's Francine. Tits out to here."

The stranger nodded and smiled. "I remember. I'd sure like to get next to her again. Funny, I can't recall her last name. Began with a P or a D or a . . ."

"Del Fazio," said the bartender. "Francine Del Fazio. She's in here every Tuesday and Thursday night just about. Her old man works the night shift at Grumman. God damn! The shit's gonna fly if he ever figures out what she's doing while he's humping rivets."

The stranger got off his stool and left a ten on the bar to pay for his two beers and waved away the proffered change. The bartender grinned and said, "Hey, thanks! You want me to tell her you're looking for her?"

"No," said the stranger, "I'll find her."

Peter Schick was panting and sweaty when he got to the room in Bellevue's prison ward where they did the mental health competency hearings. It was a hair past ten in the morning. Schick was often out of breath in his job, which consisted largely of having to be in widely separated places at close to the same time to deliver formalized statements on issues he barely understood. This was called representing the People. He had been told that everybody had done this on first arriving at the D.A., and that they had survived. He was young and tough and thought he would survive too, if barely.

The room he entered was painted institutional green and floored with shiny brown linoleum. The windows were barred with heavy grilles. The room was, in fact, a ward day room, which was this day being devoted to competency hearings. It had in its temporary function none of the usual trappings of the law's majesty, being furnished, at the front, with a large rectangular table and wooden chairs and at the rear by several battered brown couches and an assortment of plastic chairs. It stank of steam heat and Lysol.

At the table sat a judge, a stenographer, a court officer, a Legal Aid lawyer and a psychiatrist. There were vacant chairs for a defendant and an assistant district attorney. On the couches sat a dozen or so men in bathrobes and paper slippers, waiting their turn to be told if they were crazy or not.

Schick introduced himself to the gathering. The judge, a grumpy black gentleman in his late sixties, scowled at him and said, "Call the first case." The judge was anxious to move through his list of defendants because when he had disposed of these hearings he would be free for the day. The competency-hearing duty was a prize distributed by rotation, and the judges regarded it as the next thing to a day off.

Schick sat at his place and arranged the stack of files he had brought with him. He shuffled through them to find the one the bored psychiatrist was talking about: Mendez. OK, Mendez, here it was. He read the complaint sheets while trying to concentrate on what the shrink was saying, and glancing briefly at the dulled-out tan man in the defendant's chair.

What he was hearing made no sense. Shit! The wrong Mendez. More shuffling. The doc finished. The judge said, "All right, on the basis of this report I'm going to rule this man competent to stand trial. Objections?" Schick found the right file, heard the Legal Aid say, "No, sir," and heard himself say the same. The judge said, "Next case."

After six cases had come and gone, Schick was somewhat more on top of his job. They were mostly of a piece: the individuals had committed crimes of violence or passion while under the influence of booze or drugs or both, or when driven by some irrational impulse, such as (in one case) a fixed belief that his wife was having sexual intercourse with every male person of his acquaintance during every waking moment she was not in direct sight. Nevertheless, they all could, according to Bellevue, assist in their own defense, and so were competent to stand trial, if not to live life to its fullest.

The court officer called, "Phelps." This was what Schick had been waiting for, and for once he was well prepared. A gray-haired, chubby man in a white coat sat down in the psychiatrist's chair and consulted his notes through half-glasses. Schick searched the couches for the spare, dark-haired figure of the Chelsea Ripper. There were only eight men left and none of them was Phelps.

The court officer called the name again. The judge looked at the shrink, who shrugged. The judge said, "Put him on second call. Next."

Next was Mendez, the other Mendez, who proved a true wacko and was remanded to the state institution for the criminally insane at Matteawan. Other cases came and went, until second call came around. Still no Phelps.

The judge looked meaningfully at his watch. It was nearly eleven-thirty, and he had labored for the People for over an hour. If he closed this out now, he could get a quick bite in town and be home in Teaneck in time for eighteen holes that afternoon, before the autumn light faded.

"No Phelps," said the judge. "I'm going to put this case over for the next hearings."

Schick said, "Ah ..." The young man knew that something was wrong, that he should do something, but he didn't know what it was or what he should do. Everyone around the table was looking at him, with expressions ranging from the bored to the hostile.

What was wrong was this: it is the heart of every legal proceeding, even one as sloppy and rushed as this one, to produce the body of the defendant: not a name on paper, or a record, written or electronic, but the actual living, breathing, sweating lump of flesh attached to the name, and to show the same to the actual living beings representing the prosecution, the defense and the court itself.

This is the reason, and the only reason, for the elaborate and tedious charade of the criminal courts, that these bodies, however cynical, bored, corrupt or vicious the spirits animating them had become, might by this simultaneous conjunction be touched by the holy miracle of justice. It happens.

So what Peter Schick should have done was to look in the eye of the representative of Bellevue and speak some version of that ancient and portentous phrase, *habeas corpus:* "You have the body." He had every right and a positive duty to view the body of Martin Phelps at that moment.

But the judge said, peremptorily, "Mr. Schick, did you have any applications at this time?"

Schick flushed. He did not shout *habeas corpus* at Bellevue. He did not shout at all but instead in a low voice said, "No, sir," and the sacred moment passed away.

Bellevue did not in fact have the body of Martin

Phelps. That body had walked free out of the prison ward that morning because of a clerical error. Another M. Phelps (case dismissed) was still safely, and illegally, under lock and key.

The body of Martin Phelps was at that moment alighting from a 23rd Street cross-town bus at Eighth Avenue, while his mind was occupied in receiving directions from his masters, the Metaloids of the planet Trigon. The Metaloids had enlisted him years ago in their campaign to rid the earth of the agents of the Punox protectorate. They spoke directly into his head, sometimes painfully, but always with truth and complete authority.

They provided him with money, and a place to stay, and his special tools. They had released him from the clutches of the evil Punox that very morning. They pointed out the agents for him to kill.

He was following one now, a particularly vicious agent disguised as a pretty young woman. They were clever, the Punox. And tough. He had to stab them many times, sometimes hundreds of times. And he had to eat various parts of their bodies, so that they could not reconstitute themselves, and keep other parts to show to the Metaloids. He did not particularly like this, but the Metaloids were adamant. It was a hard job, but somebody had to do it. He followed discreetly behind the woman, listening to the Metaloid signals, securely under guidance.

CHAPTER
five

The first sign that Karp's life was about to unravel came during a brief conversation he had with Peter Schick two days after the competency hearing. Bloom had asked Karp when, and if, Martin Phelps would be brought to trial, as he did every other day, and, spotting Schick scurrying down a hallway, Karp grabbed him and asked him the same thing.

"Nothing yet," Schick responded. "The next hearing is next Tuesday. It should come up then."

"He wasn't called?"

"Yeah, he was called. He just didn't show." Schick looked at his watch and hefted his stack of legal folders. "Jesus, I'm late for court. . . ."

He started to move away, but Karp stretched out a long arm and held him hard by the shoulder.

"Wait a minute. What do you mean, he didn't show?"

Schick glanced meaningfully at the hand holding him and then looked at Karp impatiently. "Just what I said. They called his name twice and he wasn't there. So the judge put it over."

"And what did you do?"

Schick shrugged, unsure as to where this was lead-

ing. "Do? What could I do? The guy wasn't there.
Hell, Butch, witnesses miss court all the time—"

Karp exploded. "Christ! *Peter!* He's not a witness.
He's the fucking prisoner! He has to show up. Where
the fuck was he? On the can? Jogging in the park?"

Schick essayed a weak smile. "C'mon, Butch. He's
locked up. He's in the prison ward."

"How do you know? Did you see him?"

"No, but—"

Karp cut him off with a curt gesture. "I've told you
before, it's your responsibility to make sure every defendant in a competency hearing is where he's supposed to be. Don't ever let me catch you leaving any
judicial procedure again without seeing a breathing
warm body in the chair! Now call Bellevue and make
sure he's still there!"

Karp stalked away, leaving Schick standing there,
pale and gaping. Karp was furious, but more at himself
than at Schick.

In fact, he knew he had just lied. In fact, he had not
made this point to Schick at all in reference to the
competency hearing. The kid could not be blamed for
not doing something Karp had never told him to do.
Karp felt something, some primary competence, the
sense of being more or less on top of things, slipping
away. Too many balls in the air, too many balls by far.

His mood did not improve when, on arriving back at
his office, Connie Trask handed him a stack of yellow
phone call slips as thick as a pastrami sandwich. It had
been that way since the article had come out, the price
of fame. Crime was much on the minds of the city's
rich, and a genuine crime fighter was a desirable dec-
oration for a party or salon, much as bootleggers, coke
dealers, and black revolutionaries had been in their
season.

Karp, ever the good public servant, returned all

these calls and turned down all the invitations, pleading the press of work. Those refusals, however, merely added the pique of elusiveness and mystery to people whose invitations were otherwise eagerly sought, and simply made Karp more of a challenge. The calls continued.

People called him at home too. That was new. Cranks, people wanting favors for incarcerated friends, people with good ideas about what to do to criminals, felons with threats: the public exerting its ownership. Karp bought an answering machine, an object he had thought he would never own, but still felt harassed and invaded.

He was just coming to his last few calls, talking to other people's answering machines, of course, when Schick stuck his head in and said, "It's OK, they got Phelps. He's still locked up."

Karp smiled and said, "Lucky you. Go, and sin no more."

Schick vanished and Karp picked up the next slip. Good. Not a hostess. Pagano.

Tom Pagano was the head of Legal Aid for the New York County courts, for years Karp's nominal adversary. Karp had a better relationship with Pagano than he did with many of his nominal allies, however. He had a lot of respect for a man whose job was even more thankless than his own, and who had been copping thugs to a lesser when Karp was still in high school. They ordinarily spoke to each other at least half a dozen times a week.

"What's up, Tom?"

Pagano's deep voice boomed over the wire: "How about a suit for unlawful imprisonment?"

"We never do that. You must want a different department."

Pagano laughed. "No, I gotcha this time. Guy's case

was dismissed three days ago and they won't let him out of Bellevue. My kid's been pounding on Bellevue, and of course they won't do shit unless they hear it from you."

"Who's the A.D.A.?" Karp asked, reaching for a pencil.

"Well, as a matter of fact, it's you," said Pagano, chuckling.

"Me?" Karp tried to think who he had in Bellevue and came up blank. "What's the guy's name?"

"Phelps, Martin C.," said Pagano.

"Phelps? What? What're you talking about? Phelps is the multiple killer with voices from Mars in the head."

"Different Phelps, Butch. Our guy was up for assault one, only the vic decided not to press and we got a dismissal."

The first thrill of icy fear started to twist Karp's belly.

"Uh, Tom," he said, trying to control his voice, "why won't they release him? At Bellevue."

"Because they claim he's already been released, day before yesterday. But it was a different Phelps. We need you guys to go down there and clear up the confusion."

Karp felt like his face was covered in steamed towels. "OK, Tom, I'll get right on it. I'll see to it personally."

Fifteen minutes later, after a siren-screaming ride uptown, Karp was in the prison ward at Bellevue staring at a porky, middle-aged and irate citizen who, whatever his other defects, was not the Chelsea Ripper. The Bellevue staff was embarrassed and frightened, making excuses and telling cover-up lies as fast as they could think them up. Karp was not interested in that.

He signed the papers that would enable the wrong Phelps to rejoin his loved ones, and wandered out, down green, smelly hallways, through swinging doors and out onto First Avenue, where Doug Brenner, his driver, was waiting.

Brenner saw Karp's face and asked in alarm, "What's wrong? Somebody die?"

"Yeah. Me. We seem to have misplaced the Chelsea Ripper." He gestured at the police radio. "Look, patch me in to Zone Three homicide. I want to talk to Sonny Dunbar."

Dunbar was a talented homicide detective with whom Karp had worked a number of cases in the past. He had also led the team that had tracked down the real Martin Phelps.

"You what!" said Dunbar. "How the *fuck*—"

"Never mind that. The point is to pick him up before the goddamn Martians do."

There was a pause on the line. Dunbar said, "Well. About that ... it's the Metaloids, not the Martians. And I think they already did."

Karp closed his eyes and took a deep breath. "Tell me."

"Last night in the Penn Station houses. A girl cut to pieces. The M.O. was pure Phelps. He turned her into dog meat and took the tongue and a kidney along. I thought it was a copycat at first, but now ..."

"Sure," said Karp dully. "OK, I'll write up the warrants. Just find him."

He put down the radiophone. "Where to?" Brenner asked after a minute or so of dead silence.

"Centre Street," said Karp. "Use the siren."

Karp went back to his office, got the warrant processed and made some necessary calls. Then he had Peter Schick sent for and told him what had happened in blunt, merciless phrases.

"I'm sorry," said Schick, his voice cracking. He had gone so pale that the little shaving cuts and pimples on his face stood out like stigmata.

"Bad luck," said Karp, turning gentle. "It could happen to anyone. OK, here's what's going down. I've made arrangements with Jim Vincetti for you to move over to the appeals bureau. It's nice quiet paperwork and you'll have a chance to get yourself together out of the shit that's going to come down about this. Keep your mouth shut, and if there's any official investigation of this, which I very much doubt, just tell the whole truth and nothing but. They'll have their fall guy and the press will be satisfied."

Schick cleared his throat heavily. "What fall guy?"

"Me," said Karp.

Karp waited for a half hour after Schick left and then the call from Dunbar came through. Martin Phelps had been discovered in his mother's apartment in Peter Cooper. He had been in the little kitchen, slicing a human kidney up with onions and green peppers, the fat simmering in a pan. When the cops arrived, he had obeyed the final order of his masters and teleported himself to the planet Trigon by way of the living room window and the pavement nine stories below. The press had been informed.

Karp left and rode the elevator up to the D.A.'s office on the twelfth floor. Bloom was meeting with some civic leaders when Karp barged in and whispered a few words in his ear. The meeting ended more abruptly than Bloom's meetings usually did. When they were alone, Karp explained in outline what had happened, leaving out nothing but Schick's name.

The first thing Bloom did after hearing Karp's story was to call Kevin McHugh, his p.r. man. While they waited for him to arrive, Bloom paced nervously back and forth, glancing at the door as if he expected the arrival of irate hordes of citizens.

"The main thing is to control this situation from the get-go," Bloom said. "Keep our stories straight. This is on Bellevue, right? They can't blame us."

"The original mistake was clerical, but they *can* blame us. Like I said, there was a competency hearing on the day he walked out. We, I, didn't insist on having him in the room."

"Then the judge . . . or Legal Aid. He's their client."

"True, but it's our responsibility legally," said Karp.

While Bloom was pondering this unpleasant news, Kevin McHugh walked into the room, excited. "What's going on? I'm getting calls from the press about Phelps. He escaped and killed somebody? We got ABC and CBS here already."

Karp said, "I was just explaining the situation to the district attorney." McHugh took notes and asked intelligent questions while Karp gave a brief summary of what he had told Bloom, concluding, "So there's really nothing to do but tell the story. We screwed up."

McHugh and Bloom exchanged one of those embarrassed smiles that men of affairs share when they have heard some astonishing naïveté. Neither of them was a truthful man, but that only meant that McHugh was a good public relations officer and Bloom was a bad district attorney. McHugh caught on first. He asked softly:

" 'We' screwed up? Who was that exactly?"

Karp had been waiting for this. "It was me. I was responsible." He spoke calmly. He was calm, to his surprise. It was like being in a high school play, or a morning dream.

As he delivered his line, he looked over at Bloom and watched the words strike home. But the combination of fear and naked glee playing on the D.A.'s features was so repellent that he had to look away.

"Well, in that case, um, I think our duty is clear," Bloom said. "Of course, we can keep this between ourselves." He smiled broadly. Karp merely nodded, knowing well what was going on. Some years ago, he had caught the D.A. conspiring, for political reasons, to destroy a case against a man who had murdered a policeman. Karp's possession of this knowledge had, in Bloom's mind, limited his options in dealing with Karp. Bloom now obviously believed that the books were balanced, that he had something equally damaging on Karp, and was now enjoying the contemplation of a long-deferred revenge.

McHugh picked up a phone and began dictating a press release and a statement for the D.A. to his secretary. The burden of the statement was that Bellevue was culpable in releasing a homicidal maniac, and that the district attorney would do everything in his power to insure that it did not happen again. The statement was terse, strongly worded and clear, if entirely misleading. McHugh really was a good p.r. man.

Karp sat in Bloom's office as the typed scripts were borne in by frenzied aides and secretaries. When Bloom and McHugh trooped out to the press room, Karp followed, barely noticed.

The press room was an undistinguished closet with chairs and a podium at the front, nearly filled now with a dozen reporters and five TV camera crews. When Bloom and McHugh entered, the place lit up like a nuclear test.

McHugh said a few words about the press release and turned the podium over to his boss. Karp had to admit Bloom was good at this. He radiated sincerity and concern as he delivered his statement without a hitch. There were questions; Bloom fielded them with pat answers. The TV had their five-second sound bites.

The lights started to flick out and the murmur of departure rose in the room.

Then Karp stepped forward to the podium and cleared his throat.

"If I may, I'd like to clarify some of the district attorney's remarks," he said in a loud voice. Bloom and McHugh looked at him, the false smiles freezing on their faces. The lights flicked on again.

"I am Roger Karp, chief of the Criminal Courts Bureau. I want you to understand that the responsibility for all prisoners in custody lies ultimately with the district attorney's office. There was a mental health competency hearing for Martin Phelps on the morning of the day he walked out of Bellevue. He was not produced for the hearing.

"At that point it was the duty of the district attorney's office to insist on the physical presence of the prisoner. It failed to do so, and as a result, a young woman was brutally murdered. I personally accept responsibility for this mistake, and hereby announce my resignation as chief of the Criminal Courts Bureau."

Stunned silence. Then a bellow of questions. Karp ignored these and pushed through the mob, out into the corridor. He heard McHugh shouting for order as the door closed behind him.

He went up the stairs, one flight to his own office, where, in ten minutes with Connie Trask (she weeping openly, but taking notes) he terminated his management of the bureau in a crisp set of dictated memos.

He was taking leave, he said, as of that moment. He hadn't had a real vacation in over six years, and he had accumulated over three hundred hours of paid leave. If Bloom didn't like it, he could call and complain.

Trask supplied a shopping bag, into which he threw the few strictly personal furnishings of his office. They filled barely half the bag: some framed diplomas and pictures, a baseball on a wooden stand, signed by the 1952 Yankees, a Lucite paperweight containing a bullet dug out of Karp's body, some private letters. The remainder belonged to the People. Karp slunk away before anyone else could learn what had happened.

Marlene, meanwhile, was having a rather more pleasant day. She lounged like a pig in bed until eleven, when guilt flogged her out on deck and into the bath. Then, throwing on one of Karp's huge T-shirts and a pair of disgusting maternity jeans, she entered a frenzy of straightening things, cleaning the loft as well as it could ever be cleaned, and catching up on several years' worth of correspondence.

Two hours of this, and she was famished. One avocado and a half package of frozen crab: crap! no mayo; no eggs, even.

She walked over to the lift shaft, swung open its wide iron door and yelled down, "Stu! You home?"

An agreeable shout came up from the open shaft door on the floor below. The shaft was cool and empty, except for its cable and the pallet hook hanging three floors below. Marlene stepped carefully into the open shaftway and climbed down the steel ladder bolted to the shaft wall, swinging wide over sixty feet of nothingness to clear her big belly, a maneuver that, had her husband observed it, would have sent him into foaming fits.

But he was not there, thought Marlene, and one could not, after all, become an absolute slug. The loft she entered was, of course, the same size as her own loft, but configured quite differently. The sculptor, Stuart Franciosa, had built a neat two-bedroom apartment with all modern cons out of approximately one-third of his space, and left the rest raw as a studio. Into this studio Marlene stepped from the maw of the lift shaft.

He waved to her from behind a plywood workbench, one of several placed around the loft in the good northwest light from the huge windows. Franciosa was a slim, dark, saturnine man, dressed in a black seaman's sweater and clay-encrusted jeans. He had flecks of clay drying in his short dark hair.

He embraced her warmly, then stood away and looked her over with a professional eye. "Stupendous! You've never looked better—glowing like a ripe apricot."

"A palpable lie. I look like shit warmed over."

"Who's the artist here? In point of fact—you know, it just occurred to me this minute . . ." He pushed her hair back and tilted her head up and to the left. "Let your mouth fall open and close your eyes!" he ordered.

"What?"

"No, really, just do it, like you were getting your jollies." Marlene obligingly mugged an orgasmic expression.

"Amazing! You look exactly like the statue of St. Theresa of Avila by Bernini."

Marlene laughed. "I came to borrow some mayo."

"Take." He watched her as she went into the apartment and returned a few moments later with a paper cup.

"Working on anything interesting?" she asked, glancing at the forms standing draped in damp cloths on the worktables.

"Not really. I'm doing mostly jewelry commissions. One must eat."

Stuart Franciosa was doing the kind of sculpture Rodin might have been doing if he had lived to be a hundred and forty: graceful yet massive pieces based on the human body, but subtly modified, antic, self-parodying, referential, romantic: in turns, or all at once. These were starting to sell, but slowly. He earned his rent by making tiny virtu objects and jewelry, witty and erotic, that had become the rage among the upper crust of New York gay society. He manufactured them himself out of gold and platinum, which was why his loft was built like a fort: strap barring on the windows, thick steel door, industrial locks, alarms.

"Where's Larry? At work?"

"No, he has the swing shift tonight. He's lolling in bed, the slut." He was looking at her peculiarly, in a way that might have been misinterpreted as evincing lust. Marlene was starting to wonder if he might be bisexual when he blurted out, "Look, Champ, will you do something for me?"

"Will it take long? I'm going to have a spontaneous abortion if I don't get something to eat."

"I have half a sausage and pepper hero from Paoletti's."

This proved a sufficient bribe. She sat on a stained, legless Chippendale sofa, eating her sandwich, and watched as Franciosa worked. He moved a worktable close to the sofa, placed a wooden turntable on it, constructed an armature of aluminum tubing with the speed and dexterity of a balloon-animal artist, and began to slap masses of ochre clay from a bucket onto the armature.

"What are you doing?"

"Just a little sketch."

"I used to model in college. For some friends."

"Do tell. Now, that's about ready." He had constructed a rough mass about two feet high approximating the shape of a reclining woman. "Now," he said, "take off all your clothes."

Somewhat to her own surprise, Marlene did so. Franciosa arranged Marlene and some soft pillows on the sofa, moving her so that she was seated with her head thrown back and her left arm and leg trailing limply. It was a fairly comfortable position, the loft was warm, and she found it amusing to look exalted while Franciosa sculpted away at the clay mass.

After perhaps an hour had passed, Marlene was roused from her pleasant, if guilty, somnolence by the sound of someone entering the loft, someone who issued a delighted shriek.

"Marlene! What a tummy! My dear, let me look at you!"

These words were delivered in the sugared accents of Louisiana, and shortly thereafter their author appeared before her, beaming. Larry Bouchard was a small, elegant tan person, whose fine-boned Creole features were perpetually lit by the apprehension of some delicious surprise, which, if he liked you, he would communicate in the most extravagant and amusing language. He was dressed in a beige leather coat over medical whites.

He strode over to Marlene's sofa and without asking placed his hands on her naked belly, pressing gently and skillfully on her womb.

"I beg your pardon!" she said in astonishment.

"Oh, don't be silly, dear. I do this all the time. Yes, it's right in the groove. Four weeks, I'd say. Not more than five."

"Larry, I'm working here, huh?" said Franciosa grumpily.

"Oh, be quiet, Stuart! Always flashin' out these peremptory orders—I mean to say! I was just leavin' fo' the mill anyway."

He blazed his remarkable smile at Marlene and said, "Just imagine! The patter of tiny feet in this *grim* environment! An' ah shall be a godmother at last."

Marlene laughed. "Larry, you're too much."

He strolled toward the door. "Not at all. Ah am barely sufficient." He blew a kiss and vanished.

Franciosa was smiling and shaking his head. Larry was not the first Larry that had lived in the loft; Marlene had met at least two previous others. But she liked Bouchard the best, and she suspected that Stu Franciosa did too, which was fine with her.

She stretched and said, "I'm out of position. Do you want to keep going?"

"No, let's call it a day." He threw a damp cloth over the work before Marlene could get a good look at it. "Drink? Dope?"

"No, thanks, I'm supposedly off everything until after. God! Four weeks! I can't believe it! Do you think he's right? My doctor says more like five to six."

"Oh, I'd believe Larry. By all I've heard, he's a formidable nurse. Put in something like eight years in obstetrics. Getting a little burnt out now, unfortunately. He's working the children's cancer ward at Presby."

"Oh, God!" said Marlene, vibrating with the increasingly familiar pangs of Parent Fear. Suddenly she needed a cigarette and a drink, neither of which she was likely to get. She had just hauled herself to her feet and begun to look around for her clothes when she heard the unmistakable heavy tread of her husband on the stairs.

"Agh! It's Butch!" she cried. What was he doing home so early? She dressed in a flash, stuffing her underpants into a pocket, and headed for the lift.

Franciosa, an amused look on his face, remarked, "Hurry home before hubby finds out you've been doing naughty."

"Oh, fuck you too, Franciosa! He can't get in because the bolt's on the door." Then she giggled. "Yeah, secrets of a housewife's day."

"I'll never tell," he called as she clambered up the shaft.

Karp was standing in the doorway, playing Death of a Salesman with his pathetic shopping bag.

"What's wrong? Are you sick? Come in! Sit down! What happened!"

Karp moved silently through this rush of exclamations like a specter through a graveyard mist and collapsed on the red couch. He kept his shopping bag between his feet, like a refugee from an undeclared war.

"I quit," he said. "Resigned. Bang. End of story."

To her credit, Marlene said nothing at this but, prompted by generations of working-class genes, went to the cupboard and poured out a tumbler of red wine from the half gallon and handed it to Karp. That was what was done when the man of the house was on the bricks.

Karp looked at the glass as if he had never been handed a stiff one before, which was nearly the case, and drank half of it down. He made a castor-oil face, then dutifully chugged the rest.

"Now, tell!" said the wife.

Loosened by the wine, he told, succinctly and fairly, blaming no one but himself. It was the death of the girl. He couldn't allow it to be passed off as an unfortunate error, or made into a political football. A sacrifice was required.

Marlene said, " 'Now all the truth is out, be secret and take defeat from any brazen throat, for how can you compete, being honor bred, with one who, were it proved he lies, were neither shamed in his own nor in his neighbors' eyes? Bred to a harder thing than Triumph, turn away, and like a laughing string whereon mad fingers play amid a place of stone, be secret and exult, because of all things known, that is most difficult.' "

Karp looked at her open-mouthed, in frank amazement.

"Yeats," she said. It's called 'To a Friend Whose Work Has Come to Nothing.' Sister Marie Patrick made us memorize it in tenth grade."

He shuddered: the wine and the reaction from the day's events. "Guy knew what he was talking about. Place of stone is right." He looked at her looking at him with her steady if skew-eyed gaze. "I guess you think I'm a schmuck for taking the fall for Peter. With the baby coming."

"That's almost insulting," said Marlene.

"Sorry."

"You should be. My father was on the street for nine months in '51, and he had two kids and one on the way. We always had food on the table and a roof—which reminds me, it's a good thing we don't have a mortgage on a house in the suburbs. Anyway, if worse comes to worst, in six months I'll go back and you can watch the baby."

"A cheerful thought," he said, but the idea amused him. "From putting asses in jail to putting asses in diapers."

She smiled. "Serve you right. But really, what will you do? Go private?"

Karp let out a gush of breath, pursed his lips and considered. "No, I don't think so. I'm still a little confused. It was like—I don't know—having a sort of low flu for weeks, years maybe, and then suddenly it lands in your gut and you puke everything up without warning. Then it's over and you feel kind of light-headed, weak, but basically OK. You just have to sit in bed and it'll be OK."

The phone rang and the message machine recorded a plea to call from a reporter on the *Post*. It rang a minute later. Ariadne Stupenagel wanted a word. Neither of them made a move to answer it as it rang at intervals thereafter.

"Ah, fame," sighed Marlene. "So you're going to take to your bed?"

"No, I don't mean literally. I mean I'm going to take some time. We have about eight weeks' paid leave, so we can coast a little on the money end. Then we'll see." He smiled in a way that Marlene had not observed often enough, a relaxed expression instead of his usual tight grin. She knew it wasn't just the wine. A new Karp was emerging.

"So what will you do with your well-earned leisure?"

"Oh, hang around the shanty. Pinch your ass in the morning. Work on my jump shot. Shit! That reminds me . . ." He looked at his watch. "I have a basketball game to go to tonight. Want to come?"

"Well, you've recovered fast. I thought you'd mope more."

"Yeah, well, I'm basically shallow, Marlene. I put my career in the toilet—what the fuck, right? Tomorrow's another day. Besides, these are gonna be great seats. Bernie Nadleman is holding a couple of tickets. Hustlers and Sixers. We can see Dr. J. So, want to come?"

"Only if he's an obstetrician," said Marlene.

CHAPTER

six

By the end of the first quarter, it was obvious to Karp that the New York Hustlers, while possessing talent and speed, were not a very good basketball team. He had a fine view of just how bad they were, because Bernie Nadleman had provided a seat in the second row behind the Hustlers' bench. The team played in a decrepit arena in Flushing Meadows, a part of the old 1939 World's Fair construction. It was small, dank, and smelly, like a two-thirds scale Madison Square Garden without the memories.

Karp had not attended many basketball games in the past decade, but he had not lost his appreciation of the game, or his skill in assessing a team. The Hustlers were playing well as individuals, but lacked the unspoken, nearly mystical connection between players on the court that separated winners from losers in the pros.

Fred James, the power forward who had replaced the slain Marion Simmons, had been shooting well all through the first half, racking up eighteen points by halftime. But when the Sixers inevitably discovered that he had no idea where the open man was, they double-teamed him continually, and since one of the men working him was Julius Erving, he got only six points in the second half.

The small forward, Jim Lockwell, was an aggressive rebounder, who got the ball a lot and lost it a lot too on unwise passes. He also could have used some free-throw practice. He missed five straight shots in the first quarter.

The Hustlers' center, Barry Croyden, seemed to be competing with Darryl Dawkins for who could make the loudest slam dunk, but in nothing else. At post, he seemed confused, as if he were playing by himself against five people. He was an effective rebounder, but three of his outlet passes were stolen. Croyden fouled out at the beginning of the fourth quarter. He did, how-ever, score sixteen points.

Johnnie Bryan, the point guard, and at an even six feet the shortest man on the court for the Hustlers, was probably the best all-around ball handler on the team, but seemed incapable of using these skills in coopera-tion with his teammates. He did a lot of fancy drib-bling that did not lead often enough to plays or points.

To Karp, the most interesting man on the court was Doobie Wallace, the shooting guard. Wallace was an exciting player, an in-yo-face competitor with enor-mous natural athleticism. Fast, a great jumper, he seemed to radiate energy as he penetrated and went up for flying, twisting shots. His problem was that, for a guard, he was not all that interested in guarding. He scored points, but the people he was supposedly in charge of, working off their more tightly knit team, scored somewhat more points than he did, which was not the way to win basketball games.

And, in the event, the Hustlers lost, 118–98; toward the end the team became shockingly dull, barely going through the motions. The dispirited fans shuffled toward the exits, to which they had started a few minutes or so before the final buzzer.

When Karp stood up, Nadleman spotted him and gestured, pointing to his open mouth. Food. Karp nodded and the coach said, "Ten minutes."

It turned out to be twenty-five, but Karp had nothing better to do. They got into Nadleman's black Chrysler and drove to a big, brightly lit pastrami emporium on Queens Boulevard. Seated and chomping immense sandwiches, they discussed the game. Nadleman seemed eager to talk, although frustrated and irritable.

"I tell them, watch the ball, watch the ball. What ball? They're fuckin' snoozing out there. Bryan watches the ball, I give him that, but one, he's six foot tall and unlike Cousy he's got no shot. What he has got is attitude. You see him out there in the third quarter? The NBA record for dribbling without moving the ball."

"Wallace looked good. James has a lot of talent there," Karp offered.

"Wallace always looks good. It's his main thing. He's good for eighteen, twenty-two points, you could put it in the bank. On D he takes a vacation. He won't fill the lane. He won't go for the loose ball. You know what his assist average is so far? Point nine.

"James, I agree, talent up the wazoo. If he would start thinking, we might start winning games again. You notice how he goes up in the air and hangs there for about a minute or so while he figures out what he went up there for?

"So to make a long story short, my D is in the toilet, nobody's rotating to the open man, my center isn't blocking shots the way a guy that big should be. Our fast break is sluggish. I mean the kids are physically fast, but they get up court and sort of mill around. I got no transition game to speak of, and if I see one good secondary break a game, I'm lucky."

"What's the story on your bench?" Karp asked.

Nadleman shrugged. "Run-of-the-mill, except for Murphy, who's a pain in the ass."

"No, what I meant is it seems to me that if your people aren't playing ball the way you want them to, then park them. Give somebody else a chance. You got Murphy. You got that other big center, what's-his-name."

"Blanding."

"Right, Blanding, and you got that rookie forward from Temple, the kid, Kravic. You can't lose any worse than you already are, and you could put together a different chemistry. Anyway, the starters will get the point. Play my way or don't play."

Nadleman nodded, frowning. "Yeah, I could do that, but if I didn't show some wins right away, Chaney would be all over my ass. How come I'm not using his expensive players? Wallace gets his million per for sinking shots, not for warming the bench. If I had a winning season, then maybe I'd have some clout with the front office. Meanwhile . . ." He shrugged helplessly.

"I take it Mr. Chaney is not all that sensitive to what it takes to run a ball team."

"You could say that," Nadleman agreed. "Sensitivity is not Howard's long suit anyway. Besides, he's completely focused on the new arena. You saw the pit we play in. Chaney's working with the city to build a new one; it was part of the deal he cut for bringing the Hustlers to New York. He's a businessman, as he's always telling me. He expects value for money; he pays for good players, he expects good play. He also seems to think they'll play better in a fancy new arena."

"You tell him about the Celtics and Boston Garden?"

"Hey, I'm worn out talking to the guy," Nadleman replied. "Like I said, he's a businessman."

They finished their sandwiches and Nadleman called for the check. Karp sensed that he did not want to talk any more about the shortcomings of his team. It was unusual in any case for a coach to have been as frank as Nadleman had been already.

Still working on a decade-long sports-talk deficit, Karp said, "That Dr. J is a hell of a ball player anyway."

"Yeah, pure class," Nadleman agreed. "But let me tell you: Marion Simmons definitely came out of the same box. You ever see him play?"

"Not really."

"You missed something special. He could fly. He could penetrate. OK, lots of guys nowadays can do that. But he had something else. He had a sense of the game in his head, like I've never seen in a young kid. He was everywhere he had to be. He was getting ten, eleven assists a game the week before he died. You ever hear of a forward doing that?"

"There's Bradley. And Elgin Baylor."

"That's right. Classic players. But they're six-five and Marion was six-eleven. Personally, there was no limit to where he could have gone. Remember, this was just his second year in the pros. But the point is, from what we were talking about, the whole team just came together around him. He made stuff happen. What you saw out there tonight—that was a wheel without an axle."

"Yeah, I can understand," said Karp, and then he asked, "Anything new on the investigation?"

"What investigation?" Nadleman said bitterly. "Everybody's too busy whining about another brilliant athlete lost to drugs. The cop in charge has got his head up his ass and nobody'll listen to me."

"You sound like you still don't think Simmons was a doper," Karp ventured.

"No fucking way, like I told you on the phone. The kid wouldn't even take pain pills. I'm not saying my guys never touch the stuff—shit, this is New York and they got plenty of money. I'm not their fucking nanny. The way I figure it, if they show up and play good, the rest is up to them. But not Marion."

"How can you be so sure?" Karp asked.

"Hey, I'm around them, I keep my eyes and ears open. I've heard stuff go down, locker room stuff," Nadleman said darkly.

Karp caught something in the coach's voice that decided him against pressing the point. "And Chaney?" he asked instead. "He must be in pretty good with the city. How come he's not pressing the investigation?"

Nadleman glanced at Karp quickly and then away, hiding something in his eyes. "Yeah, well, Howard has already written off his investment there. No point in stirring up more trouble. He tends to be, ah, focused on getting his stadium built."

Nadleman threw some money on the table and walked out to the parking lot. "I heard you didn't have much of a day yourself," he remarked as he opened the car door.

Karp got in and Nadleman took the driver's seat and cranked the engine. Karp said, "Yeah, well, it happens. Some days the bear eats you."

"You're sure you did the right thing?"

"Yeah." And after a pause, "I don't know." Laugh. "I'll let you know in a week."

Nadleman pulled the car out of the restaurant lot. "I'll drop you off."

"You're sure? I'm in the city."

Nadleman looked at him oddly. "This *is* the city."

"No, Bernie, we're in Queens. In New York 'the city' is Manhattan. When you're in L.A., 'the city' means New York."

Nadleman the Californian chuckled and headed the car west on Queens Boulevard.

"So," said Karp as they drove toward the Queensboro Bridge, "if it wasn't dope, why was he killed? Any ideas?"

"Beats the hell out of me," Nadleman replied. "The kid didn't have an enemy in the world, far as I know. And why did whoever killed him want to make it look like a dope-business hit?"

"That's easy. So we would have the kind of situation you've got now. Simmons was carrying heavy weight of prime uncut coke in his car. Heavy weight means serious dealers, which means professional shooters. The cops figure whoever did it is back in Palermo or Colombia by now. Why bother putting a big investigation together? On the other hand . . ."

"What?"

"The investigation is a little too light. One cop, and apparently a rummy. The Queens D.A. doesn't want to know about it. I made a couple of calls. It smells wrong." Karp stared out the window at the grimy industrial blackness of Long Island City. "Tell me, how bad do you want to find out what really happened?"

"Real bad," said Nadleman vehemently. "It's not right, a talent like that, a decent kid like that just . . . wasted. I get dreams about it." He looked inquisitively at Karp. "You're not just asking."

"No. I'd like to look into it. It can't hurt, and it might do some good."

"But you're out of the business . . ."

"True, but I have a lot of connections. I can still work the system. And the fact that I'm not active with the Manhattan D.A. may not be all bad."

"So you'll really do it? Find out what happened to Marion?" Nadleman's horse face lit up like a lantern as they crossed the bridge. In his excitement he let the car swerve momentarily out of lane.

"Yeah, I will," said Karp. "There's a little catch, though."

"Whatever you need . . ."

"OK, I want to be on the team."

Nadleman stared at him, and this time the car really swerved, enough to draw an ensemble of angry horns. "You're not serious."

"I'm dead serious. If Simmons wasn't killed for dope dealing, then it was something else in his life. This wasn't an anonymous street mugging. Somebody set him up."

Nadleman absorbed this as he negotiated the left onto Second Avenue. "But why . . . ?"

"There was a secret. He knew something. He had an enemy. He was going to do something that someone wanted to stop. Whatever—the team knows. There aren't any secrets on a team, as you know."

"Except from the coach."

"Right. Which is why I have to be on it."

Nadleman gave him a long look at a stoplight. "Be honest, Butch," he said. "Do you really think you're a plausible professional ball player? How old are you?"

"I'm exactly the same age as Bill Bradley, who is still playing for the Knicks. I'm six years younger than Bob Cousy was when he played his last game."

Nadleman raised a dubious eyebrow. "Um, yeah, but that's pretty fancy company. And besides, Bradley isn't starting anymore."

"Did I say 'start'? Look, you got plenty of talent on the team if you use it right. You need a twelfth man, and I could do it. And as far as company goes, check out your *Sports Illustrated,* February 1963, the college All-American team picture. I'm the guy between Bradley and Cazzie Russell."

"That was a long time ago, Butch. And you got a bad knee."

"My knee is fine. I'm not going to be mixing it up under the boards in the playoffs. I said twelfth man."

"It's still the pros, Butch. It's not the same game as college in the sixties."

"It's the same game for the player, Bernie. And with all respect, from what I saw tonight, I can play on your team."

Back and forth this way, inconclusively, until Nadleman dropped Karp off on Crosby Street. In overtime, Karp managed to extract from the coach a promise to talk to Howard Chaney about it.

"You have seven thousand messages," said Marlene as Karp entered. "The tape is all used up."

"Screw the messages."

"You should talk to the guys in the bureau. Guma, V.T. and Hrcany all called. They're worried about you."

"They're worried about their own asses is more like it," said Karp unfairly, kicking off his sneakers and climbing up the ladder to the sleeping loft.

"That's stupid and you know it; they're your friends. Besides, Bloom will be begging you to come back before long. I was listening to a talk show on the radio. Everybody thinks there's some kind of big cover-up going down and you got sacrificed."

Karp grunted noncommittally. "Who won?" Marlene asked.

"Sixers, 118–98. Bernie has some serious problems with that team."

"So what was so important about this shitty team that you had to run off to see them play on this particular night of all nights?"

"Well, as a matter of fact, Bernie asked me to look into the Simmons murder."

Marlene sat up with a jerk and stared at him. "And ... ?"

"And I said I would, if he'd take me on the team as a player."

"A good idea," said Marlene after a significant pause. "And as soon as I drop this kid I'm going to start getting on some flyweight cards. I think this Espadas guy is overrated and I could be a contender."

"Nobody thinks I'm serious when I say I want to play basketball," said Karp. "Why is this? I'm a good basketball player."

"I thought you had to be young to play professional," said Marlene and regretted it instantly as unkind.

Karp didn't seem fazed. "It's more important to be smart. Anyway, there it is. If Chaney goes for it, I'm going to do it: my life's ambition, suppressed all these years."

"God, you *are* serious! Can I be a cheerleader? That's *my* life's ambition. Leaping around, assuming I will ever be able to leap around again, waving a what-d'you-call-it. . . ."

"A pom-pom."

". . . a pom-pom, in a tiny white skirt, maddening the crowd with glimpses of plump crescents of creamy buttock."

"I like it," said Karp, running his hand under the blanket and fingering the referenced flesh. "We'll make a great team in pro athletics."

"Speaking of which, what about the murder? You're going to need some help there too."

Karp gave her a look. "Yes, and your end is gestating our baby. That'll be a big help."

"That's the fucking chauvi-est thing you've ever said, and if that's the way you really feel you can take your hand out of my crotch."

"I don't really feel that way, I swear," answered Karp quickly.

"Seriously, Butch, I'm going bonkers waiting around for the blessed event. If there was a baby to take care of, it'd be different, but as it is ..." She brightened with an idea.

"Look, I could at least make calls, set up appointments—you won't have any support, especially if you're spending most of your time running around in your shorts throwing push-ups."

"Lay-ups," said Karp automatically, but he was thinking. Marlene was right. He needed at least somebody to take messages and make calls. The kind of people who were usually helpful in murder investigations were not usually the answering-machine type of caller. Besides, it would keep Marlene at home.

"OK, you got it," he said. "An upwardly mobile secretarial position with the world's only detecting point guard."

"Every girl's dream," said Marlene, sliding into a fetchingly supine secretarial position. Before she lost herself in sexual heat (especially lubricious when you didn't know if it would be the last for some time, with the baby and all), her mind flicked past some intriguing thoughts.

A remarkable chain of events had turned her life upside down. Instead of stretching into a career-centered, bland infinity of petty cases and small administrative advances, it had suddenly become almost picaresque. She found herself having an entirely unplanned baby, married to a semi-famous man who had just walked away from his career, and was now attempting to simultaneously become a professional athlete and solve a major homicide mystery. Which she intended to dive into, with no damn nonsense about taking messages.

What next?

"So what's Butch doing these days?" asked Peter Balducci.

"Playing basketball. And trying to pull my pants off every minute."

Balducci snorted around a mouthful of food, coughed and wiped his mouth, laughing.

"It's not funny," sniffed Marlene, "and 'why' is the question since I'm such a whale—"

"C'mon, you're a knockout."

"You're a liar. God, this is terrific! I haven't had cappelletti in years. He never takes me anywhere."

The two of them were seated in the cool, oil-redolent basement of Paoletti's on Grand, a short block from the loft, Marlene scarfing down antipasto and little gobbets of pork and spinach wrapped in pasta, Balducci grinding through a huge plate of ravioli alla genovese. A neighborhood place, nothing fancy, frequented by Little Italy locals, the more respectable strata of SoHo artists, police officers, and a discreet group of mobsters.

Balducci, a detective in the first year of his retirement, remembered the place from when NYPD headquarters was in the baroque palace down the street on Centre. He was a stocky man in his late fifties with a pleasantly battered face the color of weathered grocery bags, thinning slicked-back dark hair and a liquid glance deep-set in brown pouches. Marlene had saved his life once by shooting the man who had just shot him, and he had appointed himself her uncle. They tried to have lunch every few months.

"So besides your sex life, everything OK? What is this with basketball?"

"Oh, he talked the coach of the Hustlers into letting him play a little on the team, if he would look into what happened to Marion Simmons."

"You're joking."

"Yeah, that's what everybody says," said Marlene, "but there it is. The man is a stone jock. Anyway, he hasn't had a heart attack, yet."

Balducci said, "I never followed basketball. Baseball and football. What about this murder—they don't have cops working Queens homicides anymore?"

"Not on this one, apparently. The word is Simmons was dealing serious weight and he got hit for it. The cops figure it was a pro job and aren't bothering to look very hard."

Balducci's face clouded. "What, if it's a pro job it doesn't count anymore? We give discounts?"

Marlene shrugged. "C'mon, Peter, you know how it is. Besides, there's no juice in the case. The team and the press just wish it would dry up and blow away. It's bad for the image of the sport, as they say. So, the cops got some rummy handling the case all by himself, and the coach is the only guy in town that seems interested in finding out what happened. And now Butch."

"Some rummy, you said?" asked Balducci reflectively.

"Yeah, guy named ... I can't remember—Italian—Bellone, Bella ... ?"

"Not Harry Bello?"

"Yeah, that's the guy. Do you know him?"

"You could say that. We been neighbors for the last fifteen years. Talk about a damn tragedy!" Balducci shook his head sorrowfully.

"What happened?"

"Everything. First his wife, Doris, a real sweet lady,

got cancer. Harry started drinking. I mean more than cops usually drink. OK, one day him and his partner, Jim Sturdevant, had to go into this shithole building in Bed-Stuy to talk to a witness and they walk into a burglary. A couple of kids ripping off an apartment. Right away, no warning—bang! Jim takes one through the head. Lights out.

"Harry goes crazy, tracks down one of the kids and aces him on the spot. A big cloud over the whole thing—did the kid pull a gun on Harry? Was it the same gun that killed Jim, or did Harry use a drop gun? Was Harry in the bag at the time?

"Anyway, a serious mess. Harry stuck to his story and they never found the other kid, so who knows, right? So they finish the investigation, and Harry winds up transferred out of Bed-Stuy to the farm, the one-oh-five out in Queens, and right after that Doris goes. Harry climbs into the bottle and stays there."

Marlene nodded sympathetically. It was a familiar story, although usually it was divorce, not death, that broke the cop. "Was he good?" she asked.

"Huh!" Balducci snorted. "Top of the line, the best. If Harry was still in gear, you would've had the damn killer on a plate last Tuesday."

Marlene considered this for a moment and said, "What do you think, Pete, does he have any stuff left at all?"

Balducci waggled his hand like an airplane caught in a wind shear. "Who knows? He's a sad case."

"We could find out."

Balducci gave her a sharp look. "What is this 'we'? I'm here having lunch."

"You're finished."

"I want coffee and something," said Balducci defensively.

"OK, but then will you at least call him?"

"Marlene, what're you talking here, huh? I'm retired and you're pregnant."

"Peter, if I was retired and you were pregnant, I'd make the call at least."

He grinned and chuckled, shaking his head. "You're a pisser, you know that?"

She stood up. "More than I would like, as a matter of fact. I got to go to the ladies'. Make the call, Peter."

Harry Bello had the day off, as he did most days. He worked nights a lot. He was always available to fill in a swing or graveyard shift for another man, a man who might want to spend some special time with the family. Harry didn't care when he worked.

Nobody had been by the house for over a year. After Balducci called, Harry made a halfhearted effort to clear up the worst of the mess. He got the bottles and the glasses and the frozen dinner trays with their plastic forks stuck in ancient grease, and shoved them into the trash. He thought vaguely of running a vacuum and a dust rag around the living room, but he hadn't gone in there since they took Doris away, after the wake. The sunporch was clean enough. Not that he cared. The doorbell rang.

The smell was the first thing that hit Marlene, coming in from the crisp air of the street: an undertone of spilled beer and scotch and over it something sharper, the ketone stink that an abused liver blows off through the sweat glands: Eau de Drunk.

Wordlessly, Harry led them through a dark hallway to the sunporch at the back of the house, and the three of them sat down in dusty rattan armchairs upholstered in green and purple flowered cotton.

The room might have been cheerful once, the brightest room in the house, looking out at a little garden full of flowers. Now, with the steely light of a late November afternoon coming in over a plot of wet and ragged weeds, it was funereal, a tone augmented by the dozens of dead and shriveled potted plants on shelves and in hanging baskets. There was a clock in the shape of a comical cat on the wall. Still stupidly grinning, it had stopped, its pendulum tail covered in dust. Marlene caught Bello staring at her in an odd way. It's her chair I'm sitting in, she thought.

Nervous small talk. How ya doin'. Fine. How ya doin'. Lies. Balducci was embarrassed and regretted that he had agreed to bring Marlene here. Bello wasn't a close friend; they had never even worked in the same borough. But he was a cop and Balducci could not help feeling the reflected shame.

Marlene described her interest in the Simmons case, and Karp's connection with the Hustlers. She started asking basic questions about his progress. She was amazed that Bello didn't object to this amateur meddling by a Manhattan A.D.A., as he should have, as any normal cop would have. Information was gold; you didn't give unless you got some back or unless you had to, and often not even then. More than the dead plants, it confirmed that his spirit was broken.

And there wasn't much information. Bello had examined the crime scene. He had not attended the autopsy, but he had looked at the M.E.'s report, he thought. He had talked to Nadleman, the coach, and to Marva Simmons, the dead man's mother. He had attended the funeral.

He hadn't talked to any member of the team, or any other of Simmons's relatives, or checked out the drug lead with Narcotics, or ordered a canvass of the neighborhood around the parking lot where Simmons's car had been found, to see if anyone had seen anything that night. Worst of all, it turned out he had made no effort to find how Marion Simmons had spent the last twenty-four hours of his life.

This was too much for Marlene's patience. "Harry," she said. "What's going on? You want to find this guy or not? For chrissakes, they teach little kids in school to check out the vic's movements the previous day. It's like page three in the crime-stopper's handbook—"

"Marlene . . ." Balducci warned.

She ignored him. "So what is it? You think that it's a professional hit and it's not worth the trouble? Because you sure as shit haven't taken any."

Harry just looked at her, as if she were talking about the weather on Mars, something unconnected to him and far away. Marlene stood up abruptly, or as abruptly as she could manage in her condition. Harry Bello started at the movement, like a sparrow beneath a moving shadow.

She said, "Let's get out of here, Pete. This is horse-shit." And then to Bello, "Look here, boss—you had some rough hits, fine! You want to drown your sorrows—great! But do it off the job, OK? Maybe you have to be drunk, but you don't have to be a clown too."

That was stupid, Marlene, she thought as she waited for Balducci to emerge from the little house. It was a post-war brick cottage with peeling white trim, not un-like the one she had grown up in, not five miles from here. Vet housing. No blue madonna in the tiny front yard, though; a clogged bird bath instead, with a tarnished mirror ball in it.

Stupid to get angry like that. She should have worked him, coaxed. Even blind drunk he should have ab-sorbed more than he had apparently picked up. She knew how to work a lush. The truth was, she had been oppressed by his passivity and silence. It frightened her too. On the ride over, Balducci had described some of Bello's exploits, feats of detection and courage that had become famous throughout the Department. If a guy like that could go down the tube, then nobody was safe. Not even Marlene her own self.

The raw wind chased her into Balducci's car. She wished she still carried cigarettes. She rummaged in Balducci's glove compartment and found an open six-pack of Roi-Tans. She lit one on the car lighter and puffed, filling the car with ashy smoke, like the color of the sky above Queens.

Balducci got into the car after a while, frowned at her, and when she knotted her brows and frowned back, he laughed out loud.

"I can't take you anywhere," he said. "Enjoying my cigar?"

"I prefer Macanudos."

"Yeah, well, I'm on a pension. You know, kid, you were way out of line back there."

She nodded and blew a plume of smoke. "Agreed. I embarrassed you and I'm sorry. Blame it on my delicate condition."

"On the other hand, a little good-cop, bad-cop never hurts if you're trying to promote cooperation. Give me one of those cigars."

While Balducci lit up Marlene said, "He talked to you after I left?"

"Yeah. It'll take a lot more booze to turn Harry Bello into a complete fuck-up."

"So give already!"

"First of all, Harry's pretty sure Simmons didn't drive the car to Queens. He thinks the guy was shot someplace else, driven to the lot, placed behind the wheel and finished off with two in the head."

"Why does he think that?"

"Because Simmons was shot once through the lung *before* he was put in the car, and then twice through the head. He only found two casings in the car; that's what got him suspicious in the first place. Also, there's an exit wound in his back and no marks on the seat and no slug from that wound. That confirms it. Another thing: no prints on the steering wheel. It was wiped. As was the driver's door handle. Simmons was put in the car. Oh, yeah, and no coke in the kid at all."

"Interesting. So how come he didn't bust a gut trying to find out where the vic took the first shot?"

Balducci shrugged and blew a long stream of smoke, like a visible sigh. "Ran out of steam, I guess. Harry is not hitting on all eight lately, as you saw."

"Yeah. Is that it?"

"No, something else. A little vague here. Harry says he was checking out the photographs they always take of the funeral. He says he was wondering why there wasn't a girlfriend or two among the chief mourners. An attractive, famous, rich, unmarried guy should have a girl, right? Anyway, in the back of the crowd there's a white woman nobody seems to recognize."

"Whoopee!" yelled Marlene. "A missing bullet. A mysterious woman! Am I in heaven or what?"

"I'm taking you home," said Balducci. "You should start making dinner for your husband."

Marlene ignored the avuncular advice. "You come too, Peter. We need to get our heads together and figure out how we're going to approach this case."

"Again with the 'we,' " he said. "I don't like that, Marlene."

"Of course you do. You're bored shitless sitting around the house, getting in Marie's way. This'll make a new man out of you."

"It'll kill me, is what it'll do," said Balducci, trying to be glum and failing.

"Nonsense, you'll love it," she said.

* * *

Francine Del Fazio, a homemaker on the census forms, had been a semi-pro prostitute for nearly five years, working out of several bars in Bayside, although she would have been appalled and insulted had anyone actually called her a whore. She had a nice little bungalow on a quiet street in Little Neck, a car of her own, and a husband who left her more or less alone, didn't drink and made a nice living. Queens paradise, but . . .

Of course, she didn't have any kids, which was the main problem. Frankie wanted to adopt, but she thought, The hell with it, I'm gonna bust my hump wiping up somebody else's kid's shit, and that idea had been quietly dropped.

So, time on her hands. She was thirty-two and bored out of her mind. He made enough so she didn't have to take a dumb factory or clerk job, but not enough so she could buy anything really nice. She was thirty-two, and the lines were starting to bite around the eyes and the corners of her mouth. Of course, she still had those nice tits, and she had kept her weight down, and she took good care of herself. Still, it made her cry sometimes, early in the morning, looking in the mirror.

On the other hand, she was not one to brood, nor was she interested in making a break from Frankie. Although the cool hood with the lilac Bel-Air and the duck's-ass haircut that she had loved and married out of high school had metamorphosed into a jowly, pear-shaped machinist who fell asleep in a lounger in front of the TV every night, being married gave her a certain status. Her family, her friends, would not comprehend leaving a good provider because of . . . what? It wasn't rough, she couldn't complain, it was just zero, and it was hard to get up and go from one zero to what figured to be another zero, where she would also have to bust her ass paying the bills.

Francine, in any case, was too shrewd for that. There were no flies on little Francine, her mother had declared from her early childhood.

It had started with a guy in a bar; he ran a carpet-cleaning operation, nice car, dressed sharp. A hot affair, Tuesdays and Fridays, for a year. Then the guy kissed her off—his wife was getting suspicious, he had kids. She understood, and to tell the truth, she had been getting a little dragged behind the whole thing too—it had started to feel like being married to two guys.

But, to her astonishment and delight, he had made her a parting guilt offering, a twenty-four-karat gold bracelet with a little diamond in it. She had pawned it for four hundred and fifty dollars the next day, and it had struck her forcibly that there was no need to go through the whole year-long song and dance, the bitching and the boredom, before getting the little giftie at the end. You could shorten the whole process considerably.

There were rules, she told herself, that marked a distinction between what she was doing and the girls did out on the stroll. One guy, no, make that two guys, or at any rate never more than three or four guys on the string at any one time. No cash money, just little gifts, either real jewelry or unopened and, hence, exchangeable, brand-name luxury goods.

She learned not actually to ask for these things, but how to make them appear without asking. Men were schmucks after all. She was clearing eight hundred, twelve hundred a month at the end of her third year.

Stan Malinski was a recent conquest; she'd known him for around three weeks. He had a free hand with large bottles of imported perfume, which he got from a friend who drove for Bergdorf's. She'd been a little uneasy about doing it in the sleeper of the truck, but after a while she got into the kinkiness of it. Thrills were, after all, part of the secret life.

That night when they had heard the cars coming into the alley, Stan had frozen in mid-screw and put his face to the truck window. He was paranoid about the possibility that his wife might hire a private detective to follow him around. When he saw the guy walking over, he had jumped back into the sleeper and put his hand over her mouth; that had pissed her off, like *she* was going to yell and attract attention. When the guy climbed down from the step and walked away, they had relaxed and had a giggle.

Her heart almost stopped when they heard the two booming reports. OK, somebody had whacked a guy out. It didn't concern them, and they sure as hell were not going to call the cops. In fact, she hadn't seen anything, having spent the whole episode flat on her back. But Stan was practically gibbering with fear. She calmed him down a little, but not nearly enough to get him back in the saddle. They waited until the killers had driven off and then separated, she driving away in her Toyota and figuring that she'd never hear from old Stan again.

And she hadn't, and hadn't thought about him at all for the next two days, although she had followed avidly the press coverage on the Simmons murder, and then she had seen the little two-inch piece in *Newsday* about the cops finding his body. She hadn't known Stan Malinski very well, but she was a good judge of human nature and she didn't figure him as somebody who would blow his own brains out.

She surprised herself that she was not in terror, that she was thinking calmly and rationally about the murder of an acquaintance by professional hit men (for what else could they be?) and about the possibility that they might be interested in her.

The good news was that they hadn't seen her. They might not even know she had been there, unless Stan had volunteered the information, and why should he have? Even if he had, he hadn't known her last name, or her address, and there were a lot of Francines in New York. There was the car—they might have noticed that. It might be wise to get rid of it, on the off chance, and she had enough stashed away to get another car, a better one, maybe a late-model T-bird.

As she thought it through, there seemed no need to get all that excited—yet. They were just men, after all, and she hadn't met one so far that she couldn't outsmart.

CHAPTER
seven

"So, are you mad at me?" asked Marlene, the first words out of her mouth after Balducci had gone.

"Why?" asked Karp as he began clearing the table. "Am I showing anger or resentment? Being surly?"

"No, but I thought you might be hiding deep reservoirs of rage that might burst forth when a girl least expects."

He smiled benignly at her and stacked dishes. "Well, now that you mention it, when you walked in with Balducci and it became clear that not only were you messing with this case in a way I thought we had agreed you weren't going to, but also that you had roped Peter into it, without discussing it with me, yes, I did feel a flash of red-hot fury."

She said, "Which, however, passed away because of the terrific dinner I whipped up. No, don't scrub out the pot, let it soak; I'll take care of it tomorrow."

"Yes," Karp agreed, "the dinner was great, but the real reason was that it suddenly occurred to me that you were going to do what you were going to do and there wasn't anything I could really do about it." He put down his sponge and turned away from the sink, looking straight at her.

"And then I thought about my dad. He liked things done his way too. Gave my mom hell when she didn't toe the line. I'm starting to recall that he might have popped her a time or two. He sure had a heavy hand with the kids. In any case, what happened was that she became a sneak, and she got me to be a sneak's helper. Little lies about where she was and what she had bought and how much it cost.

"I've just started to remember a lot of stuff like that. And so I started thinking maybe I was a lot more like him than I wanted to be, as far as being king shit went, and that you were coming back at me in the same way—getting into sneakiness. And I didn't like it."

She stared at him in happy amazement. "God, Butch! Insights flow out of you as from Montaigne. I'm astounded. And delighted. I thought we were in for a screaming match."

"If you thought that, why did you do it? Maybe you like screaming matches?"

"There's also such a thing as *excessive* insight, Dr. Freud," she sniffed. "What ever happened to the simple jock I married?"

"He has become a complicated jock," said Karp. "I guess I never had time to think about all this stuff when I was working at the D.A. Workahol is a great drug. Since I quit, and since I started playing ball again, I've had more time to . . . it's not just thinking. My head feels like an empty balloon. All that space that used to be full of schedules and hassles and preparing cases, it's working on life. *People* v. *Karp*."

"I can live with that," said his wife, and gave him a hug, which turned into a longish smooch among the steaming dishes.

Later that evening, Nadleman called and told Karp that Chaney had agreed to let him play.

"I sold it as a gimmick," Nadleman said.

"A gimmick?"

"Yeah, I said the town is full of guys who played some college ball and who think they could have played in the NBA if they just had the chance. I said you'd be a draw for those guys, and he bought it. Also, I said I was going to keep James in the power slot and that we didn't need a franchise player, which meant our replacement could be a twelfth man, and that you were the cheapest twelfth man we were likely to get. Howard loves cheap."

"Stop with the flattery, Bernie, I'm blushing all over. OK, I'm a gimmick. What about the investigation part?"

"Uh-uh. That's between you and me."

"Oh?"

A pause on the line. "Yeah, well, in the first place, Howard is not what you would call tight with information. He's got a mouth on him, so if he's in on it, it's all over town, which probably would not help our game all that much. Also ... I get the feeling that he would like to put this Marion thing way behind him."

Again, that odd tone. Karp decided to push it a little.

"Bernie, do you mean he's just cutting his loss like a businessman, or something else? Like he knows something about the hit?"

Nadleman laughed uneasily. "No, the businessman thing. Howard doesn't like unpleasant stuff. Speaking of which, he said he wants you on ten-day contracts, the usual minimum. We'll renew as needed. I assume that's OK."

"Let me get this straight," said Karp. "You're gonna pay me to play basketball? What's the usual minimum?"

Nadleman laughed. "It's 2,700 bucks for the ten weeks."

"You mean $270 a week?"

"No, dummy, $2,700 a week, each week."

"Holy shit!" said Karp with fervor.

"Welcome to the big time, sport," said Nadleman. "There's a press conference at eleven at the Hilton; he wants you there. Practice starts at three, at Memorial."

Karp had not been treated like a piece of meat since the age of nineteen, and he had never been treated as a clown. Chaney was master of ceremonies for the circus. He was wearing a double-breasted blue blazer with a yacht club crest on the pocket, over a white shirt and a yellow spotted tie. His face was ruddy under a five o'clock shadow of Nixonian density, and he had a fleshy nose and prominent, almost floppy ears. A memorable face, and no stranger to the press and cameras.

He made a little speech to the small group of assembled journalists and TV crews in which he expressed his pleasure in inviting one of New York's finest young men—well, he wasn't that young—har-har—to play with the Hustlers. While Karp writhed, Chaney went into a sentimental flight about how it was never too late for a dream, how Karp represented all the good school players of the past who never got a crack at the pros, all the schoolyear champs who thrilled . . .

The questions were even more embarrassing. Somebody brought up Bill Veeck's old stunt of hiring a midget to play for the St. Louis Browns, a man supposedly guaranteed a walk every time up because his strike zone was so small. Did Mr. Chaney feel that it was the same kind of stunt? Chaney laughed and said something about show business being show business and that he had always admired Bill.

It was inevitable that the Simmons case should come up. A man from CBS asked if putting a D.A. on the team was part of the investigation. To Karp's surprise, Chaney answered, "Why don't we let Butch answer that himself?"

Karp explained that he was on leave of absence from the New York D.A., was not interested in pursuing any investigation officially, and that, in any case, the Queens D.A. was in charge of the case. Somebody asked how he felt when the Chelsea Ripper had claimed his last victim. Karp ignored him. The *News* guy asked nastily whether he seriously thought he could compete in the N.B.A. Karp said, "No, I don't. Neither can twenty per cent of the players in the N.B.A. I'm not here to start. I'm here to fill a twelfth man slot, and I think I can do it."

Murmurs and snickers, but something about Karp's carriage and perhaps something in his eyes stayed any further sneering attacks. He was not after all a midget. After a few more questions directed at Chaney and Nadleman, the conference began to break up. Karp walked out without another word to anyone.

Three hours later, Karp arrived for his first practice at the appointed three p.m. to find the stadium locked and deserted. He hung around in the doorway, questioning his sanity, until let in by the trainer, a hefty, balding man, a little past three.

The Hustlers, it seemed, did not start practice on the dot.

"You the new twelfth man, huh?" said the trainer, unimpressed, and issued Karp a red practice uniform. Karp undressed, wrapped his bad knee in an Ace bandage, put on the uniform, took a ball out of a net bag and walked onto the court.

Karp did stretches and one-footed deep knee bends. The problem joint was holding up nicely. It hurt, but just enough to let him know it was there. Then he picked up his ball and started throwing it through the basket.

He was still sinking shots, still deep in the semi-trance this sort of practice induced in him, when he became aware of other people moving about the court.

The Hustlers, all eleven of them, had drifted onto the court. The five starters, John Bryan, Barry Croyden, Doobie Wallace, Fred James, and Jim Lockwell, were wearing white uniforms. The remaining six were dressed, as Karp was, in red. Nadleman came onto the court wearing a white short-sleeved shirt and electric blue sweatpants. He spotted Karp and nodded, and then there appeared on his face a puzzled frown, as if he had forgotten that Karp was really going to be on the team.

Not precisely playing on the team, of course. An N.B.A. roster has twelve men on it, although even practice scrimmages require but ten on the court at any one time. The two extra warm bodies exist to fill the place of their betters when these are bushed or injured. On this particular day, the first and second teams were in the pink of health. Karp and the other spare guy, a thirty-year-old journeyman named Chas McDoul, were required for the first drill, which involved three groups of four doing two-on-two, pick, pass and shoot, and then toward the end of the practice they got to take their place on the line to shoot fouls. Otherwise, they sat on the bench, and waited for someone to pull a muscle.

The practice, as it unfolded, confirmed and helped to explain Karp's prior analysis of the New York Hustlers. The team had no cohesion, no spine, and the players knew it. There was little (so to speak) hustle; nobody dived for the loose ball. The four-man drill had been conducted at a pace that Karp thought inferior to

what you could pick up any Saturday at the 4th Street
playground.

Nadleman yelled advice from time to time, but it
was clear that his heart wasn't in it. Karp had to admit
that his friend did not have the moral dominance that
a coach needed to make a bunch of good athletes into
a winning team.

The scrimmages were the proof. Scrimmaging with
one's own team is in many ways harder than playing
an opponent. All the plays, all the endemic weaknesses
are known. That is, in fact, the point of scrimmaging—
to make you play with no advantage, to push you
against yourself, like boxing with weighted gloves.

The Hustlers' scrimmage resembled a badly organized playground game. Fouls everywhere, shoving,
cursing. The second team was putting somewhat more
into it than the starters, obviously trying to impress the
coach: Karp thought Ed Murphy showed more hustle
than John Bryan, his starter opponent at point guard.
Phil Kravic, the big forward, had nowhere near the raw
athletic talent of Fred James, but he seemed anyway to
be snagging more rebounds.

Sutter Blanding, the second center, and at seven-one
the team's tallest player, was nothing like the whiz on
D that Barry Croyden was, but he would at least move
without the ball and try to hustle plays. Stu Elmore, the
second team's shooting guard, was a terrific defensive
player, guarding Doobie Wallace with an aggressive intensity that made sweat skitter off his shaved skull and
stuck a permanent scowl on his face.

Not that it did a lot of good. Wallace was just a better player, a better ball handler, a devastating shot from
twenty feet out, and, to Karp, the most interesting
player on the court. He threw convincing three-pointers
too. Karp had to admit that as a shot, Wallace was as

good as Karp, and with legs besides: he was releasing his jumpers from nine and a half feet in the air.

The result of this talent was that Wallace was often good for thirty-odd points a game, Fred James for a bare twenty, the rest of the Hustler starters around a dozen each, and with various contributions from the subs, the Hustlers were regularly scoring ten to twenty points too few to win games in the N.B.A.

After five minutes of scrimmage, Karp also knew how to fix the team. Wallace was the key. An outside shot as good as Doobie Wallace was like a knife in the heart of any opposition team. He simply could not be allowed to shoot at will, and so whenever he got the ball he would draw defenders like a magnet pulling paper clips.

By the ineluctable, but eternally neglected, arithmetic of B-ball, two men guarding Doobie meant that one Hustler was being guarded by zero men. Passing to the open man was the obvious move, but the passing was not working. The open man wasn't moving to Wallace's passes, and the passes were to the wrong man or wide or slow.

But worse, besides wasting Wallace's talent, the Hustlers were also wasting the talents of Fred James, because they were not using him in intelligent alliance with Wallace. James had no ball-handling skills to speak of, but if he was given the ball anywhere in the lane he would fly through the air unstoppably and drop it into the basket.

A dead shot and an airborne penetrator should have been a decisive combination. That they were not, that the team could not coalesce into an effective unit, puzzled Karp; it annoyed him, like a loose thread in a suspect's story. He glanced over at his neighbor. McDoul was deep in a prep book for the New York state real estate broker's license. Karp sighed. It was, after all, not his concern. His wave-making days were over; let Bernie run the team. But what a shame!

The scrimmage ended. They took a short break. The Hustlers ignored Karp pointedly, except for McDoul and Wallace, who at thirty were the team's oldest members (besides Karp himself) and remembered Karp's college career. Wallace had played at Oregon State, and so had been on teams whose older players recalled Karp's Pac-10 glory very well.

Wallace seemed fascinated by Karp's background; he thought his belated return to the world of big-time ball was a sketch.

"So how come Bernie let you on the team?" Wallace asked. "He lose a bet?"

He would learn, thought Karp, when he read the papers tomorrow. "Something like that. He saw the thing in the papers. We knew each other from Pac-10 ball. He looked me up. I was tired of being a lawyer. He needed a twelfth man, and the rest is history. Oh, yeah, Mr. Chaney thought it was a good gimmick."

"A gimmick? Oh, like a girl or a guy with one arm." Wallace didn't appear surprised. He laughed and said, "Yeah, well, you were great then, is what they say. Hey, just don't make us old bastards look bad out there, give the owner ideas."

"Not that I'll get to play," said Karp.

"Who knows?" said Wallace, bulging his eyes and waving his hands like a stage wizard. "Anything can happen in the mysterious world of the Big Time."

The coach called the team together for a brief talk about the game with the Knicks that night in the Garden. Karp couldn't fault Nadleman's strategy, although it was not at all clear whether he had the authority to enforce it.

Karp lined up with the others to shoot fouls. Wallace was at the head of Karp's line, and Karp watched him

flawlessly sink ten in a row. Karp had warmed to the
man spontaneously. He was much like Karp physically,
about the same size and build, with the same ability to
concentrate his entire being on creating a perfect ge-
ometry of force, ball, gravity and the hoop. If Karp had
been born black in Compton, like Wallace, and had
kept his knees, he might have been standing there in
Wallace's skin, a real pro, a star.

This thought disturbed him. He wasn't a ball player;
he was a prosecutor investigating a crime. No, actually,
he wasn't that either. He had spoken truly at the press
conference. What *was* he doing here? He felt a queasi-
ness of soul, a little softening of the identity. Although
the sages tell us such qualms are the beginning of true
wisdom, Karp was not buying any today, and as his
turn came up, he lost himself instead in the discipline
of the foul shot.

He sank his ten, and then moved to a vacant basket
and took some more shots. He sank twenty in a row,
then missed, then sank ten more from the top of the
key. He was vaguely aware that some of the other
players were watching him silently as they drifted toward the showers. The court cleared out. Karp was
alone, still shooting.

Calmer after fifteen minutes of this, he went back to
the now deserted locker room, showered, changed, and
then found that the doorway he had used to enter the
stadium was now locked. He wandered around the unfamiliar corridors for a few minutes when, attracted by
the sound of voices, he mounted a flight of stairs and
came to a suite of offices.

Four doors opened off the corridor, and these were
glass-fronted and labeled "PUBLICITY," "BUSINESS
MANAGER," "COACHING STAFF," and "GENERAL MAN-
AGER," of which only the last was lit. At the end of the
corridor was a red-glowing exit sign and a likely way

out. As Karp headed toward it, he passed the lighted door and glanced in.

Bernie Nadleman was in the throes of a violent argument with Howard Chaney. Karp could not hear, through the glass, what the argument was about, but he could guess it had something to do with the Hustlers losing five straight games. Such confrontation was a part of pro ball that Karp didn't care to think about, and he moved quickly past the window and out of the building.

The dead man's mother, Marva Simmons, lived in a large, well-kept Tudor house in the Forest Hills section of Queens, not far from the famous tennis courts. Her son had bought it for her with the proceeds from his first pro contract, making her one of the few black women in the neighborhood who was not wearing a white uniform.

Harry Bello's car crunched over the fallen leaves of the driveway and came to a stop in front of the two-car garage. Marlene had called him the day after their first, unhappy meeting, and asked the detective to arrange an interview. Bello had complied, without enthusiasm and without objection. Marlene had wanted to apologize to the man, but something about his desperate passivity had prevented her, as if, in retreat from his personal hell, he had placed himself beyond all human intercourse.

Mrs. Simmons was tall, about five-ten, heavily built, and wore a black pants suit. Her hair was a tidy set of gray bristles; her yellowish face was trenched with darker lines, especially around the eyes, whose underpouches seemed to be eroded by tears.

She led them into a draped and darkened living room, and sat them on new plastic-covered royal blue velour armchairs. Marlene noticed that she walked stiffly, as if hurt.

One side of the spacious room was taken up with a bookcase crammed with trophies and awards from Marion Simmons's basketball career. A long side table held a dozen or so framed photographs of Simmons and another child, a girl, at various stages of life, from babyhood through youth. The opposite wall was nearly covered by an unnaturally bright depiction of the Last Supper, done in tapestry.

Marlene introduced herself, disingenuously, as from the district attorney's office. Mrs. Simmons looked at her suspiciously.

"I already talked to them." She had a low, hesitant voice, and her gaze flickered away from Marlene's, darting between the Last Supper and the memorabilia of her dead boy.

"Yes," said Marlene, "but you haven't talked with me yet. I'm working another angle on the case. The, ah, drug angle."

This was Mrs. Simmons's cue to blaze out that her boy had never used drugs, as she apparently had done when last interviewed by Harry Bello and the folks at the Queens D.A. But she did not. Instead she seemed to shrink into herself. She mumbled something.

"What was that, Mrs. Simmons?"

"I don't know about those drugs. I don't know where he got them."

"But you're not surprised he was using? And selling?"

A mumble that sounded like "I knew" came from the woman.

"Excuse me, Mrs. Simmons, but that's not what you said earlier. When Detective Bello here interviewed you right after Marion was killed, you said you were sure he never had anything to do with drugs."

The woman shrugged heavily. "I was wrong," she said. "What does it matter now, anyway? Let the boy rest in peace."

"Well, it matters a great deal, Mrs. Simmons, if we're going to find the people who killed your son. You want us to find them, don't you?"

This was, of course, meant as a rhetorical question, and was a commonplace in the armory of prosecutors trying to get bereaved kin to give details about the less savory activities of their freshly killed relations. Mrs. Simmons, however, seemed to give the question serious thought. Or perhaps she had drifted off into a deeper trance.

Silence hung in the room, and so they easily heard the approach of an auto, the slam of its door, the entrance of its putative passenger into the house, the approaching steps in the foyer and hall. The three of them turned toward the open doorway of the living room like an audience cued to the entrance of a star on stage.

The newcomer had planned on a furtive entry; her head was down, her raincoat collar was pulled high, a black beret was jammed down low upon her forehead, and her booted steps were quick. But as she passed the doorway and became aware of her audience, she froze for an instant and turned to them, like a jacklighted deer.

Marlene observed her with interest. This was obviously the daughter and sister. She was tall, about five-eight, Marlene reckoned, with her brother's elegant long-necked grace. But she was bone thin, and her face under the beret was an unhealthy yellow-tan, with smudges under the eyes and a sore at the corner of her mouth.

Marlene waved and called out, "Hi!"

The young woman broke and ran for cover. They heard a door slam deep in the house.

Marlene turned back to the mother. "That's your daughter, isn't it? Leona." Mrs. Simmons nodded hesitantly, as if even this admission would open her family to further violation.

"Would it be OK if we talked to her?"

"No!" she shouted, so loud that Marlene jumped involuntarily in her seat. Some deep current of anger had been released by this outburst, and Marlene found it directed at her. "I don't want you bothering her any more, do you understand? She's sick. She's been through enough."

"What has she been through, Mrs. Simmons?" asked Marlene as mildly as she could.

"Don't play with me, miss! Don't you people have any feelings? What more do you want to take from me?" Mrs. Simmons was truly agitated now, and Marlene, although completely baffled as to its cause, had interviewed enough people to know when it was time to cut and run. She rose abruptly and said, "Thank you for your time, Mrs. Simmons," and in two minutes was out of the door, with the shuffling Bello in tow.

"What was that all about, Harry?" asked Marlene when they were back in Bello's car.

Shrug. "Flipped her lid or something. It happens."

"Yeah, but why did she roll on her kid using drugs?"

Shrug. "Who knows? People change their stories."

"And how about the daughter? You think she might have been involved with drugs too?"

"Could be," he said flatly. "Where did you want me to drop you?"

"My mom's. It's off 97th. Take Woodhaven south. What do you mean, 'could be'? Did you see her eyes? Her pupils were the size of neutrons."

After a long moment, and in a voice that seemed dragged out of him, Bello said, "I'll try to find him. Check the sheet."

Marlene looked at him in astonishment. For someone who appeared until that moment nearly brain dead, it was a remarkable statement, compressing at least three logical jumps, and assuming she was capable of grasping that leap. She felt oddly flattered.

"OK. I'll do it," she said.

"It was fucking eerie, Butch," said Marlene that evening. It was late and she had just gotten back from Queens, where she had dined at her parents'.

"Here the guy was a rutabaga, and all of a sudden he's talking in code. For a second I thought he had slipped his gears. I mention the sister's got her eyes pinned, and he says, 'I'll try to find him.' It took me a second. He was saying, *of course* the sister's a junkie, so *of course,* if the bro is into drugs, she's connected that way, so *of course* if he was really killed in a sour dope deal, whoever supplies her with dope has got to be a key player, so the next move is to find her pusher."

"Very fancy," said Karp, "and also he's got you checking to see whether she'd ever been arrested."

"Right, and I will."

"No, I will. You look wasted. I noticed it when you walked in. I don't like you running around Queens this close to delivery. And, as I recall, you were supposed to stick by the phone on this deal."

"I'm OK," Marlene bristled.

Karp patted her shoulder and looked her in the face, his expression grave. They were seated together on the red couch. "Yeah, you're always OK," he said. "You eat dynamite. You shoot bad guys in the head. Soon you're gonna have a baby in a cab on Linden Boulevard in the middle of rush hour. No, don't argue, let me finish.

"Like I told you before, I know you're gonna do what you're gonna do; I accept that. But let me just appeal to your rationality. One, in re: checking out the sister's situation, I will get more out of the Queens D.A. than you will. That's a fact; it's unfair and unwoman's liberated, but there it is and you know it's true.

"Two, I'm going to have to travel with the team starting in two days. I may be picking up important stuff. Peter'll be working the street, checking up on Bello or whatever. There's no way we can coordinate things except through you, which means you have to stay put. Does that make sense?"

A long sigh emerged from Marlene, and she slumped more comfortably into the crook of his arm. She couldn't argue. He was right. The day had given her shooting pains up her thighs and back, and the fact that she had to urinate every five minutes or so put a serious dent in her investigative zeal.

"Whatever you say," she said wearily. "Christ on a crutch! Defeated by biology—who would've thought it? OK, no more running around until the baby comes. Knitting booties. Cooking nutritious and satisfying meals for my jockoid hubby. A full life."

"Sounds good to me. And you left out terrific, soul-scorching sex every single night without exception."

"In your dreams," she said. "I'm surprised you have any energy running up and down the floor all night to no good purpose. By the way, John and Peggy were at Mom's for dinner, and he said he watched the Nets game on TV and spotted you on the bench. He was so jealous he could hardly eat."

"Yeah, at least it was a good seat for the game."

"Will you ever get to really play?"

"Oh, sure," Karp said with a sour laugh, "if a mete-
orite came down through the roof and squashed the
five starters, I might have a chance to play." He
shrugged. "Meanwhile, leave us not forget the point of
this exercise, which was to find out who killed Marion
Simmons, which is not a game."

The following morning, Karp dressed in his lawyer
outfit for a meeting with the Queens A.D.A. in charge
of the Simmons case, Jerry Thelmann. He had had no
difficulty getting the appointment. The secretary had
recognized his name.

Thelmann proved to be a stocky man, perhaps half a
dozen years younger and ten inches shorter than Karp,
with thick, prematurely graying hair, heavy black
hornrimmed glasses, and an expression that tended toward the pugnacious. He wore red suspenders.

He greeted Karp cordially, reaching over his desk to
administer a handshake perhaps a trifle too firm. Short
perhaps, but no one to be fucked over, was the clear
message.

Karp announced his purpose frankly: he was on
leave from the New York County D.A., but a friend,
the coach of the Hustlers, had asked him to look into
the murder of his star player. He described Marlene's
observations at the Simmons home and suggested that
Leona Simmons might be an interesting lead.

Thelmann nodded. "We know her. We're on top of
that already," he said confidently.

"She's got a sheet?"

Thelmann waved his hand dismissively. "Petty shit.
Boosting. A couple of lightweight possession charges.
Typical rich junkie."

"Who'd she buy from?"

The same gesture. "Street guys, locals. Nobody who
could even touch the weight Simmons was carrying."

"So you don't think that she was involved in any way with her brother's murder?"

"I didn't say that. We're working the connections."

"I see," said Karp. "And who's this 'we'? I thought that Harry Bello was handling the investigation on his own."

This brought a snorting laugh out of Thelmann. "Hey, give me a break, all right? Bello can barely find his car keys."

"There's another investigation?"

"In a way. The Simmons murder is, uh, associated with a complex and highly sensitive multi-borough narcotics investigation."

"Conducted by ...?"

"Conducted by a task force under the direct supervision of Mr. D'Amalia." Having mentioned the sacred name of his boss, the Queens D.A., Thelmann took a deep breath and looked uncomfortably around his office, his eyes falling on a variety of interesting objects before returning to Karp.

He continued, "Look, Mr. Karp, don't think I'm trying to be uncooperative, but this is locked up tighter than Murphy's asshole. It's my own white butt if it gets out. I mean, I respect your rep and all, but ..." He gave a helpless shrug.

Karp said, "I understand."

Encouraged, Thelmann went on, "And look: I appreciate what you're trying to do for Nadleman, but this is really at a delicate stage. I'm not saying you would necessarily screw it up ..."

"But you want me to lay off?"

Thelmann smiled in relief. "It'd be the smart move. Look, I'd like to talk with you more, but I got a lunch at noon."

Karp rose. "Yeah. Hey, I appreciate it. It's a lot clearer now."

"A pleasure," said Thelmann and gave Karp another manly shake.

In times past, Karp might have been fuming at this point, for there was nothing that irritated him more than seeming a fool in areas where he considered himself a master. But he had relaxed enough to enjoy the role of clown: a fuck-up at the New York D.A., the goat on the team, and now a bumbling amateur about to mess up someone else's carefully constructed case. The beauty part was that it would keep Marlene on ice indefinitely. He couldn't wait to tell her.

As he emerged from the Criminal Courts Building, he spotted a line of blocky off-white vehicles purveying food to the lunchtime masses. The day was clear, and mild for late fall, with high veil-like clouds and chunks of unfamiliar blue sky sitting above the bare trees of Forest Hills. Karp headed for a cancer wagon and purchased a sausage, onion and green pepper hero with a bottle of Yoo-Hoo to wash it down. He found a sunny bench and sat down to eat and watch the crowds. Not one of them, he thought with real pleasure, represented a case he was responsible for, not one of them wanted a deal.

One of the crowd was, however, a familiar face. Jerry Thelmann was hurrying down the steps of the courthouse like Bojangles, glancing up and down the boulevard as if trying to spot a friend. He waited on the pavement not twenty feet from where Karp sat. A minute or so later, a big limo, a Lincoln, oozed silently up to the curb in front of him, and he got in. The license plate on the car read "B-BALL 1."

Karp's sandwich stopped abruptly halfway to his mouth. His stomach flipped, and not from the toxic qualities of his meal, for the man in the backseat of the Lincoln, with whom Jerry Thelmann was engaged in excited conversation, was Howard Chaney.

CHAPTER

eight

The third time she saw the Chevrolet, she knew it was following her. Francine Del Fazio had continued with her regular activities, except, naturally, hanging out in bars and going with men, and had spent considerable time in the driver's seat, watching her mirrors. An anonymous blue sedan, but it always had the same two guys in it, and they were that kind of guy.

She had been driving east on Northern Boulevard, en route to do a little Christmas shopping at Mays in Great Neck Plaza, when she spotted them. The car behind her had passed, leaving them exposed. Francine accepted this discovery without much apprehension. If they knew who she was and they hadn't killed her yet, they probably weren't going to. No, they wanted her to know they were watching her, in case she decided to be a jerk and go to the cops. Francine was not a jerk, so she really had nothing to worry about. Nor did she see any reason to change her plans. She took the exit for the shopping mall, parked, and went off to spend her hard-earned money.

"So the question," Karp finished, "is what do we do now? Do we believe Thelmann? If we believe

Thelmann, do I tell Bernie? What if we pull back and nothing happens?"

"I could ask around the cops," offered Peter Balducci.

"Yeah, so could I, Peter," said Karp. "Plus I know people in the Feds, but the problem there is that if it's this tight, if they're so worried about leaks that they stuck that poor bastard out there with a phony investigation, then there's no reason they're gonna talk to either of us."

Karp and Balducci were sitting in the loft, at the round oak table in the dining area. Marlene was sitting disconsolately in a shabby bentwood rocker, literally knitting a bootie and attempting to ignore the discussion, as agreed.

After a moment Karp said, "Thelmann was pretty convincing. If I hadn't spotted him with Chaney, this whole thing would be history. What the hell were they talking about?"

Balducci smiled and said, "How about basketball? Thelmann is a Hustlers fan—he won first prize with the lucky soda can, an hour in a limo with Chaney discussing team strategy."

"Yeah, and the second prize is two hours," said Karp. "No, it's crazy. It had to be something to do with the murder. But why Chaney? Bernie says he's a loudmouth, one, and two, he was trying to forget the murder. The last person a tight-ass like Jerry would talk to. Unless . . ."

"What?"

"Unless Chaney is involved in the investigation. As a witness, say. Or an informant."

Balducci considered this. "It would help if we knew where Simmons was the night he got killed. We know he was shot someplace else besides that car. But . . .

shit, we're back to the same place; if you buy Thelmann, we can't risk doing squat."

Silence, and the maddening click of knitting needles. Then Marlene cursed vividly and threw her bootie across the room.

"Something wrong, dear?" asked Karp mildly.

"Yes, my knitting is not going well," said Marlene icily.

Karp rose and picked up the bootie, a gnarled pink lump the size and consistency of a softball, and placed it back on her lap.

"I couldn't help noticing you haven't mentioned Bello," she said. "Before we give up, we should talk to him, find out if he had any luck."

"Marlene, he's a lush. A stooge," said Karp.

"He's a genius," Marlene shot back.

"Peter," he said wearily, "talk to her."

Balducci rubbed his hand over his bald spot. He seemed embarrassed. "Well, kid, the thing of it is, he's been hitting the sauce pretty hard. I found him sleeping it off in his car on a couple of these mornings. I don't think he's doing much police work."

Marlene set her jaw in an expression Karp knew well. "I still say we don't bail out until we talk to him. We're just taking Thelmann's word for it. Did you actually see Leona's sheet?"

"No, but—"

"See? Something's fucked up. They're shining you on. I want to talk to Harry."

Karp nodded sharply and he rapped his knuckles on the table.

"OK! Fine! Get Bello up here and talk all you want, assuming he can climb the stairs. I'll be gone with the team until next Thursday: Boston, Cleveland, Indianapolis, Chicago, and we finish with the Hawks in Atlanta on Thursday night. I'll see what I can find out

from the players about Simmons's last night and anything else that seems connected. But let's agree that if
we don't get something really convincing by then,
we're closing the store."

He glared at both Marlene and Balducci until they
each nodded solemnly in agreement.

"Follow her, Joey," said Carmine when the woman
had left her car.

"I whack her in the garage?" asked Joey.

"No, Joey, you just follow her and find out what
she's doing in there, if she meets anybody, whatever,"
explained Carmine patiently. "And, Joey—keep away
from her, like I told you," he added.

Joey grunted noncommittally and strode off in pursuit of the woman. Carmine cursed forcefully in Italian
for half a minute, then lit a large cigar and tried to relax. In one ear and out the other, that kid. He explained, he argued—the only thing he hadn't tried was
the last resort, fear, and Carmine wasn't even sure *that*
would work: the asshole was too dumb to be afraid.

Carmine himself was not exactly afraid, although he
retained a bad feeling about this entire operation. They
had hit two people to protect it, with the prospect of
more. Not that Carmine minded killing, but every hit
increased the possibility that the operation would be
compromised, an operation that depended for its very
success on utter secrecy. That was why he couldn't
hire any local talent, why he was stuck with this
scemo, why he couldn't put together an adequate watch
on the woman.

He couldn't just whack her, not before he had determined whether she had told anyone what she had seen
in the interim between the shooting of Marion Simmons and the present. It had taken him a week to find
her, even after learning her name. The city was full of

Del Fazios. She could have told her husband or some other man or her priest or . . . there was no point in thinking about it. They would have to pick her up and ask her. Joey could do that part; he liked that part, and it suited his talents.

It took Harry Bello five days to find out where Leona Simmons got her dope. It would have taken only a day or so, but he had been sick a lot lately, a couple of blackouts, and once, in the night, dozing fitfully on the sunporch, he had seen Doris come through the door and sit in her old chair. Which wouldn't have been so bad, but then he had to go and pick a fight with her, on account of her leaving him, and the more she explained that it was the cancer and it wasn't her fault, the more he shouted and said she was getting back at him because of what happened at the place on Lewis Avenue. After a while he was really screaming, and lights were going on all over the neighborhood and people were yelling.

Bello had shut up then. He didn't want to explain to other cops about Doris.

The next day he had driven to Leona's house and parked down the street and spent a pleasant morning in the car listening to the radio, and popping the engine and heater every once in a while when it got too chilly. About eleven-thirty, Leona came out, entered her little yellow Datsun and drove off.

He thought she would go south to Jamaica or St. Albans, where the drug markets were thicker on the ground, but instead she turned west on Jamaica Boulevard and then onto Fulton toward Bed-Stuy. Bello felt a pang of dread. He had not been in this area since the thing on Lewis Avenue, and he was always careful to skirt the neighborhood on the rare occasions when business forced him into Brooklyn.

It hadn't changed. Street after street of brownstones and short tan apartment houses, some of the best housing stock in the city slummed out. Gaps where burning had cut the losses of some landlord, leaving lots occupied by shanties and fire barrels surrounded by ragged black men. Broad commercial streets, slowly dying, every third storefront empty and the rest more like demi-fortresses than stores: the liquor stores with their windows filled with concrete blocks, the dry cleaners barred with iron gratings, the small convenience stores manned by fearful Asians who kept one hand under the counter.

But nearly every block held a tiny record store, blasting music out to the street, and a couple of nail-and-hair parlors: life went on. Fulton Street was full of people and traffic. Bello ignored the sights that had once been his daily study and concentrated on the yellow car, his fingers gripping white on the steering wheel. It turned right on Ralph Avenue and pulled up double-parked in front of a high-stooped brownstone. Leona Simmons got out and pushed her way through the black-coated, rag-headed players who adorned its steps, and entered the building.

She was in there ten minutes. When she emerged, Bello let her drive away. It was getting late to go back to the office, and besides, he had nothing to do there anyway. And after the cruise through Bed-Stuy, he badly needed a drink. He went back to his house in Queens, had a big scoop of J&B and called a couple of old friends in the 79th Precinct. They were surprised to hear from him, but they told him what he wanted to know, what he had already suspected from the look of the men surrounding that brownstone on Ralph. Then he called Marlene Ciampi.

"John Doone," he said without preamble when Marlene picked up the phone.

"What?" she said, and then after her brain stumbled into gear and she realized who was talking to her and what the name meant, she said, "Great, Harry—way to go! So what's this guy's story?"

"Jamaican. Runs what they call a posse. A dope gang. Major handler citywide. Got a rep."

"What kind of rep is that?"

"They say he's a jointer."

"I never heard that one," she said. "What's it mean?"

"A Jamaican specialty. They get pissed at you, they take you apart joint by joint. The good ones keep you alive until the last one, your neck. Then they throw the parts in a trash bag and leave it in a can. They get real pissed, they might throw in your wife and kids too."

"Harry, this is for real?"

She could almost feel the shrug over the line. "Bags of parts turn up. Sometimes not all the same person in them. And never the head."

"What do they do with the head?"

"You'd have to ask them about that. It explains the other day. And it buries the case."

Marlene was getting used to this jumping from track to track. Bello was talking about their visit to the Simmons home. If Leona was involved with a guy like John Doone, she and her mother had every reason to be frightened and to resist questioning by the police. And if admitting her son's drug involvement would take that pressure off and maybe keep her daughter from getting hurt, then it all made sense.

It also tended to support what Karp had learned from Thelmann. If Doone was a serious cocaine merchant, and a killer, then there was every reason to believe that a citywide operation might have him as a target.

Marlene's mind raced. What to do now? What did

she tell Bello? That he was a distraction for the real investigation?

To delay this embarrassment, she said, "Um, Harry, so what do you think? You want to talk to this guy?"

It was a stupid question, and she knew it. There was a long pause on the line. When he spoke his voice was flat. "Yeah, I'll ask him did he shoot Simmons. Maybe he'll confess out of remorse."

More silence. What was he waiting for? She thought, Oh, what the fuck? and said, "There's another investigation, Harry. Out of the Queens D.A. It's a big sweep, and I think Doone is involved in it. They were just letting you be a ... distraction."

He said, "Yeah, I figured. What've they got?"

"This I don't know. I just heard about it. What do you mean, you figured?"

"Come on, Miss Ciampi! I may be a lush, but I'm not an asshole." He paused and she heard a clink that could have been a bottle hitting a glass. "So what do we do now?" he asked. "Whoever told you about it must have told you to lay off, right?"

"Right."

"You gonna?"

"I guess. I said I wanted to talk to you first."

"That must have gone over good," he said.

For some reason she couldn't define, she did not want this final conversation to end, and so she ignored his last comment and said, "So, anyway, you think it's this Doone character did it?"

"Well. Since you ask. No."

"Why not?" The line crackled silently. "Harry? Are you there?"

"Yeah. So. Why not, right? Why not?" A pause, and then, "You home now?"

"Yeah, Harry, that's how I picked up the phone when you called me."

"Oh, right. What're you doing? Making dinner?"

"No, my husband's out of town. I was just going to grab something from the fridge."

He said, "Doris used to make this big kind of lasagna with sweet sausage in it. It would last for days. I used to heat it up if I came home in the middle of the night. Last all week. We never had any kids. You're pregnant, aren't you?"

"That's right, Harry."

"Jim Sturdevant had three kids, Francie, Jim Junior, and . . . Mack. He got shot. Jim, not Mack."

"Yeah, I heard," she said. His pain radiated through the tinny sound of the earpiece, through the drunk talk. Her eyes smarted as she listened to him ramble, disconnected things about his wife and his partner and his partner's kids, about buying them presents, about parties they had been to together, Jim and Doris, and Jim's wife, Maggie, and the kids. It all came oozing out, helped by the ersatz intimacy of the telephone. He called her "Doris" twice and she didn't correct him.

At last and without an obvious break, he started talking about the murder. "Why not? I'll tell you: because it's not a Jamaican hit. Leaving fifty large worth of prime rock in a glove compartment is not Jamaican. Two in the head in a Caddy in a parking lot is not Jamaican. Shooting him someplace else and bringing him to Queens is not Jamaican. It's Mob, or some asshole who wants it to look like Mob, or . . ."

"Or what, Harry?"

"Nothing, forget it. I forgot what I was gonna say. I gotta go sleep. You gonna brush your hair?"

"Yeah, Harry, I might. Why do you ask?"

"Nothing, just . . . check the pictures. It's the woman with the head scarf."

"What woman, Harry? Harry . . . hello?" But the phone was dead.

Marlene took a deep breath, hung up her phone and poured herself a tiny glass of red. The baby kicked her, as it was doing with increasing frequency.

"Come on, kid," she said aloud, "give Momma a break."

Sighing, she sat down on the red couch and, taking up a yellow pad, began to make notes on the conversation she had just had, including what seemed to be extraneous details and ravings. With Bello, you could never tell what was extraneous, what was message and what was static. Listening to him was watching a play illuminated by a very slow strobe light, or listening to one side of a conversation between two people in an intimate relationship: twins, or a married couple, or two detectives who had been partners for a long time. The unspoken context, the net of associations, was absent, and with it, clear meaning. Marlene sensed that Harry Bello, or some part of him, his analytic genius perhaps, was attempting, in a hesitant and boozy way, to establish another context, with herself as the other partner.

The baby kicked again. That's all I need, she thought, another parasite. No, a symbiont. But what's my end? Fascination? A case to work? Not being Mom-at-Home?

Marlene looked at her notes. The woman with the scarf. Bello was referring to the funeral photographs. She vaguely recalled that off to the side in one of them was a group consisting of a man in a hat, a man with sunglasses, and a woman with a scarf, none of whom had been identified as yet. Balducci was supposed to be working on this problem.

It was nine, not too late to call Peter. When he got on the line, Marlene summarized the conversation she had just had with Harry Bello, leaving out the loonier segments. Balducci listened in silence. "So what do you think, Peter?" she asked.

"I don't know, kid. It's just speculation. I mean, he doesn't have any real reason for thinking it wasn't this Doone mutt. The girl is in with a heavy dealer, the victim's got a ton of drugs . . . it's starting to look *more* like a coke war, not less, if you want my opinion."

"The thing is to see the girl again, alone. And we should talk to Doone."

"We should definitely not do that, Marlene," said Balducci with some asperity. "We agreed, you and I and Butch agreed, that we weren't going to take this thing any further. You had your talk with Harry, like we said, and that's it. Case closed."

Marlene took a deep breath to stifle a harsh reply. She heard voices and the clinking sound of people eating and drinking.

"Having a party, Peter?"

"Yeah, just a couple of people over. So how you doing? A basketball widow, huh?"

"I'm doing fine, Peter. I've been living by myself for ten years and I've been married six months. Look, about this woman with the scarf and the two guys—did you get anything on them?"

"Zilch."

"Nothing? Where've you looked?"

Balducci sounded embarrassed. "Well, the truth is, Marlene, I haven't been feeling a hundred percent this last week. I got these chest pains, got no energy—"

"Oh, no! Did you see a doctor?"

"Yeah, sure, what're they gonna tell me? My pump's shot? I already know that. Meanwhile, Marie goes apeshit every time I get up from the lounger. I think my days of working the street are over, doll."

"Yeah, well, I'm sorry, Peter. Look, could you just

get all the stuff you have back to me—the photos, any
notes you took—"

"Why? It's over."

"Just humor me, Peter. You never can tell. Maybe
when this big investigation breaks, we can make a con-
tribution, however small. You know how it is, some little connection . . . it could help."

Balducci agreed to humor her, and after a mutual
pledge of concern for each other's health they hung up,
after which Marlene cursed imaginatively and did a
foot-pounding dance of rage for about thirty seconds,
until the baby kicked her yet again and she stopped,
suddenly sad and exhausted.

A nice bath was what was needed. She stripped, tot-
tered up the little step and folded the insulated cover
back from her huge tank bath. A column of dense steam
arose. She switched on a small black-and-white TV
resting on a bookshelf within easy viewing distance of
the bath, and entered the steam like a Wagnerian heroine making an exit.

She floated in the semidarkness, her attention drifting between an old Betty Grable movie and literally
contemplating her navel, now swollen and bobbing
above the ripples like a pink Malomar. The film ended
and the news began. Politics and crime. A tittering feature about teenagers with green hair. She was distracted from her reverie by her husband's name. The
sports announcer was saying something about the
game between the Hustlers and the Celtics that night.

She saw a tiny Karp, looking strange in his uniform
(like an old clipping brought magically to life), take
the ball from a teammate, drive past an opposing
player, his face intense, his hair dripping sweat. Then
the camera cut to a full-court view, and she saw Karp
heave the ball all the way to the opposing basket. It hit
the rim, bounced high, and went in. A buzzer sounded.

Cheers. And then the blow-dried blonde was back saying that the Hustlers had broken their five-game losing streak, the first game they had won since Marion Simmons's "tragic death."

Karp had apparently done something remarkable. She wished for the first time that she knew something more about basketball. Karp would call later, as he always did, and he would explain it in profuse detail.

She leaned back and immersed her head in preparation for a slow and luxurious shampoo. When she broke the surface, a loud bell was ringing. She swore and climbed out of the bath. Head wrapped in towel and robed in a tattered black and red silk kimono, she marched over to the street-side windows, heaved one up, and stuck her head out to see who was ringing the street-level bell.

A man was standing in the light of the street lamp grinning up at her.

"Raney!" she cried. "What the hell're you doing there?"

"Can I come up?" He waved a manila envelope. "Pete gave me some stuff for you."

"Sure. Here's the key." She picked a split tennis ball with a key inside it from a table and tossed it down.

A few moments later, Marlene opened the door to James Raney, a NYPD detective out of Zone 6 homicide in Manhattan and the former partner of Peter Balducci.

"Well, well," said Marlene, offering a cheek for a kiss, "to what do I owe the pleasure?"

"Delivery boy. I was over Pete's for dinner and he said you wanted this stuff." He placed the manila envelope on a side table. "I got the midnight tonight and I wasn't going to go the hell back to Malverne anyway, so I said I'd drop it off."

He reached out casually and rubbed her belly. "This is coming along pretty good."

"Yes, it is," said Marlene curtly, "and I'd like to know why every Tom, Dick and Harry feels entitled to palp my womb. Christ! People on the goddamn bus do it."

Raney laughed and sidled a hand around where her waist used to be. "Hey, I'm a friend. Mmm, you're not wearing anything under this kimono, are you?"

She slapped his hand away in annoyance, partly feigned, and looked up at his grinning face. Raney was about thirty, with red-gold hair, skim-milk skin, turquoise-chip eyes—her type, for sure, so why, given her taste for (and track record with) guys who looked like they entered stage left on a wire, did she end up with a hulking Jew, inclined to the morose? A mystery of life, or maybe because Karp was earthy, of the earth, and a necessary anchor. A month with Raney, or the other Raneys of her past, was a guaranteed case of the screaming fidgets, and she'd done that already. Still, the old tug was there.

Slightly flushed, she moved away from him, playing respectable matron. "Have a seat, Raney. Want a drink?"

He sat on the couch and patted his lap, which she ignored. She poured him out a Miller. He asked, "What's in the envelope?"

"Let's see." She sat down next to him and dumped the contents of the envelope on the black door coffee table. A thick stack of eight by ten glossies of the funeral party, both the original shots and blow-ups showing individual faces. Blow-ups too of the license plates of the vehicles used. A printout matching plate numbers with registered owners' names. Balducci's sketchy notes.

The individuals in the close-ups were all identified

with big red numbers, and a hand-written list linked
these numbers to names, except for the two men and
the woman Marlene had mentioned to Peter. She
glanced through the notes, then shook out the envelope
to see if something was stuck within it.

"Shit!"

"What's the matter?" asked Raney.

"Oh, Peter didn't chase down the plate numbers on
the rental cars. This trio I'm interested in must have
rented a limo. Somebody has to go to the livery companies, find out who was driving that day, and show
them funeral pictures. That's the only way we can find
out who these folks are."

"Can't you do it by elimination? It looks like Pete
ID'd most of them."

"No, because half the people there came in hired
limos, and a lot of them were hired by firms." She
shuffled out a sheet of paper. "Here, look! LP Products. The Menton Agency. Marpol, Inc. Which people
came with who? It's impossible to tell."

"You want to tell me what this is all about? I
thought you were taking a break."

Marlene offered a wan smile. "OK, you asked for
it . . ." She told him the whole story, up through her
conversation with Bello.

"So there it is," she concluded, "a dead end. But not
a dead end if I could get some help." She gave Raney
an appraising look. He laughed and stood up. "No
fucking way, honeybunch. I love you and I still got
dibs on your first extramarital affair, but this is a loser.
In the first place, they're screwing up the ongoing investigation. Hubby and Pete are dead right on that, and
I wouldn't touch it with a pole. Second, you don't want
to go anywhere near John Doone."

"You know him?"

"I heard the name a couple times. A buddy of mine,

Tony Draper in the three-oh, was interested in him for a pile of soup bones somebody made out of a small-time dealer up in Inwood. Got nowhere. Man is a stone killer."

"Can you get me in to see him?"

"Who, Tony?"

"No, Doone."

Raney laughed again and rolled his eyes. "You're a sketch, you know that, Ciampi? Doone, my sweet ass! Go to bed." He walked out of the loft, still chuckling.

Marlene jumped a little as the baby kicked again. "Who the fuck asked you?" she shouted at her central bulge.

Riding back to the Sheraton, the Hustlers were raucous, yelling out the windows at the few women strolling on the chilly Boston streets and raising their index fingers in the familiar "number one" sign. The team had never beaten the Celtics in the Garden before, nor had they very much expected to this time, but they had, and it was Karp's doing.

Karp, however, was not joining in the fun. He had no great wish to scream obscene invitations to women or stick his index finger in the air, and besides, he knew what a fluke it had been.

He hadn't expected to play at all. But John Bryan had shown up that morning with food poisoning, and Stu Elmore had banged a knee badly in practice, and Ed Murphy had been hit in the face by a charging Celtic and retired with a broken nose. Nadleman had looked at his bench and, forced to choose between McDoul and Karp, had given Karp the nod, and so he made his pro debut on the sacred parquet of the Boston Garden, playing against the likes of Jo Jo White and John Havlicek.

He went in with two and thirty-two left to play in the second quarter with the Hustlers down by seven. His man was understandably more interested in guarding Doobie Wallace than an unknown white guy, so Karp broke free easily and made himself so open that Barry Croyden couldn't help hitting him with a pass just outside the three-point circle. Unbothered, unrushed, he swished it through.

Then Croyden blocked a shot and Karp was there where the ball came down. He whipped it across to Wallace, who took it down court, faked a shot, and then (amazingly) *passed* it to James, who dunked it. Karp felt fine, more detached than nervous, surprising himself (*I'm playing the Celtics in Boston Garden!*); after all, it was just a game.

The Celtics scored, then Wallace scored, then Croyden, with an assist from Karp, a fancy, blind behind-the-back pass. Croyden grinned at Karp after that one and held up his thumb. Lockwell stole a Celtic pass and the Hustlers took off on a fast break that ended with James dunking another. Tie score. The Garden was rumbling. The momentum of the game seemed to have passed to the visitors. The Celtics tightened their defense and picked up a foul off Lockwell, which they converted to a two-point lead with ten seconds left in the half.

Karp by this time had his basketball *nous* cooking, and had entered that peculiar state where he seemed to be able to see a half second into the future. He knew, for example, that the Celtic forward was going to throw up a brick; before it had flown a yard from his fingers he knew where to pick up the rebound. As he rushed past Fred James, he said, "Fast break. Go!"

James took off like a deer the instant Karp had the ball. Sixty-two feet from the basket Karp heaved a baseball pass. It was supposed to fall into James's hands right at the foul line, and he should have had no trouble making the shot to tie.

But as soon as Karp released the ball, he knew it was going to be too high. He watched, open-mouthed, as it flew over the forward's straining fingers, hit the rim, bounced twenty feet in the air, and went in.

Stunned silence from the crowd for an instant, then the buzzer, and the Hustlers were all over Karp, slaps and fives and hugs. The remainder of the game was anticlimax. The Hustlers' game came together, the ducklings became swans all, and they beat the Celtics by eight. Karp played twenty-two minutes and got fourteen points, ten assists and five rebounds. His knee hurt like hell and he wanted to call Marlene and go to bed.

This was hardly possible. The Hustlers were in the mood to celebrate. At the hotel, Karp headed straight for his room, which he shared with Chas McDoul. McDoul wasn't there and Karp turned off the lights, threw himself down on his bed and closed his eyes: just a moment to relax and then he would call Marlene and get undressed.

He woke with a start, in the dim glow from the bedside clock, his nose filled with unfamiliar perfumes. There were two women in bed with him, one chocolate with her hair in beaded cornrows, the other a strawberry blonde with purple lipstick. The blonde was nuzzling his ear; the other one was rubbing his groin. He sat up straight, knocking them both aside, to the sound of giggles and male laughter. The room lights went on.

McDoul and Doobie Wallace were standing there, grinning. Wallace was in a white hotel robe and McDoul was wearing slacks and a T-shirt.

"What the fuck . . . ?" said Karp. "What time is it?"

"Lovin' time," said Wallace. "Welcome to the fringe benefits of the N.B.A."

"Um, not right now, guys," Karp said, rising from the bed. He smiled politely at the giggling women.

"In that case," said McDoul, "I was wondering if you could ..." He made a flitting motion with his hand.

"Oh, sure," said Karp, hiding his annoyance. He was no stranger to what big-time athletes do in the off hours; he had done his share. But he was grumpy at being tossed out of his own bed and irritated with himself at having failed to call Marlene.

He went down to the lobby to search out a phone and ran into Bernie Nadleman.

"Butch! I was just starting to look for you. Come and have a drink."

"Bernie, I need to call home—"

"Just for a minute," said the coach, grabbing at Karp's arm. He led Karp into the hotel's lounge, a dark place done up in mock colonial: artfully scarred wooden tables, brass lamps, and smudged portraits of eighteenth-century personages. The waiters didn't wear wigs and knee breeches, but you could figure that the owners were considering it.

Nadleman steered Karp to a round table in the corner whose half-dozen seats were occupied by men of a characteristic type. Karp had met their clones before at booster rallies and sports award dinners, clustering importantly around every major center of professional and (as if there was a difference) high-end college athletics. They were often beefy and always loud. They demanded the best service and got the best seats and never waited on a line. They owned teams.

In fact, Karp observed, one of them owned the team he was on. Howard Chaney had been vigorously celebrating the victory of his boys, and his broad face was flushed with drink. He hailed Nadleman heartily and grabbed his hand. He raised his glass in a clumsy toast, sloshing liquor on the table and his sleeve.

"Heyyy, Bernie!" he cried, "way to go, Coach! Fuckin' Celtics, way to win 'em." The power boys around the table bellowed agreement. Nadleman said, "Howie, this is Butch Karp. You said you wanted to . . ."

Chaney stared up at Karp for a moment before he recalled why Karp had a claim on his interest. "Oh, right. Hell of a shot, Karp." To his friends: "Hey, guys, this guy just shot the second longest basket in N.B.A. history—fuckin' amazing! You do that every game you can have my daughter." Loud laughter. "Twice, you can have my wife." More laughter. Chaney seemed to remember something and peered at Karp narrowly through the fumes of cigar smoke and booze. "Hey, guys, this is the fuckin' D.A. I was telling you about! The boys kill anybody out there on the court, I guess you can take care of it, huh?"

Chaney beamed at his cronies, his hand extended palm out toward Karp, as if presenting for approval an unusually large bass. Everyone laughed, including, Karp was unhappy to see, Bernie. Karp allowed a tight smile to crease his face, nodded to the company, and began to pull away from Bernie's steering hand.

"Hey, where you going, Butch? I thought we could have a drink." They moved away from the power table, which ignored them.

"I'm tired, Bernie. I'm an old man, remember?"

"Just one, OK?"

Karp sighed and followed the coach to a booth. They ordered beers. Bernie grinned at him and said, "Old man, my ass! You were unbelievable out there tonight. I just wanted to tell you I was wrong. You turned the whole team around."

Karp gave him a sour look. "Bernie, I did not turn

the team around. What I did was I heaved a high pass that went in by a fluke. What turned the team around was that Doobie started passing and moving without the ball. He had more assists tonight than he's had all season. Why he should start now, I don't know, but there it is."

Nadleman smiled and shook his head. "You were great."

"Yes, I was great. I'm a good point guard. But Bryan is a good point guard too, minus his attitude, which by the way might improve if you yanked him occasionally and put in Murphy or McDoul when he gets up to his tricks. The thing is, I'm a good point guard for ten minutes. There's no way I can do consistently what I did tonight." He indicated his knee. "It won't take the pounding. And besides, we shouldn't forget why I'm really here."

"Oh, that." Nadleman's face darkened and he took a chug of his beer. "So. You learn anything?"

"Some. You ever hear of a guy named Thelmann? Works out of the Queens D.A."

"Yeah, I think I met him once, just after Marion got killed. Short little guy?"

"Yeah. Does Chaney know him?"

Nadleman shrugged. "I don't know. He could. Why?"

"Because I saw Thelmann last week and he gave me a line about not fucking with the Simmons case because it was part of a big citywide investigation that was coming to a head. And later, outside the courthouse, I saw him getting into a car with Chaney."

Nadleman's jaw dropped. "Are you sure?"

"Positive. So what's the story? Is Chaney into something with the Queens D.A.?"

"Christ, Butch! It's hard to believe. The last time I

suggested that he use some of his clout with the City to get more action on it, he went ballistic on me."

Karp thought of the argument he had overheard on the night of his first practice. He said, "Well, who knows? Maybe it was something else."

They finished their beers, making desultory small talk, and Karp went back to his room, where he found McDoul in bed reading his real estate book.

"I see the party's over," said Karp.

"Yeah, they're down with Doobie now. Man, that mother never gets enough."

"Well, I hope you didn't use my bed." Karp sat and picked up the phone, then paused. "Fill me in here. The whole team indulges in these parties?"

McDoul snorted. "No, Blanding's a churchgoer. Kravic's just married. Some guys got regular girls in this town or that."

"How about Marion?"

"Marion?" McDoul's brow knotted. "Well, he hung with Doobie and Jamesie pretty much, and those two were basically the team's crotch commission. But the last couple of months he dropped out."

"He had a girl?"

"That's the story. Doobie saw him outside a club with this incredible fox, a blonde, and we started to rag him on it, you know? And he wouldn't bite. Like, one time, in Atlanta I think it was, we got us a couple of chicken buckets, and Doobie says, 'Hey, save the white meat for Simmons. That's what he likes.' Some shit like that, and Marion gets real pissed and walks out. So we left off of him after that."

"Uh-huh. She have a name, this girl?"

"I never heard it. He wouldn't talk about it. The rumor mill says she was married, but I can't vouch for that. How come you're so interested?"

"I'm not. Just bullshitting. But I hear Simmons was a hell of a ball player."

"You hear right, son. And it wasn't just his talent. I mean, the girl—it's fucking amazing he had anything left to prong a chick. Like, we all joke—'basketball is my life'—but it was true on Marion. Hey, I dig the game and all, but Marion could be a little boring on the subject, if you want to know."

"Not as interesting as real estate."

McDoul chuckled and looked at his book. "Yeah. But the difference is, when your legs go, real estate don't give a good goddamn."

CHAPTER

nine

"It's me," Karp said. "Is it too late?"

"No, I've just had a bath, and then Jim Raney dropped by."

"Oh?"

"Oh me no 'oh's' in that tone of voice, my boy," said Marlene. "He was over at Pete's and did me the favor of dropping off the funeral photos."

"So he didn't join you in the bath?"

"No, I just stuck my creamy butt out and we did it fast dog-style in the doorway, like always. How about you? I heard about you big-time pro stars. Getting any?"

"No, but everybody else is and it's making me horny. What's this about the funeral pictures? I assume you talked to Bello."

Marlene told her story, focusing on the discovery of John Doone and Bello's doubts about Doone's involvement in the murder, and about the unidentified trio. "So that's that," she concluded. "The obvious next steps would be to talk to Doone, talk to Leona, and run a serious check on the livery companies, but I obviously can't do that without Balducci and Bello, and besides, there's your famous secret investigation—"

"It's not mine, dear," said Karp, "and whether it's Jerry Thelmann's or not remains to be seen. But for your information, I think I found your blonde."

"No kidding! Who?"

"No name yet, but the word is, Marion was seeing a white woman, blonde, possibly married."

"Hmmm, enter a host of additional motives, from a jealous husband to the K.K.K. Of course, that doesn't explain the coke."

"Unless the husband is a coke dealer named Bubbah Jim Bob. Look, we can't do anything right now. I'll be back on Thursday. I'll show the pictures to a few people, maybe get a confirmation on the girl. I also want to see whether we can pin down where Marion went on the night of. I looked it up, and it was a game night. He might have told someone where he was going.

"The weirdest part is, I'm not tripping over anyone. I've talked to one or two people on the team, and kept my ears open; Marion's still a subject of conversation. Nobody has talked to these people. If Bello is just a distraction, where's the *real* investigation?"

"Maybe Chaney is the only one in on it."

"Um, yeah, but you haven't met Chaney. He drinks and gets drunk. He pals with a bunch of guys who look like they get around. He's the last person I'd use in a confidential investigation, unless he's an actual eyewitness to the murder, in which case, why haven't they arrested someone? It doesn't make sense, and it's starting to piss me off. This sucks, even for Queens."

"And what should I do meanwhile?"

Karp was about to say, "Gestate," but stopped himself in time. Instead he said, "Use your imagination, anything you can dig up, but, um, avoid anything official. If Thelmann *is* running some game, I'd rather he didn't hear about it. If he's kosher, we'd be in serious shit."

" 'Use your imagination'! Gosh, what confidence in little wifey! This is a change. It must be true love at last. Mmm—my nipples are stiffening with desire, my lush thighs slide together under the sheer silk of my kimono. Tiny droplets of love juice start to pearl on the matchless coral of my nether lips . . ."

"Good night, Marlene," said Karp.

The next morning Marlene was up early and feeling perkier than she had in weeks. She slipped into her kimono and after breakfasting on a large pot of tarry Medaglia D'Oro and a square of warmed-up Sicilian anchovy pizza, attacked her home with energy. She made the bed, swept and damp-mopped the entire loft, dusted surfaces that seemed to need it, gathered and filed the funeral pictures from the night before, pinning the blow-up of the mystery trio to the corkboard next to the refrigerator, wiped down the stove, watered the plants, left out cat food on the fire escape for her wandering cats, sorted and bagged the week's laundry, collected the trash in plastic bags, and then, having worked up a fine sweat, lay down on a mat in the middle of the floor to do her Lamaze natural childbirth exercises.

You were, of course, supposed to have The Father there to coach you along; the line drawings in her book showed a generic husband being a perfect modern man. Karp was, however, not a perfect modern man, which, all things considered, suited Marlene pretty well. He was willing to do the necessary, but she could see his heart was not in it.

Nor was hers. Her image of an appropriate accouchement involved grave elderly Sicilian ladies (in rustling black with jet ornaments and cameo pins), steaming caldrons, secret herbal drinks, and herself on a brass bed, gripping the bars, screaming curses at God and men, while the ladies crossed themselves and gave conflicting advice. The men, of course, would be out in the yard with the other animals, smoking yellow cigarettes and discussing politics and extortion. *That* was childbirth.

Nevertheless . . . she puffed and panted, counting appropriately, for twenty minutes, then arose and turned to a more interesting sort of practice. Marlene had been introduced to sleight-of-hand by a physical therapist several years back, when a letter bomb had damaged her hands, especially the left one, which lacked the ends of the two smallest fingers. She had worked at it diligently during her therapy, then dropped it, and had recently taken it up again, thinking that she could delight little children at birthday parties with magic tricks, and thus become a more nearly perfect mom for little whomever.

She also found it marvelously relaxing, this endless repetition of finger moves, like a drug that shut off the worrying centers of the brain. You couldn't look at your hands; that was the key, except in the mirror, when you had the trick down; it had to be unconscious action, like Zen archery.

Marlene sat at the dining room table with a small tinfoil ball, a steel thimble, and a nickel laid out before her, facing a framed mirror propped up by a couple of bricks. She took the ball and practiced French drops, seeming to grab the ball out of one hand with the other, but actually palming it. Then she ran through a sequence of top-of-fist and bottom-of-fist vanishes, then fingertip productions, where the ball appears at the fingertips out of the seemingly empty hand, and finally, the more difficult ball acquitments, where the artist seems to show the audience that there is no ball in either hand. Done properly, the illusion is startling: the audience swears that it saw both hands exposed and empty simultaneously.

Then she did palms, switches and the standard vanishes with both coin and thimble, ending with the thimble walking from thumb to pinkie on her good hand and back again. Not ready for Vegas, Marlene thought, but it should baffle a four-year-old.

Now she found, as often before, that the blank concentration of the sleight-of-hand session had been a fertile void. She walked down to her desk, a beat-up wooden office model, three-quarters covered with houseplants, and pulled out the file where she kept the things Balducci had given her and her notes on the Simmons case.

Reading them through again, she wrote rapidly on a legal pad, putting down ideas, crossing them off, substituting others. Then she took a fresh sheet and condensed the rambling notes into a few terse lines:

1. Where was he killed? Where did he go after game? (Butch)
2. Girl, cars—check limos. (Bello)
3. Drugs—Doone (? hold off)
4. Sister (A.S.)

Satisfied with this effort, she put the rest of the files away, and after checking numbers in her little address book, she dialed Bello's office. He was not there, and she left a message. Then she dialed the number Ariadne Stupenagel had given her. It was a service, and she left her name there too.

So much for crime. She put on slippers and belted her kimono tighter and began to climb down the ladder to Stuart Franciosa's loft, as she had every Karp-less morning since Stu had started his sculpture.

The phone rang. She ignored it, and continued down.

"I'm here for my immortalization," she said as she

entered the loft. "You better hurry it up if you want to capture the noble swell of my *labonza.*"

Franciosa smiled at her from behind the low bench where he worked on jewelry. He had a set of magnifiers strapped to his head and was working with concentration on some glittering object.

"Come over and check this out. Want some coffee?"

"No, I had already. What is it? Wow, that's pretty!"

He placed the object in her hand. It was a thick medallion, done in massive gold with silver inlays, of a beautiful boy's face in high relief. His curls, the angelic mouth, the flared nostrils, were all done in remarkable detail, and though derived from the *kouros* portraits found on Hellenistic coins, it was a modern face, the kind you saw getting off the bus at Port Authority every day. "OK, now press in on the nose," said the sculptor. Marlene did so and the face folded in on itself with a click. She was now holding in her hand a perfectly modeled set of male genitalia, the penis erect.

"Stu, this is amazing," she shrieked, and laughed so hard the baby started kicking. "You *made* this? I love it! How do you make it go back to the face?"

"Put it in your mouth and slowly run your tongue . . . no, I lied—you push down on the tip of the prick."

"Gosh, I was taught as a girl never to do that."

"Me too, but that's how it works," said Franciosa. Marlene pushed and the face reassembled itself. "I have to have this," she said.

"Well, it's a pricey item, but we could talk about a deal. This is the Mark I version, actually—"

"Mark who? Do I know him?"

"Shh! It's got some flaws that I've worked out for the model I'm going to market. You can have it for the price of the metal; I was going to give you something for modeling anyway." He named a figure and Marlene readily agreed.

"OK, put it down and let's get to work," said Franciosa, walking over to where the statue lay under its damp sheet. Marlene dropped her robe and assumed the familiar position; Franciosa lifted off the sheet and picked up a glittering instrument.

The glitter caught Marlene's eye. "What's that you're using on it?"

"Don't move your head, please. It's a curette, as a matter of fact. Larry brings home all sorts of goodies from the hospital. A lot of them are useful to me—curettes, probes, hemostats. Lift your chin a bit. Good. Theft, I guess, but I think it's entirely innocent. You know Larry—absentminded as a clam. He shoves them in his pockets and walks out with them. If the sculpting business ever collapses, we can open a hospital."

"How is Larry?"

The sculptor shrugged. "Need you ask? The man has the most even disposition in the hemisphere. A little ray of sunshine. They shit all over him at the hospital, and I, being me, have done the same on occasion myself. Sado-mas: it's too trite for words."

"Sounds like true happiness."

"I guess. Chin up a little, please. Good. Yes, happiness. Yet one wishes to be surprised on occasion. I'm never surprised any more. And how is your marriage, dear?"

"Low-key, as a matter of fact. He's out of town and I'm fairly immobile. I had a dishy cop up here last night who was about to hit on me, but I spurned him, which was my romance for the month."

"A cop?"

"Yeah, it turns out that Marlene is on the trail of a vicious killer. A busman's pregnancy leave, so to speak."

"How exciting! Tell us more!"

"Uh-uh, it's too early and . . . it could be anyone. Even you."

He laughed. "No, not me. I only kill with a kiss." He worked in silence then for nearly forty-five minutes and then tossed his instrument aside with a metallic clatter. "You know what?" he said. "I think this little number is soup now. I have that familiar feeling of wanting to fuck with it forever, which is the signal to stop."

Marlene rose from the couch and stretched, then walked naked over to the turntable. Franciosa spun the clay model slowly. "Well, what do you think?"

"I'm gaping with admiration. It's funny and sexy at the same time, and it looks . . . soft, like flesh, like she's going to get up and scratch her crotch."

"It's all in the wrist," said Franciosa, wriggling his. "Well, my dear, a million thanks."

"What do you do with it now?"

"We add sprues for the pour, then plaster it and after the plaster cures we cut it apart and take it down to the foundry and pour bronze into it and patina it and then sell it for lots of money."

"Sounds good," said Marlene. "Maybe someday it'll be famous and grandparents will buy bookends of it for high school graduation. Like 'The Thinker.' "

"My devoutest wish," said Franciosa. Marlene dressed and headed for the shaft. "Don't forget your medallion," he called.

In reply, Marlene squatted down, made a chicken sound and seemed to pick the golden object off the floor beneath her crotch.

Franciosa grinned in delight. "Now, that's surprising," he said.

When Marlene arrived back in her loft, Ariadne Stupenagel was just leaving a message on her answering machine. Marlene snatched up the phone in time to catch her. After the usual pleasantries, Marlene invited the reporter to lunch.

"Lunch? Well, dear, it's short notice—"

"Stupe, I *know* how busy you are, and I'm a mere housewife, but I need some help and there may be a major story involved for you."

"Ah, you said the magic words. Where at? I'm Midtown."

"No, it has to be here," said Marlene. "The kid isn't moving far from home these days."

"Home cooking, eh? OK, it's eleven-fifteen now. Say one? But the story better be what happened to Jimmy Hoffa. What's the address?"

That accomplished, Marlene ran through the rest of the message tape. The machine had answered the phone a dozen times, but the callers had left no message. Odd—maybe the machine was on the fritz? She reset the tape, threw on disgustingly soiled maternity jeans, a sweatshirt, and Karp's blue duffel coat, tossed the bagged trash and the bagged laundry down the lift shaft and left the loft.

She picked up the bags from the bottom of the shaft, threw the trash in an industrial dumpster, dropped the laundry off at a Chinese pound laundry on Mott off Grand, and went to shop in Lucca's on Grand.

She bought a pound each of calamari and sweet pepper salad, a loaf of Tuscan bread and chunks of Bel Paese and asiago cheese for lunch, which would go well with a bottle of good verdicchio she had in the fridge. On impulse she bought the makings of a sausage lasagna—fresh pasta and two kinds of sausage, plus pancetta, with fresh ricotta and mozzarella cheese.

While this was being wrapped, a gravelly voice behind her said, "What did the Nazis use Italians for in concentration camps?"

"What?" she asked without turning around.

"Every thousand Jews, they used to run an Italian through to grease the machinery."

Marlene turned around and scowled into the leering face of Raymond Guma. "Guma, that's disgusting," she said. "What are you doing lurking around here? Why aren't you in court fighting crime?"

"Hey! I'm on my lunch hour, all right? I'm Italian, I could go to Little Italy for lunch? Also, I heard you were going to drop your kid in Lucca's *salumeria* this afternoon, and I thought I'd come down and catch the show. I hear you took the razor blades out, the kid won't get scratched or anything."

"That's so typical of you, Guma, a vicious and un-provoked attack on a helpless pregnant lady. OK, just for that, you're gonna help me schlep this stuff back to the loft."

Guma looked around as if she had addressed some-one else. "Me? What, I got a medallion on my ass now? I'm a cab?"

Marlene said, "And that's good because I can pick up a bunch of heavy stuff now like milk and beer and canned—*and* don't say another fucking *word* to the person who helped you pretend that you were her own brother at her wedding so you could go on schtupping a Supreme Court judge, who, in case you forgot, at this moment is still only a phone call away."

A strenuous half hour later, Guma was sitting on Marlene's couch, breathing heavily through his mouth between sucks on a can of Schaeffer. "I'm having a heart attack," he gasped. "Let me teach you a new word—'elevator.' How the fuck does Karp let you live on top of the fucking Statue of Liberty?"

Marlene, kneeling on the floor in front of the refrig-erator, distributing groceries, shot him a sharp look over her shoulder and said, "Karp has nothing to say about it. So tell me, what's happening back at the courthouse?"

"The usual horseshit. Everybody's talking about bailing out. Bloom's got Ehrengard in there as acting chief."

"Shelly Ehrengard? But he's a nincompoop."

"Yeah, like Connie says, the laziest white man in North America. It's true he can't find his ass with both hands, but on the other hand he has the personality of a dog turd. The guess is Bloom put him in as a fumigator. He wants all of Butch's gang out of there."

Marlene shook her head and began to lay out the lunch she was going to give to Ariadne Stupenagel, while Guma chatted to her about the decline of the Criminal Courts Bureau.

"You wanna hear the living end? I got this case: a mutt tries to rip off a car. What car? An unmarked police car parked in front of the Sixth Precinct with a fucking uniformed cop sitting in the passenger seat. The cop couldn't believe it. He watched the guy hotwire the ignition and crank it up before he put the collar on.

"So of course, I figured I had a pretty good case. The kid had been boosting cars since he was ten, right? So I said, 'Kid, the top count is grand theft auto and you're gonna plead guilty, right?' The kid says no way, he wants a deal. I laughed in his face. The Legal Aid practically laughed in his face.

"The punch line? I go to Ehrengard with the trial and he says, 'No trial. See if he'll cop to petty larceny and vandalism.' " He sighed. "Fuck me! I'm getting too old for this shit, you know? Hey, mind if I grab another beer? It's not like I'll need any advanced mental resources this afternoon."

Marlene said, "Help yourself." She finished setting the table, laid out the food, put the wine with ice in a big tarnished trophy cup that Karp had won in some contest, and went behind the screen that divided the bath area from the kitchen to dress and primp. She had chosen her only dressy non-office maternity outfit, a Chinese jacket in heavy crimson brocade with frogging, over loose silky trousers: a borrowing from her suburban sister Anna.

She was just shrugging into the jacket when Guma said, "How come you got a picture of Frankie Mack on your wall?"

"Who?"

"This picture by the fridge. Frankie Mack, and that looks like Carlo Parmagianni behind him."

In an instant Marlene was beside him, hastily buttoning her jacket. "You know these people?"

"Yeah, well, I wouldn't say 'know,' but I know who they are." He placed a pudgy finger on the chunky saturnine man standing next to the woman in the scarf. "This is Francesco Maccaluso, known as Frankie Mack when he was in South Philly. He calls himself Frank Mackey now."

"He's a Mafioso?"

Guma frowned at her. "No, he's not a fuckin' 'Mafioso,' Marlene. He's just a guy who hung around with some hard guineas when he was a kid. Like we both did. Am I a Mafioso? Are you?"

"OK, enough! So tell me, what's his story?"

"His story is, he was associated with the Scarfi mob in Philly, a little of this, a little of that. Not a made guy; he's a Neapolitan anyway. Got sent up for some piece-of-shit federal charge. Did a year in Allentown, got out, decided he'd do better away from South Philly and moved to the City, it musta been, fifteen, eighteen years ago. Got into hauling, bought some trucks, made some dough, bought some real estate cheap in the sixties. He made out pretty good is what I hear. He's got his own company, Mar- or Mol-something."

"Hold on," said Marlene and trotted down to her filing cabinet. She returned with the list of limo renters from Simmons's funeral.

"Yeah, that's it—the Morell Company," said Guma. "So, you gonna tell me what's this about?"

"In a minute. Do you know who the woman is?"

Guma peered at the grainy image. "I never dated her that I remember," he said, then shook his head. "Could be the bimbo of the month. Frankie's a killer with the women, is what I hear."

"Could it be his wife?"

"I guess. Why?"

"Nothing, just a thought." She quickly explained the connection between the blow-up and the murder of Marion Simmons.

When she had finished, Guma said, "And you think this lady was involved with the vic?"

"How do I know? I just want to find out who she is and why she was at the funeral."

"Maybe Frankie's a Hustlers fan."

"Maybe," Marlene said thoughtfully. The street bell rang. She said, "Oh, shit! She's here. Look, Goom, I hate to kick you out, but I invited this old girlfriend of mine over for lunch, and . . ."

"Yeah, I get it. I'm not good enough to meet your fancy friends."

"Fuck you, Guma," said Marlene, smiling. "I really appreciate this information, though. It's really helpful." She gave him a generous kiss.

"A little more tongue on the next one and I'll tell you who did the job on Simmons. And by the way, I wanted to say your tits haven't sagged all that much, in case you were worrying."

"Scram, *schifezza!*" said Marlene, shoving him toward the door.

The phone rang. Marlene answered it, and a woman's voice said, "Is this Marlene Ciampi?"

"Yes, who's this?"

"Did you go to St. Joseph's in Queens?"

"Yeah, I did; who *is* this? Hello? Hello!"

The line was dead.

Irritated, Marlene slammed the phone down, and had no time to contemplate this mystery, because just then the bell rang and Ariadne Stupenagel waltzed in the door, knee-booted and dressed in a flowing black maxi-skirt and a man's ruffled formal shirt. She carried a stained canvas bag and a gray Soviet army greatcoat marked with colonel's flashes hung from her broad shoulders. "Champ!" she cried in greeting and enveloped Marlene in an enthusiastic hug and a cloud of Arpege. She briefly fingered Marlene's jacket, palped her abdomen, assured her she looked gorgeous and whirled to take in the loft. "Great loft! It's going to be terrific when you fix it up. Have you seen Diana Bullet's place on Great Jones Street? No? She got Victor to do it for her."

"Victor?"

"Yes, this marvelous faggot—he's doing everybody in SoHo. All the Warhol people use him. So!" She flung her coat onto a chair and turned a bright gaze on Marlene. "Here you are—still preggers. I can't believe it we're back in contact again—little Champ from my long ago school days. Well, better you than me, darling."

Marlene hung up the greatcoat on a bentwood coatrack by the door and said, "I bet there's a story behind this thing."

"God, is there! Don't ask, dear, I'm in enough trouble with the State Department. What's for lunch? I'm starving, and please don't let it be pregnancy health food."

They sat at the table. Stupenagel pronounced the meal edible and dug in with both hands, talking between mouthfuls. She was still a voracious eater. Marlene recalled from her college dormitory days that her friend would arrive unannounced at midnight, fresh from some outrage or hilarious debacle, with a pizza or a load of Chinese take-out, there to sit on the floor, and gorge, and laugh, and wake half the hall.

A session with Ariadne was still exciting, like being caught in a sudden thunderstorm with a cheap umbrella, although ten years of hard experience had tempered Marlene's enthusiasm for the other woman's hectic personality. Charm does not season well. Still, she was able to value Ariadne as the only person she had yet encountered who could make Marlene Ciampi feel prim.

The plates empty, Stupenagel poured out the last of the wine, of which she had consumed three-quarters, and said, "You said a story. I'm all ears."

Marlene picked up her Simmons file with its photographs, which she had laid ready on a nearby bookshelf, and proceeded to fill her friend in on what she had learned in the past few weeks. Stupenagel made notes on a cheap steno pad.

When Marlene was done, Stupenagel said, "You're figuring it for a triangle, huh? That's why the blonde's so important. I love it: Gang Lord Slays Blonde Bombshell's Black Lover. Not exactly my line, actually. I start writing shit like that and I'm off the political pages and back to the women's section. On the other hand, you say there's a cover-up going down."

"We don't know, but it's possible. We have the Queens D.A. in charge palling around with the team owner. We get warned off because of a big-time investigation that nobody else has ever heard of. Also, where does this John Doone fit in, and the bag of coke—"

"Speaking of which, do you mind if I do a couple of lines? I was up till all hours last night."

"Ladies can do what they wish in my toilet," said Marlene, attempting, not very successfully, to keep the edge out of her voice.

"You're joking," said Stupenagel. She had already taken a glass vial and a hand mirror out of her bag.

"'Fraid not, girl," said Marlene, meeting the other woman's eyes, in a manner that left no room to doubt her seriousness.

The journalist shrugged and replaced her paraphernalia. "OK, go on, then. What do you see me doing in this?"

"For starters, see Mackey's wife. Cook up an excuse. You're doing a story on, um . . ."

"Famous mobsters' wives who fuck basketball players?"

Marlene laughed. "Yeah, that should get you in the door. No, something social: she's rich, she'll be interested in something. I don't have to tell you how to barge in. Now, if she turns out to be the blonde in the photo, we're home free. If not, we'll have to punt."

"Assuming it's the wife, what do we want to know?"

"Well, obviously, whether there was any relationship, and particularly, if she saw him the night he died." Marlene frowned and added, "Of course, there's no reason for her to tell you any of that, is there?"

"No, but you'd be surprised what people spill to the press," said Stupenagel briskly. "Or what they can be made to admit. Don't give it a thought, dear: a rich bimbo like this, I can suck her brains into a jar without raising a sweat. And, if it *is* the wife, it makes a nice frisson, doesn't it. He slays the boyfriend and accompanies the wife to the funeral. How Italian! I like it more and more. In fact"—she picked up the blow-up and studied the face of Frank Mackey—"he looks like a killer. And I've known a few."

"I'm sure you have, but probably not as many as me. Let's not get carried away here, Stupe. We just want to find out who she is for starters."

"Fine," said Stupenagel impatiently. "Just so I don't have to say she has a right to remain silent. Anything else?"

"Yeah. The other thing is Leona Simmons, the dead man's sister. She's a junkie, so you two ought to get along real well."

"I'll ignore that. What does she know?"

"She might have some idea where the dope in Simmons's car came from. For starters, we should take a look at her arrest record."

"Surely you can get that easier than I can."

"I could, but there can't be any ties back to me or Butch. We've been warned off, remember."

"Oh, yeah. You know, Champ, I can't get used to you as the careful bureaucrat. This is your hubby's influence, I gather. Don't want to rock the career boat."

Marlene laughed uproariously. "What's so funny?" asked Stupenagel, disconcerted.

"Nothing, Stupe. It's a long story. The idea of Butch controlling my behavior to advance his career just struck me as so weird. . . ." She wiped her eyes with a napkin and continued, "But you're right, I guess, in a way. One mellows. Also, what most people don't understand is that the job isn't finding out who done it. It's making a case, which is not the same thing at all. Usually they don't confess in court, like on *Perry Mason*. In order to make a case you have to do things a certain way. One of the big rules is no overlapping investigations. It's not just procedural. If it comes down to dark alleys, all the good guys have to know who all the other good guys are. We're talking sudden death here."

"I can dig it," said Stupenagel. She made some final notes on her pad and put it away. "So what goes on here when you're not crime fighting? I mean for fun. I mean, you don't get out, do you? I'm in SoHo a lot and I never see you at the places to be seen at. I guess it's just being wifey, now, hey?"

"Well, actually," Marlene answered, "most New Yorkers don't show up at the places to be seen at."

"What do you mean? They're all New Yorkers. I'm a New Yorker."

"No, in point of fact, Ariadne, you're a hick from out of town, from where-was-it? East Crotchburg, Ohio?"

"Please, East Crotchburg, Pennsylvania."

"Exactly, a hick in the City, like, I would guess, ninety percent of the people you hang out with. Me and Butch, on the other hand, are New Yorkers. This is my neighborhood. It's Little Italy, not fucking SoHo. Both my parents were born less than a quarter of a mile from here, on Elizabeth. Butch's mom was born another quarter mile uptown and east, on Rivington Street. This food we just ate, it's from a store, my grandmother used to shop there. So, the thing is, we all don't glitter that much. In fact, I guess for most of the City it's a lot like East Crotchburg, with more crime and fewer plumbers."

"Very impressive, Marlene! I am put in my place. Can I use some of that?"

Marlene laughed. "Be my guest. On the other hand, to be absolutely frank, I *have* lost a little edge, in a way." She patted her belly. "This takes energy, which I have a lot of, but there's a limit. The hormones are yelling, 'Nest, nest!' I decided not to fight it anymore."

"As long as we're being frank, tell the truth—don't you fucking dread it? I mean the actual—uh!—event. All the pain and the *fluids*."

Marlene leaned back and looked up at the skylight while she considered this. "No, I don't think so. Not to mention that it's Woman's Highest Calling. At this point I'd want to get rid of it if it was going to emerge out of my left nostril. Another goodie, of course, is you get to see the kid and find out how you did in God's big lotto.

"What else? Intense curiosity? One of the tickets you punch: I got laid; I did drugs; I graduated college; I graduated law school; I got a job; I got blown up; I roller-skated naked down a New York street; I killed a man. Fuck, what's left? And you know what Isaac Singer says, something about 'Women see marvels when they give birth, but they never tell men about them.' Maybe it's true, like he'd know."

"Will you tell *me*?" said Stupenagel. She had a smile on her face, but Marlene, not for the first time, saw something odd flickering behind her eyes, like a reflection of some deep fracture, or an unfillable pit.

"I might," said Marlene. "It depends on what you find out about the presumptive Mrs. Frankie Mack."

"Oh, what a big meanie!"

"Well, we humble matrons must have our secrets," said Marlene airily, "just like you big-time girl reporters."

Francine was frightened now. It had happened so quickly that she still could not quite believe that the shaking, weeping body she now occupied was the same one that had, barely an hour past, driven so blithely into the Great Neck Plaza shopping center.

She fumbled at her pile of change, and some coins fell off the phone booth's little shelf and rattled on the floor. She put a dime in the slot and dialed the number yet again. This time the phone was answered and she found out what she needed to know. She hung up and immediately dialed the number of a cab company, arranging to be picked up at a nearby intersection. Then she walked shakily out of the shopping center, avoiding the parking lot where her Toyota was parked, and where she knew the men were watching.

CHAPTER

ten

Not two hours had passed since Marlene's lunch with Ariadne Stupenagel. She was stretched out on the red couch with *The Mill on the Floss* balanced on the crest of her belly and a jar of Jordan almonds within easy reach. She had promised herself to cover the classics during the last month of her pregnancy, and was enjoying it more than she had expected. Provincial Victorian England had become a lot more interesting, it seemed, since she was a girl.

The phone rang then, and Marlene immediately recalled the odd, questioning phone call she had received just before lunch, and was struck with the certainty that this call was the same person calling again.

It was the same voice, breathless but oddly familiar. "Is this Marlene?"

"Yes, it is. You called before. Please, who is this?"

"Marlene, this is gonna sound crazy, but it's Francine Del Fazio."

"Francine ... ? Oh, my God! Frannie Ciccolino!" Marlene's mind immediately filled with a memory from childhood: the chalk-and-floor-wax smell of a fourth-grade classroom, a nun droning away at the front, two dark-haired little girls in blue jumpers and gray stockings, seated at adjoining desks, Ciampi and Ciccolino, locked together since the first grade by the order of the alphabet, best friends.

"Wow, it's what—fifteen years!" said Marlene.

"Yeah, you went to Sacred Heart and I dropped out and got married."

A vague guilt tugged at Marlene. Puberty had struck both girls like a thunderclap, and both of them had indulged in weekend activities not on the approved list for Catholic teenagers in late 1950s Queens. The difference was that Francie had been less discreet, less careful. St. Joseph's had given her the boot in ninth grade. On Monday mornings, therefore, Francie had walked off to public high school, where she had become a fixture among the motorcycle-riding, car-boosting, leather-jacketed fraternity that the era called "hoods," while Marlene, armed with a full scholarship, had hopped the train for Manhattan, garbed in the sober livery of the most prestigious Catholic girls' school in the United States. It was inevitable that she should then see less of her friend, and then want to see less of her as her world expanded and she was invited to parties on Park Avenue and dances at the Biltmore and the Plaza.

"Yeah, well, so how are you, Francie?" asked Marlene after an uncomfortable pause. "You married that guy, Frankie, right?"

Francine laughed. "Yeah, the dream boat. I guess you don't see much of the old gang?"

"No, not really," Marlene admitted. "You?"

"I see your sister, Annie. We get together maybe once a month."

More guilt. Anna was Marlene's older sister, a housewife in Hempstead with four kids, with whom Marlene got together much less frequently. She vaguely remembered a relationship between the man Anna had married and Frank Del Fazio. Cousins?

But Francine went on, "Yeah, that's what got me thinking about you. Annie said you were some big shot with the D.A."

So that was it. Marlene had suspected that her old playmate had called her for something other than nostalgia or the gladness her voice might bring. She said carefully, "Yeah, I'm with the D.A., but just a little shot. Why, you in some kind of trouble?"

"Uh-huh. I mean, I haven't done nothing wrong or anything, but ... look, could I, like, see you? Now? It's kind of complicated to talk over the phone."

"Sure. No problem, Francie. Where are you, out in Queens?"

"No," said Francine, "I'm in a booth on Lafayette, around the corner. I'll be there in five minutes."

Joey came back to the car out of breath and smiling in a way that Carmine did not like.

"Where is she?" he asked. Joey grinned and said, "Hey, she's right behind me. Maybe she had to stop off at the ladies' room. Quit worrying, will ya? She ain't gonna give us any problems."

Carmine's suspicions were confirmed. "You grabbed her, didn't you? I fuckin' told you just to watch her, but you hadda grab the bitch."

"Hey, she spotted us anyway—what the fuck, Carmine! I just let her know what would happen to her if she talked. It's no big deal!"

Not to Joey, in any case. "Talking" to her consisted of him throwing a choke hold on Francine Del Fazio in the parking garage, slamming her up against a rough concrete wall a couple of times, and, with a hand around her throat, hiking up her skirt, tearing her underwear and thrusting two fingers deep inside her vagina. After that he entertained her for ten minutes with a description of what he was going to do to the various orifices of her body when he got her alone. He urged her to say how much she would enjoy this when it happened, and she did. He had left her in a weeping heap on the greasy floor.

Carmine was silent for five minutes, fuming and chewing on his cigar, now dead. Joey searched through the windshield for the returning woman. "Where the fuck is she?" he complained. "I swear she was right behind me."

"She make any calls in there, Joey?" asked Carmine mildly.

"Yeah, she made two. What about it?"

The older man said nothing but headed for the mall entrance at a trot. Joey cursed and followed.

In the mall, Carmine got Joey to show him the phone booth the woman had used. He inspected the walls of the booth carefully and then looked through the Yellow Pages hanging there. He made several calls. Then he came out of the booth in a rush and headed toward their car. He still hadn't said a word to his companion.

They entered, and Carmine started the Chevy. "Hey, you gonna tell me what the fuck is goin' on or what?" Joey demanded.

"She called a cab, Joey, and she went out the back after she left you. She would've taken the car if you hadn't shown up, but she's a smart lady and she set up another way out, so that when you did fuckin' show yourself, she could double around out the back way and leave us sitting here like a coupla assholes.

"OK, so what I did was, I started calling local cab companies, starting with the top of the list. We got lucky on number three. I said I was a cop and did they pick up a woman at the Great Neck mall and where did they take her?"

"And they told you?"

"Fuck yeah, they told me. How the fuck they supposed to know who I am? You got the right voice and you know how cops do stuff, you can get people to tell you any fuckin' thing you want on the phone."

Carmine burned rubber getting out of the lot and exceeded the speed limit on the Expressway inbound to Manhattan.

"So, where're we goin'?" asked Joey after a while.

"Spring and Lafayette. That's where she told the cab to take her. Of course, if she gets there before we do, she could go anywhere."

They rode in uncomfortable silence west on the expressway, through the Midtown Tunnel and south on FDR Drive to the Houston Street exit. Carmine was worried. If he had a whole outfit to command, finding the woman would have been a trivial task. But he did not, which made the task tedious and nearly impossible. He would have to trust that the fright that Joey had laid on the woman would suffice to keep her quiet until the whole misbegotten thing was over and done with. Carmine hated to leave things to chance, however, and thus, by the time they got to the correct intersection, he had worked himself up to a towering rage.

Joey yelled, "Look! Carmine, there she is! It's her!"

She was just leaving a phone booth on the west side of Lafayette. She walked quickly south. Carmine parked the car instantly and illegally, and they both gave chase. Following her was easy on the crowded commercial thoroughfare. She turned left on Broome, and now they had to be more careful, letting her lead by half a block and hiding themselves behind the trucks unloading on the narrow street. She turned onto

Crosby, where she rang a bell at a dingy factory building.

From their vantage point deep in a doorway, they saw a window in the building's fifth floor open. A woman's head appeared in it and some words were exchanged with their quarry. Then Francine Del Fazio entered the building.

"Now who the fuck is that?" asked Joey aloud.

Whatever had gotten into the New York Hustlers in Boston stuck with the team in Buffalo, Cleveland, and Indianapolis. They pulled into Chicago behind four straight, with Karp playing ten to fifteen minutes in each game and racking up double digits in points and assists.

Now that he had shown that he was a clown who could play basketball, he started to get a more sympathetic press. The sports columnists wrote a spate of sentimental columns about the All-American who had lost his career and become a famous crime fighter and then picked up his sports career again, thus verifying the classic American myths of It's Never Too Late and Anybody Can Be Anything. The sportscasters started calling him "D.A. Karp" right off, as if those were his personal initials, and of course, whenever he stole the ball, which was more than occasionally, there was a little witticism about a life of crime.

The team, relieved to see that Karp was neither a drag on their chances nor, of course, a threat to their jobs, accepted this odd notoriety with good humor; they were constructing their own myth: zany, murder-haunted, unpredictable, raffish; hard-luck kids making good. Karp's story fit perfectly into this larger tale. Beyond that, the players understood what Karp had contributed to the team, something only the more perspicacious sportswriters mentioned.

"Listen here, D.A.," said Doobie Wallace, flapping his newspaper into position, "this is about you. And me, of course."

The team was breakfasting in the Chicago Hyatt on the Monday morning before their game with the Bulls. Karp was sitting at a table with Wallace, Croyden, Lockwell, James, Kravic and McDoul.

This had become something of a ritual: Wallace ate faster than anyone else and devoted the end of the meal to the edification of his teammates, reading from the morning paper. Sometimes it was a comic strip or some editorial matter, but most often he did the sports pages.

" 'Why have the Hustlers become so hard to stop?' " he read. " 'Several things come to mind. Of course, the teamwork has vastly improved. The young front line, led by Fred James, is moving the ball well, getting the rebounds and getting them away down court. Doobie Wallace has taken the team spark plug role over from the slain Marion Simmons: he could always shoot, but now he's passing as well, as witness the triple doubles he racked up in the last two games. But what really makes the difference is the unexpected strength the Hustlers have found in their bench—' "

"Yo! Let's hear it for the bench!" said Kravic.

" '. . . especially the amazing old man of the team, "D.A." Karp,' " Wallace continued. " 'With Karp and Wallace on the floor, New York has two credible three-point threats. Although Karp can't move or jump much, he doesn't have to. Get him the ball and it goes in.' " Wallace put the paper down and grinned. "There's more, but I don't want the second team to get big ideas."

"That's a true thing about Karp's legs," said James. "The bionic man, but his warranty run out."

There was more good-natured joking of this sort as the team finished and drifted out to the lobby. Karp thought the columnist had been right about Wallace being the team spark plug, and he felt an affinity for the other player for that reason. Although Karp had never owned the pure athletic skills Wallace possessed, he was essentially the same all-around sort of player. Even Wallace's previous no-pass chuckmanship sounded an echo from Karp's own high school career. It was a kid's failing. In Karp's case, a sharp personal shock, the death of his mother, had matured him at fourteen. He wondered what had changed Doobie Wallace.

Karp decided to ask him. He had meant to get with Wallace to ask him about Marion Simmons's sex life. He figured that the team's premier swordsman would have a reasonably good idea of who was getting it and from whom. He finagled his way into a seat next to Wallace on the bus out to the practice gym.

"So, Doobie," Karp said, "you like what they're saying about you now? The next Elgin Baylor, right?"

Wallace grinned engagingly, showing gold. "Yeah, man. You had any legs and Jamesie had any smarts, we could win sixty-five games this year."

"Fuck you, Wallace," said James sleepily from the seat behind.

"I couldn't help noticing you looked a lot better the last couple than you did against the Sixers."

"Yeah, we were fucked up then, man. Marion getting killed—it did us all in. I mean, you know: it was like the Sixers getting Dr. J. killed, or the Lakers losing Kareem."

"He must have been something," said Karp. "I don't think I ever saw him play."

Wallace looked at him strangely. "You never saw . . . ? Where were you, man? Afghanistan?"

"No. I kind of turned off basketball for a while. Anyway, I hear he was real good."

Wallace looked out the window at the slushy roads of Chicago, as if contemplating the lost goodness of Simmons. "Yeah, he was. More than good. You know it's a joke, 'Basketball is my life,' when we say it. But Marion, he really meant it, you know?"

"That's just what McDoul said. Devoted to the game, as they say?"

Wallace laughed. "Yeah! It was like he was only alive when he was playing. He wanted to play every forty-eight minutes, every game. On a practice, he would stay on, taking shots after everybody else left for the showers, you know? Had to drag him out of there."

He lowered his voice to a conspiratorial tone. "Now, you know and I know that the game is fucked up. We got all these white coaches go into the ghet-to, 'Hey, boy, you want to go to college? You want you a Thunderbird? All the pussy you can eat?' It's show biz, right? A fucking game. Four years of kindergarten and you get the shot at the pros. OK, then you're on TV, making half a mill, a mill every year, playing a kid's game for whitey, plus endorsements. Hey, I'm not complaining, but I'm realistic, you dig?

"Not old Marion, though. It was like basketball was fucking church for Marion. Pissed people off too."

"How so?"

"Oh, you know—somebody fucked up a play, or he thought they weren't hustling a hundred percent. Didn't matter if we were ahead by fifteen with a minute left. He didn't actually say shit, but you could feel it, you know?"

"That must have made him unpopular," Karp observed.

Wallace shook his head. "No way, man. Funny thing. We all thought Marion was right on. More than the coach, if you know what I mean. A classy dude. Weird maybe, but classy as hell."

"Weird?"

"Yeah, like he was always writing in this little book. Like part of it was an appointment book and the other part was a notebook. Scratching away all the time. We asked him, What you writing, Marion? And he would say, 'Observations on life and the game.' Never showed it to anybody that I heard of."

"Wanting privacy isn't all that weird."

"Yeah, but you don't see Jamesie writing in no little book. Or me. We used to kid him he was writing love notes to the mystery girl."

"Oh, yeah, McDoul mentioned that too. You ever meet her?"

"Matter of fact, I did once. I was going into this club uptown, and he came waltzing out with this blonde. A killer fox. Very white."

"Who was she?"

"Well, we was not formally introduced. I said hi and he said hi and then he hustled her past me into the cab I just came out of. She gave me a nice smile, though."

"Any reason why he should be so secretive?" Karp asked.

"Well, there *has* been a lot of speculation over that. The rumor is, she's married to a big shot, and they wanted to keep it cool. Which doesn't make a whole hell of a lot of sense, follow? I mean, a nigger that's six-ten and has his picture on TV and the papers every other day, plus cereal boxes, who's tramping around the clubs with a white lady, is not something you can hide under a Dixie cup. If there's a husband, either he's deaf, dumb and blind, or else doesn't give a rat's ass his old lady's into chocolate syrup."

"So why?"

"Since you asked, the mom is why. Mrs. Simmons don't approve of catting around, one, and two, especially not with white trash. Oh, yeah, that was another weird thing about Marion. His family. Like their shit didn't stink."

Wallace thought for a moment, then chuckled. "Like the motherfucker business. OK, a lot of black guys use the word without thinking too much about what it means—motherfucker this, motherfucker that. Like 'oh, shit!' you know?

"OK, we're playing Portland, and Marion goes up for a rebound and the Portland center, Beale, goes up too and he gets an elbow in the face. The whistle goes, Portland gets the foul, but Beale ain't half satisfied. Marion's walking off the paint and Beale yells out, 'Hey, motherfucker . . .' and some other shit. Marion just hits the pivot, takes one big step and coldcocks the guy. Bang! He goes down like a tree."

"Basketball and family, huh? Sounds like my kind of guy."

Wallace hooted. "What! Tell me basketball is *your* life too."

"I wouldn't go that far. I will say it's something that I don't get anywhere else. When everything clicks, when I'm inside the game. What, you don't?"

Wallace was shaking his head. "Hey, man, my daddy humped crates for Allied his whole life and I hump baskets. Same difference, but I make a shitload more money. Only thing clicks for me is when I write big checks for nice stuff. That's the part I like."

"But you were saying . . ." prompted Karp.

"Yeah, right, the family. Him and me had words on the issue."

"You insulted his mom?" Karp asked, startled.

Wallace laughed out loud. "Shit, no! His sister. Pretty little thing. He brought her to a party once, and needless to say, the Doob threw a couple of moves on her. Nothing heavy, but Marion didn't like it. It was like, I could marry her and then after a year, if it worked out, I could kiss her a time or two."

"They were close, him and his sister?"

"I guess. He used to let her use his Caddy. When we played home, she used to pick him up at the stadium. Shit, I love my own sister, but I wouldn't let her drive my wheels, so I guess they were close."

Karp felt a familiar stirring, the presentiment of a revelation. "So," he began with studied casualness, "she always picked him up after home games?"

Wallace shrugged. "I guess, most times." Then he gave Karp a sharp glance. "Why you so interested?"

"Well, if she picked him up the night he got killed, it could be important."

"Uh-oh, the D.A. strikes," said Wallace in mock horror. "You searching for clues, man?"

"Force of habit," said Karp. "I presume you told the cops about this."

"Shit, nobody asked me and I didn't volunteer. What happened on the night of, though, is Marion did a fast break all on his own. I figure he was the first one left the locker after the game. It was the San Antonio game—we whipped their ass, so we were feeling pretty good. Marion had a nice triple double, so there was press all over the fucking place, wanting to talk to the *star*. And nobody could find him, man."

"He must have had someplace to go."

"Yeah, to basketball heaven," said Wallace lightly and then, more gravely, "Shit, when I heard, the next day—I couldn't fucking believe it. It blew me away."

"You were surprised about the dope?"

"Surprised ain't the word. Hey, let me tell you something—off the record, right? No D.A. horseshit?"

"Sure. No problem," said Karp, with all the sincerity he could muster.

"There's plenty of dope around this team, like every team in the pros. Coke, speed, you name it—not to mention steroids and all the trainer shit. I'm not saying it's a serious problem—like it's not like we're all junkies. It's not even like pro football. But you want to get yourself keyed up for a game, you take a snort, take a pill, you dig? After the game, maybe you pop a downer, get you relaxed. Or if you're wiped out and you want to party a little, there's stuff around. Shit, we got money up the ass, it's New York—maybe next year we're not here, you know? Rip a ligament or some shit, and it's bye-bye black boy. So it's live while you can, you follow?

"OK, two guys on the team that I know are definitely totally straight. One's Blanding—he's a fucking deacon or something. The other was Marion. I mean, if he had bigger nostrils he would've snorted basketballs, but aside from that . . ."

"So you don't believe he was involved with drugs."

"I didn't say that. I just said he never did any that I know of. It wasn't his thing. Little Leona, on the other hand . . ." He waggled his fingers in the air.

"The sister."

"The sister. Girl didn't *need* to drive no Caddy. She could've *flown* anytime she'd've wanted, you know what I'm saying? OK, you want to know how I figure it? Marion's pissed off little sister is doing skag, so he decides he's gonna—I don't know—scare off the bad guys. So she's making a deal, or whatever, and Marion busts in. Bang, bang! End of story. And end of ride, we're here."

The team bus had pulled up into a driveway. Players

were standing up and pulling their bags down from the racks. Karp wanted to talk with Wallace some more, but he felt he had learned enough for the present. Wallace's theory was at least plausible. If you believed it, you also had to believe that Leona Simmons was at least an accessory after the fact. That was the weak part. On the other hand, she was a junkie. Maybe that was what was keeping her mouth shut, or maybe she might have talked had she been interrogated.

And another thing: Leona was a heroine addict. What was the industrial-grade cocaine doing in the car? As Karp walked off the bus, these and other puzzles surrendered their hold on his mind, as it began to adjust itself to the narrow focus required by first-class basketball. He'd feed all this to Marlene and let her wrestle with it. After the game.

Francine Del Fazio walked through the door of the loft, cried, "You're pregnant!" and immediately collapsed in hysterics. Marlene spent forty minutes, two hefty shots of Johnnie Walker, and half a box of Kleenex getting Francine to the point of rational communication.

The first thing she said was "This can't get out. Frankie'd kill me. I mean, seriously, he'd kill me."

"What did you do, Frannie?"

Francine seemed surprised at the question. "Do? I didn't do shit! They're after me because they think I saw something. But I didn't see nothing, I swear. Zero. I didn't even look out the window. But they think I saw it."

"Hold on, Frannie—you're saying you're a witness to a crime?"

"No, I'm *not* a witness!" shouted Francine, and the tears started again. "That's the point! They think, but I'm not."

She's losing it again, thought Marlene, and laid a calming hand on the other woman's arm. "Frannie, listen to me! Some people who committed some crime think you saw something and—what?—they're harassing you? Following you?"

"Worse than that," Francine mumbled.

"They assaulted you? OK, then we got enough to pick them up on. All you got to do is swear out a complaint."

Francine started and shook her head vigorously. "I can't do that."

"You can't? Why the hell not?"

"I just can't." She let out a long sigh and was silent for a few moments. Her fingers played aimlessly with the strap of her purse. When she spoke again, she seemed deflated, exhausted. "I can't get involved, with the cops, with court. It's too complicated to explain. I fucked up my life, Marlene, and it's all landing on me."

"Come on, Francine! There's got to be something we can do. What the hell did they think you saw? At least you could tell me that."

"It was a murder."

"A murder," Marlene echoed, nodding, keeping herself calm. "Who got killed?"

Francine opened her mouth and then closed it to a grim line. "No. I'm not gonna get involved. I just want out of the whole stinking mess. Jesus, Marlene! What the hell happened to us? Who thought we would end up this way!"

The "us" startled Marlene, until she realized that Francine saw Marlene's peculiar dwelling as a pathetic slum, evidence that Marlene had not, as expected, risen in the world. It was a small thing, but it added to her growing irritation with her old schoolmate. In a colder voice she said, "Look, Frannie, if you won't tell me anything, I can't help you. You won't tell me who was murdered. Can you tell me where it happened? No? OK, the people bothering you, can you tell me anything about them?"

"There are two of them. In a car," said Francine in a whispery croak. She was crying soundlessly, the tears falling in thick runnels down her cheeks onto her blouse.

"What do they look like?" Marlene pleaded. "Black? White? Young? Tall? Short?"

"Evil," said Francine. And then she shuddered and heaved herself to her feet. "Marl—you got any cash? I'll give you a check."

"You're going to run?"

"I got to, kid. It's the only way. Poor Frankie, the slob! It'll take him a week to realize I'm gone."

A certain determination, a hardening of the eyes and chin, had crept into Francine's face, and Marlene recognized the expression as one that her friend had often worn in childhood when thwarted or unjustly accused by one of the nuns. There was no arguing with it. Marlene got her bag and raided the various mad money stashes she had around the loft, coming up with $216.

"You won't get far on that," she said.

"Far enough. I can get more by wire from the bank," Francine answered, scribbling out a check. "I'm sorry I bothered you," she added, "but, you know, it just hit me that the last time I felt things were OK, like I had a life? It was in the seventh grade. Funny, hey? So I thought of you. Look, after a while, when I'm far away, I'll write you, tell you the whole story. That's fair, right?"

She hugged Marlene tightly for a moment, and was gone. Marlene collapsed on the red couch and sank quickly into a profound sleep. Karp called around ten and told her what he had learned from Wallace.

Francine's visit seemed like part of a dream, and she did not mention it. She made herself some cocoa, watched twenty minutes of Carson and went back to sleep.

From which she was awakened again by the ringing phone. The loft was pitch dark. Cursing and stumbling, she answered it.

"Get this," said Ariadne Stupenagel without preamble, "the girl is a mule."

"What the fuck, Stupenagel! It's one in the morning. Who's a *what*?"

"Hey, the press never sleeps, Ciampi. It's the sister, Leona. She was picked up three weeks ago at Port Authority with five kilos of heroin. Arrested, charged, but—get this—never tried."

Marlene was by now fully awake. "Holy shit, Stupe! They're using her; she's an informant. Christ! No wonder she's terrified. How did you find this out?"

The reporter laughed. "Confidential sources. But the information's good. I saw the actual sheets. So what's the next move, counselor?"

"Obviously, to get the two of us alone with Leona Simmons."

"Hmmm, that could be hard to arrange," said Stupenagel. "She seems to have dropped out of sight. Her mom won't talk to me. I went out to Forest Hills— shudder—and her little yellow car was still in the drive. Today I watched the house until the mom went out and then I pounded on the door, but nobody answered. The house felt empty. I stuck around until just a little while ago. She never came home.

"I figure either she's cracked and is on the run, or the cops have her, or . . . shudder, shudder."

"Yeah, there's that. I got an interesting call from the hub tonight. He says one of the players told him that Leona could have been the last person to see Simmons alive. She was in the habit of picking him up after games. Also that he disappeared real fast from the stadium the night of the murder, like he had somewhere urgent to go.

"It turns out that our vic was a real straight-arrow and devoted to his family. The player thinks that Marion tried to get his sister away from her dealer, maybe stumbled into a drug deal, and that's why he got killed. It's a plausible idea, and what you just found out about her working as a mule tends to support it.

"Oh, another thing: Butch says that Simmons kept some kind of diary or journal. I checked the inventory sheet from the search of Simmons's house that the cops did, and it's not on it."

"A journal? I didn't know those guys could read, much less write. Mmmm, one wonders at the style: 'January 12. Me eat. Me play game. Me fuck. Sleep. Ditto, ditto, ditto.' "

"Yeah, well, it'd be nice to find it anyway," said Marlene abruptly. Ariadne's humor in the wee hours was more wearing than it had been at school.

"OK, that's the Leona part," Marlene continued. "What about the blonde? Incidentally, Butch also says he has confirmation about Marion having a blonde girlfriend."

Stupenagel said, "No problem. First of all, the woman at the funeral is definitely Julia Mackey, ex-Maccaluso. A buddy of mine who knows the social climbers in town ID'd her for me."

"She's a social climber?"

"Of the lower slopes of the Nouveau Range. She's on a couple of charity ball committees, a couple of museum boards. That's as far as former gangster molls are allowed to go. Their little girl is at Miss Finchley's; she'll go a little further. But Julia still entertains hopes."

"How did you get in to see her?"

"We just spoke on the phone, actually. I told her I was doing a feature piece for *WWD* on the women behind the men who built New York."

"And are you?"

Hysterical laughter. "Marlene! Bite your tongue! I graduated from doing puffs for floozies years ago. Do you chase ambulances?"

"You're going to burn in Hell, Ariadne," said Marlene, vaguely irritated for reasons she could not quite grasp. "She's probably told all her friends already."

"Hey, everybody's got a sad story," said Stupenagel briskly. "So. I'll do the interview and we'll take it from there. Anything else?"

"Yeah. I want to make sure that you understand that if Leona isn't dead already, she will be if anybody who shouldn't finds out what you learned. It's not just her reputation that'll suffer."

Stupenagel answered testily, "Don't teach your grandmother, Miss Priss. I was in Chile, remember? I know how to keep it buttoned up."

"Sorry, Stupe, I'm just nervous about it. The guy we're dealing with here makes General Pinochet look like Edmund Gwenn."

"Who, the Jamaican, what's-his-face?"

"John Doone," said Marlene. "I'd give my left tit for five minutes with him where he had to talk to me."

"Why don't you call him up and make the offer, Marlene? That kind of guy, he might be interested." Stupenagel gave a sharp, hoarse laugh and broke the connection.

Marlene hung up the phone, lay back, and attempted to re-enter the Land of Dreams. She had only indifferent success, dozing and waking through the long December night until, at seven-thirty, as crepuscular beams lit the upper edge of the huge eastern windows, the lift-hoist motor snarled into action, unbelted itself, and set off the clanging of the alarm.

With further sleep now doomed, Marlene hauled herself out of bed and, robed and slippered, descended the sleeping platform ladder to await the arrival of the metalworkers. They were unforgivably cheerful as they made their repairs, and Marlene was short with them.

She was in any case consumed with worry; her semi-sleepless night had granted neither surcease nor any morning wisdom. The situation of Leona Simmons had ended her peace. Marlene had imagined that she could arrange a meeting with the sister through Ariadne Stupenagel, and then convince the young woman to reveal what she knew about her late brother's last evening. Marlene had a lot of confidence, bred in hundreds of post-rape interviews, about her ability to winkle information out of people, especially nervous, frightened women. She had been sure that, once comfortably settled with Leona Simmons, over coffee or a drink, the story would have flowed.

This possibility had vanished with Leona. And now, growing in Marlene's mind was the necessity of pursuing an alternative course, one that was far more dangerous than an interview with a frightened girl. She tried to put it out of her mind, tried to read, to watch TV. Cursing her helplessness, she called Karp's hotel in Atlanta and was told that the team's flight had been delayed in Chicago. Suddenly the loft seemed unbearably confining. After throwing on a bulky outfit that made her look not quite like a pregnant bag lady, Marlene hit the street.

She walked east up Grand Street, moving from the early morning hustle of industrial SoHo to the relative quiet of Little Italy. Along the venerable street shopkeepers were taking deliveries, and Marlene waved to several that she knew, while dodging around gaping trucks, burly men with crates or sides of meat on their shoulders, and the open steel gates of basement storerooms.

At last she reached Ferrara's and ordered a double-shotted *café latté*, which she drank down immediately, and then another with, this time, a truncate cone of the establishment's legendary rum cake. This produced in her an effect similar to that which drug scene habitués achieve by downing Quaaludes and amphetamines together, although with considerably less fetotoxicity: a lightness of mind that is all the more beguiling because it precedes total oblivion.

Thus primed, she found herself able to arrive at a course of action. She still had some misgivings; the plan might require her to dissemble just a trifle with Karp. This was her chief concern, that and the possibility that she might end no better than she started with respect to information. That she might be killed in the process barely crossed her mind.

When she returned to the loft, she called Harry Bello at home. The phone rang for half a minute before Bello's whispery voice came on the line. Without preamble she invited him to dinner that evening, lasagna. She doubted that he would plead a previous engagement, and he didn't.

He said simply, "Thank you," and she said, "Around six-thirty," and that was it. My most gnomic relationship, she thought, and started to arrange her little kitchen for serious cooking.

They picked Francine Del Fazio up easily at the corner of Crosby and Howard, whipping the car swiftly around the corner—a leap, a muffled scream, and it was over. One second a woman was striding along a dingy street and the next she was gone. Carmine had to admit that Joey was good with his body.

He heard the struggles in the backseat subside. "Joey," he said, "we need her alive. We gotta talk to her, remember?"

"Hey, she's fine," said Joey happily. "She's gonna stay alive and awake for the whole thing, as long as I want. Ain't you, sugar?"

CHAPTER
eleven

Bello arrived, fashionably late at seven, looking worn and smaller than she remembered, clutching a bottle of Bardolino. He was only mildly drunk. Marlene was wearing her red Chinese jacket outfit for the occasion, giving her the look of one of those toys that pops up after you knock it down. He offered the wine wordlessly as he moved into the loft, his deep-set eyes taking in the room in one sweep. Marlene saw his eyes cast around again, more slowly this time, and when his eyebrow moved up a fraction of an inch, she said, "He's in Atlanta. Just us burnt-out Italians tonight. You hungry?"

"I could eat, yeah," said Bello, and she ushered him to the dining zone. A dinner with Harry Bello, she found, was easily distinguishable from one with Oscar Wilde; the cop ate steadily and with good appetite, acknowledging Marlene's comments with monosyllables between bites, and succeeded in consuming two-thirds of a lasagna the size of the Manhattan Yellow Pages.

Marlene talked throughout the meal, about Italian cooking, about Queens and cops she knew that Bello might know, trying to draw him out, to find the person beneath the cryptic style. She also filled him in on

what she'd learned through Karp and Stupenagel about
Leona Simmons.

In the end, after having eaten all he could, and having drunk five-sixths of the wine, with the espresso and
biscotti on the table, Bello, who might be a drunk but
was no boor, began to yield before Marlene's assiduous
pumping.

He had, it emerged, been married to the same
woman for twenty-six years, had been with the cops
since he got back from Korea, and still lived in the
same house he had bought on the GI Bill the year after
Doris and he were married. Doris had wanted him to
go to college on the Bill too, but he liked the cops and
he thought he was too antsy to sit in a classroom.

Doris had taught first grade. They never had any
kids, a buried sadness. But two city paychecks—they
had a nice life, and Marlene sensed that the romance
that had blossomed in high school had never faded,
preserved, as by a minor miracle, through the sexual
katzenjammer of the sixties and despite the many
temptations that drop in the path of New York police
detectives.

He also talked about working Brooklyn homicide in
the old days, watching as wave after wave of gangsters
succeeded one another, keeping time with the changing
demographics of New York: Irish, Jewish, Italian, now
American and Jamaican black; even more recently various new immigrants from the mysterious East—
Odessa to Saigon—had cut into the action. They all
seemed to affect the same style of flash and often
chose the same corpse-disposal areas as their predeces-
sors. They talked for a while about the blackened un-
derside of the famous melting pot; the old days were
better.

Harry told a good story when he got warmed up.

The star of all the stories was Jim Sturdevant, the dead partner, the bravest, the best friend, the best cop. . . .

After one of these tales, Marlene said, tentatively, "Yeah, it must have been a real shocker when he died. How did it go down?"

Bello's face froze and the life seemed to vanish from his eyes. His eyes closed in a long blink and then he looked away from her. He cleared his throat. He cleared his throat again, but nothing emerged.

Marlene reached across the table and clasped his hand. He started to jerk it back, then relaxed and let her hold it.

"What do you want from me?" he said, his voice husky and strained.

"You want to know? I'll tell you," she said. "OK, two things. One is, I feel for you. You had some rough knocks. Your wife dies. Your partner gets killed, and not only does he get killed but in a way that you can't even think about, much less talk about. You were . . . you think you fucked up in some way, that's why he died. You're carrying the guilt.

"No, let me finish. This isn't cheap psychology. I'm feeling this. I look at you, I see my brother, Dom. I don't know what happened to him in the fucking war, because he won't talk about it any more than you'll talk about what happened with Jim, but I know he went away a bright, funny kid and he came back like you are now. He does odd jobs our dad gets him. He could drink you under the table, believe me.

"So we have this case dropped in our laps. I'm in it because—I don't know—I can't just *sit*. I thought I could, but I'm not made that way. I've got to find out. I got to! You're the same way, except you don't want to know what happened to your partner. You killed your curiosity. So you've retired from the detective business. You can't really work on the Simmons case.

It's too painful to use that terrific mind you have, so you're kicking it to pieces. It's like watching a moron child tear apart a beautiful antique clock. So cut it out! That's the first thing. Cut it the fuck out!"

Bello didn't say anything for a long time. The only sound was breathing and the refrigerator's cycle and the distant traffic on Broadway. At last Marlene said, "You want some more coffee?"

Bello nodded and she rose to fill up the little stove-top espresso maker. Then he said, "What do *you* believe in?"

Marlene was used to the elisions and non sequiturs that passed for conversation with Harry Bello. She could fill in behind them. She turned to face him and patted her belly. "I believe in this. Plus love, I believe in the healing power of it. At moments I believe in the Holy and Apostolic Catholic Church. Family. A short list."

"The job?"

"Oh, yeah, how soon we forget," she said with a grim laugh. "Do I believe in Justice? You know, Karp gives a little speech to the green attorneys we take in every year. Something like, abandon hope all ye who enter here. *Lasciate ogni speranza.* You're not going to change things, you're not going to stop crime, things will get worse with every passing year. Being a pro is doing the right thing despite all that. It's its own reward. And so on."

Bello's eyes narrowed and his mouth relaxed into a shadowy smile. "Does it work?" he asked.

Marlene shrugged. "Fuck if I know. It works for me. Butch believes it." The coffee was ready and she poured the inky brew into regular cups. She placed a cube of sugar on her tongue and drank, letting the coffee swirl past its sweetness.

Bello smiled again. "My grandma used to do that."

"Mine still does. So. What's it gonna be, Bello? You gonna straighten up? Get it together? I tell you what, and this is my final offer." She pointed to her belly with her thumb. "You got nothing to live for? I'll let you be a godfather to the kid here. Take an interest. Protect her from the devil and all his works. And we'll catch the bad guy. What d'ya say?"

Bello laughed, a soundless chuckle, shaking his head. Marlene giggled. He said, "You're a piece of work, you know that, Ciampi?"

"And you too, Bello," she said.

He sobered. "The thing is, though, I'm off the case."

"You're what!"

"This morning, after I talked to you. McKelway, the watch commander, called me in and told me to turn all the Simmons stuff over to Darryl Fence. No, Marlene, I didn't fight it. Face facts, I been fucking the dog for a year now. Like you said a while back—maybe there's this big investigation and Simmons is part of it. It means amateur hour is over."

"Shit, Bello, what'll you do now?"

"I don't know. Same as always: sign in and sign out. Cash my check. They got me helping the arson squad—somebody's torching buildings over by Long Island City. I'll live."

"But . . . ah, shit, Harry! We were doing good."

"Yeah, well, not good enough. McKelway said the decision came down from way, way up." He finished his coffee. "What the hell, I don't sleep anyway," he said, half to himself.

"I'm going to keep at it," Marlene said, her jaw stiffening.

"You can try. Fence is pretty good. A couple of nice collars. But he's not gonna give you the time of day."

"I wouldn't ask him," Marlene snapped. "What about Leona? Did somebody pick her up?"

"I guess not. Fence didn't mention it."

Bello stood up and looked around for his coat. "I got to go," he said. "Thanks for the lasagna. And the rest of it."

"The two-dollar lecture. You think I'm a schmuck, right?"

"No, I don't. You know something? Since Jim and Doris passed away, I haven't touched anybody I wasn't arresting, or a stiff, until tonight."

"That's shitty, man. Enough to drive you to drink." She handed him his coat and kissed him on the cheek. He put on the coat, and as he turned to go, he asked, "What was the second thing?"

"Huh?"

"The second thing. You said you wanted two things from me, but you never got to number two."

"Yeah. Number two was I want you to set up a meet between me and John Doone."

He stared at her. Behind his eyes she could almost see the stainless steel gears whirling as he calculated, balanced, figured, ran through conversations, and came up with the answer.

A full minute passed. Then Bello nodded slowly and said, "Wednesday."

Marlene expected Bello to call the next day, Saturday, telling her that the meet with John Doone had been set up. There was no call. By noon on the Tuesday she was getting worried, but had resolved to trust Bello and not to nag.

She was called instead by Ariadne, this time at a decent hour, the early afternoon.

"Stupe, it's two in the afternoon. I thought you'd still be in bed."

"How do you know I'm not?" she replied, and then

in a shrill, breathless tone, "Faster, Duane, faster! Use your tongue."

"Duane?"

"Just a little jest, Marlene, to enliven your dull days. Actually, I'm calling from the St. Regis, where I have just had my second interview with La Mackey."

"How did the first one go?" asked Marlene.

"It was beyond boring. Names dropped like rain. And clothes. We toured the wardrobe. It took forever and a day."

"It sounds like fun. You always did like clothes, Stupe."

"I won't dignify that with a reply, especially coming from someone who positively lusted after my closet for years. . . ."

"And did we find any little clues amid the Diors?" asked Marlene sweetly.

"No, no, Marlene, what we were doing, if you remember, was establishing a premise for our growing intimacy. Which I did. Now we meet for drinks at the dear old Saint R. to exchange girlish confidences."

"And were there any?"

"As a matter of fact, after the fourth stinger there was a modest gusher. Things are not terribly House and Garden *chez* Mackey. He doesn't know how to treat a woman. He plays around. She found Someone, but It Was Not to Be. How deeply shocked she was when he was *murdered*. I was suitably impressed. No names mentioned, but I was assured that he, the slain lover, was well-known."

"Does she have any ideas about who whacked Mr. Wonderful?"

"Yeah, that's interesting," said Stupenagel. "I said, 'Who could have done such a terrible thing?' and she gave me a knowing look and said, 'He's insanely jealous. Insane!' Then all of a sudden she realizes what she's said and she goes dead white. She goes, 'Oh, God, oh, God, please don't ever say I said that—he'll kill me,' and so on, the tears flowing like rain, as they say. Very impressive."

"She likes the husband for it?" asked Marlene.

"Let's say she'd like it to be him. She'd also like it if he got poked in the eye with a lit cigar. Not a reliable judge."

"What's your take on her, in general?"

"Mmm ... your basic bimbo, with delusions of cultural grandeur; insecure; self-dramatizing. The background is: from a little shitheel town in P.A.; went to Philly to be a 'dancer,' although where she actually danced was left vague."

"The horizontal foxtrot maybe?" asked Marlene.

"I doubt it. She doesn't have that whore's edge. I'd guess she'd want a ring and the hall hired before spreading the golden thighs. Anyway, met the asshole in Philly, married, one kid, a girl. Besides that, I think she's really scared shitless. She's a good little actress, but not that good."

"When did she last see Simmons?"

"This we haven't determined yet. She was blubbing so much that I figured if I brought Simmons's name up, I'd need to shove a wooden block between her teeth. Later I'll call her up and say that a rival reporter is about to link her name with the Simmons murder and the only way to avoid a major scandal is for her to give me the full story, to insure sympathetic treatment."

"Sounds good, Stupe. Then we can both drop by Elizabeth Arden to have the slime removed. I love this work!"

"Leave sentimentality to the bimbos, dear," said Stupenagel. "The only thing that keeps this affair from degenerating into a sleazy triangle murder is the dope angle. I still have hopes in that department."

"Yes, me too," said Marlene. "I'm trying to wangle an appointment with our local kill-crazy drug baron to see about just that. Also to find out what happened to the flying Leona and, if possible, talk with her."

"Sounds interesting. Can I come?"

"Not a good idea. I think it'll be hard enough to get him to see one stranger, never mind two. Keep in touch, kid."

"Yeah, well, watch your ass. If you get killed, can I have your toys? Or your husband? I still can't believe *you* got a tall one. A nice body too, I saw him play on TV. He must be a total schmuck."

"Far from it; he is the embodiment of every human virtue, and God's gift to women," lied Marlene smugly, thinking, "Or soon will be."

Stupenagel sighed. "I must be doing something wrong. Maybe I should turn to the church in my despair. I have a neat diamanté cross somebody gave me. I could start right now by praying to St. Regis over vodka gimlets. Hey, you're a Catholic; is there really a St. Regis?"

"Yes, he's the patron saint of rich assholes. So long, Ariadne," said Marlene and hung up.

Barely pausing to take a breath, she called Harry Bello's office and found out why she had not been able to reach him for three days. A cop at the 105th told her that he was in Bellevue, the detox ward. Cursing vigorously, she struggled into warm clothes and hopped a cab uptown to the hospital complex.

"How did you get in here?" asked Bello sourly from his bed.

"That's nice," she said. "No 'Good to see you, Marlene.' No 'Thanks for the flowers, Marlene, twelve months pregnant you shouldn't've dropped everything and come running up through the fucking sleet to my sickbed, Marlene.' " She tossed the plastic-wrapped bouquet she had purchased at the shop downstairs onto his bed. "You know what you can do with these," she said.

Bello put a hand over his eyes and shook his head. He looked even more pasty than usual, and the tendons stood out in his neck, like those of a much older man. "I'm sorry," he said. "Sit down."

She pulled a guest chair up to the head of his bed and sat.

"What happened?" she asked.

"I got drunk," he said.

"So I assume. Would you care to elaborate?"

"I left your place after dinner. I got in the car. I was feeling groggy, so I pulled over on the other side of the tunnel, in Sunnyside, and took a nap. I slept for about an hour and a half, and then I figured I'd drive over by Long Island City, take another look at the fire scenes. I told you about that?"

"Yeah. They took you off Simmons and put you on this arson deal."

"A piece of shit," said Bello contemptuously. "You never catch these guys unless it's some bozo who's got insurance up the ass and a gas can in his trunk. The owner, understand? But here there's no reason. One building, a glass jar factory, last boosted the insurance in 1949. The rest of the buildings're tenements, absentee owners, shitty insurance. Tough for the folks thrown out on the street, especially for the ones that died, but no angle, except a nut, or some kind of fucked-up revenge. I mean, what can you do, arrest everybody in town with matches and a gas card? But it's arson homicide, so they got me in on it. Detached duty. It means: Keep the asshole out of my hair.

"Anyway, there I am at five in the morning cruising down 31st toward Astoria, when this car passes me going fast, runs a signal, and he's out of there. A late model Chevy Malibu, dark blue."

"And you gunned your engine and began a thrilling high-speed chase?"

Bello's lip lifted a fraction of an inch: for him, a grin. "Yeah, right. I figure the guy's heading for La Guardia by Grand Central Parkway, he doesn't want to miss his plane. OK, fifteen minutes I hear sirens, I switch on the radio, it's a fire, two-alarm, right across the street from the last burnt-out building. I was just there. They must've been pouring gas while I was out in the street.

"So I think about my Malibu. It's worth a check, so I drive to the precinct and call in the plates, and . . ."

"You remembered the plates?"

"Yeah, well, the last three numbers were 756. My shield number is 21657. So it stuck. You want me to finish this story? OK, so the car's a rental, Hertz out of La Guardia. Rented by a James Cross, from Philly. I run the address past the Philly cops and it's a phony; no such address. I find the clerk that rented it and I go to see her. She remembers the customers. A short guy with a round face and a heavy five o'clock shadow. Like Nixon, she says. And the other guy, a cigar smoker, big, older, gray sideburns, wears a plaid hat, glasses, dark eyes. A good witness. She remembers because of the cigar. She hates cigars.

"And also because she's seen this pair before. At least twice: in late at night, out on the first shuttle the next morning. Always a Chevy, always paid in cash. I call Hertz back and check the records. This Cross rented a car on the same nights three of my buildings burned. This is number four."

"Nice work, Harry," said Marlene.

He grimaced in distaste. "It's still horseshit, though. It's no crime to come into the City, or to drive through Long Island City at night. I doubt I'm gonna catch them in the act."

"You could tell the car agencies to look out for them. Put up a description."

"Yeah, yeah, I did that already. So big fucking deal, Marlene. I pick these guys up and let's say it turns out that they're professional torches. I still got shit. You think they're gonna be carrying a notarized contract that says burn down such-and-such a building?" He settled back into his pillow and sighed.

"You don't get it yet, do you?" he said. "Face it, if you were the brass and wanted a case shit-canned, who would you give it to?"

"Come on, Harry, you know that's not true."

"No? I haven't lost that many marbles. OK, forget that. The rest of my weekend. I go down to Bed-Stuy and I look up an old snitch of mine, a Jamaican guy named Lamont, and I tell him about your little problem."

"What did you tell him?"

"I said you wanted to see Doone. And that you knew who hijacked his dope."

"What! Harry, I don't know shit about who."

"Yeah, I know." He looked at her appraisingly. "You're not slowing down on me, are you? I have to draw a map?"

Marlene was about to protest, then checked herself and tried to make a Harry-type jump. She figured it out and her palms started to sweat. "Jeeze, Harry, that's really fancy. If it doesn't work out, it's my sweet ass. What makes you think he'll buy it anyway?"

"I got no idea if he'll buy it. You're the one who wanted to see Doone, and that's how you get in. How you play it from there's up to you. Meanwhile, Lamont got back to me Sunday afternoon. It's on, tomorrow. Tomorrow's Wednesday, right?"

"All day long," she said.

He gave her an address. She wrote it down and gestured at the hospital room and said, "So you worked so hard, you decided you had to take a rest?"

"No. I didn't drink all weekend. Didn't need it, want it, anything. Then I'm sitting around the house Sunday, thinking about Bed-Stuy and Doris and things. And thinking about you, as a matter of fact. A nice dinner, laughs, human life, like that. So I got out a gallon of red I'd been saving for a special occasion and I drank it."

"The whole gallon?"

"For starters. By the time I finished it, it was Monday, my R.D.O., so I walked down to Queens Boulevard and went into Phil's. You know it?"

Marlene nodded. "I ordered a double scoop of Canadian, Schlitz on the side. That's the last thing I recall, ordering that drink. I woke up here, last night. The Department is not pleased. They don't like blackouts, especially not by armed officers. They want me in a thirty-day program."

"A good idea," said Marlene.

Harry sniffed. "I'm not an alcoholic, Marlene. I don't have deep inner problems. Just bring Doris and Jim back and I'm a one-drink-with-dinner guy."

Marlene didn't say anything. She just looked at him and waited for his mind to digest what he'd just said. It took a while. Then he sighed deeply and in a choked voice said, "I don't want to end up on a slab."

Marlene leaned over and grasped his hand. "Harry, I promise you, you avoid the medical examiner, I'll make sure you go out by way of St. Joe's, with a Mass and a wake and the whole nine yards. Provided I survive myself."

Harry Bello looked her in the eye and said in a tone of the utmost gravity, "He touches you, there's no place he can hide. I told Lamont. The fucker will never see a courtroom."

The intensity of his gaze unnerved her. She said lightly, "Come on, Harry, I'm a D.A.; don't say shit like that."

"Just so you know," said Bello, turning his face away, squeezing her hand.

While Carmine waited for Joey to finish in the shower, he made calls to boat liveries in Sheepshead Bay. He knew a dozen guys who would do the job, just as a favor, but he couldn't use any of them. Nobody was supposed to know he was in town on business. He engaged a twenty-one-foot Bayliner inboard-outboard for some night fishing that evening.

Joey came out of the bathroom with a towel around his waist and a grin on his face. "Hey, Fish—so, we goin' fishing?" he said brightly.

"I told you, don't call me Fish. Just Carmine, OK? Yeah, we're goin' tonight. She wrapped?"

"Yeah, she looks like a big turd. She sure could move it, though. Probably the best fuck she ever threw in her life. Funny, they really put out if they think you're gonna let them go."

"Any mess?"

"Nah, I used the plastic sheet. So what about this Ciampi cunt? She said she didn't say anything to her, but . . ."

"You said you believed her."

"I did. By the time she was finished she wasn't bullshitting about nothing. I guarantee it."

"We'll check her out a couple of days," said Carmine thoughtfully. "See who she is, what she does.

Tell you the truth, I'd be just as happy if we didn't have to bother anybody else."

"Listen," Marlene said to Karp, "do you mind if I do something a little risky?" His nightly call, and through the conversation, as she filled him in on what she had learned from Ariadne Stupenagel, she had been building up to this and then saying something else. It was so easy, so wifely to tell him little lies, to omit details. Why make him worry? What he doesn't know won't hurt him. It was the way she was raised, the way Karp was raised, and harder than she had thought to change. Still, now it was out.

Karp paused meaningfully. "Um, how risky would that be, Marlene?"

"Risky like going to see John Doone."

"The cops picked him up?"

"No. I'm going to see him in his lair. In Bed-Stuy. Bello set up the meet."

"I presume he was drunk at the time," said Karp acidly.

"It's within the realm. But be that as it may, it's set up."

"But he's going with you, right?"

"No, it's a solo. Just the kid herself."

"What! Marlene, where's Bello while you're in there?"

"He can't come; he's in detox, drying out."

"Oh, uh-huh. He makes an appointment with a crazed killer for you and then relaxes on the pillows. What do we buy for this, Marlene? Could you tell me that?"

She ignored the irritation in his voice. "We buy the sister. The sister knows the whole story."

"The sister? What, your intuition tells you this?

Marlene, for crying out loud, you got no evidence for that, you—"

"Wait!" she shouted. "Listen, will you? OK, one, we know the sister used Simmons's car all the time; two, we know the sister was a mule, probably for Doone; three, there's a strong likelihood that Leona picked up Marion after the game—she did it before.

"OK, something happens: Marion gets shot, someplace, we don't know where, and carted off in the car. Leona's scared stiff. Why? Who's after her? Doone, for losing the dope? The D.A., for clamming up? The killers? Maybe she saw something."

Suddenly, Marlene thought of Francine Del Fazio. Whatever weird mess she had fallen into, Marlene had not been able to help her. She realized that the intensity of her desire to get close to Leona Simmons owed something to that failure. She continued, with renewed fervor. "So we've got to have Sis. She's got the answers. And my gut feeling is, she's with Doone."

"How do you figure that?" asked Karp. "Why isn't she running from him?"

"You forget: Harry followed her to Doone's place *after* the murder, *after* the dope was lost. She walked out. They must have made it up some way."

Karp's sigh whistled in her ear over the lines. "OK, you go in there, assuming he's got the girl, what makes you think he's gonna deal with you? You want Sis, but what have you got to trade for her?"

"Harry told him we know who did Marion. No, calm down! I didn't see it right away either. OK, the presumption is it's Doone's cocaine, so he's got to be dying to know who got in the way of his delivery. A rival? An accident? If it was a rival, why'd they leave the dope in the car? It doesn't make sense. It's as much of a mystery to him as it is to us.

"So there's a point to his cooperating. As far as he

knows, we're the law, we got all these resources, we're going to find his bad guy for him. That's what pulls him in. He doesn't need to know we're running our own game."

"Uh-huh, and suppose we find the killer, what happens then?" asked Karp, his voice unnaturally calm.

"Nothing happens. Once we have a suspect, we can start to build a case. Leona's probably a witness—"

"Stop! Marlene, this is the most fucked-up thing I ever heard of. Since when do we finger suspects to killers?"

"Who said finger? Did I say finger? All I want is for Doone to be interested enough to give me a lead on Leona. Then he's out of it."

Karp gave the inarticulate cry of a man stuck in Atlanta while his wife was doing something crazy and dangerous in New York. *"Out of it?* You're fucking *out of your mind, Marlene!* What makes you think that your charming partner is going to roll over and let the law take its course when he finds out? By his rep, he's not into probable cause or trial by jury. Of course, we know where he stands on capital punishment."

"Butch, that's not fair, we do deals with the bad guys all the time."

"Deals? Yeah, we use a little fish to catch a big one, but then *we're* in control of the investigation. We are preparing a fucking case. What you're doing is farting around because you're bored, putting yourself in danger and maybe screwing up something you don't even know about—"

"I'm going to hang up," said Marlene. "I don't have to listen to this shit."

"Wait! Wait, don't hang up," Karp cried into her ear. She paused, waiting. She heard him catch his breath, and then he said in a voice creaking with strain, "Look, OK, you want to play detective, fine. You're a grown-up. Do me one favor, though, please? Take somebody with you. Besides going to see Doone, that's a rough neighborhood. I'd rather not be worrying about somebody sticking a gun in your face. And face it, you're not as limber as you used to be."

"That's a point. OK, I'll take somebody."

"Somebody reliable," added Karp.

"I'll take Rin-Tin-Tin's *father,* OK? Jeez, Butch, a girl gets knocked up, you think *she's* the fucking baby."

"I wonder why. Ah, shit, if I think about it I'm gonna get pissed again."

"I know what I'm doing, Butch," said Marlene.

"Yeah, right," said Karp sourly. "Anyway, I'll be back home tomorrow, early evening. Assuming you're still alive and not in jail, I'll see you then."

Marlene hung up and then, on impulse, called her sister, Anna.

After the usual pleasantries and family chat, Marlene brought up Francine Del Fazio, saying she had come by but omitting any details.

Anna said, "Francine! God, Frankie Del Fazio called too. She hasn't been home and he's worried sick. Do you know where she is?"

"No, but I got the impression she needed a separate vacation. Look, Annie, if she shows up, let me know, huh? I'd like to talk to her again."

The next morning Marlene rose early. Nervous and jumpy already, she made herself eat an English muffin and swallow some coffee. Then she got on the phone and reached Raymond Guma, not at his office but at Sam's, a luncheonette off Foley Square, where he and his various cronies fortified themselves for their several days in court.

She got swiftly to business. "Goom, I got a date

with John Doone this p.m., in Bed-Stuy, and I need a
baby sitter."

"Doone, Doone . . ." mused Guma. "B. and E. guy?
Used to work the diamond district with Shorty Paltz?"

"No, Guma, this one's a Jamaican dope dealer.
Chops people up."

"Oh, that Doone. You better take the whole Fifth
Precinct, honey. Does Karp know about this?"

"Yeah, Guma, he does. What, I need his permission?
Check my ID—I'm a grown-up, all right?"

"Hey, get off my case, Marlene! Anyway, why call
me? Just buzz Fred Spicer and he'll send one of his
guys with a car—"

"No, it can't be cops, Goom. This is seriously unofficial. Nobody respectable need apply, you know? I
was thinking of one of the street people. Somebody
reliable."

"A reliable street person, huh? Isn't that a whadya-
callit?"

"An oxymoron," said Marlene. "Somebody intimidating. Just for the cab ride down, back and hang
around to scare off the mutts. For a twenty."

"A twenty'll buy you a lot of oxymoron," said
Guma. "I'll work on it. Where and when?"

Marlene gave him the information and then called a
gypsy cabdriver whose girlfriend's mugger Marlene
had once sent up for a three-to-five. He was available
and glad to help.

At noon, therefore, Marlene was sheltering in the
doorway of her loft, wrapped in a maroon quilted
maxi-coat, leather knee boots and a black wool scarf,
trying to keep out of both the harsh wind and the way
of the men with handcarts servicing the local industries
and wholesale merchants. At ten past, a battered black
Dodge, bearing no visible mark of its trade, edged to
the curb between two trucks.

Marlene darted forward. "Poco, my man!"

"Marlene! Lookin' good, *guira!*" answered the skinny Nicaraguan in the driver's seat, leaning over to roll down his passenger window. They shook hands warmly and the driver said, "Hop in."

"Just a sec, Poco. We got to wait for somebody, my, um, assistant."

"No problem, *guira,* I got all day. Get inna car, though; 's cold as a bitch out there."

Marlene sat next to Poco in the front seat. They spoke briefly about family and general conditions and then remained in companionable silence for about ten minutes. Marlene felt no particular pressure of time, since neither the person she was waiting for, nor those who were expecting her, were likely to be keeping Date-Minders.

The engine murmured, the car heater strove to replicate the climate of its owner's homeland, and Marlene settled into a pleasant semi-doze. Then, through half-closed eyes, she spied a familiar shape walking rapidly toward the entrance to her building. Her heart sank. "Guma, you bastard . . ." she mouthed, and then stopped when she reflected that he had done what she asked—provided her with a reliable escort.

She heaved herself out of the car and approached the being that stood waiting on the sidewalk. He was nearly seven feet tall and built like a coal-fired home furnace. He had a bushy gray-black beard twenty inches long, which object was so heavily encrusted with dank organic matter that it resembled the floor of an Amazonian rain forest. He was dressed in a hooded ensemble, constructed mainly of green industrial canvas wrapped with thick cords and wire, that covered him from the crown of his head to the bulky wrappings in which his feet were shod. A greasy leather letter-carrier's bag completed his outfit. His face was so black with filth that only his red-rimmed blue eyes evidenced his original race.

"Hello, Booger," said Marlene, moving casually into an upwind position.

"Ahrrng gong, hn mmnf," replied the creature, grimacing horribly, revealing an astounding mass of naked flesh and gum. He had no front teeth and a spectacular harelip and cleft-palate combo.

This person was known in the environs of Foley Square as the Walking Booger. The D.A.'s staff swore he was a former defense attorney who had chosen a nobler life. Reliable all right, thought Marlene as she directed the huge man into the backseat of the cab. The Walking Booger was used by the seedier bail bondsmen and lawyers as a courier, especially when cash had to be transferred across town. The Booger was both as honest as a brick and as unstoppable as an armored car. And he was cheap.

"Jesu Maria!" gasped Poco when the Walking Booger entered the car. The stench was like a living being.

"Quick, roll the windows down!" Marlene cried, "and get moving!" The cab leaped into traffic, and they pointed their noses gratefully into the icy wind. Marlene wrenched a purse-sized sprayer of *L'Air du Temps* out of her bag and frantically doused the air with cologne spray. The Booger settled comfortably into the backseat, grinning and humming to himself; he didn't get many rides.

CHAPTER

twelve

Poco made the trip to Brooklyn in twenty minutes, running more lights than even gypsy cabs usually do. The location Bello had mentioned was a rubble-strewn vacant lot at the junction of Gates and Ralph avenues. Despite the cold and wind, a dozen or so well-wrapped black men were grouped around a fire barrel; others were standing around on the street, talking to people cruising by in cars and shaking hands unusually often with passersby.

"This is a bad area, Marlene," observed Poco. "You see those guys aroun' there? They dealin' drugs."

"No kidding?" said Marlene. "Good thing I'm not on duty or I'd have to lodge a criminal complaint. OK, Booger, we get out here."

On the street, she leaned in the window and said, "Poco, stick around the neighborhood, OK? It'll be two, three hours max. Say forty on top of the regular hire."

"Thass cool, *guira*. I'll be aroun'."

The Dodge drew away, and Marlene walked up to the closest vendor, a short yellow man wearing four sweatshirts in layers, who immediately hit his pitch. "Whachoo, whachoo, I gottit, skag, ludes, reds, I got crank, I got flake . . ." Then he saw her companion. "What the *fuck* is that!"

"He's my cousin Lewis from Westchester," said Marlene demurely. "I'm showing him the sights. He'd like to see Lamont," said Marlene.

"Lamont? I dunno no Lamont."

"Yes, you do," said Marlene. She leaned closer and said confidentially, "Honestly, Lewis has been looking forward to this for weeks. You definitely don't want me to have to tell him you're not being helpful. He has a real problem controlling his temper when he's disappointed."

"Bitch, listen close, I don' fucking know any damn Lamont—" the man began, and at that moment a tall teenager darted forward from the drift of men and grabbed Marlene's shoulder bag.

She pulled back instinctively on the strap and was yanked off her feet, crashing into the stinking canvas of her companion's chest. The Booger instantly whipped a huge arm around her, holding her a few inches off the ground against his left side. With his right hand he grabbed the strap of the bag and stopped the kid dead in his tracks.

The kid's eyes widened and he pulled out a six-inch gravity knife. With a curse he lunged forward and sank the knife into the Booger's wide belly.

The Booger roared, "Nnngah nunka orgh!" and, releasing the bag strap, seized the wrist of the purse snatcher's knife hand. The kid tried to jerk back, to no avail, and then kicked his captor twice in where his groin might have been expected to be. For all the effect it had, though, he might as well have been kicking a utility pole.

The Booger placed Marlene gently back on her feet. Then he reached out, grabbed the kid's forearm with his other hand and with one violent twisting motion snapped both bones. The kid let out a single shriek and collapsed onto the pavement.

This whole sequence of events had taken not twenty seconds, and the sweatshirt man Marlene had first addressed was still standing there as if fastened to the pavement, his jaw gaping. Two gold teeth glinted in the dull afternoon light.

Marlene smiled tightly at the man, and then, taking a deep breath through clenched jaws, tugged at the knife sticking from the Booger's chest. It came free with a soft crunch. She examined the blade briefly; it was not clean, but it was not bloody either. She dropped it into the Booger's mail bag.

She looked the man in the eye. "Lamont?" she said.

"By the b-barrel," the man stammered. "Yellow cowboy boots and the long suede coat."

"Thank you. Come on along, cousin Lewis."

Lamont had observed the events on the sidewalk, as had his peer group. A path magically cleared before Marlene.

"Bello sent me," she said to Lamont. "I want to see Doone."

"Bello din say not'ing about dat one. Joncrow, 'im a go dead me I bring dis bwai up 'im ranch deh."

"He'll stay in the street," said Marlene reassuringly.

Lamont licked his lips nervously but nodded. "Follow me, den."

He led them down Ralph Avenue across the streets named for Revolutionary heroes, toward Crown Heights. In Marlene's girlhood this had been a respectable, even an elegant neighborhood. The housing stock, large brownstones set back from the street and ringed with low stone or cast-iron fencing, had been cut up into rooms by slum lords who had purchased them from the retreating bourgeoisie. They were tatty now, painted with graffiti and with their little front yards choked in trash. But some of the streets were still reasonably pleasant, tree-lined with old sycamores and inhabited by people among whom hope had not entirely died.

Lamont turned down one of these streets and stopped before a large house faced with reddish rusticated stone. He opened the waist-high iron gate and said, "Wait 'im here. You come wit' me."

Marlene said, "Booger, wait here. If I'm not out by dark, come in." The big man grunted assent and began to root through a sidewalk pile of trash.

She followed Lamont down the path. They climbed the broad marble steps. The house still had its heavy glass and wrought-iron doors. Lamont rang the bell. After waiting several minutes, he rattled the bars, calling out, "Yo, Coolie! Open de raas door dem!"

More minutes passed and then the door locks clicked and it swung back revealing a barrel-chested yellow-skinned black man with an oriental cast to his features, wearing dreadlocks and a red, green and black wool tam on his head.

"Is what fe you bangin' den, Lamont?" he asked.

"I brung de Babylon woman Joncro want fe see."

Coolie looked Marlene up and down and then stepped out of the doorway. Marlene crossed the threshold and was led through another glass and iron door into a dark and different world.

As she stepped past the inner door, she was struck, to her great surprise, with a sense memory from her childhood. Her grandmother had had a sister, Tanta Nina, who seemed to the six-year-old Marlene impossibly ancient, a contemporary of the saints on the holy cards she won in school. This old Sicilian woman, dragged reluctantly to New York in late widowhood by her American family, had taken one look at the New World and rejected it. She had created in her tiny

Canarsie apartment a reproduction of her life in Palazzolo.

Entering her apartment hallway was like entering another world; even the air was different, alien, laden with exotic odors—steam heat, rotting paint, anisette, singed feathers, vinegar, garlic, camphor. All the kids, Marlene and her contemporaries, had hated to be brought there for holiday visits. It wasn't the frail, toothless old lady in rustling black that was frightening; it was the air itself. The air made you believe that the rest of the world might have vanished, that the only reality left was these cramped and overheated rooms, densely impregnated with the foreign, and filled with the hollow scratchy sound of old records in Italian, played on a huge mahogany wind-up phonograph.

John Doone's house had the same sort of air: tropical in temperature, laden with exotic aromas, conjuring up not rural Sicily but West Kingston, Trenchtown, and the jungly villages of the cockpit country—cooking rice, curry, hot grease, goat meat, the heavy stench of white rum, a sweet, cloying perfume Marlene could not identify, and (overlying all) the fug of marijuana.

And there was the music too. A rhythmic thump permeated the house, a sound felt through the feet and belly as much as the ears. Someone was playing reggae over a set of very serious speakers.

She was led up a dark stairway, down a darker hall, into a brightly lit room. Three dark women, their heads wrapped with bright scarves, were doing something at a table. Brown children played on the floor or ran in circles. The music was louder here and she could hear the scratchy singing, and the bass guitar, although the words were unclear. The beat was clear enough—*deh deh Dum de DAAH, de de Dum de DAAH*—the women were working their shoulders to it as Marlene passed them. They didn't look up from what they were doing.

They went through another door into a much larger room, high-ceilinged and shadowy, thickly carpeted, with an ornate fireplace. Here they stopped. Marlene's eye took a moment to adjust to the relative dimness; the room seemed inordinately crowded with furniture, like a Levitz showroom: several sofas, stuffed arm-chairs in numbers, coffee tables in marble and wood, leather recliners, table and standard lamps. There was no pattern or design to the arrangement; the stuff had just been shoved where it would fit.

There were also people in the room, perhaps twenty-odd, men and women and some children, as if a party were in progress. They were well dressed, in the player style. The men favored leisure suits or bush-jacket out-fits in pale pastels or white over open silk print shirts. They wore knitted tams or floppy caps. The women were in bright print dresses, and some had their heads wrapped in scarves, as in tourist posters of Jamaica.

But the atmosphere was not party-like, despite the heavy smell of marijuana and white rum, and the pen-etrating bump of the reggae. People were speaking in lowered voices, with the occasional louder expostula-tion of argument. Once again the scene plucked at Marlene's memory, but from a different era of her life: this wasn't a party or a family gathering. It was court.

"Wait, you!" said her burly guide, and he moved away toward the far end of the room, under the large, curtained windows, where the crowd was thicker. Shortly he re-emerged and gestured to Marlene. The people made way for her and she found herself stand-ing before a broad mahogany table, on which sat a desk lamp, several account ledgers, an ashtray holding a smoldering cigar-sized, newspaper-wrapped reefer, a bottle of white rum with no label, two glass tumblers, and a large nickel-plated .38 revolver with engraved pearl grips. Behind the table was John Doone.

He was a black man—that is, his skin was not one of the infinite shades of brown called "black" by Americans but literally black, the matte, light-absorbent color of soot or of a CIA spy plane. His hair was cropped short and his skin had the fine, slightly oily texture of well-worn leather. There was a deep scar on his cheek that glinted blue highlights when he moved. The nose was thin and hooked, and the mouth was deep-lipped, wide and tightly held.

Doone's eyes were a surprising golden-brown color, particularly striking in their matte setting, like topaz inlaid in ebony. These regarded Marlene coldly. Without preamble he said, "Woman, they tell me you know who make me lose my property."

Marlene coolly returned his gaze. She said, "I'd like a chair."

Conversation halted in the room. Then there were surprised murmurs. Doone opened his mouth as if to issue a retort, then gestured to one of his satraps. An armchair was thrust forward and Marlene sat.

"Thank you," she said. "I'm here to propose a deal, Mr. Doone. As you say, I have some information you want. You have something I want. We can both benefit—"

"Doone 'im make no deal with Babylon, yaah," Doone interrupted. His finger slowly reached out and played with the barrel of the revolver on the desk, rocking and spinning it on its balance point. He gave it a last casual flick and the barrel ended up pointed straight at Marlene.

She ignored this demonstration. She said, "I'm not from Babylon. I'm from Ozone Park. Babylon is way out on the Island."

Doone frowned, his brow knitting itself into a mass of thick channels like a truck-tire tread. From his crowd, murmurs.

"It was a joke," said Marlene. The frown deepened. This was not a great start. She drew a deep breath and tried to recoup. "Look, Mr. Doone. I have no bone to pick with you. Trust me on this. I don't care what you do for a living. I work in Manhattan, not Brooklyn. I came here because I want to talk to Leona Simmons, that's all."

He glared at her for a long moment. Then he said, "You got somet'ing you gone a tell me, tell! If not, get de fuck outa me house!"

"That's really nice, Mr. Doone. You ought to talk to the guy who writes the ads for Jamaica. I thought it was supposed to be the friendly island."

There was a mass intake of breath and all talk ceased. Marlene gathered that this was not the way John Doone was ordinarily addressed in his inner sanctum. She thought she saw a smile play around Doone's lips, which may or may not have been a good sign. He said, "Daughter, listen me! You playin' wit fire you don' understand, yaah. You t'ink, cas you white gal from big Babylon office, nothin' can happen a you here. It not so, gal. Coo yaah! Dis house, I make de law. I say you go out, so you do; I say no, you disappear, nuh?"

Marlene nodded impatiently. "Yeah, yeah, I know. You cut up people and throw them in the trash. OK, you're terrifying me. I tell you what, though." She wagged her left hand in his face, so he could see where the two smallest fingers were partially missing. "I'm already started, see." She tapped her false eyeball with her fingernail. It made an audible click. "This too. You want to pay somebody to cut me up, I wouldn't want you to get ripped off. I mean, you could probably get a discount."

Another moment of stunned silence, and then John Doone's face split apart to show a set of large teeth, impossibly white against his skin, a dental strobe out of the blackness, and he laughed long and hard. Everyone else in the room suddenly thought it was pretty funny too. When the noise died away, John Doone said, "What you name, daughter?"

"My name's Marlene," she said. "Why do they call you Joncrow?"

"Cho, gal, where you heard dat?" He laughed again, then followed it with a rapid-fire exchange of patois, unintelligible to Marlene, with the nearest of his companions, producing more laughter. Marlene didn't know whether this changed mood was a good or bad sign. Maybe these people got happy before they killed you.

Doone said, "Some o' dem say, dem call me Joncrow, cas I black like de joncrow, wha' unu call de buzzard in Jamaica, nuh? An' another reason, dem say, cas, dem say in Jamaica, 'How fas 'im run, de joncrow beat 'im, how strong 'im be, de joncrow eat 'im.' You understan'?"

"Yes, it means death comes to all and the buzzards feed on it. I like the second reason."

This seemed to please Doone. He smiled at her and said, "Cho, you right, gal, to raas!" He leaned back in his chair. "So now we mo' friendly, nuh. You a tell me what you want."

She glanced around the room. "I'd like to speak with you alone."

A momentary frown crossed Doone's face, but it passed, and he made a swift dismissing gesture, followed by a rustling, chair-shoving exeunt all. In thirty seconds they were alone in the room with the reggae. Marlene played her ace.

"OK, look, the big question in the Simmons murder is the dope stashed in the glove of his car. At first we thought it was a plant, to throw the cops off the trail, and take some of the pressure off the case. A sports hero who's also a dope dealer—people don't want to know about it. The problem with that is that nobody will associate Simmons with dope. He was pretty clean as far as his teammates can tell."

Unless they're lying, thought Marlene, but plunged on. "But that leaves us with another problem—who'd want to kill Simmons bad enough to ditch fifty grand worth of good cocaine as a scam? It was worth at least that, wasn't it?"

Doone shrugged. "Say it so. Den what?"

"So rethink it. What if the target wasn't Marion at all. What if the target was you? Leona worked for you. She used Marion's car all the time. Maybe they figured Marion was in with her. Anyway, Marion's sitting in the car somewhere, and somebody who doesn't like you figures he'll leave you a message. Bang bang."

Of course, they knew Simmons had not been shot while sitting in the car, only finished off there, but there was no need to let Doone in on that bit of information.

Doone said, "Cho, you doan tell me nuttin I doan know already. But is you can name names?"

"You'll never know unless you let me talk to Leona," answered Marlene.

Doone leaned forward menacingly and pointed his finger at Marlene. "To raas! Gal, you a go make me rahtid wi' you. Coo yah, I talk a dat gal a'ready. She doan know raas 'bout who dead her brudder. Dis I know, nuh."

"I still want to talk to her."

"Yah, unu want fe put her in de jail. What, you t'ink you playin' wit' some quashie, nuh? You t'ink I doan know de D.A. got her, 'im reduce de charge, 'im want her fe spy on me? An' now you come, you t'ink you trick me wi' dis talk 'bout you know dis, you know dat. What I t'ink? You doan know shit."

"You can think what you want," said Marlene calmly. "But whoever hit Simmons isn't going to stop there. I would think you couldn't afford to turn down anything that would let you find them before they find you. And another thing: if the D.A.'s got his eye on you already, maybe he likes *you* for the Simmons murder."

Doone laughed. "If 'im t'ink so, 'im dam' fool. On de night dat bwai 'im shot, I in de jail, nuh, in de City."

Marlene, nonplussed, continued, "Good for you, then. I, on the other hand, have no beef with you at all. I doubt you had anything to do with Simmons's death. I think that, between the two of us, we can figure out who did. But you have to trust me. Let me see Leona."

He scowled and pointed his finger again. "Huh! Trust you? To raas, trust you! You mus be t'ink me stupid bungo, nuh. What reason me got fe trust you, Babylon? You not oppress me? You not cheat me? You not hunt me like de beast? Now, so little white-white gal, come a me, tell a me dis yah sweet tale, trust me, Ah doan do no harm a John Doone, jus lemme see de girl. Shit! You know wha it take fe me a trust you? Black you skin and live in dat Trenchtown fe twenty year, nuh! Den we see. Now, you go home little white gal, go have dat white baby fi you. You damn lucky you funny you, dis time. Anudder time, I a go show you somet'ing you doan like." Doone swiveled his chair around so his back was to her. She was dismissed. She heard a door open, and a large man stuck his head in and glared at her.

She had seconds before the crowd returned and hustled her out. A phrase popped into her head and she spoke it, almost without volition, pitching her voice to carry. "You'll trust me because I'm not afraid of death."

The chair swiveled around. Doone looked at her oddly. "Is wha' you talkin', gal?"

"Very simple, Mr. Doone. I said that to impress you. You don't think I'm reliable. I'm white and soft. Well, I'm not soft. Let me put it this way. If I put my life on the line, will you go for a deal?"

Doone narrowed his eyes and pursed his lips. "Wha' you gon do, nuh?"

In answer Marlene reached out and picked up the .38. She was aware of hurried movement and excited voices behind her, and footsteps, and clicking sounds that she knew to be weapons cocking, weapons pointed at her.

John Doone raised his hand in an arresting gesture. The noises stopped. She said, "May I?" and, carefully not pointing the gun at Doone, pressed on the cylinder release. The cylinder fell open and she worked the ejector rod, dumping six fat hollow-point bullets out on the desk.

She lined them up like toy soldiers and selected one. It disappeared into the cylinder and she snapped the gun closed. She looked into Doone's eyes as she spun the cylinder three times. The ratchet noise it made was the only sound in the room, besides the constant dulled beat of the reggae. She continued to look into his eyes as she raised the pistol to her temple and squeezed the trigger.

The revolver said, "Click," and the room sighed with the mass release of breath.

She broke the gun again and placed it on the desk. The single cartridge was in the next chamber to fire. "Looks like my lucky day, Mr. Doone," said Marlene. John Doone threw back his head and laughed until the tears flowed.

Marlene waited until she was out of the house before allowing herself the luxury of a tremble. Her steps down the entrance path were unsteady, and the cold breeze dried the sweat on her brow. She found the Walking Booger sitting on the curb in front of the house. He had found a Kentucky Fried Chicken box in the trash and was eating the scraps, crunching up the bones like a dog and licking his fingers, as advertised.

"Booger," said Marlene, "I believe I have set a new Olympic record for free-style stupidity, but I pulled it off. You should've been there. It was like Vegas. Now you see it, now you don't."

"Ngorn 'on mang."

"Good point," said Marlene cheerfully. "Now we have to find a phone so we can call Poco. Come on. You can take your lunch."

The giant rose from the curb and stuck the chicken box into his mail sack. At the corner, Marlene found a heavily barred convenience store manned by two suspicious Pakistanis, a store that held a working pay phone. She called Poco's service and gave him the pickup address, and then went out to loiter under a large, elaborately graffitied NO LOITERING sign.

They waited twenty minutes, during which time the Walking Booger rummaged happily in a dumpster and nobody bothered Marlene. When Poco arrived, she noted that he had at least a dozen fiber deodorizers shaped like little pine trees hung on every available purchase of his cab. A valiant effort, although the Booger's pong would have challenged the Snoqualmie National Forest. Within the steamy interior, therefore, a faint pine scent fought a losing battle with dead dog (the base note of the Booger's fragrance) and was totally overwhelmed when the street person climbed in again.

"Holy shit, Marlene," he complained, "I gonna have to steam-clean the whole car." Marlene calmed him with kind words and folding money and they set off. At Fulton and St. James, Poco hung an unexpected right, instead of heading straight for Flatbush Avenue and the Manhattan Bridge approaches, and weaved through the streets around Pratt Institute before returning to De Kalb going west. His eyes met Marlene's in the rearview and they were worried.

"Hey, Marlene, you know a coupla white guys drive a late-model Chevy, one of them smokes cigars?"

Marlene fought down a stab of fear. "Um, why do you ask?"

"Because they been followin' us, man."

"What? Are you sure?" asked Marlene, resisting the impulse to look over her shoulder.

"Yeah, they been on our tail since Fulton. They don' seem to mind if we seen 'em either, you know. Wan' me to try an' lose 'em?"

"No, just get us back home as quick as you can."

This was jarring. And confusing. Two men in a car had been following Francine. Marlene also recalled her last meeting with Bello and his description of the two putative arsonists. She wracked her brains but could come up with no rational explanation for why two Philadelphia torches, if her pursuers were indeed them, should be following her around. If the followers were also Francine's persecutors, then ... something clicked. Francine had seen the fires set. Arson murder. It was the only plausible explanation.

Back at Crosby Street, she paid off both Poco and the Walking Booger and stumped slowly up the stairs, cursing her bulk. When she reached the loft, she called Bello at the hospital, but the nurse there said he was in group therapy. Marlene tried to imagine Bello spilling his guts, his secrets, to a bunch of strangers. She left a message, hung up, and flopped on the red sofa, where she fell into a profound sleep.

From which she was awakened by a kiss.

"Butch! You're home!"

"That, or you're having a particularly intense sexual fantasy," he said.

She struggled to a sitting position and rubbed her face vigorously. "Blaagh! What time is it?"

"A little after seven."

"My God! I just collapsed." Then, turning to him, "That was a nice wake-up. I missed you. Mmm, what a day!"

"You're still in one piece, anyway. I checked the dumpster next door before I came up."

"Oh, that! He's just a big teddy bear. No problem. He's going to let me talk to Leona when she gets back. He's keeping her on ice somewhere."

"Oh, yeah? And how did you convince him to do that?"

"The truth? You can take it, without having a paranoid shitfit?"

Karp gritted his teeth, squinted and clenched his fists, in a caricature of a man about to be shot from a cannon. "OK, hit me!" he said in a strained voice.

"I pretended to shoot myself in the head."

Karp looked at her to see if she was kidding, and determined that she was serious. "Oh. Well, that's always a convincer. What do you mean, shoot yourself, Marlene?"

"I set up a Russian roulette with a pistol he had, but I palmed the cartridge. Worked like a charm. The fans went wild."

Karp leaned back against the cushion and let out a long sigh. After a minute's silence she said, "You're mad at me, but honest to God, he was going to kick my ass out of there. It was the only thing I could think of to do that would convince him I wasn't just another candy-ass college grad. You understand? Butch? Talk to me . . ."

He sighed again and his voice, when it came, was cracked, despite the effort he was making to control it. He said, "I'm not . . . I understand that it's something that I'm going to have to get used to. You're not going to change. Hell, if you carry on like this when you're eight months pregnant . . . anyway, it's real hard for me. It's like being blindsided, catching an elbow in the guts." He spread his hands helplessly and she saw, with no little shock, that his eyes were soft with tears.

He shrugged. His head nodded as if he had reached a decision. "I guess I'll get used to it."

He sounded and looked so woebegone that Marlene had to suppress an urge to throw her arms around him and promise to reform her ways, and forever after cross with the green and not in between. This would, however, have been a lie, and Karp would have known it. He *would* have to get used to it. She felt odd—both frightened and exhilarated, as if she had left a small, stuffy room filled with women and had entered an enormous room occupied only by Mr. Death.

It also, paradoxically, made her feel intensely domestic. "You must be hungry," she said, rising. He nodded and let his tongue loll comically.

She gave him a squeeze and then stumped over to the refrigerator. "I got fresh linguini and I have some sausage sauce left over from Harry—"

"Left over from Harry?"

"Yeah, I had him over, the poor bastard. Before he went on a binge. What's that look for?"

"Hey, what do I know? You're queer for cops? First Raney, now Bello. Fine, but if one day I'm taking a leak in a station house and somebody's got 'For a good time, call Marlene' written up there, I just want you to know, I'm gonna be pissed off."

"That's fair," she said cheerfully, glad that he was joking. You had to give it to Butch, she reflected: he bounced back.

"OK, dinner. Linguini and sausage. There's a melon, there's prosciutto, I could make a little salad, there's what's left of the cannolli—"

"How come we always have to eat Italian food?" asked Karp.

"How come?" asked Marlene in mock amazement, and then, shifting accent to Low Queens, " 'Cause you married an Italian, you bum, that's why." She opened a drawer and took out a wooden spoon, which she brandished, her other hand clenched on her hip. "Whassamatter, you don' like it? You don' like Italian food, you shoulda married a Joosh goil, huh? Huh!"

Marlene's voice now went up in pitch and volume, to a fingernail-on-blackboard screech, and she made a hook of her finger and placed it over her nose. "Yah wanna a Joosh goil? I'll give yah a Joosh goil. Make more money! I wanna car-ar! I wanna mi-ink! Oy vey, I broke a nail!"

"I can't believe this," said Karp. "Anti-Semitism, right in my own home."

Marlene looked startled. She laughed nervously. "Oh, don't be silly, I'm not anti-Semitic."

"Oh, no? What about this performance? How come you sort of slurred my name when you introduced me to your folks?"

"I did not," cried Marlene with an embarrassed giggle.

"Did too. Your grandma still thinks my name is Carpa. She keeps asking me how's Giuseppe and them down by Sheepshead Bay."

"Oh, don't! I was just kidding."

"Uh-huh. That's how it starts: first jokes, then the camps," lectured Karp. "However, now that I've established moral ascendancy, I forgive you." He patted the sofa. "Come here, my little Himmler."

Marlene complied, and poked him viciously in the ribs. "You're the shits, you know that?"

Karp put his arm around her and drew her close. "Mmm, that's better. Now that you've revealed yourself, are you going to show up in one of those tight black leather girls-of-the-S.S. uniforms, like they have in men's magazines? And torment my flesh?"

"Tight is not a word I can deal with right now. Ooo, what are you doing?" She slapped facetiously at his hand. "You can't be interested in this body."

"You'd be surprised," said Karp, fumbling with a hook. "Of course, we don't want to Injure the Child."

"Don't worry about that," said Marlene as she wriggled free of her slacks. "Vee haff our vays. I thought you wanted supper."

"That too," said Karp.

The next morning, early, Marlene slipped from bed, and the snoring Karp, to the telephone, where she called Bello. This time she was put through.

She quickly covered her interview with Francine, her experiences at Doone's and the sight of the shadowing car.

"The same guys?" said Bello doubtfully.

"I don't know," said Marlene. "Two guys, a late-model Chevy, one was smoking a cigar. It could be anybody, but the question is why are they following me, except . . ."

"Yeah, the arsons."

"You figure she saw the arsons, came to me, and they saw her at my place . . . ?" She left it open. She had a bad feeling about what had become of Francine Del Fazio.

A pause. Bello thought. Then he said, "You got a camera?"

Forty minutes later, Marlene had slipped out, dressed in her maxi-coat over boots, two sweatsuits and boots. She carried her big leather bag, into which was tucked the Polaroid camera she had received as a wedding present.

The day was clear and chilly. As she stepped out into the street, she cast her eye along the blank windows of the loft buildings on both sides of the street. If she was really being followed, there would be eyes behind one of them. Somebody would be making a call.

She walked slowly to Grand Street, went into a store, bought two lemons and a pound of butter, and then stopped on Lafayette Street and hailed a cab. She told the driver to head up Broadway.

"Where you goin', lady?" the man asked.

"I don't know yet. Just drive."

The cab headed north. After a few blocks Marlene was gratified to see the familiar Chevy slip into position, keeping two cars behind in the thickening morning traffic. They were still locked in as they passed Herald Square, and at 35th Street, Marlene told the cabbie to hang a left.

"Lady, I don't know where you're goin'," said the cabbie patiently, "but I hope you ain't in no hurry."

The street, as ever, was packed with cars and trucks delivering merchandise to the firms of the garment district. By the time they passed Seventh Avenue, they had slowed to a walking crawl. Marlene paid the driver and added a five on top of the meter. She leaned forward and checked the cab's rearview mirror. When the

Chevy was wedged tightly between double-parked trucks on either side, she got out of the cab.

She walked east on the packed sidewalk until she reached the stationary Chevy. Then she stepped out onto the street and, standing in front of the car, took a photograph of the startled pair in the front seat. Then she spun on her heel and disappeared into the crowd. It took the men in the car a few seconds to react, and nearly a minute before Joey could wriggle out from behind the passenger seat, to stand cursing on the sidewalk. There was clearly no point in trying to follow on foot. Traffic had moved and horns were already starting to honk. Joey got back in the car.

"Fuck it," said Carmine, puffing his cigar. "We know where she lives."

"This fucking city!" said Joey. "I wouldn't fuckin' live here if you paid me."

Marlene walked quickly around the corner, went a block south on Eighth Avenue and caught the IND southbound to the East Houston station. A three-block walk down Crosby Street brought her home.

Her back and thighs were aching powerfully as she clumped into the loft, breathing hard. Karp was relaxing with a cup of coffee and reading *Sports Illustrated*.

"You OK?" he asked with concern.

She dropped her coat on the floor and collapsed into the rocker with a groan. "I want to give birth," she said. "Hello? You can come out now. Ring-a-levio, one-two-three! Home free all!"

"Why did you have to run out?" Karp asked.

Mutely she held up the bag with the lemons and butter.

"Damn it, Marlene, why did you have to schlep downstairs? I can drag stuff up from now on."

"Yeah, well, it wasn't just that." She pulled a Polaroid snapshot out of her bag and held it up for him to see. "You ever see these guys before?"

Karp came over and examined the photograph. "No. Should I have?"

"Not really. They've been following me around for the last day or so."

"Following you?"

Sighing, Marlene told him the story Bello had told her, about the two probable arsonists and Francine Del Fazio. When she had finished, Karp said, "I'm missing something, right? Aside from how incredibly dumb it was for you to do what you just did, it doesn't make any sense. Why would a couple of out-of-town torches follow you around? Because they maybe thought that somebody you saw once in the last twenty years spilled her guts to you. Why the hell would they do that? There's no case—you're not a witness to anything."

She shrugged. "Sure, and guys like that know exactly what counts in court and what doesn't. Maybe they want to light my fire. Meanwhile, I can't think about it anymore. I'm going to bed again. Wake me when I go into labor."

Marlene shrugged out of her clothes and into a flannel nightgown, and climbed grumbling up the ladder to bed. Karp made himself a bowl of raisin bran and ate it while thumbing idly through his magazine. Once again it was brought home to him that being inside something made it nearly impossible to read about it credulously. For years that had been true for him in reference to crime reporting; now it was true for pro sports as well. At best, they always got it a little wrong. It made it hard to believe anything you read. Of course, nearly everyone was an expert on something, so that everyone should have had that realization, yet everyone still read and watched the press and quoted it as an authority. Go figure.

He cleaned up, put on a duffel coat, and went out for a walk. He looked around the nearby streets for a lurking Chevy with two men in it, but spotted nothing obvious. There was too much traffic in any case. He stopped by the Chinese candy store and bought the *Times* and the *News*. Force of habit.

Back at the loft, he tossed the papers aside. He was too twitchy to read. Practice started at two; it felt unnatural to be idle on a workday morning. He considered calling up one of his friends for lunch, then remembered that all of his friends lunched on sandwiches at their desks, with a phone shouldered into their ears. As he had, most days, back then.

Instead he walked down to Marlene's office and leafed through the Simmons file she had assembled. He saw her note to herself:

1. Where was he killed? Where did he go after game? (Butch)

2. Girl, cars—check limos. (Bello)

3. Drugs—Doone (? hold off)

4. Sister (A.S.)

Well, Marlene had certainly done her bit. The sister was missing and it was not likely that Stupenagel was in a position to find her. He crossed off item four. Number two was solved, although Bello was no longer in the play. He crossed that one off too.

He himself had drawn a partial blank on number one. It seemed almost certain that Simmons had gone away from the stadium with his sister. The question was where did they go. Was she with him when he died? If she knew something, and she was really a snitch for the Queens D.A., why wasn't she in protective custody now, spilling her guts?

He looked at the list again. His vague boredom and irritation began to coalesce, and became focused for the first time on whoever had dealt this mess. Like ev-

eryone else in the criminal justice system, Karp hated
a mystery. They were rare enough, in fact. The identity
of the perp in ninety-five percent of criminal cases was
perfectly clear. Joe and Sally fight. Joe buys gun from
Jim, announcing that it is for killing Sally. Joe shoots
Sally five times in the head. Joe is found with the gun,
his Nikes full of Sally's blood.

The art was in building a case that would stand up to
legal challenge and, if need be, before a jury. In this
case, however, somebody was screwing with the process, throwing out false leads, gumming the works.
Karp's pride in what was, if not a machine of justice,
at least a smoothly working sewage plant, had been
touched now.

As he thought about it, doodling on Marlene's note,
he confirmed in his mind the notion that the mess was
the fault of the Queens D.A., either through incompetence or worse. In the note's margin he wrote:
"Chaney-Thelmann/Bello—no pressure on cops/sis-
ter—rap sheet— informant— why no follow up?" It
was as good as an indictment.

Marlene always wrote the names and numbers of
case contacts on the inside of the case folder. Karp
found the number of Jerry Thelmann at the Queens
D.A. and dialed it.

He got Thelmann's secretary and misidentified himself as a New York D.A. bureau chief. It seemed that
Mr. Thelmann was not in. What was this in reference
to? The Simmons murder? Oh, then he would have to
wait. Everyone on the staff connected with the Simmons case was at a press conference. They had arrested the killer that morning. Who was it? A man
named John Doone.

Karp thanked the woman and hung up the phone. He
looked at the list again. In large letters he wrote on it,
"WHY???"

CHAPTER

thirteen

"They did what!" Marlene came up out of her doze like a breaching whale.

"I said," Karp repeated, "that they just picked up Doone for the Simmons killing. I just got off the phone with Thelmann."

It was past four and the December light was thinning out. Karp was lying on top of the covers next to Marlene, who, though she had scarcely stirred since returning from her thug-photography session, had come alive in response to the mysterious instincts that let her know when Karp was doing business on the phone in the loft.

"What'd he say?" Marlene asked. She rubbed the sleep out of her eyes and sat up expectantly in bed.

"He said they'd been watching him for a while on the thing anyway. They knew Leona was carrying dope for him and they figured that was the connection—"

"Who's this 'they'?"

"Queens homicide detective named Fence. Thelmann told me he's the one in charge of the real investigation. Anyway, they got a tip and they went into his car with a warrant. Found an automatic, nine-millimeter, the ballistics check out. It's the gun that did Simmons."

"And what does Leona Simmons have to say about this?" Marlene asked.

Karp nodded. "Yeah, I asked him that too. He said she wasn't material to their case."

"Wasn't material! Christ, Butch, she could've been an eyewitness. Does he even know where she is?"

"He didn't say and I didn't ask. He was not that anxious to talk to me in the first place; he sounded real nervous—excited but scared. Long pauses."

"I bet," said Marlene, then, "Wait a second: they like him for the actual trigger?"

"So I'm told. Why?"

"What about Doone being in jail on the murder night? How did he explain that?"

Karp was startled. "Where did you hear that?"

"From Doone. Don't give me that look! Why the hell would he lie about something like that? It's easy enough to check. And Doone isn't stupid."

"No, but if he's not, then Thelmann is. I can't believe the little putz wouldn't check something like that." He looked at Marlene, who had risen from the bed and was shuffling through her dresser drawers. "You don't like him for it anyway, do you?"

"No, I hate him for it. Bello had it right. It's the wrong kind of hit, and the dope in the car makes no sense at all. Why would Doone have seen me, have listened to me for two seconds, unless he was genuinely concerned about losing his stuff, or about somebody trying to do him dirty?"

"That's a point," admitted Karp. "But the thing that really stinks out loud is the business about Doone being locked up. You going somewhere?"

Marlene was struggling into a pair of red wool tights. "Well, I'm not going to lounge in bed while they railroad my own personal vicious drug lord. What about you?"

"I'm beat for today," said Karp, leaning back and flexing his bad knee carefully. "Tomorrow I might make some calls. Find out about that arrest anyway. You know, this is starting to stink worse all the time. What I can't figure out anymore is why they killed him. And why somebody is setting up this elaborate scam. What could be so important?"

"That's the toughie, all right," said Marlene. She pulled on a bulky black sweater and wriggled into a denim maternity skirt. "And I think I know who to talk to about it."

She dropped down the ladder and went to her office. There she dialed a familiar number and was quickly connected to the woman who was holding down her job while she was on maternity leave, Luisa Beckett.

"Luisa, I got a problem," she said after the usual pleasantries. "Are you free later this afternoon?"

"I could shuffle some things. Why? Is it important?"

"Yeah, I think it is," Marlene replied and then gave Beckett a brief description of her involvement in the search for whoever had killed Marion Simmons.

At the first mention of Bello's name, Beckett interrupted her.

"That's Harry Bello? Used to work out of Brooklyn homicide?"

"Yeah. You know him?"

"Um, you could say that. Working in the Brooklyn D.A. back when I did, he was hard to miss. I knew his partner, Jim Sturdevant, a lot better. Jim was one of those cops who keep baby D.A.'s from making assholes of themselves, you know? A sweetheart. I broke down when he got killed. Harry, on the other hand . . ."

"What about him?" asked Marlene anxiously.

"Well, the word on him around the courthouse was

that he wasn't that tightly laced to begin with. Smart as
hell, but he wouldn't talk to anybody but Sturdevant; I
mean literally. He had a temper on him too. Some mutt
would tell him a stupid lie, like they all do, and he'd
go batty. Jim kept him in line, and when Jim got it, he
went out of control. Went on a rampage looking for the
shithead all over Bed-Stuy. A kid got shot dead under
suspicious circumstances. Self-defense according to
the inquiries, but it left a stink. The D.A. had words
with the commissioner, I understand. Anyway, he got
transferred out."

"What was the story on how Sturdevant got shot?"

"Yeah, that too. Bello's story was him and Jim were
checking out a witness at a building on Lewis Avenue.
They surprised two kids busting into an apartment.
One of them pulled a gun and shot Jim, and then they
both escaped while Harry was getting help for Jim. So
he knew what they looked like."

"And Harry tracked down and killed the gunman?"

"Well, he killed a black teenager all right. Whether
it was the gunman remains to be seen. The dead kid's
mother swore he was out of town when it all happened. But, given the circumstances, case closed. I
mean, what's another dead black scumbag more or
less? So, Harry's back in action, huh?"

"Yeah, to an extent," Marlene replied, and finished
the story of the case.

Beckett laughed and said, "That's some vacation
you're taking, Marlene. How would you distinguish it
from work itself?"

"I don't wear makeup or panty hose," said Marlene.
"Look, here's the point. I need to go back and see Mrs.
Simmons again. She was locked up tight when she was
interviewed before, because she was afraid for Leona.
Probably somebody was pressuring her to keep her

mouth shut and to go along with the story that Marion
was involved with the drug business. If I go to her now
and explain the situation that's come out in the last
couple of weeks, I'm pretty sure we can get her on our
side."

"I don't follow," said Beckett.

"It's because of the problem of protecting Leona. If
she really did see something, we're not just talking
about a stretch upstate. Somebody might try to hit her
too. It's a different ball game now, and the mother'll
see that."

"Why not let Queens handle it?"

"Luisa! *Queens* is the fucking *problem*! If they're
trying to frame a guy who was in jail during the murder, they must be getting desperate. I'm talking massive corruption here."

"Fine, fine," said Beckett. "Where do I come into
this?"

"I want to go down to Mrs. Simmons this evening,
with you, and pump her. Maybe we'll even get a line
on where Leona is."

Marlene heard the flipping of pages. Luisa was
checking her calendar. Marlene could sympathize: running the rape and sexual violence bureau was a job and
a half. On the other hand, Luisa owed her a big one.

Luisa said, "Mmm, yeah, I could, after six. But I re-
peat my question, Marlene: why me?"

"Because you're another woman. Because you're a
good interviewer. Because I don't have a car and you
do—"

"And I'm black."

"Yeah, right, Luisa. There's that."

The Simmons home was dark when the two women
arrived in Luisa Beckett's yellow Firebird. They had to
ring several times before a hall light came on and they

saw the older woman's face peering anxiously through the tiny square window set in the door. When she saw Luisa, her eyes widened and she flung the door open.

"Honey, where've you—" she began, and stopped abruptly when she was able to see in the light from the hallway that the thin woman standing there was not her daughter.

Mrs. Simmons put her hand to her throat and took a stumbling step backward. Beckett said, "Mrs. Simmons, my name is Luisa Beckett. We're here about Leona."

"Jesus God, she's not—"

"No, as far as we know she's still all right," said Beckett quickly. "But she may not be if we don't get some information from you. May we come in?"

Mutely, Mrs. Simmons drew back from the door, and Beckett and Marlene entered.

They sat in the living room, with the Last Supper and the memorabilia of the Simmons children. If Mrs. Simmons recognized Marlene from her previous visit, she did not mention it.

"Where's my baby?" she asked.

"We don't know, Mrs. Simmons," said Marlene. "I think she's being hidden by a man named John Doone."

Mrs. Simmons grimaced as if she had swallowed bile. "That evil, evil man!"

"I agree, ma'am," said Marlene. "He is an evil man, but killing your son was not one of his crimes. Somebody else did it, and I think your daughter knows more about what really happened to him than she's told anyone so far. That means that as long as she's on the loose, she's in grave danger from whoever really did it."

"I don't understand," said Mrs. Simmons. "The gentleman from the D.A., he said that pusher killed my boy. He promised nothing would happen to Leona. Now you're telling me ..." She threw up her hands and turned a stricken face to Luisa Beckett.

Beckett rose from her chair and sat on the couch next to Mrs. Simmons. She held her hand and spoke softly. "Ma'am, this has been confusing for everyone. Ms. Ciampi here has been working on your son's case all by herself, nearly, and she's found—well, it may be hard for you to believe, but the Queens district attorney may not want to find your son's killer."

This did not seem to surprise Mrs. Simmons. She rose heavily and went to the shelf where the pictures of her family were assembled. Selecting one in a silver frame, she returned to the couch. "They were both such good babies," she said softly, staring at the photograph. It showed Marion and Leona at ages ten and eight, dressed in elaborate Easter get-up, the boy in a white suit with bow tie and the girl in a white foam of ruffles. "I honest to God thought we had crossed the river." She looked seriously at Beckett. "He wasn't one of those playboys on those teams. Trained monkeys! Marion had brains. Always did well in school. Leona too. I can't understand it." She shook her head in confusion.

Beckett said, "Mrs. Simmons, can you tell us what happened on the night Marion died?"

"I don't know what happened. She took the car, the Cadillac. Said she was going to pick up Marion and bring him home. About ten I went to bed. In the morning I went out to get the paper and I saw the Cadillac wasn't in the drive. I went to Leona's room. She was using that poison.

"I screamed at her. We had a terrible argument, terrible. We said terrible things. She said I never cared for her, only for Marion. That's not true. I said to her, you're both my babies ..." She paused. "You don't want to hear all this.

"When we settled down, I asked her where Marion was. She started in crying. She said she didn't know. She said she was driving him home, and he said for her to go on the highway to the City." She was silent for a long time, and Beckett had to prompt her.

"Why did he want to go to the City, Mrs. Simmons?"

"He wanted to see that woman. That whore."

"Julia Mackey," said Marlene.

"Woman got a husband already, what does she want with my Marion? I told him, I told him, but once he got under her clutches it wasn't no use. A boy doesn't listen to his momma when he's that way."

"You're sure it was Julia Mackey," Marlene pressed.

"Yes, I'm sure. Leona told me. She brought him there a lot, she said. That's how I know, from her. I told him it was breaking my heart. Why couldn't he find a nice girl and settle down?"

She was crying now. Beckett reached into her bag and gave her a package of Kleenex. Marlene waited until her weeping had subsided into snuffles, and then asked, "Did Leona say what happened that night?"

"No. Not really. She was scared to talk to anybody, after what that D.A. said."

"What was that?" asked Beckett.

"That they would put her in jail for a long time if she didn't help them catch that man. The drug man. The Jamaican. She had to pretend that Marion was using drugs, and keep up with that man, and to do what they said."

"But she did say something to you."

Mrs. Simmons nodded. "Yes. After we settled down she did. I'm her mother. Leona said something about Marion being very nervous and excited. He said he had found out something bad, something about the team. She didn't understand what it was, and he wouldn't talk about it. He said she'd see all about it on TV. What happened was she let him off at that woman's building and went to get something in a drugstore, and when she came out, the Cadillac was gone. She thought Marion had just driven off, so she took the subway home. That's what she said, but ..."

"But what?"

"I know when my children are lying to me."

Marlene said, "One more thing, Mrs. Simmons. Marion had a kind of diary that he wrote in and kept appointments in. Do you know what happened to it?"

The woman shook her head. "No. I never did get his things back. That book. He was always scribbling stuff down, from when he was a little boy. He always had it with him. But I don't know. It must have been in his bag when he left, but they never gave it back."

Mrs. Simmons knew nothing more of relevance, and with many promises to keep her informed and many half-believed assurances that everything would be all right, Beckett and Marlene finished the interview and walked out to the Firebird.

Marlene said, "Baby, can I drive your car?"

"You serious?"

"Yeah, I love to drive and I never get a chance. Especially a hot machine. What have you got inside?"

"Damn if I know," said Beckett. "I liked the color and my brother said it was a good deal." She handed Marlene the keys. "Here. I'm beat anyway. Just remember it's not my car, it's the bank's car. Hey, can you drive with that eye?"

"No problem. Half the drivers in the city are blind in both eyes."

Down at the end of the darkened street, two men sat

in a blue Chevrolet. One of them was having a tantrum.

Carmine was venting his rage and frustration in a stream of curses, in both English and Sicilian dialect, impressing even Joey with its virtuosity and fluency. It was especially impressive because Carmine was usually so cool. It was why, Joey supposed, they called him the Fish.

"What the fuck, Carmine. So she goes to the momma, so what? Don't mean she knows shit about us."

"Us!" Carmine cried hoarsely. "Us ain't the point. She's talking to the momma, it means she's nosing around the deal. She saw the nigger who got the sister one day, the next day here. It means she could get close enough to fuck it up."

"So we whack her?"

"Fuckin' A," said Carmine, starting the car.

Marlene got into the Firebird and rolled the seat far enough back to accommodate her girth. She cranked the engine and pulled out onto the street in a scatter of gravel.

When she was headed north toward Queens Boulevard, Luisa asked, "What was that about a diary?"

"Oh, Butch found out Simmons kept some kind of date book, diary; I thought it might have turned up. That was interesting what she said about Simmons finding something out about the team."

"You mean somebody wanted him not to say what he knew?"

"Yeah. It's a reason for the hit, which we haven't had before. By the way, you were great. I really appreciate it."

"No problem," Beckett said. "Sad woman. So fucking hard to raise black kids to begin with, and she does it, and one's a junkie and one's dead. At least she's got some money out of it."

They drove along Queens Boulevard, talking desultorily about office politics and the perfidy of men. Marlene decided to take the Long Island Expressway and the BQE back to the city. It would be the world's longest parking lot eastbound at this hour, but virtually deserted in the other direction.

Driving with no right eye, Marlene was particularly sensitive to the usual blind spot to the right rear, which she tried to reduce by canting the rearview mirror to the right and using the side mirror to check her left rear. She also kept in the right lane most of the time.

As she had expected, traffic was light and she barreled along at a good speed. She passed a beer truck, pulled back into lane, and then cursed softly. Beckett said, "What's wrong?"

"Oh, this jerk was tailgating me behind the truck. Now I passed and he's up on my butt again. Pass, asshole!" she snarled, as if the other driver could hear. On their right was the vast darkness of Calvary Cemetery, and Marlene was just getting ready to make her exit to the Brooklyn-Queens Expressway when the trailing car made its move.

Marlene saw the headlights pull out and the car draw up beside the Firebird, on the left. It was too close. Marlene cursed and edged away from it. But instead of pulling ahead, the car stayed even with the Firebird and edged even closer. Marlene glanced at it in annoyance. The overhead lights of the highway gave only fitful illumination, but it was enough to see that the man in the passenger's side was one of two who had been following her.

Marlene hit the brakes at the instant before the Chevy swerved right and slammed into the side of the Firebird. The beer truck following hit his own brakes and leaned on his horn. Marlene heard the screech of metal as the right flank of the yellow car tore itself to pieces against the guard rail with a broad shower of sparks.

The wheel twisted in Marlene's hand. She felt the rear of the car slide out into the road and heard the shriek of the beer truck's brakes. She saw its headlights veer wildly left. Then there was a thump and a crash, and her head was slammed against the backrest as the truck sliced off the rear left quarter of the Firebird.

The next instant, the pressure of the Chevy was gone as its driver burned rubber to get out of the way of the onrushing beer truck. Marlene fought the Firebird to a rattling stop on the narrow shoulder.

"Jesus! What happened! Are you OK?" Beckett's voice was cracked with strain.

"Yeah, I think so," answered Marlene.

"Somebody just tried to run us off the road, didn't they?"

"Yeah. Those guys following me around just upped the ante. Sorry about the car—"

"Fuck the damn car! How're you feeling, the baby and all?"

"Nothing's changed that I can tell. Shit, if this didn't induce labor, nothing will," said Marlene, and fainted dead away.

"You're sure it was the same guys?" asked Karp.

"I'm positive," answered Marlene. "In fact, if I hadn't spotted weasel-face in the passenger seat and tromped on the brake a second before he slammed us, there's no question we would've been wrecked. That and the beer truck happening to come up behind, with a smart driver . . ." She shuddered and sipped tea.

After three hours of energetic hustling involving ambulances, tow trucks, the police, insurance companies, hospital emergency rooms, all linked by frantic phone calls and desperate cab rides, Marlene and Karp were together again in the loft, exhausted and telling each other over and over that it could have been worse, in the midst of Marlene communicating what she had learned at Mrs. Simmons's.

"Well, it could have been worse," said Karp. "The question is, what to do now."

"Bed. Sleep for a week. I feel like a giant bruise."

"Yeah, you say that now, but wait till next time. Don't look at me like that! I know you won't listen, but—"

"I'm listening! I'm listening! OK, here it is." Marlene raised her right hand and intoned, "I do solemnly swear that notwithstanding any undertakings heretofore entered into, I will not leave this loft until I drop this kid, without a police escort, so help me, God. You're on your own, boss."

"What happened to not being afraid to die? Doone's gonna be all disappointed you turned into such a pussy."

Marlene looked at him sourly. "That's right, gloat! Now that I'm a helpless lump, you finally got what you really wanted all the time, a totally passive woman. I hope you're satisfied."

"Not really," said Karp. "My appetite for passivity has barely been tapped."

"Help me into bed," sniffed Marlene, "and watch where you put your hands!"

The next morning, it was Karp who rose early and dressed silently in his lawyer's outfit, while Marlene slumbered on. He paused only to slip the Polaroid Marlene had taken of her two tails into a pocket, and then rode the subway to Queens, there to beard the disingenuous Thelmann in his den.

"He's in a meeting," said Thelmann's secretary when Karp arrived at the office in the Queens Criminal Courts.

Karp replied breezily, "That's OK, I'm in the meeting too," and brushed past her, flashing his Manhattan D.A.'s ID card.

Thelmann was at his desk, polished Oxfords propped up on its cluttered surface, apparently expounding the law to a couple of junior attorneys. He looked up, startled, as Karp barged in.

"I beg your pardon—" Thelmann began.

"And well you should," snapped Karp. "I'm here to prevent you from making an embarrassing and expensive mistake."

Thelmann opened his mouth to say something and then thought better of it. He smiled falsely to his two acolytes and begged them to excuse him for five minutes. They scurried out and he turned his most intimidating stare at Karp. "Well?"

Karp, however, had been intimidated by real experts and was not impressed. His anger at what had happened to Marlene, having at the moment no other outlet, directed itself like a scarlet laser beam at Thelmann.

"*Well,*" said Karp mockingly. "*Well*, Jerry, just tell me one thing: when you arrested and charged John Doone with the murder of Marion Simmons, were you aware that he spent the night of the murder in a precinct lockup?"

"Who told you that?"

"Never mind who told me. Is it true?"

"Of course not! Yeah, he claims that he was, but there's not a shred of documentary evidence of any arrest." This last was delivered with such confidence that Karp's suspicions were confirmed.

"Well, maybe you didn't look in all the right places," Karp suggested quietly.

"What the fuck is this, Karp?" Thelmann exploded. "You accusing me of suppressing evidence?"

"Not me. But that's just one of the many peculiarities of this investigation. Another is, why haven't you questioned Julia Mackey?"

Thelmann's gaze dropped nervously for an instant, and his mouth became tight. "Who's Julia Mackey?"

"Who's Julia Mackey? Come on, Jerry! The victim's girlfriend. With whom he spent his last hour on earth, maybe. What's the matter? Somebody tell you to lay off?"

"Nobody told me anything," snapped Thelmann. "I'm in complete charge of this investigation. We have physical evidence linking Doone to the crime. We have motive, means, and opportunity, and there is absolutely no need to bring Mrs. Mackey into this case at this time."

"Mrs. Mackey? So you do know who she is."

Thelmann swung his legs down from his desk and sprang to his feet, his face reddening. "Get out! Get the fuck out of my office! I'm going to report you to the New York D.A. for interfering with an investigation."

"You do that, Jerry. And I'm sure it'll break his little boy's heart to hear bad about me. But one more point to keep in mind—this started as a private thing, a favor. I was just interested in gathering some information and passing it onto you. But yesterday some shitheads tried to kill my wife, shitheads who have got to be involved in this mess you've created. Now it's personal. No more amateur hour, Jerry." Karp turned on his heel and left.

He went down to the lobby, where he made several phone calls. At a local instant photo lab he had several enlarged color copies made of Marlene's Polaroid photo. Then he hopped the IND subway back to the city.

His destination was a small luncheonette located on one of the twist of streets leading to Foley Square, where the courts are. The place was called Sam's, its owner was called Gus, and it had been serving breakfast and lunch to the denizens of the criminal courts since before the invention of the electric coffee maker.

When Karp entered, a little past noon, Sam's was just changing the flavor of its air from coffee and toast and grease (a.m.) to bacon and mayo and grease (p.m.). It was a long, narrow place, with a counter running half its length on one side and the other side lined with steel tube chairs and tables done in salmon Formica. There were four booths upholstered in red vinyl occupying the rear.

Two of the three men Karp had phoned were already waiting for him in one of these rear booths. "Uh-oh, here comes the star," said Ray Guma. "Could you autograph my menu? Right under where it says bologna."

"Could you autograph my jock strap?" said Roland Hrcany.

Karp slid into the booth next to Guma and said sourly, "What is this, I'm not entitled to any respect? I'm not a sports hero? You guys commies or what? Is V.T. coming?"

"He'll be along. He's probably flossing his teeth," said Guma. "Oh, yeah, big sports hero," he resumed in the same tone. "Does he remember his friends, though? Do we get front-row tickets at the Garden? Do we even get calls returned? No. Of course, when the big shot needs our help, that's a different story."

"Are you finished?" asked Karp. "What do I have to do, crawl on my belly?"

"For starters," said Hrcany.

"Stipulate it," said Karp. "Tickets, no problem. We go to Philly day after tomorrow and then play the Knicks Friday night. Probably be my last game, as a matter of fact."

"Yeah?" said Guma. "They finally figured out you don't have a jumper?"

Karp hesitated before answering. He mentally discarded several light or sarcastic remarks and then with a sigh responded, "No, as a matter of fact, it's because I really can't play anymore. I hurt all the time. The trainer is pushing pain pills at me and they're starting to look good."

"Take 'em!" said Hrcany. "Drugs are the answer. Why should you be different from everybody else in New York?"

"Pussy!" said Guma, sneering. "I always thought you were a real man."

"Thanks for the support, guys," said Karp. "Yeah, I guess I should risk permanent physical damage to sell beer and snow tires. Chaney'll probably spring for a cane. Hi, V.T."

The man who had approached the booth while Karp spoke nodded and slid into the vacant space next to Hrcany. V.T. Newbury was small, blond, classically handsome, and very rich. A sprig of an old and distinguished New York family, he stood out from his present company like a Reine des Violettes rose among dandelions.

"Are you considering carrying a cane, Butch?" asked Newbury. "Good idea. You could cultivate a little waxed mustache as well, sort of an acromegalic Adolph Menjou effect."

"How's the Fraud Bureau these days, V.T.?" asked Karp.

"Booming. I still haven't figured out why someone with an income of fifty million dollars would risk going to jail to make another million, but I'm working on it." He gave Karp a long, considering look. "You appear well, Butch. Fame and fortune agreeing with you?"

"He's quitting," said Guma.

"Yeah, the rat," said Hrcany. "Just when I was starting to make serious money off the Hustlers."

"I hope you were betting *on*, Roland," said Karp. "I'd be deeply hurt if I thought you were on the other side."

Hrcany offered a superior smile. "No, no, that's not the way it works, Butch. Only suckers bet the team. You wanna make money, you got to beat the line."

"Come on, Roland," said Guma, "you think you can screw Vegas?"

"Yeah, why not? They're just guys, put their shorts on one leg at a time, just like everybody else. But it's not really screwing Vegas in the first place. Look, the thing to remember is that bookies don't bet; they're not gamblers. What they live on is their vig—you got to bet eleven to make ten, and so on. So the line is not a reflection of who they think is gonna win—they could care less who wins—it's just a way of balancing the action.

"I mean, you got a team that's hot—like the Hustlers have been hot—nobody wants to bet against them. So they suck out the money by giving the other team points."

"We know this, Roland," said Guma impatiently. "What's your point?"

"The point is that it's not just that the Hustlers are hot. Basketball don't work that way because there's too many games and there's too much action, especially with the N.B.A. expansion. Nobody can stay hot for eighty-two games. Who the hell can figure out what a team is gonna do on a night?

"OK, but there's two other things working here. First of all, the Hustlers are a New York team. That means more fans and more money bet on the team to win. Everything else equal, Vegas'll give them more points than they deserve on talent, on home-court advantage, whatever, just to draw money against. The other thing, the Hustlers are a popular team; people like to see an underdog make good, like the Mets were a couple years ago. And they're colorful, like the Dallas Cowboys. That pulls more money. The books don't want to get sided, so the point spread gets more favorable for a bet against the Hustlers."

Hrcany leaned back and smiled knowingly. "So the real point is that in their last five games, the Hustlers haven't made their spread, and I cashed in."

"I knew it! You bet against," said Karp.

"See, you're talking like a fan," Hrcany protested. "You're just putting money in my pocket."

"I don't bet on games, Roland," said Karp. "And besides, I don't believe the line wouldn't catch on eventually."

"Yeah, but until—" Hrcany began, when the waitress, a cast-iron New York type with dense wrinkles and a hair net, arrived to take their order. Guma said, "This is on you, right, Butch?"

Karp nodded and waved his hand in a gesture of liberality. The waitress wrote and departed. Newbury said, "I assume that this betting talk, fascinating as it is, was not the reason we are gathered."

"No," said Karp. "I need some help." Succinctly he laid out Bernie Nadleman's original request, together with his and Marlene's discoveries of the several weeks. The food came. He continued to talk while the others munched.

When he had finished, he studied each face for a reaction and found blankness, and some confusion.

Guma spoke first. "Ah, let me see if I understand this, Butch. Your big guy got wasted in Queens. Looks like drugs, but it ain't drugs, or maybe he wasn't dealing, but his sister was. The old lady thinks, *thinks,* he went to the girlfriend's and thinks he knew something important. Queens homicide likes a dealer for it, who we know was in with the sister, but you don't like him. Meanwhile, we got a friend from parochial school says she saw something, a murder, but she doesn't say anything else and skips.

"But you think, maybe, what she saw might have something to do with some torches from Philly who're burning up Long Island City. For some reason Marlene thinks the guys following her are these guys. She gets run off the road and she thinks, *thinks,* these guys did it." He shrugged apologetically. "It's—I don't know—fruit salad, you know? Bits and pieces. I don't see the angle for us."

Karp looked around the table. "Anybody else?"

Hrcany said, "I'm with Goom, Butch. I mean—ah—besides, it's Queens, right?"

Newbury said, "I notice you didn't say anything about why you think he was killed. Maybe that's where to start."

"Thank you, V.T.," said Karp emphatically. "Yeah, you're right. OK, the question is why should you give a rat's ass. I'm surprised nobody picked it up. It's fruit salad, Guma says. He's right, but let's see if we can pick out the cherries. One, somebody is seriously fucking the system over on this one. It pisses me off. Queens D.A. is laying down on this and I want to know why, because somebody on our side of the river has to be involved.

"Why? Two reasons. One, Doone was arrested in Manhattan, he says. Why should he lie? Thelmann sounded pretty confident that there was no documentary evidence of the arrest, which means somebody in the New York D.A. is covering up to frame Doone for a Queens murder. This piques my interest, to say the least.

"Two, Simmons was shot someplace else before he was taken to that parking lot in Queens. His mother says he was on his way to visit Julia Mackey the night he died. Unconfirmed, right, but Thelmann almost choked when I suggested he talk to Julia Mackey—"

Hrcany broke in incredulously, "You think Queens is covering up a murder to protect the husband?"

"I don't know what they're covering up, Roland, I just know they are. That's what I need you guys' help for."

They thought about that for a while, and then Guma said casually, "Well, I don't know, Butch. I mean public spirit and all that shit, but I don't see the percentage in it for us, you know? I mean, what do we get out of it, busting our hump on the off-hours?"

"I can't believe I'm hearing this," said Karp. "A possible serious miscarriage of justice, corruption in high places, and nobody's interested?"

"Miscarriage of justice is our business," said Hrcany. "And besides, like I said, this cockamamie mess is in Queens. That's why they draw those dotted lines on the map. They don't fuck with us, we don't fuck with them."

"And what about the real possibility that Simmons was shot in New York County?" said Karp, his voice rising. "That's on the right side of the goddamn dotted line, Roland."

Guma raised his hands, palms out. "Calm down, guys. Butch, you made your point. But, you know, you gotta give a little to get. Now, I think the guys here would be more than willing to help out if we got something solid out of this."

"Such as?" snapped Karp.

"Such as getting Sheldon Ehrengard's lard ass out of the bureau chief slot and off our backs. Jesus, the guy is a lunatic! Everybody worth a damn has got their nose in the want ads."

Hrcany nodded vigorously and said, "I'll take a piece of that."

"How am I supposed to get rid of him?" asked Karp. "You think Bloom is about to do me any favors?"

"He doesn't have to do you any favors," said Guma vehemently. "You resigned as bureau chief, but you forgot one thing. That was an acting position because fucking Bloom never confirmed you. But you're still assistant bureau chief. You got that on a permanent basis from Garrahy. Just come back. Shelly'll crumple. He's scared of you. So's Bloom, for that matter. You get back in there, things'll start to happen. I mean it, Butch, it'll work."

"And you'll help on this if I do?"

"Whatever you need," said Guma, and Hrcany nodded in agreement. Newbury said, "And I'll help too, purely out of a profound love of justice."

Almost before he knew it, Karp found himself saying, "OK. Deal."

CHAPTER
fourteen

The waitress came and cleared away their plates. Karp looked at his three companions. The relief shown on their faces affected him strangely. He had no false modesty about his skills, but he had not realized that he could be missed, that his presence imparted a quality to the work of the D.A.'s office that could not easily be replaced. Like many natural leaders, Karp despised the accouterments of leadership: posh furniture, deference, flattery, speeches and honors. He thought in terms of function, and he insisted on flawless preparation and aggressive prosecution. When he thought about it at all, he supposed that his staff regarded him as an annoying son of a bitch. It was a shock, and not entirely a pleasant one, to realize that he was part of something that wanted him for his inherent qualities of mind and spirit, that depended on him.

It was quite different, he realized, from being part of a professional athletic team, and that difference sprang from something essentially wrong at the heart of pro ball. Ball could be thrilling, dramatic, even beautiful, but—the realization struck him now with implacable force—*it was just a game.* Suddenly it was unbearable to him that Doobie Wallace and Fred James each received for "playing" (the irony of the word!) twice the annual salary that his entire (former) staff at the Criminal Courts Bureau got for helping to keep a city from falling into lawless chaos.

"Ah, Butch . . . ?"

Karp snapped to with a start and looked at Guma. "Sorry, guys, I was just thinking." He extracted from his breast pocket the enlargements of Marlene's photo and laid them out on the table. "Do we know these guys? Anybody?"

The three studied the shot. One, the driver, the cigar smoker, was about fifty, with bushy gray sideburns and a pitted potato nose. He wore hornrimmed glasses. The other was younger, had a rounder face and a thinner, hooked nose over fleshy lips. Neither of them would have been easily mistaken for professors of comparative literature. Both were deeply tanned.

"I'm drawing a blank here, Butch," said Guma, whose memory for faces was legendary, and whose knowledge of the Mob was no less impressive. "Sideburns looks a little like Solly Rocks, but Solly passed on in sixty-eight, I think it was. The other guy? Young . . . I wouldn't know him, probably. I'll show this around. You say they're Philly guys?"

"Maybe," Karp said cautiously. "The question is, what does a series of torch jobs have to do with Marlene? Or with Simmons? V.T.?"

"We could look at the burned properties," offered V.T. "See if anybody is making buys or collecting big insurance in the area. That'd be a start."

"Good," said Karp. "Do that, and also check out Chaney's business interests. And Frank Mackey's. See if there's a connection between them, especially with reference to the team."

V.T. made notes in a slim leather book. "What are we looking for?" he asked.

"I don't know—that's the problem," replied Karp in frustration. "It's a fishing expedition, which is why it can't be official right now. Be discreet."

"My middle name," said Newbury, smiling. Very little went on in the New York financial community that was beyond the ken of V.T. Newbury and his vast tribe of relatives and acquaintances.

Karp turned to Hrcany. "Roland—OK, the key for you is Doone. Assume he's being framed. Assume he was in jail on the night of, and somebody had to hustle to suppress the records. Find out who his lawyer is."

Hrcany frowned. "That's a lot of work, Butch. The logical place to start is to find the cop that pulled him in, see if we got anything at all, or if your guy is just blowing smoke. That means going up to the three-oh and going through their duty logs, talking to the shift sergeants, and pray that the cop remembers. You got any idea how many traffic stops and DWIs they got up there? Not to mention, if we don't have the docket number on the complaint, we'll never find the records. You can't find shit if you don't have a number."

"You'll manage, Roland," said Karp confidently. "I'm sure there's a cop up there you got something on. I tell you what, though: get Peter Schick on the records end of it. You remember him—he's over at Appeals now."

"He'll do it?"

"Guaranteed. Tell him it's for me. He owes me one." Karp hesitated for a moment and then went on. "Oh, one other thing: get a car and a police driver. Marlene's going to want to talk to Doone, and I don't want her out of the house alone."

Hrcany laughed knowingly and said, "I don't blame you. Let me start on the records end here. Tell her to

find out as much as she can about the circumstances of
the arrest. It'll help to find out what really happened."

Marlene was still lounging in bed when Karp returned to the loft.

"I'll have my cappuccino now," she called out when
she heard him enter. "And an assortment of tiny
cakes."

"How about instant and some old Oreos?" he replied, plopping on the red couch and massaging his
knee. "And if you come down here, I might tell you
what I've been up to this morning, concerning the
case."

Bed springs creaked and fabric rustled. Marlene appeared, a kimono draping her bulge. "Give!" she demanded. Karp gave.

"That's terrific, Butch," she exclaimed when he
wound to a halt. "The old gang! It's like the movies,
except you have to win the big game."

Karp laughed without humor. "There's not much
chance of that."

"Oh? Your old knee?"

"Yeah, that and ... the whole thing. The pros. It's
the game itself. It's changed, or maybe I have. It's not
that I don't love basketball. Getting back into it, it's
been a good thing for me, picking up a thread of my
life. Today, like, when I was talking to the guys, I realized that one of the things I tend to do when something goes sour is I cut it totally out of my life.
Big-time basketball was finished when I was a kid, so
I cut it out. I didn't play, I didn't watch games, I didn't
want to know from it. Same with the D.A. just a while
ago. I didn't call Guma, V.T., anybody—people I
worked with for years. It was shitty and I regret it.

"But ... there's something wrong with the big time.
I don't know if I can explain this right. Basketball is a

head game. I mean, you need physical talent and all, but basically, in the game I learned, the point of it was pattern and plays, being somewhere and *not* being somewhere else. And the heart of the game, what makes it different from football and hockey, is the fact that you're not supposed to touch the other players. OK, that's always been ignored in the clutch, you have to take a foul.

"But the tone of the game has changed. It's hard to find a good half-court game now. Nobody wants to drill on the plays. It's all fast break: run like a rabbit, fly through the air, slam it in. That's what the fans like to see. Plus giants cutting each other up under the boards, fistfights, pushing. Guys give each other the elbow when there's no point to it. And the refs are scared to call half the fouls."

He shook his head and looked down at his huge hands. "It's playground stuff. No, it's worse than playground ball. In a schoolyard, guys won't play with you if you're rough like that. You get your head beat in. But these guys in the pros, they're millionaires, which is fine, but they have the arrogance of millionaires too—and it's going to get worse."

"Are you sure it's not just 'When I was a boy . . .'?"

Karp laughed. "Yeah, maybe. But meanwhile . . . you know my grandmother used to say something, whenever us kids would tell her some news about the modern world, anything—Sputnik, politics, some scandal—she'd always say the same thing, *'Ohne mich.'* It means 'without me,' the perfect solution. That's how I feel about professional basketball."

"You're quitting. Well, a short and brilliant career. That's something. When?"

"Oh, I'll do Philly, and then the Knicks game. I always wanted to play in the Garden. I'll guard Bill Bradley maybe, thrill of a lifetime, a pair of *alte co-*

chers. The team's heading west after that, and I don't see any point in being away from home this close to the baby."

"My hero," said Marlene, beaming.

"My heroine," said Karp. "Speaking of which, I got Roland to have a cop with a car lined up, assuming you want to go to Riker's and see your mutt."

Marlene groaned. "Cripes, oh, not today! I feel like I've been beaten with rods, and my legs are all swollen."

"Poor baby!" said Karp sympathetically. "OK, we can put it off. Or I'll go myself . . ."

She groaned again as she heaved herself upright. "No, this is breaking now. If they went so far as to plant evidence and falsify records, the longer we wait, the more chance they have to solidify the frame-up. And I doubt if he'd talk to you. He may not even talk to me. For all I know, he thinks *I* framed him."

Carmine and Joey watched Marlene drive off in an unmarked police car. Carmine had done some looking and knew the worst.

"Ain't you gonna follow her?" asked Joey.

"No, Joey, the fuck I care where she goes anymore. All I want is to get her alone."

The guard at Riker's Island jail looked at Marlene and at the visitation form she had filled out and did a double take. "Relative?" he asked.

"Lawyer," she replied, truthfully, if not relevantly.

Clang of doors, the walk through the dank corridors stinking of disinfectant and that monkey-house smell— primates in captivity—and the sound, a continuous low bellow of rage. She'd been here many times before and it was always a real treat.

Doone was in his yellow jumpsuit when she arrived

at the other side of the glass interview box. The color of the outfit against his skin gave him the look of an exotic tropical bird, one with ruffled feathers.

Marlene sat down in the hard chair with relief and said immediately, "I know they're trying to frame you, and I intend to get you out of here."

He looked at her for a long, cool moment. "Why you care, Babylon?"

"Why do you think, Jamaica? We had a deal, and this isn't part of it. OK, you got a lawyer?"

"Yah."

"You tell him you were arrested and in custody the night Simmons was shot?"

"Yah. Den dey tell 'im dat dere ain't no records fo no arrest. So 'im say dem steal de arrest records or some t'ing; I say yah, yah, is always de same, to press de people. Same t'ing dem do in Jamaica, nuh. So wha' we gon do?"

"Well, we gon do one t'ing first—shit! you got me talking like that."

He cracked a thin smile. "Dat our liltin' island speech. It gets in your blood, mon."

"That should be 'it *get* in your blood.' Try to stay in character, Mr. Doone. OK, here's the thing. I can find stuff out that your lawyer might not be able to. I've got people working on this. The first thing I need is the complete story of where, when, how and by whom you were arrested and what happened after that."

The story was quickly told. On the night in question, Doone had gone to do some business in Harlem. Afterward, he had gone drinking at a club that featured Jamaican music. He had downed a good deal of white rum. An acquaintance had invited him for a ride in his new Cadillac El Dorado. Along with two women, the two men had gone roaring up St. Nicholas Avenue, passing a bottle around the car.

At Fort Tryon Park, the acquaintance had lost control of the car and gone off the road into the bushes. No one was hurt, but after that Doone had insisted on driving; he was well oiled, but a lot less so than the other man. With Doone at the wheel, they had just turned south when a blue-and-white out of the 30th Precinct pulled them over. Doone didn't have a license, didn't pass the breathalyzer test, and the car was stolen. They were both arrested without incident.

Marlene asked, but Doone didn't remember the name of the arresting officer. It was dark. He was drunk. A white bwai. The companion he knew only as Corky—a small-time dealer and hustler. He'd seen him around, but knew little about him. Harlem was far from his home ground.

Doone and his companions had been taken to the 30th Precinct, where the women were let go and the two men booked and sent to the holding cells. They had been kept there overnight and taken in the van early the next morning for arraignment at the criminal courts, Centre Street. Doone was charged with DWI and driving without a license, his companion with receiving stolen property. Doone had pleaded guilty to both charges, peeled the $250 fine from his money clip and walked out.

Marlene noted with interest that Doone was capable of shifting his language easily between an incomprehensible patois and something close to standard colonial English. He told his tale succinctly and without embarrassment. Just another uptown Saturday night, except it was a Tuesday.

Marlene finished writing her notes and looked up to find Doone staring at her, a quizzical expression on his matte face.

"What?" she said.

"Is whe you get dat cantin eye?"

"I got blown up by a bomb," said Marlene.

"Cho, I been shot, nuh, an cut, an beat on, but I never been bombed," said Doone, a hint of admiration in his voice.

"You're not missing much," said Marlene, and then, encouraged by what was, for Doone, an outpouring of the soul, added, "Is Leona OK?"

"She safe. You still wan fe see 'er, nuh?"

"Very much. You too, I guess."

"Eh? Is why you guess dat?"

"Well, she's your girlfriend, isn't she?"

Doone expelled a derisive laugh. "Is wha you t'ink? Nah, gal, I don' play dat way. She work fe me, nuh. I don get me beef whe I get me bread. Nah, see, she had 'er dis bwai, but 'im t'row her down, dese pas weeks. So I hear."

"Oh, I see. Sorry, I assumed, because you were looking out for her that—"

"Yah, you t'ink, dat John Doone, 'im jus some raas dope dealer, he don give a dam' about nobody but 'imself alone, les 'im got interes in a gal. Look, you, you see dese fas bwais around de city, dey killin each other fe nuthin. Dey kill friends fi dem, breddahs, sisters. I don work dat way, nuh. Dem people fi me, dey give me loyalty, I give dem loyalty. So I work. Is reciprocity. Like de rasta man say, one heart, one love."

"And if not, you cut them into little pieces."

"Easy to mock, yah," said Doone without rancor, "but Babylon got the bigges knife. Babylon cut up more people den ever I did, and not for no reason, no, jus fo meanness. An Babylon make de rules."

"We'll talk social policy later," said Marlene judiciously. "What did you say this boyfriend's name was?"

"I din say. But 'im star fe de team, 'er breddah's

team. Dem call 'im Doobie. So, tell me, when you spring me from heah?"

"Real soon. What's the matter, you don't like jail?"

He sneered. "Cho, gal, I been in jail in Kingston. Dis not no jail. Dis some kin o' pickney school. But I got me business a tend to."

"Yeah, I bet. OK, there shouldn't be a problem. And I expect a meet with Leona Simmons as soon as you're back on the street."

"I say I do it, it happen, soon as I'm out."

Marlene had received assurances from Supreme Court judges that she had believed less. She nodded and left.

"It's amazing," said V.T. Newbury, "how careless people are when they're under the impression that they've cozened the authorities." It had taken only two days for him to find out the connection between Howard Chaney and Frank Mackey, and perhaps others equally well-known. Karp was sitting in Newbury's cramped office at the Fraud Bureau having it explained.

"The center of it," Newbury began, "is this operation called Long Island Properties, Inc., incorporated in the great but lax state of Delaware. They went into business about a year ago. The president and chairman of this corporation is that titan of industry, J.C. Maccaluso."

"J.C.?"

"For Julia Carole. Miz Mackey. The wife fronts. Nice touch using the old name. Vice-president is Sandra P. Chaney, wedded to guess who. The secretary is Charles Parmagianni, the well-known and semi-literate associate of Mr. Mackey, and the treasurer is one Denise P. Metcalf."

"Who is ... ?"

"Surprise! The longtime secretary of Dan Logan, the borough president of Queens. I wonder if he knows she's dabbling in real estate. To continue: Long Island Properties is in the real estate business. It has purchased during the past twelve months a scattered checkerboard of lots in Long Island City, in a fairly run-down industrial and residential neighborhood between 14th and 31st streets, north of Broadway. Including the lots that were burned out, as it happens. They bought low too. The owners were glad to sell.

"So I wondered, what's the point of buying a scatter of lots in Long Island City? Check this out. I traced it out of the plat books."

V.T. brought out a large sheet of tracing paper and spread it on his desk. On it was a tracing of the property lines in a twenty-square-block area of Long Island City. A scattering of properties was shaded in red pencil.

"The red ones are what L.I.P., Inc., has bought," said V.T., "a dozen or so unconnected pieces of property in a run-down neighborhood. Or so it seems. But look at this."

He lofted another piece of tracing paper up and aligned it on the first. "The red shadings here are properties owned by the Morrell Company. Mr. Mackey himself." The new properties fit neatly into the L.I.C. holdings, forming extensive swaths of red pencil shading.

"Interesting," said Karp. "But it looks like he still has a ways to go." His finger indicated a salamander-like zone still showing white.

"Not as far as you might think," said Newbury. He pulled a third sheet out and tugged it into position. "This is owned by the Viva Corporation. Where do they get these names? See what happens?"

The red zones on the third map covered up all but

two tiny slivers in what was now a red quadrilateral about five acres in extent in the center of Long Island City.

"And who is this Viva?" Karp asked.

"Viva is a Long Island developer. Homes of distinction. It's owned by a man named Salti, who must be a far-sighted businessman, since he is obviously not going to build $175,000 split-levels with car ports in the middle of Long Island City. I had somebody look into it. It seems that Mr. Salti, besides his business acumen, had the taste and good fortune to marry a perfect peach named Rose Maccaluso."

"Don't tell me ..." said Karp, feigning astonishment.

"Yes, the sis; it's all in the family," said V.T., "except for the two properties you see here."

Karp studied the map in silence for a moment. "Tell me, V.T., I can see the point in blocking up property like this. You want to do a big project and you don't want anyone to know about it, so you use multiple purchasers or fronts. But why the arsons?"

"That's easy. The places that got burned were mostly tenements. New York has the strongest tenant-protection laws in the country. It can take years to move people out legally. A fire does it overnight."

"So what's wrong with waiting years?"

"Nothing. Zeckendorf does it all the time. Except if, one, you've got to have the property ready for something that you know is going to need a home within a tight time frame, a parkway interchange, for example. A civic center. Or two, you've got notes due. You borrowed big and short to buy the land, and you've got to move it fast."

"Uh-huh," Karp nodded. "And that would go double if the folks you borrowed it from were not as friendly as the folks at Chase Manhattan."

"I see a light in your eye, Roger," said V.T.

"Yes, it's the light of understanding. I just recalled something Bernie said, that the Hustlers have been wanting a new stadium. Wouldn't it be convenient if when the city gets around to building it, a major site in Queens should suddenly become available for immediate occupancy. And not only the site itself, but a sufficient buffer zone around it so that there's no pesky citizens to complain about the neighborhood or people being displaced. We're talking serious money here, aren't we?"

"Gravely serious," said V.T. "I'd estimate, judging from what they paid for these properties, that if a sports and commercial complex was built there, the profits could easily run into the hundreds of millions."

"Worth burning a few buildings for," said Karp. "Worth killing a basketball player for."

V.T. looked puzzled. "The buildings, yes. But Simmons? What's his connection?"

Karp shrugged. "It's not totally clear. But we know he was involved with Julia Mackey. Say he found out about the real estate scam. Say he was talking about it, maybe he flipped Mackey the bird. Mackey gets worried . . ."

"Mackey had him whacked?"

"I'm not saying that, although given that Simmons was *schtupping* the wife, he was probably not on Mackey's All-American list. I'm more concerned with Mackey's associates. He's an old Scarfi alumnus. The two characters that apparently have been lighting buildings are from Philly, so maybe the connection is still live. If there's Mob money in all this, and if Mackey happened to mention that some guy was close to queering the deal of the century, they'd take Simmons out in a New York minute."

"It's fancy, but it makes some sense," V.T. replied.

"Yeah, and it ties up a lot of things. We have motive. We don't have to worry about the drug angle anymore. That was a fluke. The sister was making a delivery and the stuff just happened to be in the glove of the Caddy. A stroke of luck for the bad guys. It gives them their excuse to fuck up the investigation, and it gives them their patsy, Doone."

"But that doesn't answer the question of why they're bad guys in the first place. Queens D.A., I mean."

"You went to Yale," said Karp. "Give it a try."

V.T. leaned back in his chair and simulated deep concentration. "Hmm, I'm going to go out on a limb and blame it on insensate greed. A handsome if slimy profit from blocking a likely site and selling it to the taxpayers. The cast of characters would have to include ... let's see, Dan Logan, the Queens borough president—we know he's in it; D'Amalia, the Queens D.A. himself; the cops, maybe up to the level of borough commander. There'd have to be a majority on the Board of Estimate too, although that's probably assured with normal procedure. They'll logroll if Queens is backing something as important as a major stadium.

"OK, the problem is that while I am shocked—shocked!—at the possibility that New York's civic leaders are prey to corruption, it's hard for me to see these guys going along with a hit. Sure, they're despicable slime balls, but they kill with a ballpoint."

"I'm not saying the pols ordered the hit," said Karp. "I'm not even saying Mackey ordered it. But once it happened they fell all over themselves covering it—the Watergate effect. Because, figure it out, a real investigation of Simmons's murder would've uncovered the connection with Mackey's wife, and probably the connection between Mackey and Chaney, not to mention that a serious canvass of people Marion talked with, plus using what they got on the sister to make her cooperate rather than cover up, would have spilled probably everything that the kid knew about the stadium deal. Not to mention a major search for the diary. And that leads back to the arsons, and arson homicide, and the end of the deal and the end of Mr. Mackey and all his political friends. It ties together. What d'you think?"

V.T. chewed on his lip and his pale blue eyes went blank. He hummed tunelessly for a moment and then expelled a gush of air and shook his head, as if to rattle his brain into more efficient action. He removed his gold-framed half glasses and said, "It's not very elegant, Roger," he said. "It doesn't sing 'Dixie.' Whodunit is all well and good, but as you yourself have often said, whodunit is bullshit unless you can build a case out of it. What's the case?"

"That's what we're going to work on now. For you, the first thing is to pull complete financial histories on the principals involved: Mackey, Logan, D'Amalia, and Chaney. We're looking for loans or any unexplained big-money transfers. Let's find out why they were in such a burning hurry."

V.T. replaced his glasses and looked at Karp over their tops, his eyebrows rising and a smile creasing his lips. "So to speak," he said. "But, excuse me, surely you don't want me to violate the financial privacy of a group of prominent citizens, without charge or warrant, using my personal contacts. You couldn't have meant that, could you?"

"Absolutely not," said Karp. "Perish forbid!"

Karp's next stop was Roland Hrcany's office, which was identified by the large picture of Arnold Schwarzenegger taped to the glass window of its door. Karp rapped on Arnold's pecs and entered.

Hrcany was at his desk, in shirtsleeves, doing slow curls with a thirty-pound dumbbell. Peter Schick was sitting in a side chair, looking grave, arranging a stack of papers on his lap.

"What's up, guys?" said Karp, perching on the edge of the desk.

Hrcany set the barbell down on the floor with a clong, and worked his massive shoulders. "Well, this is quite a thing we got here, Butch. I found the cop, first of all. He remembers the stop, all right, but not the names. That's understandable.

"But somebody got to the precinct files and pulled the blue sheets on the arrest. The log book's been doctored too. You know how they white the whole entry out when they make mistakes? What they forgot was that the other guy, this Corky bozo, was arrested with him. Levar Williams, street name Corky, possession of stolen vehicle, et cetera. He was there, all right, but there's a whited-out entry just after the one for Williams, at the date and time we would expect for our arrest. For Doone, there's *nada*.

"A lot of sidelong looks and not meeting of eyes up at the old three-oh. I talked to one of the detectives, guy I know, he said that an order came down from way high up to bury the arrest."

"Did he say who, way up high?"

"No, and I didn't press him on it; I don't think he knows. This isn't the first time this has happened, you know. Cops forget lots of stuff."

"Yeah, they do, like when one of the cardinal's or the mayor's people get caught with their zippers open. This is a little different."

"Yeah, it is," said Hrcany. "But that's the bad news. Peter's got the good news."

Karp had not spoken with or seen Peter Schick since that dreadful day when his goof on the Chelsea Ripper had revealed itself and Karp had thrown his own body on the resultant legal grenade.

"That's good," said Karp. "I'm ready for some good news."

Schick cleared his throat nervously and consulted a notepad. "Um, the first place I checked was the calendar courts. We don't have the docket number, so I had to go through all the cases for the morning in question. Just to make sure, I checked the ones for the next two days as well. Drew a blank."

Karp nodded, impressed. Schick must have gone through over a thousand case files.

"So then I pulled the docket number for the Williams case. I figured it had to be pretty close in sequence. I pulled the ten numbers on either side of that. There's a gap, a number missing: 7718732."

"Good, but that's not proof of malfeasance. The clerks void numbers all the time."

"True," said Schick, "but then I realized that if it *was* our guy's docket number, I could use it to check the paying desk records. The guy paid a fine, right? So I check it out: another blank. They never heard of the docket number."

"I thought this was good news," said Karp impatiently.

"Yeah, I'm sorry," said Schick, flushing. "Here it is. When I was at the paying desk, I remembered. The fine clerk generates a form that goes back to the Tombs, so they can clear their daybook: the guy's paid his fine, or he's posted bond, don't expect him back at the cells."

"They didn't get that?" exclaimed Karp.

"No. I have it here." Schick waved a form, Karp took it and studied it and gave it back. Schick continued, "But the best part is, although they stole the intake form they didn't get to the daybook. The Tombs receipted for Doone by name, and then when he cleared, they recorded the missing docket number that's right on the paying clerk form. So we have documentary proof not only that Doone was arrested and in custody when the murder happened, but that somebody actively suppressed a file."

Karp smiled and said, "Very classy, Peter. Nice piece of work."

Schick nearly writhed with pleasure. "Glad to help, Butch," he said, and after a pause added, "It's the responsibility of the D.A.'s office to keep track of everyone in custody."

Karp laughed ruefully. "Indeed it is. And we can assume that whoever ran this scam was less familiar than he should have been with the various procedures by which this is done. Who do you like for it, Roland?"

"Oh, as to that, I don't think we need to look further than our own Sheldon Ehrengard," Hrcany replied with a savage grin. "Means and opportunity—no problem. He's a bureau chief, the whole case file is within Criminal Courts, he controls the complaint room, he has open access to all the fourth-floor court files. As for motive, Fat Shelly does what he's told. As a matter of fact, I've noticed a certain cat that ate the canary about Sheldon recently. He's started to refer to the D.A. as 'Sandy.' I think they've grown closer."

"Well, I'm sure we're all very happy for them," said Karp. "Bloom has to be involved, hey?"

"I'd bet on it," said Hrcany decisively. "What're you gonna do, Butch?"

"Do? Nothing, for now. Remember, I'm on vacation. But, Peter, get notarized copies of all that stuff for me, would you? And stash another set in the safest place you can think of, preferably out of the office." Schick ran off on this errand. Karp paced the little office in silence for a minute or so and then said, "Tell me, what do you think happened to the original case file?"

Hrcany snorted. "Deep-six. They'd be fools to hold onto it. If anybody found it, it'd be disbarment for sure, maybe jail."

"Yeah, right, but we're *talking* about fools here. If I was Shelly and I had something that hot, involving really major players, I'd hang onto it. You know, V.T. said something really interesting just now. Something to the effect that when people think they've got the law wrapped up, they get real careless."

"Yeah, the Watergate effect. Christ! You think he hung onto it?"

"We shall endeavor to find out," said Karp blithely, and left.

He stopped by Guma's office and was directed to one of the grand jury rooms. He found Guma in the tiny antechamber, waiting for the jury's deliberations.

"Big case?"

"Yeah, sure," said Guma, wrinkling his nose. "The usual garbage. We don't have big cases anymore. Shelly doesn't like big cases. What's up?"

"Oh, just checking on things. Any luck with our Chevy-driving twins?"

"Nah, and I showed it to people who would know. There's an old mustache who used to run with the Scarfi outfit down in Philly. He never saw them before. They're not New York guys. I'm planning to put the pictures out on the wire to Chicago, Detroit, Boston— what's wrong?"

"No, don't do that, at least not yet. The less official this is, the better. We got bad guys among the good guys, and I don't want to risk a wire photo being seen by the wrong people. And you know, when you said Chicago, the thought occurred to me. We got two classic out-of-town torpedos, who're both wearing heavy tans and who think it's cute to run somebody off the freeway. What does that suggest to you?"

"What do you mean? Oh, I get it. You're thinking Miami, Phoenix, L.A.?"

"Yeah. You know people there?"

"If I don't, I know people who know people. It'll take a couple of days. And it ... the people I'll be dealing with ain't that comfortable doing favors for the law. It might cost some chips."

"Do it," said Karp. "And use all the chips."

CHAPTER

fifteen

Karp walked out of the New York County Courthouse with a thick manila envelope under his arm
and took the IND subway to the Queens County
Courthouse. There he presented himself at Thelmann's
office.

Thelmann's secretary brought out her most hostile
expression and placed her hand on her telephone. She
said, "Mr. Thelmann told me he doesn't want to see
you, and if you came by again I should call security."

Karp placed his envelope on her desk. "I don't really
need to see him," he said equably. "Just give him this."

She snatched it and tossed it contemptuously into a
plastic in basket. "I meant now," Karp said, his voice
hardening. "I'll wait, if there's a message. Oh, and tell
him I have another copy that might be on its way to the
Times."

He stared her down, feeling faintly ashamed about
playing the heavy with a secretary, until her gaze broke
and she picked up the envelope and trotted down the
hall to Thelmann's private office. Karp settled himself
in a vinyl-covered armchair and leafed through the
sports section of *Newsday*. He didn't have long to wait.
Thelmann's secretary emerged after less than five min-

utes, looking distraught. She said, "He'll see you now." Karp said, "Thank you," and walked down the hallway.

The first thing Thelmann said when Karp walked in was "I had nothing to do with this. This was a New York thing."

"You were misinformed, is that it?"

Thelmann attempted a manly glare, and then his eyes dropped. His typical pugnacity appeared to have deserted him. "What are you going to do?" he asked in a low voice.

"I'm not going to do anything, Jerry," said Karp. "It's not my problem. Of course, if Doone isn't instantly released from jail, I'd feel obliged to turn this material over to his lawyer and the press, simply as a good citizen and an officer of the court. But I'm sure you'll do the right thing."

"Yes! OK, I'll do it, all right?" snapped Thelmann. Karp smiled benignly, and Thelmann added, "How come you're so interested in Doone? You got any idea what kind of shit we're dealing with here?"

"I'm not interested in him at all," said Karp. "But what fascinates me is why two prosecutorial offices should be organizing a frame-up to protect the real killers of Marion Simmons, including the suppression of police and court records. Would you care to fill me in on the background?"

"I told you, I didn't know anything about it—"

"Yeah, you were misinformed," Karp broke in, "but look here, Jerry: when you play dirty, you stay dirty. This isn't going away, and when it's over there's liable to be a line of ex-lawyers sitting on the sidewalk out there with tin cups and cardboard signs. You could be one of them."

"Don't threaten me!"

"No threat, Jerry. Just a reasonable prediction from

the facts at hand. So tell me, was Chaney involved from the beginning?"

He had to give Thelmann credit. He didn't flinch. "I don't know what you're talking about."

"Yes, you do. You hopped into Chaney's car minutes after I spoke to you that first time, in the days of my innocence. Did you concoct the frame right then and there, or did you have to bring in the big players: Mackey? D'Amalia? Logan?"

Thelmann said nothing, but Karp could hear his breathing, rough and heavy, and he was white around the lips.

"Jerry, this is coming unglued," Karp continued in the same pleasant tone. "The big boys are going to start searching for a fall guy, and it's going to be the littlest fish in this dirty pond. I wonder who they'll pick. Think about it, Jerry."

Karp waited for Thelmann to say something, but nothing emerged. Smart boy: when in doubt, keep your mouth shut. Karp rose and walked out of the office.

Once again he rode down to the lobby and made for the bank of phones. Here he called Marlene. The phone rang five times, and when Marlene answered she sounded drowsy and confused.

"You OK?" Karp asked. "Is anything, um, happening?"

"No, nothing is happening, except I can barely drag myself out of bed," she replied grumpily. "I would jump up and down to induce labor, but I don't have the energy. If men had to do this the human race would've ended long ago. I hate men."

"Except me," he said lightly.

"Especially you. So, what have you been doing while I've been on my bed of pain? Hitting the hot spots? Enjoying the company of slender women?"

"That's on for later. I've been by the courthouse." He quickly summarized what he had learned.

"God, I'm throwing up," said Marlene. "Those bastards! So now we know. It explains the Bobbsey Twins too: they probably used the same guys for the arsons and the hit on Simmons. Interesting about the tans and where they come from. But why did they always get on the flight from Philly, and why did they flash a phony Pennsylvania license?"

"All this will emerge in time. Look, I'm going to read you off two addresses on the same block in Long Island City. They're two apartment buildings, the only property our friends don't own in their site."

"OK, shoot," she said and wrote down the addresses. "You think these'd be poor risks for Allstate?"

"Very poor," said Karp. "Get them to Bello as soon as you can. He might want to keep an eye on them. Any sign of your mutts?"

"No, but I haven't been out, and I'm not going out. I still feel watched, though."

"You probably are. If wise guys are involved in this it's probably not all that difficult to find somebody to watch you. I mean, we live in Little Italy. So keep the door locked."

"Yes, Daddy," said Marlene. "Where are you off to?"

"Practice. I'm in Queens, I'll cab over to the stadium."

"You going to talk to Wallace about what Doone told me? About him and Leona?"

"I might," said Karp, "if the opportunity comes up."

Marlene put the phone down and headed for the couch. She had taken to dozing away the day there, reading a few pages of Eliot during her intermittent moments of consciousness. From time to time she also thought about Francine Del Fazio. The promised letter had not arrived, and Marlene was beginning to fear that it never would.

She had just gotten comfortable when the phone rang again. Marlene put a pillow over her head and waited for the ringing to stop. The answering machine clicked on. She exposed an ear and heard Ariadne Stupenagel's voice, sounding testy: "Marlene, I know you're hiding there, you miserable wretch! Come to the phone." Pause. "Really! I have to speak to you. I have Julia Mackey at my place and she wants to spill her guts."

Cursing vividly, Marlene rolled off the couch and toddled to the phone. "Stupe! What's up?"

"Thank you very much," said Stupenagel. "I can't stand it when people purposely keep out of touch. It's medieval."

"I'm a medieval sort of girl," replied Marlene, "as you yourself never fail to point out. What's this about Mrs. Mackey, or was that a scam?"

"No scam, dear. She's here at my place turning on the water works. She's ready to rat out the world and she'll talk about you-know-who."

"Simmons? That's great, Stupe! Can you get her down here?"

"What! To your place? I think it would be unwise. She's comfortable, she doesn't have to leave her own turf—I'd hate to give her time to reconsider. Also, I'm not sure she knows how to climb stairs. So, with all due respect to your condition—"

"Can it, Stupenagel!" Marlene snarled. "My fucking condition has nothing to do with it. Somebody tried to run me off the road the other day, and I think it's the guys who did Simmons and I'm not moving out of the house."

Stupenagel expelled a burst of astonished laughter. "Marlene, you're imagining things; it *is* your delicate condition. In the Pleistocene, a lady as knocked up as you would be making a nest in the bushes and defending it with a sharpened stick."

"Very amusing, Ariadne. Now let me tell you the actual situation. You've just given me probable cause for a warrant. You can get your sweet asses down here *this very minute,* or I can get on the phone and have the two of you handcuffed and brought in on a charge of obstructing justice."

A nervous giggle. "Marlene! You wouldn't!"

"Try me, honey!" said Marlene, her voice tight.

A pause. "Well, OK, but don't blame me if she clams up. Honestly, this is just like Chile."

Marlene hung up the phone, took a deep breath, and tried to compose herself. She had let Ariadne get to her again, the digging little comments about motherhood, as if Marlene had not more than proven . . . there, she was doing it again! Insidious, it was—little all-girl guerilla demolition teams from the patriarchy inside her very skull. She shook herself into action.

First a bath—no, there wasn't time. But she'd have to dress. She marched to her full-length mirror; what she saw brought out an involuntary yelp of dismay. She was in an old blue plaid flannel bathrobe of Karp's, virtually the only garment in the loft that she could bear to wear. It had several large stains on it; tiny crumbs perched on the lapels. Her hair was dull and arrayed in random coils like old extension cords at the bottom of a storage carton. Her face was puffy and sallow, and her eye patch looked pathetic rather than romantic.

OK, elegance was out. Arty squalor, then. She splashed water on her face, wrapped her foul hair in a big antique paisley scarf, pulled on black tights and a denim maternity maxi-skirt stained with white paint from when she had repainted the crib, and grabbed a clean white dress shirt from Karp's side of the closet. Her good amber necklace, some religious medals on gold chains and—a prize—Stuart's dirty boy pendant. Dance slippers. She stood in front of the mirror again: there! Fuck 'em if they can't take a joke!

A glass of wine, to promote keenness of mind, a gargle to mask the odor of wine, a few slaps on the damask cheeks to bring up the color, and . . . knock, knock.

Julia Mackey was the sort of woman called striking—that is, designed to strike the senses of men like a ball-peen hammer. Her eyes were green, her hair ashy blonde and arranged in a great, stiffened cascade on either side of her oval face. Her nose was long and chiseled, her lips a delicious painted pout. She was wearing a fur-lined, belted trenchcoat and buttery boots with little brass spurs on them.

Stupenagel's eyes widened when she saw Marlene's getup, but she wisely refrained from comment. Julia looked around in frank wonder, like an Omaha tourist at a punk disco. To her, Marlene seemed perfectly in place; of course, that was what someone who lived in a filthy, clanking factory would wear.

Marlene took their coats and seated them in what passed for her parlor. Julia had revealed a fawn-colored wool pants suit over white cashmere, with pearls. She sat gingerly on the old red couch, as if expecting it to exude nameless substances, all of which might be hard to dry-clean.

"Coffee, anyone?" said Marlene brightly.

"No, I couldn't possibly," said Julia. "I'm so nervous already."

"All right, then," said Marlene, and picked up a legal pad and a ballpoint. "Let's get down to business. Ariadne here tells me you have some information regarding the murder of Marion Simmons."

Julia started at this bluntness and cast a questioning

look at Stupenagel. She said, "I didn't say that. I don't want to get involved."

"But you are involved, Mrs. Mackey. In a murder case." Marlene waited for the repetition of the ugly word to sink in, and studied the woman's face. It was composed of layers, she thought. At the surface, the perfectly composed and made-up face of an aspiring young society matron, bland and a perfect screen for the projection of whatever was fashionable. Beneath that, something harder, around the eyes, the tilt of the jaw, the mouth that might at any moment curve into a contemptuous sneer and open on a barrage of street obscenity—a bit of the gun moll and demi-mondaine there. Deeper still, in the way her eyes flitted when she thought no one was watching, a kid from the sticks, way out of her depth and badly frightened. It seemed to Marlene that these layers were coming apart, like an old piece of plywood delaminating in a junkyard.

"Now, look, I understand that this began as a jour-nalistic interview," Marlene continued. "Then, at a cer-tain point, you decided that you wanted to go to the authorities, and Ms. Stupenagel here knew me person-ally and agreed to set up this meeting, on an informal basis—"

"I didn't say anything about the authorities," Julia protested. "She said she had this friend who knew her way around the system and could give me advice."

"And so I can," answered Marlene. "My advice is to tell me everything you know."

"I can't do that," cried Julia, her body stiffening. She seemed about to bolt. Marlene made her voice stern.

"Listen to me! You were damn lucky to run into Ar-iadne. Don't you realize that you were bound to be questioned on this? Mrs. Mackey, you are a material witness in a homicide case. I could have you arrested right now."

Julia stiffened her jaw. "If you're going to question me officially, then maybe I should have my attorney present."

"You can have whatever you want, Mrs. Mackey, but the whole point of the present interview is to keep this unofficial as long as possible. If you insist on a lawyer at this stage, then it does become official and a matter of public record, and that means the press and the whole circus of publicity, at a time when we haven't got our stories straight and speculation will be completely flagrant. The tabloids will go crazy. You don't seem to realize that Ariadne and I are doing you a favor."

Julia turned to Stupenagel and said petulantly, "I never should have talked to you. You got me into this."

"No, she didn't," said Marlene. "We knew who you were from other sources. We knew you were at Simmons's funeral. We knew all about your affair with him. We know who your husband is and what he's doing in Long Island City, and we know that Simmons knew it too. We know that he spent the last night of his life with you."

This farrago of truth, plain lies and suspicions had its effect. The perfect face crumpled and dissolved into tears. Ariadne put a comforting arm around Julia, while the weeper fumbled a hankie out of her elegant leather bag. Marlene rose heavily and stumped over to the cabinet, where rested the remains of her wedding booze, a dozen or so bottles containing anything from a shot to most of a fifth. She selected a bottle of Remy, poured a hefty slug into another wedding present, a Waterford snifter, and handed it to Julia.

She drank half of it in a gulp, coughed violently, and in a few minutes her hysteria had subsided into sniffles. Businesslike, Marlene took up her paper and pen once more and prompted, "Why don't you begin with how you first met Marion Simmons?"

"It was at a party for the team, last April or May," Julia began. "Frank has an interest in the Hustlers. I didn't want to go, but Frank insisted. He does that a lot.

"OK, what you have to know about Frank and me, we don't have ... I mean we get along, but there's nothing there. We have Emily, our little girl, but that's not enough, is it? He has women, and he doesn't bother to hide it either. OK, fine, he wants an armpiece he can bring to affairs, take care of the kid and the house, I can live with that, you know? But it affected me.

"So at this party, I started talking to Marion. You want to know something? I never talked to a black person before, except, like, clear the table, bring the car. I guess I started just to pi—to irritate Frank; I'd had a couple of drinkies."

She finished her present drink, as if to demonstrate the act. Marlene tipped another two fingers into her glass. Then Mrs. Mackey went on. "We were out on our terrace. We're on Sutton Place and we have a river view. The night was warm, the moon was full. What can I say? I was swept off my feet.

"He was a passionate, intelligent man, strong, sensitive. Everything a woman needs. I wanted him more than I've ever wanted anything in my life. He called me the next day, and we checked into a hotel and spent the afternoon in bed. It was paradise. I was completely fulfilled as a woman."

"Mrs. Mackey, did your husband know about the affair?" Marlene asked.

"Well, I didn't rub his face in it, but I'm sure he knew. It wasn't exactly the Manhattan Project."

"And did you and Simmons ever discuss your husband's business dealings?"

"Not really. Why should we? We were in love. We talked about us, how we could be together more."

"Were you contemplating the break-up of your marriage?"

Was that a cloud that crossed Julia's face? It passed in an instant. "We talked about it. You know, it was like a fantasy . . . dreams, you know? The whole thing seems like a dream now, or like a movie you saw when you were a kid, that affected you, but it wasn't real. Frank would never agree, and if I sued him, he'd never let me have Emily. He'd say I was an unfit mother. Can you imagine going into court and saying I wanted to raise my daughter with my black lover? Marion . . ." Fat tears crawled out of the mascara jungle, leaving tracks. She dabbed her eyes. "I'm a wreck," she said.

Marlene and Stupenagel exchanged a brief look, and Marlene resumed her questioning. "One thing, Mrs. Mackey. I understand that shortly after Simmons's murder, when Ariadne first interviewed you, you appeared distraught and frightened. You seemed terrified that your husband was going to do something to you. Why was that, and do you still feel that way?"

"Frightened?" said Julia after a pause. "Of course I was frightened. Marion was gone, my whole world was turned upside down. I was scared that the whole thing would come out in a way that Frank couldn't ignore and that he would take it out on me. And I—" She stopped, blew her nose, drank more cognac.

"Yes, go on," urged Marlene.

Julia looked away and said in a cracking voice. "I thought, my first thought was that Frank had had him killed."

"Why did you think that?"

"Because he has a violent temper, and . . . he is connected. He could get it done."

"But the question is, why wait?" Marlene said. "This had been going on for eight or nine months. Like you said, it was no big secret. Any ideas on that?"

At this, the spillways opened again and Julia blubbered incoherently, crying literally on Stupenagel's shoulder.

She rolled her eyes at Marlene over Julia's back while her blouse soaked up tears.

The story came out in bursts amid the sobbing. She had overheard details of the stadium scam when she had picked up a telephone extension on a conversation between her husband and the Queens borough president, Dan Logan. She had mentioned it to Simmons casually, but he had seized upon it as a way to winkle her away from Mackey. She begged him not to do it, but he was driven by love and heedless of danger.

When the story was all out, Marlene said, "Do you know for a fact that Simmons confronted your husband and threatened him with exposure?"

"I didn't see him do it, if that's what you mean. But he must have." She sighed. "Poor Marion, he said he would die for me . . . and he did!"

"What happened on the night of the murder? That would have been Tuesday, the twenty-sixth of last month. He came to see you, didn't he?"

"Yes. Yes, he did. About eleven. Frank was out of town. Emily was with friends. I told him it was too dangerous for him to visit me at home, but he wouldn't keep away. He came in and we . . . couldn't keep our hands off each other. We fell down on the rug in the living room, and we did it with our clothes on. Like teenagers. Then he left. I saw him go into the elevator. And that was the last—"

Wracking sobs, then, "What are you going to do? What's going to happen to me?"

"The investigation is continuing on various fronts," replied Marlene blandly. "But you should hold yourself ready to sign a formal statement encompassing everything you've told me."

Julia nodded glumly and the interview wound down. Stupenagel walked Julia down to Canal Street to catch a cab. Marlene sat in her rocker and tried to read over her notes, but found she couldn't concentrate. The interview had disturbed her more than she thought it would. The silly woman had got to her. She put the legal pad aside and drew an embroidery hoop out of a canvas bag and began to run tiny stitches into a christening gown, a project started with great enthusiasm five months ago, then abandoned and now taken up again with surprising pleasure. She was just completing the tail of a tiny bluebird when the door rocked with importunate pounding.

Marlene got up to answer it and let in Ariadne. "She's off to her happy home," said Stupenagel. "How about that—did she deliver the goods or not?"

Marlene mumbled something noncommittal and resumed her seat. Stupenagel said, "Hey, you got a beer?"

Marlene said, "The fridge. Help yourself." She picked up the embroidery hoop again. Stupenagel popped a Schaeffer can and sat down on the couch. "What's that?" she asked. "Knitting little booties? How cute."

"This is embroidery, Ariadne. The *mesdames* of the Sacred Heart do not knit, but they do embroider and they expect the young ladies placed in their care to do likewise. Sister Marie Aemilia, who taught me the stitches, once embroidered a cope for His Holiness, Pope John XXIII."

"I'm impressed," said Stupenagel. "Is what you're doing for the pope, or do you have to work your way up?"

"It's a christening gown. Don't look at me like that. It's a perfectly appropriate activity for a Catholic mother-to-be. Tell me, Ariadne, don't you ever get tired of being hard-boiled?"

Stupenagel looked puzzled. "What, you're bent out of shape because we gave that bimbo a hard time?"

"Yes, 'bimbo.' That's what I mean. Funny, I didn't tell you before, but I got a weird call a little while ago from somebody I knew in grade school. Bright girl, but she dropped out of school to get married. Some guys were chasing her because they thought she saw a killing. I let her walk out of here, and I think she's probably dead now as a result, but all I could think of at the time was, that could've been me, Marlene. I didn't want to think that, I didn't want to think about *her,* Francine, her life. It was threatening."

"There's no point in getting into a guilt trip," said Ariadne. "People make their own choices."

"Do they? That's the conventional wisdom. But you know what I was thinking during that interview? There but for the grace of God go I. The grace of God and a full scholarship to Sacred Heart. I knew a dozen men while I was growing up who would have liked to make me into a Frannie Del Fazio or a Julia Mackey. It would have been as easy as falling down the stairs."

"Yeah, but you didn't."

"No, I didn't, but the older I get the more I think it was dumb luck and not the brilliant wonder that is Marlene. Anyhow, what did you think of her story?"

Stupenagel was caught off guard by the change of subject. She had been thinking of an excessively tall and ungainly girl who had never been invited to fall down the stairs. After a brief moment she answered,

"It's hard to tell. She gets her language from the soaps. 'I was completely fulfilled as a woman.' 'He said he would die for me.' It wouldn't knock me over if I found out she got the plot from a soap too. What was all that about a stadium deal? And Dan Logan?"

Marlene ignored this last remark. "It makes some kind of sense. At least it's a motive, and it pins down the location of the initial abduction and maybe the time of the first shooting, and puts it in Manhattan, which means that we have an official reason to follow the case."

"Wait a minute: how do you know he didn't just leave the building and drive away?"

"It just makes sense. Look, he arrives at Mackey's around eleven. They go into a clinch. Squish, squish, gasp, gasp. It's got to be midnight at least. Meanwhile, the sister is waiting down in the car."

"How do you know?"

"I didn't tell you, we talked to the mother again. She spilled all this. Anyhow, the sister decides to go into the all-night drugstore. I checked: there's one a couple of blocks west on 57th. She walks up there and when she comes back, the car is gone. Or so she says.

"The medical examiner says Simmons received his chest wound approximately two hours before the head shot that killed him and that he'd been dead between two and four hours. We were lucky; we got a good body-temperature reading. So, if she's telling the truth about that at least, we have to believe either that Simmons drove off, leaving his sister miles from home in the middle of the night and immediately drove someplace else, where he was shot, or that he was shot either between the apartment and the street, or on the street between the building and the car. We know he wasn't shot *in* the car because the slug went right through him and it wasn't found in the car. I tend to believe the latter story."

"OK, say it happened that way," said Stupenagel. "What about the motive, this stadium deal?"

Carefully, Marlene said, "That's still under investigation. I can't discuss the details."

Stupenagel's eyes widened in amazement. "What! *Fuck you, Ciampi!* Can't discuss, my ass! I thought we were together on this."

"Up to a point," replied Marlene calmly. "I said you could have first crack at it when it all jelled and we were ready with indictments. But it hasn't jelled. Be patient, we're almost there."

Stupenagel rose to her impressive full height, a pugnacious expression tightening her face. "Fuck patience! I feel betrayed, you know that? Betrayed! I thought we could work together on this, make you look good, but now all bets are off. I'm going to get the whole story, *the whole story*, and print it with all the dirty laundry showing." She threw on her greatcoat and stalked toward the door, pausing dramatically at the threshold.

"You've changed, Marlene," she intoned in a voice of doom, "and not for the better. You've turned into a . . . a fucking *mom*! Go back to your goddamn knitting."

"It's embroidery," said Marlene to the slamming door.

She sat and rocked for a long time after that, her little project untouched on her lap, watching the skylight darken as the short day faded. There was a brief drumming of rain against the glass. A chill gathered in the loft, and Marlene stirred herself to turn up the gas radiators.

She was thinking "there but for the grace of God"

thoughts not only about Julia Mackey and Francine Del Fazio, but about Ariadne Stupenagel as well. The sort-of moll and the sort-of man: two options she had turned down for reasons she still could not articulate. She was brought out of her study by the baby, who took this opportunity to pop her a good one in the region of the bladder. Marlene grunted and trudged to the toilet, this making it an even dozen visits for the day.

Emerging, she paced, at a loss. She put the embroidery away in its canvas bag. The loft was as clean as it ever got. She could not bear to read *The Mill on the Floss,* and the thought of watching crap on TV was repugnant. She couldn't get drunk, and she didn't feel like going downstairs and schmoozing with Stu and Larry. She got out her sleight-of-hand kit and practiced vanishes and productions. Before long the concentration chased, or seemed to chase, the plaguing thoughts about the three women from her mind.

But they still lurked there, throbbing like an old sprain, so when the door shook to a heavy knock, and she got up to answer it, and it was the oriental-looking man from Doone's house, informing her that a car was waiting to take her to Doone and Leona, she, with scarcely a second thought, threw on a coat and left with him, into who knows what peril, leaving no note, but leaving Mom behind.

There was a black stretch limo parked on the street. A cold intermittent rain bounced off its shiny flanks and polished the ancient cobbles that showed through Crosby Street's skin of black asphalt. Marlene's guide threw open the back door and she looked in. Sitting on the far side of the plush seat was a thin youth wearing a long coat and a black, green and red knitted tam. He had a wary expression on his brown face and an Uzi submachine gun across his knees.

Marlene entered the car. The yellowish giant swung into the front seat and the car moved off.

When they were on Grand Street headed west, the boy in the back gave Marlene a black hood and told her to put it on. She did so without argument. She thought it unlikely that Doone wished her any harm, and she was well protected against the Bobbsey Twins. She relaxed in the stuffy darkness.

They drove for a period that Marlene estimated at a little under an hour, timed by her bladder. She was helped out of the car, guided down a concrete walk, and brought into a very warm room smelling of marijuana smoke. She pulled off her hood and found herself in what appeared to be a suburban living room, furnished with anonymous modern furniture—couch, two easy chairs, glass coffee table, a low cabinet with a TV on top of it. The windows were obscured by gray draperies. John Doone was sitting in one of the armchairs, smoking a joint the size of a young banana, and Leona Simmons was sitting on the couch. The young woman, in grubby jeans and a sleeveless top, looked frailer than ever. Her hazel eyes regarded Marlene coldly.

Marlene tossed the hood onto the coffee table. "Don't you trust me, Mr. Doone? I got you out of jail like I said."

Doone's eyes narrowed and he pursed his lips. Marlene had the feeling that he put a lot of energy into keeping deadpan. He said, "I trust so far, but you still Babylon, nuh?"

"Yeah," said Marlene, "Babylon to my bones." She turned to the girl. "Leona, I'm Marlene Ciampi. I'm an assistant D.A. I saw you once very briefly at your mother's house. I'd like to help you."

"That's a laugh," said Leona in a tone as blank as the recorded voices of telephone operators.

Wrong approach, thought Marlene. "I saw your mom the other day. She'd like you to come home."

"Oh, yeah?" said Leona. "Coulda fooled me."

Marlene sighed. She longed to chat with some *nice* people. "OK, a tough little girl," she said, as if conducting an interior monologue. "She's in trouble, but she doesn't want help. She doesn't care about her family. Too bad. Her mother would really like to know that she hasn't been a total failure. Well, fine, we'll try the tough-girl approach." She stared hard at Leona and said, "Listen, sister! I want to know what happened the night your brother got killed—everything you did, everything you saw. I just bought that information from Doone here. So spit it the fuck out!"

Leona glanced nervously at Doone, but received only a cold stare. Her pathetic attempt to erect a tough persona sagged. She scratched her arms and licked her lips and began speaking in a tight, dry tone, almost a whisper.

Marlene pulled a steno pad and a pen from her bag. In a loud, commanding voice she snapped, "Speak up, goddamn it! I can't hear you."

Leona jumped as if shocked and began again. "I picked Marion up at the stadium. I was on a run and I had the stuff in my bag. I figured I would take him home and then go make the delivery."

"Wait a minute, why couldn't you take your own car?"

"The Datsun's too small for Marion. Was. But then when I picked him up, he said he wanted to stop off at the city. At Julia's place. So I took him there. I figured I'd drop him off, and, like, he'd stay the night. He does it all the time when her husband's away. . . . I mean, he did.

"But we get there and he goes, 'Just wait for me,

hon. I got to tell this woman something.' So he goes into the building and I'm waiting in the car."

Marlene said, "Your mom said something about him being excited about something. He'd found something out. About the team?"

Leona's face stiffened for a moment and her eyes dropped. Then she said, "Oh, yeah, that. Julia told him some shit about a deal her old man was pulling to build this stadium. Some illegal shit or something. She said she could use it to bust out of her marriage so that her and Marion could get together."

"And Marion was going for this? This blackmail?"

Leona shrugged. "I guess."

"Leona, your brother kept a kind of diary, a notebook. Did he have it with him that night?"

"I didn't see it," said Leona. "Why? Is it important?"

"Maybe, and I'd sure like to see it. So go on: you were in the car . . ."

"Right, I was there in the car listening to the stereo and smoking and I run out of smokes." As if the mention of smoking reminded her of the act, she drew a Salem from a pack, lit it, and drew the smoke deep into her lungs. Through a cloud, she resumed. "So, I didn't know how long he was gonna be, see, so I remembered there was this all-night place on First and 57th. So I left the car where it was—"

"You shut off the engine and locked it?"

"Yeah, sure. It was my set of keys. Marion had his own keys. I put the stuff in the glove and locked it. I didn't want it on me, walking down the street at night.

"So, I went up there and bought the cigarettes. I walked back and when I got to the corner, I saw two guys come out of the building with Marion between them. There was something wrong with him—he was staggering and they had to practically carry him. I ducked back around the corner of the building and watched. They got his keys and opened the door and shoved him into the passenger side. Then one of the guys got into the driver's side of the Caddy and the other guy walked right toward me. I thought he spotted me, so I turned around and walked toward First. I looked back and he wasn't following me at all, he was getting into another car. Then he drove away. I went back to the building and the Caddy was gone too. I was scared. I wandered around for a while and then I called him"—she indicated Doone—"and he picked me up and brought me back to Queens."

"Did you get a good look at these guys?" asked Marlene.

"One of them, the guy in the other car."

Marlene brought out the Polaroid she had taken and passed it to Leona. "Is this them?"

Leona studied the photograph and nodded. "The younger guy, not the driver. That's one of them for sure."

Marlene was putting the photograph away when Doone asked to see it. He stared at it as if committing the faces to memory. "You know dese men?" he asked Marlene.

"No. Do you?"

Doone shook his head. "I doan. But wha you t'ink? Is why dey kill 'er bredder?"

Marlene said, "You heard it. He knew something the husband didn't want to get out, and he was using it to blackmail the husband into letting Julia Mackey out of her marriage. The husband didn't appreciate it and had the man whacked out."

Doone nodded: it made perfect sense to him.

Marlene said, "The funny part is these guys are following me around. They tried to run me off the road the other day. That's what I can't figure."

"Maybe dey want a dead you befo you find out somet'ing else?"

"Like what?" asked Marlene. "We know the whole thing already."

"Cho, maybe you do, maybe you doan." He handed the photograph back to her. "But I tell you one t'ing, Babylon. I know you not afraid to die, but you should pray Jah dey doan get to you befo I get to dem."

Marlene nodded absently. "Yeah, I guess. Where's the bathroom?"

CHAPTER

sixteen

"Harry," said Marlene into the phone, without preamble, "it was the elevator. They got him in the elevator."

"The blonde," said Harry Bello.

"Yes, and Butch has found out why they're burning your buildings down, and which ones are the next to go."

"We should talk."

"I'm here," said Marlene.

"Forty minutes," said Bello and hung up.

Nothing like a warm heart-to-heart between friends, thought Marlene as she replaced her phone. She had just returned to the loft from her visit to Doone's hideaway and had called Bello first thing. While she waited for him to arrive, she ran over her notes from the interview. She was physically tired, but the depression that had grown out of the interaction with Ariadne Stupenagel and Julia Mackey was gone.

She heard heavy steps and a knock. She unlocked the door and saw Karp staring down at her, his hair still damp from his after-practice shower. "Oh, it's just you," she said.

"Paul Newman couldn't make it," he said, closing

the door behind him. "What kind of greeting is that—oh, it's just you?"

"Sorry, I was expecting Harry Bello."

"Should I take a number?"

"Very funny," said Marlene sourly. "You know, as a matter of fact, this exaggerated jealousy when I'm in the state I'm in could be construed as a form of chauvinistic insult."

Karp walked over to the refrigerator and poured himself a Pepsi. "Marlene, don't start . . ." he began, and then there was a knock at the door and he said, "Ah, here's your guy."

Bello looked better than he had when Marlene had last seen him. He looked like a very sad, very tired man instead of a living corpse.

They settled around the oak table, Bello accepting a soda (which he did not touch), and Karp and Marlene told the detective what they had learned. Karp led off, explaining the link between the arsons, Mackey and Chaney. He finished by giving Bello the addresses of the two properties in the target block that were both unburnt and not the property of the syndicate. Bello wrote this down, although he had taken no other notes.

"Our guys are still in town. At least they haven't passed through La Guardia, we think," said Bello. "Have you got that picture?" Marlene handed over the Polaroid original. Bello glanced at it and put it away. He said, "This is good stuff. I'll stake out the buildings and we'll see. What about that elevator?"

Now Marlene summarized her interviews with Julia and Leona. When she was finished, Bello asked, "Do you believe the Mackey woman?"

"About what happened the night of? Yeah. She was wide open and blabbing. If she had the talent to act like that, we'd all have seen her on Broadway." A sharp look at Karp. "Not that I ever get to *go* to any plays.

"Anyway, I believe that Simmons walked alive and intact out of the Mackey apartment and was dying from a gunshot wound in the chest when Leona saw him being hustled into his car. The two stories jibe pretty well. They probably were waiting for him in the building; they knew where he was going. The shooting had to take place in the hallway, the elevator, the lobby or the street outside. For reasons of privacy, I'd pick the elevator. They got in the elevator car after him, shot him, and walked him out of there.

"On the motive angle—the business about Simmons blackmailing Mackey to let her go? I think she believes it. It fits with her personal drama. And Leona sort of confirms it. Maybe it's a case of life imitating art."

"So the husband ordered him whacked," said Bello.

"It's our only plausible line. But we've got zip without the shooters."

Bello stood up. "I need to set up this stake-out. And I'll get somebody to take a look at the elevator. See you."

He walked out. "Chatty guy," said Karp.

"Silent, but sober, you'll notice. Yes, Marlene adds brilliant therapeutic skills to her panoply of achievements."

"You think he'll stay that way?"

"Mmm, I'd like it better if he spilled his guts about how his partner died," she replied after a moment's thought. "I think he fucked up royally and it's unbearable to his sense of who he is; if he's got nothing but the job, and he screwed up the job, what is he? And so on. Unlike you, for example, who has a family, friends, a terrific alternative career—speaking of which, did you get a chance to talk to Wallace about Leona?"

Karp had fallen into a fog of thought about his own legal screw-up, and Marlene had to pluck his sleeve to get his attention. "Wallace? No, I didn't get a chance," he said. "Actually, I forgot. Is it still important?"

"Only as an indication that Wallace was lying to you about Leona, and may have been lying about other things. Maybe there was bad blood between him and Marion over it. I remember you once said Simmons was into basketball and his family and nothing else. I just wondered . . . what is it?"

Karp's mouth was hanging open in amazement and his eyes had widened. "Marlene! Let's stop for a second. This story you got from the woman is total bullshit. You're right. Marion cared about ball and he cared about his family. He wasn't into drugs, or running around, or high living. The idea of him blackmailing Frank Mackey about some real estate deal so he could marry a woman his mother couldn't stand—it doesn't make any sense."

"So he was in love," said Marlene. "He went a little crazy. It happens. I married *you,* didn't I?"

Karp's only response to this comment was a vague smile. He was deep in thought. Unconnected perceptions were flying toward one another like the gametes of some marine creature in the dark heart of the sea. But the shape that might emerge from their junction remained obstinately obscure, even to him.

Marlene poked him again. "What!"

He shook his head. "Nothing. No, something, but I don't know what. What I do know is, we still don't have the why."

The next morning, the why not having appeared in dreams, Karp was shaving in front of the loft's tiny sink, where once workmen had rinsed their grubby hands. Its porcelain was worn so thin that the black metal showed through in places. The phone rang. Karp continued shaving, thinking about murder, basketball and sex. He heard the machine click on and, after a moment, V.T. Newbury's voice, with a message that he needed to see Karp right away.

An hour later, Karp was in V.T.'s office, drinking coffee and eating a toasted bagel and listening to the strange tale of Howard Chaney's involvement in international trade. V.T. had explained that Chaney had inherited a modest beauty-products firm from his father and had built it into a substantial empire: shampoos, creams, makeup, and the various bits and pieces associated with hair grooming.

"Say that about the combs again," said Karp.

V.T. sighed impatiently. It was all crystal to him. "OK, last year Chaney buys this bankrupt hair-products company in L.A.: Baron Industries. They made combs, plastic brushes, barrettes, and other cheap crap. According to my sources, Chaney did the deal himself, which is somewhat odd, and it's an odd purchase. It'd be like the president of G.E. personally buying Joe's Appliance Repair.

"Well, it turns out that Baron is a neat little money maker. Last July it shipped an order of 2,000 gross of plastic comb cards to an importer in La Paz, for which it received the sum of $18,202,137."

"What's that per comb?"

"Um, let's see, at twelve per card, that's . . ." he calculated swiftly, "a little over $52 per comb."

"A pricey item," said Karp. "Must be really high quality."

"Yeah, well, Bolivians have problem hair, it's well known. Of course, it could also be a scam to repatriate drug dollars. I don't know . . ."

"So . . . Howard's into black money," said Karp. "Why doesn't this surprise me? Anything else?"

"Yeah. Chaney International, Inc., is privately held, so there's less information about it than for a public company, but my contacts say there was a little flurry on the Street last winter, when it appeared that he might take the company public. It came to naught, however, and the word was that his books wouldn't stand SEC scrutiny. The word also is that Howard's in serious trouble as regards his cash flow."

"Why is that?"

V.T. leaned back in his chair and made a bridge of his hands. "The beauty business is a marketing business. The stuff they sell is just goop—anybody can make it. Sales depend on image and outlets. On the image side, it's hard for Chaney to compete with the real giants like Revlon, with multimillion-dollar ad budgets. On the outlet side, Chaney was big in the little department stores all over the South and Midwest, and they're all going belly up. They can't compete with the new malls. And Chaney hasn't gotten into the big anchor stores to the extent he should have.

"More than that, I get the feeling that Chaney wasn't all that interested in the beauty business. A little pansy-ish for a red-blooded he-man like him. He's spent a lot of money diversifying. So to speak."

V.T. slipped his half glasses on and consulted a list. "A chain of hotels on the West Coast that turned out to be a money pit. He sponsored a film festival. A racing stable, also a loser. And the Hustlers, of course, which has yet to turn a profit.

"As far as private spending: Howard does not stint himself. His monthly nut must be humongous. A house in Fairfield, one in Malibu, a triplex on East 65th, a hundred-ten-foot yacht. He's spending more than he's taking in. The banks think he's poison, according to my cousin Evan at the Speculators and Peculators National Trust. The Bolivian deal saved his ass from default on some heavy notes. If this stadium thing doesn't jell, I'd say he'd be looking at Chapter Eleven in six months. Or worse."

"Meaning?"

V.T. picked up another piece of paper. "Odd little bits of cash are showing up in various places, just in time to keep him solvent. And it's not coming from sales of assets or commercial loans."

"You think he's into the shys?"

"It wouldn't knock me off my chair," said V.T., "but there's one aspect that's still obscure. Say Howard's become a wholly owned subsidiary of the Mob. They're using him as a money laundry, fine. They have a piece of this stadium deal, fine. But they're hanging out a mile on him. I'm looking at nearly twenty million in anomalous income over the past three months. What are they going to do to recoup? Break his legs? Even if they took over Chaney entirely and looted it, it doesn't make sense. Howard's looted it pretty good already; it's a shell. Are they just waiting for the stadium deal to close?" He shrugged and rubbed his face. "In any case, Roger my lad, either the wise guys have gotten more sophisticated or I'm losing my touch. I can't figure it. Any ideas?"

Karp mused. Another piece of a puzzle clicked into place.

He said, "I got a couple. But it's not soup yet." He thanked V.T. enthusiastically and left. His next stop was Roland Hrcany's office. Hrcany was on the phone when Karp stuck his head in and said, "Did you get it?"

Hrcany said, "Just a second, Bill," and placed his hand over the mouthpiece. "Yeah, we got it. I didn't believe Shelly would be that stupid, but it goes to show you. We got the whole docket, including the original DD-5 arrest form. Connie was glad to help with the keys to his desk. We found some interesting skin magazines too, but we left them there. What're we going to do now?"

"I don't know yet," said Karp and motioned Hrcany to finish his conversation.

When Hrcany put the phone down, Karp asked, "Roland, what's the line on tonight's Hustlers–Sixers game?"

"Hustlers and six. Dr. J is hurt and the Sixers have lost their last two. You all are five straight. Vegas loves you. Why, did you want to put something down?"

"Betting on sports is illegal in the state of New York, Roland."

"Oh, the shame of it!" said Roland, deadpan. "Guess I'll have to change my ways. Why are you interested, then?"

"Mmmm, just wondering. What's the betting been like?"

"Heavy. There's a shitload of New York money that sticks to the Hustlers whatever, but especially when they're favored. Of course, that's nothing to when you play the Knicks."

"Why is that?"

"Well, like I said, New York money, plus it's a grudge match in the Garden. The old favorites against the upstarts. On a smaller scale, it'd be like a Yankees–Mets world series, or a Giants–Jets Super Bowl. The Hustlers'll go in with twenty or twenty-two, and a million fans'll be praying for an upset. Meanwhile, for this Philly game the local books are laying off like crazy to the Coast."

"The Coast?"

"Yeah, that's what I hear. Serious L.A. money. Some folks out there are going to be real unhappy if the Sixers lose by five." He looked at Karp narrowly. "Is there something I should know, Butch? Assuming I was to place a hypothetical bet?"

Karp made his face neutral. "No. Just curious," he said.

But in the event, the Hustlers just squeaked by Philadelphia, winning 121–118. Karp played the game through again in his head as he stood under the pounding hot shower in the Hustlers' locker room. He directed the steaming water especially at the spreading bruise below his neck, in the tender spot just above the sternum. A Sixers guard had thrown an elbow hard into it as Karp moved toward a loose ball. Karp's vision had gone red with pain and he had fallen to his knees. The ref didn't bother to call it, and the game had swirled on around him.

Nadleman had pulled him out, and he had spent the rest of the game on the bench with an ice pack held to the spot and wincing every time he had to swallow. A hulking dark shape moved next to him in the steam: Fred James. Fred had been high scorer for the Hustlers, thirty-two points, and he was feeling good.

"Hey, D.A.! Caught you a good one, hey? Hey, don't worry, man, you get him next time. Part of the game."

"It's not, that's the fucking point," mumbled Karp and turned off his water. He looked around for Doobie Wallace. Doobie had had a good game too, but not as good as Fred's. While the Hustlers were a far more impressive team than they had been when they last faced the Sixers, the time that Karp had first seen them play, they had made a lot of dumb mistakes tonight, nearly all of which involved Doobie Wallace.

He dressed and went looking for Bernie Nadleman. He found him finishing an interview with a blow-dried man in a green blazer. Karp waited until the thank-yous and closing chat was over, and then he put his hand on the coach's arm.

"Bernie, we have to talk."

"Hey, Butch, how ya feeling, kid? What a shot!"

"I'm fine, Bernie. Look, can we go somewhere?"

"Hey, I'd love to, Butch, but Chaney's here. He's having a post-gamer in the owner's clubroom."

"I found out who killed Marion, Bernie. I thought you wanted to know."

"Jesus! You did? Who was it?"

Karp glanced around at the TV crew packing their gear and lowered his voice. "Not here, Bernie."

Nadleman nodded and led Karp to a small, empty office down the hallway from the locker room.

"So, who was it?" asked Nadleman.

"We don't have the names yet, but we're pretty sure of who they were working for. Frank Mackey. And indirectly, Howard Chaney."

"You gotta be kidding."

"It doesn't look that way, Bernie. It sort of fits, though, with what you were telling me about Howard not being all that interested in pursuing the case."

Nadleman said, "God, this is terrible. I got to sit down." He collapsed into an office chair. "Are you positive about this? I mean, it's crazy—Marion was a franchise player."

"This is bigger than the team, Bernie. The way the story goes, Mackey and Howard have a scam going to build you your new stadium. They're buying property and burning down buildings. Marion found out about it and he was going to pressure Mackey on the deal, so Mackey would cut loose the beautiful Mrs. M. All the pols in Queens seem to have a piece of it, which is why nobody was that interested in finding out who killed Marion. What do you think of that?"

"I can't believe it. Christ, Mackey's here right now."

"He is?"

"Yeah, he's from Philly. Comes to all our games here. Jesus, Butch, what the fuck are you gonna do?"

"Everybody asks me that," said Karp. "My problem is, what I told you is a great story and it fits most of the facts, but I don't entirely believe it."

"What, you mean about the stadium and the cover-up?"

"No, that's true enough. Marion was involved with Mackey's wife, and the people involved in the scheme knew that any serious investigation of the murder would center on Julia Mackey, who is not that tightly wrapped to begin with. The story she put out may or may not be entirely true, but if it came out, the stadium deal would go down the tubes. Hence the fuck-upery on the investigation. But that's not why Marion was killed."

"So why was he, then?"

Karp looked at Nadleman for a long moment, trying to read his face. He saw worry, confusion, a certain vagueness of will that was also apparent in his coaching style, but no duplicity, no corruption. Then, instead of answering Nadleman's question directly, he asked one of his own. "Bernie, tell me, did you notice anything unusual in the game tonight?"

"Unusual? Yeah. We beat the Sixers at home. Nothing more unusual than that." He laughed without humor.

Karp said, "Then let me tell you what I noticed. We won by three points. The line was Hustlers and six. Fred had a great night, everybody else did about what they usually do. Except for Doobie. Look at the game stats. Fifty-eight percent on free throws; he hasn't been below eighty and some for months. From the field he shot thirty-seven percent. It should be fifty. He tried five three-pointers and hit one. He passed to the wrong people. He was responsible for six turnovers—"

"I don't get this," said Nadleman in annoyance. "Wallace had a bad night. What does that have to do with Marion?"

Karp sighed. This was harder than he had expected. "OK, let's take it from the Marion end. The key question has always been, Why was he killed? Now we know *where* he was killed and *how* he was killed: he was shot in the elevator of Frank Mackey's apartment building after a visit with Mackey's wife. You knew he'd been *schtupping* her, right?"

Nadleman nodded. "It was no big secret."

"No, but nobody was interested in volunteering the information to me—not even you, Bernie. Little hints, but nobody came out and said it. All right, that's water under the bridge. So, first we think it's dope. But Marion isn't a user or a dealer.

"Then we think it's the sister. She's a doper, and a mule. We know Marion cared about his family, maybe he tried to make her stop and the pusher she worked for decided to ace him. But scratch that; we know the pusher now, and despite his many crimes, he didn't do it.

"OK, maybe it was Mackey in a jealous rage. But the affair has been going on for a while, so why now? Scratch that one.

"Finally, we have the motive I just told you about, the stadium. Julia Mackey likes it. And it fits all the facts except one."

"What's that?"

"It's not something Marion Simmons would do," said Karp. "Here's a man who cared about two things: his family and basketball. Those are the only two things that would have made him put himself into a position where somebody might have a reason to kill him. It wasn't the family. That leaves the game."

As Karp spoke, he was studying Nadleman to see whether the coach would light up, would come spontaneously to the same conclusion, and he was also examining himself. He did not often speculate in advance of the facts—it was one of his maxims. But once the thing was out in words, it felt right, the way it felt right when in the midst of jostling bodies twenty feet from the backboard, he released a ball, knowing that it would float in a perfect arc and pass through the net without touching the rim.

Bernie was silent. Karp saw fear building behind his eyes, and he spoke. "Bernie, what it is, Wallace is shaving points. Marion knew it, and he was going to talk, and that's why he was killed."

Nadleman sprang from his seat like a fish gaffed out of a tank. "That's bullshit!" he cried.

Karp didn't move, nor did he raise his voice. "No, it's true, and I think you realize it's true. What you don't know is that Chaney's in on it too. The Mob owns him."

Nadleman sat down again. His head waggled back and forth in a continuing gesture of denial. "Butch, for chrissake, do you know what you're saying? Shaving in the N.B.A.? It's . . . it'd be like the Black Sox."

"Exactly," said Karp. "It's unprecedented. Which is why somebody stands to make a serious chunk of money out of it."

"I still can't believe it. There has to be another explanation. I mean, for starters, why the hell would Wallace do it? He's got more money than God. What could they offer him?"

"Maybe we should ask Doobie about that," suggested Karp mildly.

Nadleman rolled his eyes. "Oh, sure, I'm just gonna

walk up to the guy and say, 'Hey, Doobie, shave any points recently?' ''

Karp stood up and stretched and rubbed his throat. It hurt him to talk, and his voice, deep to begin with, had changed into a scratchy bass growl. "OK, Bernie," he said, "whatever you say. You asked me to find out how and why Marion was killed and I did. In the process I turned up a corruption scandal, a point-shaving scandal, gross malfeasance in two district attorneys' offices, arson, and an attempted murder, directed against my own wife.

"But from my point of view, that's just the beginning. Now we know what happened, but we haven't built any cases. When we do, there's going to be a firestorm. So you'll forgive me if the possibility of insulting Doobie Wallace doesn't hang very heavy in my thoughts. Hey, are you all right?"

Nadleman had turned waxy in the office's fluorescent light, like a slab of fatback in a supermarket meat bin. His brow glistened with oily droplets of sweat. He seemed to have trouble catching his breath. He swallowed hard and said, "Yeah, yeah, I'll be fine. Everything got woozy there for a minute." He looked up at Karp, the pain standing out on his face like tattooing. "Butch, how the hell do you prove something like that? I mean, if I say something like that to him, all he has to do is say fuck you and the next game he goes for a triple double."

"It *is* hard to prove, unless somebody rats," said Karp. "What would help a lot would be finding Simmons's diary."

"It still hasn't turned up?"

"No. Any ideas where it could be?"

"Hell, I don't know. He never let it out of sight that I remember. That last night, after the San Antonio game, I grabbed him and told him to come early to the next practice, and he took the thing out of his bag and wrote in it and put it back. Then he left."

"So he must have had it with him when he died. Too bad."

"What do you mean?"

"I mean, whoever killed him probably took it."

"I guess," said Nadleman without interest. "Where're you going?"

"Up to Howard's party. I thought I'd take a look at Frank Mackey while I was here. You coming?"

"I'll be along," said Nadleman. Karp left him in the office chair, staring at nothing.

The owner's clubhouse was a low-ceilinged, paneled room, full of large, loud men and thick with the fumes of tobacco, scotch, beer and sports talk. Chaney was there, surrounded by his powerboy buddies, and in the outer circles the usual ruck of sportswriters, sportscasters, publicists and those aging rich kids that the papers still called "sportsmen." There were no players.

Karp picked up a Coke from the bar and was about to ask somebody to point out Mackey when a hand touched his arm and he turned.

There was a man behind him holding out his hand and Karp instinctively took it. "Mr. Karp? I'm Frank Mackey," the man said as they shook hands. Mackey wore an open-necked white shirt with a yellow alpaca golf sweater over it, tan whipcord slacks and oxblood tasseled loafers. He was in his mid-fifties, Karp guessed, with a full head of short, wiry, shiny black hair. The skin of his face had the tanned, perfectly matte look that wealthy men purchase at their health clubs. His eyes were dark and intelligent, his teeth were perfectly capped. Karp was interested to see that he had omitted the gold chains and the pinkie ring diamond.

"That was some kind of shot you took tonight. Are you all right?"

"I'm fine, except for my voice. And, officially, I didn't take a shot. I walked into Collins's flying elbow."

"Yes, sometimes the referees overlook infractions. If they called everything there wouldn't be a game."

"That's one way to look at it," said Karp mildly.

"Yes, well, I've been wanting to talk to you for some time, Mr. Karp," said Mackey. "I believe our wives know each other."

"Fine with me," said Karp neutrally. "Here?"

"Probably not a good idea," said Mackey. "Tell me, are you interested in antique cars?"

"I suppose I could develop an interest," said Karp.

"Good. I have a 1938 Packard V-12 in perfect condition down in the garage here. If you go out of this room and turn left down the hall, there's an elevator. Take it down to G-2. One of my associates will show you to it."

The associate, whom Karp found waiting as he left the elevator, turned out to be Carlo Parmagianni, Charlie Cheese to his friends, a man who looked like he had been carved from a large block of that hard, semi-translucent pink rubber they use to make babies' teething rings.

Charlie beckoned with a finger the size of a center punch, and Karp followed him through the damp fuel-scented corridors to an enormous, shiny, bulging black vehicle. Charlie ushered him into the gray plush rear seat. Karp barely had to stoop to enter, the car was so high and amply proportioned.

Charlie sat in the driver's seat and lit a cigarette. Karp ran his hand over the plush upholstery, and was caught up in a sense memory from early childhood: seated in the backseat of his father's 1948 La Salle, with his two brothers, driving somewhere, and his mother's cigarette smoke drifting back. He was drawing pictures and letters on the plush and then rubbing them out. Karp drew a heart with Marlene's and his initials in it. It still worked.

The rear door opened and Frank Mackey slid in. He had added a belted tan polo coat to his outfit. "Well, how do you like it?" he asked genially.

"It's impressive," said Karp. "You need a bunch of guys with fedoras and tommy guns."

Mackey laughed. "Yeah. Especially an Italian guy in the trash-hauling business. I piss in their eye with it; not many people catch the humor." He patted the plush armrest as if it were a horse. "But the real reason is when I was a kid I always wanted one of these, and here it is. So, Mr. Karp: would you care for a quick tour of my native city?"

"It's your show, Mr. Mackey," Karp answered. Mackey gave some terse instructions to Charlie Cheese, who brought the great car to rumbling life and steered it out of the garage.

They drove away from the Spectrum arena, through the suburbs, and then through the historic center of the city. Mackey pointed out the sights. Karp let him go on, waiting patiently for the point.

But Mackey chatted inconsequentially as they drove to another section of the city, a zone of squat reddish houses with stone stoops. The car slowed. Mackey said, "The old neighborhood. I was born right above that grocery store. The neighborhood's still Italian, you notice. Blacks don't like to come here, especially not at night. There's Dom Scarfi's club, where I wasted my youth. Would you like to stop someplace? Get some clams? A drink?"

"No, I'm fine, thanks," said Karp. "I'm wondering when the show's going to start."

"OK, let's start now," replied Mackey agreeably. "We have a serious mess here. I'm going to tell you my part in it, bluntly, frankly, with the purpose of seeing whether we can't figure a way out of it with minimum damage to all concerned. I've asked around about you. You're a no-bullshit kind of guy, and so am I. I figure we can do business. If not, no harm done. Agreed?"

Karp nodded and made a leading-on gesture with his hand.

"OK. You notice I don't ask you if you're wired. We're gentlemen here. I'm not a gangster, you're not some snotnose prosecutor on the make. All right. Let me start with some background. Like I say, I was born in this area. The Scarfis were gods on earth. I fell in with them, I did a few little jobs, I took a fall for one of them. I shut my yap and did eighteen months in Allenwood.

"I said to myself—fuck this, never again. I'm an example of the success of the criminal-justice system, Mr. Karp. I got caught and I was rehabilitated. There must be about seventeen of us in the whole country.

"After that I moved to New York. I changed my name legally. No disrespect for the Italians, but I wanted to say, that old life is over, you know. It was symbolic.

"I started on a truck, humping cans. It's the most dangerous job in the country for personal injury, did you know that? Not many people do: worse than coal mining. I saved up enough to buy an old junker garbage truck and fixed it up myself. I had an uncle ran some grocery stores, I started hauling for him. I got a rep for good service—polite, clean. I'm working eighteen-hour days. After five years I had ten trucks. God bless America, right?

"You haul trash in the City, it's not like running a

dress shop on Fifth Avenue. Did I pay off? Yeah, I paid
off. The cops, Tammany, the unions. It's part of doing
business in the City. And the wise guys too. But two
things I never did: I never let them fuck over my customers, and I never let them use my equipment or
property for any hard stuff. They knew the line. They
knew I was ready to bust heads if I had to. Charlie up
there still carries a piece. *He's* the gangster. Am I right,
Charlie?"

A friendly grunt from the front seat, and Mackey
went on.

"I did one smart thing. In 1947 I bought four hundred acres of land way out on the Island. I figured, I
collect garbage, why shouldn't I have my own dump?
Why pay tipping fees? You know what that garbage
dump is now? Valley Stream, Long Island. Dumb luck,
but it made me. I became a developer." He laughed.

"What I'm saying to you is, I'm no violet. I played
rough. I had to. But I'm not a wise guy. I'm a hard
guinea. You understand the difference?"

"I married a hard guinea, Mr. Mackey," said Karp.

Mackey laughed again. "Yeah, that's right. I wish
I'd done the same. That's the next chapter. So, local
boy makes good. I go back to see the folks in Philly,
this is 1963. I had a white Caddy convertible, throwing
cash around. I'm in this club one night and there she
is. Bang, I'm finished. She's waiting tables, fresh out
of some scrungy little coal town in the Mon Valley. A
bohunk. You met her? No? Still looks good, but nothing to what she was then. Kim Novak on top of
Brigitte Bardot.

"And she wasn't giving any away, or that's what she
said. You had to marry it first. And I did. OK, I can see
I'm boring you, so I'll speed it up. Not to reveal the secrets of the marital bed, but Julia is not what you call

a passionate woman, at least not with me. It hurts her, she says. So that part of the marriage didn't work out.

"OK, I asked for it, but I stick by my deals. We have a marriage. She likes being rich. She takes courses. How to fix the house, how to talk, expand her vocabulary, how to walk, how to wipe her royal ass—I don't know—the works. That's fine. I'm proud of her. I mean, a little bohunk kid like that, and now she's a queen in New York. We have the kid, God knows how. We should alert the pope—another virgin birth, practically.

"Do I play around? Yeah, I feel I'm too old for jerking off in the john. But discreet, civilized. You watch foreign films? That's how they do over there. Very civilized.

"OK, so she starts with this Simmons. Do I give a shit? Yeah, to be honest, I'm a little pissed. But there it is. I can live with it, if she doesn't rub it in my face. Which she doesn't, I'll give her that.

"I figured we had a kind of settlement. Not ideal, but what is, right? Then, one evening I happen to pick up the phone the same time she picks up the extension in the bedroom and it's Simmons. So I listen in—what the fuck, right? It's my house.

"And I get an earful. She's telling him an incredible load of horseshit. I'm this monster, a Mafioso. She's afraid for her life. I'm threatening to whack her out. I'll never let her go. Jealous rages—the works. He, on the other hand, is trying to calm her down. I was impressed: he sounded like a sensible kid. Anyway, she's made up this whole, like, *drama,* a fatal triangle or something. I'm telling you this so you don't think I was happy when Simmons got it. I figured the cops would come calling first thing."

"Why did you think they didn't?" asked Karp.

Mackey nodded and smiled, as if in approval of the

aptness of the question. "Ah, to answer that one, you got to understand about me and Howard. Howard—maybe you know this—is a rich kid. His dad made a pile in shampoos, hair dyes, that kind of stuff, and died pretty young. Howard took over when he was in his late twenties. What I'm saying is, he never had to bust his hump. He was entitled.

"We met through politics. Dan Logan put us together. We were both moving into real estate. Dan steered us to pick up some land where the state was going to put an interchange in, and we made a nice pile. Howard isn't exactly my kind of guy, but he's real friendly. He's generous, throws parties. We went fishing a couple three times. He's got a yacht so big that his fishing boat goes up on the deck of it.

"Anyway, he's always broke. He's leveraged up the kazoo. And gradually, from hints he keeps dropping, I realize he thinks I'm connected. I think maybe it's why he's so friendly. I say, Howard, I know the Scarfis, I know people, but I'm not a goombah. He doesn't listen. It's one of Howard's big problems. I explain to him, you don't want to know these people, and you definitely don't want to do business with them.

"But he keeps on with it. My theory is, he's embarrassed he's rich. He wants to be a hard guy. The beauty business—selling creams to faggots, it doesn't cut it. And so he's always with the horses, the ball clubs, the deals. Real man stuff.

"So, one night we're in Philly for a game, like now, and he says, take me to some places. So I figure, what the fuck, he's a grown-up. I take him to Vinnie Scoso's on South Hobart Street, over on the left there. I introduce him to Dom Scarfi. Tommy Fortunato, guys like that. His eyes light up. Another Mafia buff is born. It's not so unusual nowadays, this *Godfather* horseshit.

"Before you know it, he's deep in, he's talking

Jimmy this and Tony that. Street names. His buddies. I wish I'd of known how deep, believe me. OK, the scene changes. Howard wants a new stadium. Fine. He comes to me, we go to Dan Logan. It can be done. I put up some money, Howard's got this shitload of cash, I don't want to know where it's from. And we start blocking up a neighborhood in Long Island City. You know this already? Good. No crime in it, just a little honest graft.

"But we run into problems. We're evicting right and left, but it's slow. Howard's getting antsy, he can't wait for the payoff. I got a feeling I know why. The vig is killing him. So he says, we got to take care of it, Dom can take care of it. I should've pulled out then, but there it is. I didn't.

"So buildings start going up in smoke. People get fried. Dan's going batshit, but he can't stop it either. We're both in too deep. Then Simmons gets aced, the last fucking straw. We have a meet. D'Amalia's there, the Queens D.A. Dan owns him. He says, we got lucky, they found dope in the kid's vehicle. There won't be a big deal, we can keep the lid on.

"I feel like I've been rescued from a fucking plane crash. So it goes on. Then this schmuck kid that D'Amalia's got handling things, he calls Howard in a panic. You're looking into it, the famous Butch Karp, independently. Then there's this woman poking around. Turns out it's your wife. They go crazy. Later Howard tells me, no problem, they're framing this jig for the thing. Christ on a crutch! I say, Howard, this shit went out with the fifties.

"No, no, he says, it'll work out. I try to talk to him. I ask him, Howard, assuming the stadium goes belly up, are you in to the mob for the money? These guys don't send a final notice in the mail. I maybe can work something out. No, no, he's cool, he's paying the

Scarfis off. From where? I ask him. I read the financial pages too. No, he's got another deal, he won't say what it is.

"I'm almost finished. So, the other night I come home, and the wife is a wreck. Drunk, crying, the works. What's wrong? She tells me she's been meeting with this reporter and your wife. She's cocked up this story about how Simmons was gonna blackmail me, because he knew about the stadium deal, if I didn't let her go. The truth is, hey, anytime she wants out. I told her a million times. We can have a reasonable separation. Civilized. I got no hard feelings.

"But she's gotta have these dramas. Come to think of it, she's got a lot in common with Howard. Now she's in the shit and she wants me to climb in there and drag her out. The capper is, she tells me Simmons got it right there in my building."

Mackey let out a long exhalation of air. He said, "Charlie, swing over to the Schuylkill and get downtown. You're at the Hilton, right?" He fixed Karp with his eyes. "That's the whole story and it's the God's honest truth."

"It's quite a story," said Karp. "Let's assume it is true. What do you want me to do about it?"

"I don't really know," said Mackey. "For me—hell, I'm a big boy. I got lawyers—my *lawyers* have lawyers. When the time comes, we'll see. Julia, I'd like her in the background, if that can be worked out. Mainly, I want my kid out of it, no long drawn-out stuff. What do you think?"

Karp considered. "Well, if you told a grand jury what you just told me, I think it would move things along. If you want to keep the press out, a guilty plea beats a trial anytime. But we haven't even begun to construct any cases. We haven't caught the people who actually killed Simmons yet. My involvement has been a hundred percent unofficial."

"Any chance we could keep it that way? Unofficial? I won't insult you with an offer, but I'm a good friend to have in the City."

"I'm sure you are, Mr. Mackey," said Karp. "But I don't do that, and it isn't really up to me."

"I didn't think so," said Mackey sadly. Then he laughed. "One thing, though. After Julia spilled her guts there, that night I did get laid. After all that."

"Well," said Karp, "then it wasn't a total loss."

CHAPTER

seventeen

"That's quite a story," said Marlene, "especially given its delivery in that husky bedroom voice. Poor baby, do you think you'll ever recover?"

"I might, with proper support from my loved ones," growled Karp. The two of them were sitting up in bed, eating dim sum and drinking hot Chinese tea. It was the morning after the Sixers game, and Karp had whipped out early to Mott Street and brought home a big greasy bag of the little shivery gobbets.

"What is this one?" asked Marlene, brandishing an open white cardboard container.

"Human flesh. Or dog," said Karp, selecting one. "Is it OK to rest the sauce on the baby?"

"Your wife is furniture. Be my guest," said Marlene. "Support from my loved ones, eh? Would you like me to lick your wounds, like Catherine of Sienna? My Catholic girlhood fantasy."

"After breakfast. But, really, what did you think?"

"About Mr. Mackey's story? Well, my instinct was to discount it as a piece of self-serving chauvinistic horseshit. But then I remembered my own doubts about Julia's soap opera. So I really don't know. You know, I'm getting to hate this whole thing. It's like Venice under the doges: people whispering accusations and counter accusations, and the good guys are the bad guys and the bad guys are the good guys. A girl doesn't know what to think."

"A boy doesn't know what to think either," said Karp. "I tend to roll with Mackey, but then I didn't see his wife. That's another reason why this is so fucked. You're supposed to get all the people in interrogation rooms and then walk back and forth comparing stories. This, it's like trying to get a lemon pit out of your tea—there's nothing to grab onto."

"So what do we do?" Marlene asked.

They chomped and slurped, while Karp considered this.

"I don't see what we can do, legally," he said. "Doobie's shaving points, but who can prove it? The Queens corruption is going to end up in the Feds. I have a prima facie case of obstruction, misfeasance, malfeasance, and wrongful arrest against Shelly Ehrengard and unnamed co-conspirators, but it's dumb to move ahead with it until all the other pieces are in place, especially the murder piece. Meanwhile, we hang in there until Bello catches the bad guys and we can talk to them under cover of a New York County case."

Marlene grunted, moved the plastic bowl of duck sauce, which now held but a few brown smears, and rolled over on her side, facing away from Karp. "Meanwhile," she said, "would you rub my lower back?"

Carmine slammed down the phone in a rage. His boss was in a panic, and he had to fight to keep it from affecting his own equanimity. Carmine had warned him about this dumb deal a million times, and now that it had turned to shit, he, Carmine, was getting the blame. The worst thing was that there was nothing he could do to clean it up. He had hired a guy to watch the loft where the Ciampi woman lived, but she hadn't been out alone for days. He would have to go in after her, and pretty soon too.

"Hey, Marlene, is Butch there?" said Guma over the phone, without preamble.

"No, he just went out to practice. What's up?"

"Well, he asked me to find out something and I did. You know those guys? In the picture—the torches from Philly?"

"Yeah, what about them?"

"OK, funny thing—Butch said, look out West, Phoenix, L.A. So I did, but the people I talked to, when I described these guys, I was saying, these guys burn stuff down. And I was getting nowhere. Finally, I remember this old boozer, Jack Santini, he used to be a jockey, hangs out at the White Rose near the Williamsburg Bridge. You know where it is?"

"Yeah, I know," said Marlene patiently.

"Yeah, Jack used to be out there, L.A., Phoenix, Vegas. He always has a tan. Even in the winter in the City, he's got a tan. Who knows how, maybe one of these sun-lamp places. He sure isn't flying to the Bahamas. That's actually how I remembered Jack, because of Butch saying these guys who're after you, they both have tans, and in the picture too.

"And I remember he was connected, sort of. That's actually why he stopped riding. Racing commissions don't like jockeys that're connected. I figure he might know a West Coast wise guy. So I go in there this afternoon and there he is, Jack Santini. I buy him a bump, a couple, we bullshit awhile, and then I pull out the picture. Jesus, the guy gets pale, even *with* the tan.

"He says, 'Freshie the Fish.' He got his finger on the driver, the big guy with the cigar."

"Freshie the Fish? Goom, who the fuck . . ."

"Hold on, I'm coming to that. OK, Jack clams up. I never saw anybody clam up so fast. He doesn't want anything to do with talking about this guy in the picture. The other guy he doesn't know. OK, no dice there. So I go back to the office and I call a guy I know in rackets at the Bureau, and he knows a guy in L.A. and he makes a call, and to make a long story short, I'm on the line with a guy in the L.A. office.

"So, yeah, he knows who Freshie the Fish is. It turns out he's Carmine Fraschetti. He works for Jimmy Tona in L.A. You know who Jimmy Tona is, don't you?"

"Personally, I've never dated him, but I've heard the name. Some big L.A. *capo,* no? So this Fraschetti burns down buildings for Tona?"

"No, no, Marlene, that's the point! I was looking for pro torches, or for the kind of guy they would send to torch a building, which is why I didn't turn up the Fish. Not that I would swear Fraschetti never torched a building, but that's not what he does. He's Tona's main guy. He's what they call a mechanic."

"A shooter?"

"Among other things. He makes sure things go the way they're supposed to. He fixes things—a mechanic, get it? The Bureau guy was very interested to hear they were in town."

"The *other* guy is the torch?"

"Marlene, forget torches. These guys didn't fly across the country to burn down buildings. Tona can get that done with a phone call. Oh, yeah, the Bureau guy says the other one sounds like Joey Castello, a rising dirtbag, just got out of Folsom, copped to manslaughter. Another shooter. The Bureau guy wanted to know what was going on. I honestly didn't know what to tell him. What the fuck *is* going on, Champ?"

"Hey, Goom, cross my heart, all we got are theories. Butch was just saying this morning, we need these guys. Maybe they came to do Simmons, and they did the buildings as a favor. Or the other way around."

"Yeah, well, in the meantime," said Guma, "I drew up a couple of warrants for these scumbags on the Simmons thing and put their faces out. Maybe we'll get lucky." He paused, then added, "One thing, Marlene, don't fuck anymore with these two, understand? They're the worst."

Harry Bello sat in the driver's seat of a derelict Dodge van parked on 33rd Street in Long Island City, sipping black coffee and looking out at the frosty night. It had not taken him long to set up the stake-out, since he was its only participant. This was against regulations and good procedure, but Bello could not have cared less. If he caught the arsonists that was all right, and if they killed him, that was all right too. In any event, he did not trust his command in the NYPD. Anyone who had assigned the drunk Bello to catch a criminal did not want the criminal caught.

Bello thought he had a fair chance of bringing it off. He had checked out the two threatened buildings earlier, to familiarize himself with the layout of the basement, which is where he guessed they would start their fires. The other fires had been set in basements, using lots of gasoline and simple timing devices, and Bello had boundless faith in the unimaginativeness of professional criminals. All he had to do was wait for their arrival, follow them into the building they chose and collar them in the act. Or get shot.

He had already spent one full day and night watching. His presence had excited no attention. In that neighborhood, whole families might live for weeks in abandoned vehicles. He had prepared expertly for the stake-out: a dozen hero sandwiches, a gallon of coffee in a picnic jug, a can to pee in. He was dressed in two sets of long underwear, a sweater, ski hat and ski socks of heavy wool, and over all, a black snowmobile suit and fleece-lined boots.

He rarely slept much anymore, not since giving up the booze, so this duty was, in a sense, ideal. They had explained to him at the hospital that detox took awhile, that he would be irritable and confused for some time. They told him to go to meetings and take it one day at a time. He was willing to do that, as long as there weren't that many days in all. For some reason he had fixed on Marlene Ciampi as a reason not to drink himself to death, and had decided to risk some mutt's gun as a way out. It appealed to his sense of order. After all, it should have been him that got it instead of Jim Sturdevant.

Bello drifted in and out of a light sleep, waking whenever a car approached. At about three A.M. he came fully awake to the noise of a car door slamming. He looked out and saw two men standing by a dark, new Chevy. They took some equipment out of the car's trunk and marched into one of the buildings on the left, blithely, like Fuller brush men.

He stuck a portable cop radio and two sets of handcuffs in the convenient pockets of his snowmobile suit and picked up a six-cell flashlight and an Ithaca Model 37 12-gauge pump shotgun. He jacked a 00 buckshot shell into the breech. Then he followed the two into the building. He waited a few minutes in the dark trash-filled lobby, listening, and was rewarded by a faint scraping clank coming from below his feet. Men at work.

He walked down the stairs to the basement. The fire

door had been wedged open, revealing a long hallway that ran the length of the building. He could see the moving beams of flashlights coming from a storeroom whose open door gave on the hallway. The air stank of gasoline.

The faint spilled light from the arsonists' flashlights was sufficient to lead him swiftly down the hall to where they were hard at work, pouring gas and arranging their fusing. Standing in the doorway, he flicked his own flashlight on and said, "Police," in a conversational tone.

They stared up at him in stunned surprise, but their surprise was nothing to Bello's. In the cold glare of the flashlight it was perfectly obvious that the two men were not the ones who had been following Marlene Ciampi.

The next morning Bello called Marlene a little past dawn, said he had caught the arsonists during the night and was coming over. Marlene had mumbled something and fallen back into dreamland. Fortunately, ten minutes later the lift engine started up. Even without the alarm bell it was enough to banish sleep, for Marlene. Karp grunted and piled more pillows on his head.

She threw on his stained blue robe over her nightgown and stepped into pink fuzzy slippers shaped like kittens, a present from the secretaries. After six months in the loft they were encrusted with filth, like two little road kills clinging to her ankles. Fuck cleaning up, she thought; Bello was like family—I know he's a drunk, he knows I'm a slob.

Bello came in, sat at the round table, and accepted a cup of Medaglia D'Oro. "Congratulations, Harry," said Marlene. "How did it go down?"

"No problem. I braced them in the act and they gave it up. Nonviolent types."

"Nonviolent! Harry, I talked to Guma the other day, and he told me these guys were heavy hitters out of L.A." She told him essentially what Guma had told her.

Bello shook his head and brought an envelope out of his jacket pocket. "We got a problem here, Marlene." He placed her original Polaroid beside two standard I.D. shots of the men he had captured.

"We got one beefy older guy and one younger round-faced guy with more hair in both sets, but it's not the same two guys. My guys are Harry Ditmars and Jack DiBello. They're from Philly like we suspected, pros; the cops down there know them pretty well."

Marlene studied the photos, trying to cope with this new information. She drank more bitter coffee, but her mind was still half asleep. Obviously, Guma's discovery made a lot more sense now. But why in hell should two West Coast shooters come to ... it suddenly clicked, and she stared at Harry, her eyes wide. "That bitch lied to me!"

"The sister," said Bello, instantly sorting out the various bitches in the case, half a step ahead as usual.

"Give me ten minutes," said Marlene, "we're going to Brooklyn."

Splash, brush, pee, jeans, sweater, boots, maxi-coat, hat, scribble note for Karp on three pages of yellow bond, out the door. Ten minutes.

The day was dark, the sky like an army of dust bunnies. She said, "We could have a white Christmas." Bello grunted noncommittally and opened the car door for her.

She was excited and angry at the same time. As they drove toward the bridge, she began to talk. "It's my problem and I can't do anything about it, because it's

also my big advantage. I mean, sympathy for women.
I could get past it with Mackey but not with Leona. I
kept thinking about her mother and that family, what it
must have been like growing up with a superstar
brother. I never found out about the father, but I didn't
see any pictures in the house. Maybe he died, maybe
he split. The mother was focused on Marion. Or that's
what Leona thought. I forgot she was a junkie, and
junkies lie even if they don't have to.

"And then I was so full of myself for doing that deal
with Doone. Marlene gets in where angels fear to
tread. And this whole thing has been so complicated.
You know, we all hate routine and procedure. Butch
and I were just talking about that, but it has a point.
The good cop needs the bad cop. God, I feel so dumb!"

She looked at Harry's gray face. His eyes flicked
and met hers and then went back to the road. The millions were pouring into the City, but there was little
traffic going out. He said, "It happens. This case was
fucked from the beginning. We were scuffling. I think
you did real good."

"Yeah, well, we'll see how it comes out," said
Marlene grimly. "Speaking of fucked, how did the
booking go? You get any trouble from the suits on it?"

A tiny smile appeared on Bello's face. "No. Everybody was real happy. Or faking it pretty well. Surprised too. Even the A.D.A., Thelmann. He told me he
was in complete charge of every aspect of the case, as
he put it, the dumb fuck! I think it's ass-covering time.
From now on, everybody wants to be on record that
they're playing by the book."

"Did your guys talk yet?"

"They don't know nothing. The usual. A phone call.
Envelopes full of cash from somebody in Philly they
never seen before. They'll cop and do ten or so. They

never heard of Simmons either, and they say they have alibis for the night of."

"Because it was Guma's guys that did Simmons. Guys from L.A., from Jimmy Tona's operation. Butch found out that Chaney was running black money through a hair-goods outfit in L.A. When you caught the arsonists and we realized that we were dealing with two separate sets of hoods, I made the L.A. connection. Butch didn't think that Simmons was killed because of the real estate thing. This tends to confirm it. Something else is going on."

"What?"

"Butch thinks it's sports betting. I'm not sure, but I'm sure Leona knows," said Marlene.

They were driving east on Fulton, through Bed-Stuy. Bello slowed the car and made a turn and brought it to a double-parked stop in front of a dingy brownstone. "What's this?" Marlene asked.

"This is where it happened. That building, 321 Lewis. Where Jim died. It's funny, a month ago you could've broken my arms, I wouldn't have come by here, and now here I am."

"Maybe you're over it," she said.

He gave her a disbelieving look. "I'll never get over it. It's not the kind of thing you get over. What it is, is I still want to die, but I don't want to kill myself. I'm not scared anymore, just empty."

"They say that's a phase you go through."

Bello sniffed. "Yeah, they say that. But they weren't there. You want to hear how it went down? I never told anybody."

"Sure, if you want to tell me."

Bello inhaled a huge volume of air through his nose and let it out with a whoosh through his mouth, as if contemplating a dive through deep water. "I was in the bag. This was when Doris was real bad. She was down

to ninety-five pounds and crying all the time. I had her
at home with a nurse. I couldn't stand it, so I was sucking it down pretty good. Jim was covering for me.

"So we pulled up here, right where we are now. I
was paralyzed. Jim cracks some line and goes in by
himself. We weren't expecting anything—just picking
up this old lady who got herself mugged. The shots
snapped me out of it. Two shots. A minute later, this
black kid comes running out of the building, got a light
blue sweatshirt on.

"I run into the building and there's Jim, shot in the
head. My brain shuts down right there. All I can think
of is, if they find out I let Jim go in there alone and let
the killer run right past me while I'm drunk, I'm off
the force. I was thinking of Doris, how the fuck am I
gonna pay for the treatment if I'm off the force? The
benefits and all. That's what I'm thinking, and Jim's
brains are all over my hands. It shows you . . .

"So I lie. I say I was there. I say I saw the guy. So,
you know what happens when a cop gets it. We roust
every black male between twelve and forty years old in
a ten-block area. I go to lineups, I look in mug books.
He's not there, I say, like I would know him if he was
sitting on my lap.

"This is going on while Doris is dying, so you can
imagine. I went a little crazy, working the street eighteen hours and then going home and sitting up all night
with her. OK, the payoff. I'm on the street one day and
I see a kid in a blue sweatshirt, light blue, the same
color. I follow him, I find out who he is, where he
lives. The kid's got a sheet; he's not a choirboy.

"So I grab him, I drag him into an alley. I work him
over pretty good, and the more I pound him, the more
he's yelling he didn't do it. I must have lost my mind.
The kid rolls over and puts his hand inside his pants.
Before I know it, the kid's dead there, I got my gun in

my hand. He didn't have anything on him. I faked it up with a drop gun. Self-defense.

"There was a stink about it, but they covered it. The kid's no choirboy, like I said. Of course, I got no way of knowing he shot Jim Sturdevant either. They moved me out of Brooklyn, though. Doris passed on two days after that. End of story." He looked at her, but whether it was for approval or condemnation she could not tell. She said, "That's a bad story, Harry. It happened to me, I'd get drunk too."

"But you wouldn't stay drunk," he said.

"Come on, Harry, what do I look like?" replied Marlene with some heat. "You want me to tell you you're damned? Or saved? Am I wearing a black suit and a collar? All I can say is, I care about you, like you are now. You're a good guy and a great cop. I hope you stay sober. When we get to Heaven we'll find out what it all meant. Meanwhile, let's see Mr. Doone."

Doone's house was much as Marlene recalled it— the beat of reggae, the smells, the heavy reek of marijuana, cries of children—although in early morning it was less exotic, less threatening. The furniture and the costumes of Doone's retainers seemed more garish, almost tatty, like the costumes and sets of a play when the overhead work lights are turned on. The big yellow man who answered the door led them silently to a brightly lit dining room.

John Doone was having breakfast (grapefruit; a mash of scrambled eggs, dried fish, rice, and pepper sauce; fried bananas; coffee) dressed in a red brocade robe that sucked all the depth from the planes of his face, making him look like a black paper silhouette. He was not pleased to see Babylon at break of day. Marlene and Bello took chairs, uninvited.

"Is what unu want from me now, gal?" Doone growled. "De deal all done between we."

"Not quite, John," said Marlene. "Things have changed. We know who killed Leona's brother now, and we know why—really why—not what we thought before. Leona knew too, all the time, and she lied about it."

Doone narrowed his eyes and scowled. "Is what all dis to me?"

"If I'm right, Leona is an accessory to murder. She lied to me and she lied to you. She said she was through with Doobie Wallace, the ball player. That's not true. She's protecting him.

"Look, this whole thing isn't about buildings burning down—I mean, the cover-up, and you getting framed, *that* was. But the murder wasn't. That was about cheating on ball games. Simmons didn't want to do it. Wallace did. Simmons found out what Wallace was doing and he was going to talk about it. He must have told Leona, and Leona must have told Wallace, and word must have got back to the gangsters behind the deal through Chaney, the team owner. That's why those two guys were waiting for Simmons in his girlfriend's building."

"Dese de ones in de photo?"

"Yeah, we're pretty sure."

"I say I take care fe dem."

"That's not the point. I need to talk to Leona. More than that, I need her brother's diary."

" 'Er say 'er don got it."

"She's lying about that too. He always had it with him. My husband found out he was carrying it the night he went off with Leona. If she doesn't have it, she knows who does."

"You t'ink so? Fe why de men dead 'er breddah, dem no take it?"

"It's possible. But let's ask Leona."

Doone shook his head. "De breddah—is not my

business, nuh? I take care fe dem two, for stoppin me property."

"Sorry, it *is* your business, John. You're hiding a material witness. That's obstruction. It's a felony. Get her, or let's go back to jail, and this time you won't get out so fast. And besides, you want it all over town that a little girl jerked you around like that? Lying. Running her own game. Losing your dope. Her and her boyfriend are making you look like somebody just came off the farm. A quashie."

Doone sprang to his feet, knocking his chair over with a clatter. Bello tensed and crossed his arms, to get his gun hand closer to his revolver. Marlene didn't move. Doone said, "Don play wit me, gal. I not fe playin wit, yah." He stormed out of the room and returned five minutes later. "One hour," he said, and left again.

Marlene looked at Bello. "Are we supposed to wait here?"

"Beats me," said Bello. "This is your setup. I would've dragged the scumbag down to the station house."

"Well, right now I'm starving," she said. "I left without breakfast. I'm going to see if I can rustle us up something."

She stood up, took several steps, stopped suddenly and then staggered back to her chair. "What's the matter?" asked Bello.

"I don't know. Something down there. I just felt funny."

"Labor pains?"

"It could be. I've been getting these twinges in my middle and my back for the last, oh, twenty minutes. They're not exactly pain."

"You want to go to the hospital?" Bello asked, concern in his voice.

"Nah, it's probably just false labor. It happens a lot with the first kid. Besides, I want to see how this goes down."

Bello nodded and went out of the room, returning after a while carrying a tray with a pot of coffee and a big pile of toast with butter and jam. They waited, chatting companionably, while the life of the house went on around them, as if they did not exist. Marlene discovered she was not that hungry after all.

When John Doone came back, within a few minutes of the promised time, he had Leona Simmons in tow. The young woman had been roughed up: her lip was puffy and the shadow of an incipient shiner loomed under one eye. She had been crying.

Doone tossed a squat, heavy leather diary onto the table. Then he thrust Leona forward and snapped, "Tell dem!"

Leona spoke in a monotone, her voice as lifeless as her eyes. The tale was quickly told, and confirmed Marlene's conjectures in all respects. Doobie Wallace had pursued Leona. They were in love; it was a secret from Marion; that was part of its charm. Then Marion told her that Chaney had proposed a point-shaving scheme. Marion had turned him down, enraged. Chaney had then approached Wallace, who had accepted. Marion, inevitably, found out about it and confronted Wallace. He said he was going to expose the scam.

Wallace had gone to Leona in a panic. Marion had to be convinced not to talk. Leona told Wallace that Marion would be at the Mackey apartment after the San Antonio game. Marion was about to kiss her off, in fact. Leona had lied about the visit being a spontaneous decision. Marion didn't do much spontaneously. When he left the car, Leona had opened the trunk and taken the diary out of his bag and put it in her own large purse. That was Doobie's idea too. She hadn't expected them to kill her brother, just talk to him.

Marlene asked, "Who supplied you with the lie about the stadium deal?"

"Doobie. He said Chaney was always boasting to him about how smart he was, so he told me, anybody ever asked me, say that Marion was worried about that, not about the games."

A neat double cross, thought Marlene. Doobie wasn't in on the stadium deal, and it made a good secondary cover story, after the one about the dope had been exposed.

Leona had begun to cry again, not sobbing but an involuntary flow of tears. Marlene reached into her bag and handed the other woman a package of Kleenex. She said, "Leona, why did Doobie tell you to steal the diary?"

" 'Cause he knew that Marion must have written down all about the shaving stuff. He didn't want it to get out."

"But if they were just going to 'talk' to Marion, as you said, what was the point of that? He'd still be around, and he'd miss the diary and probably get mad. Isn't that true?"

Leona didn't say anything. She just snuffled and blew and every three seconds cast an apprehensive sideways glance at Doone's cast-iron face. Marlene doubted that she would say anything more. She was trembling like a rabbit in the jaws of a wolf, probably from heroin withdrawal as much as fear. She had set her brother up for a hit, and was now running away from that knowledge into some cellar of her mind.

In the silence Marlene mentally assessed the appalling legal situation. Leona was both an accessory to murder and the chief witness. That meant her testimony about the actual crime would be valueless without corroboration, which they did not yet have.

As a testifier to the shaving scheme, she was almost as useless. She was a junkie and heavily involved in the dope trade. This "spontaneous" statement had obviously been beaten out of her. She would have to be arrested, detoxed, and Q. and A.'d formally with the appropriate legalities observed.

On the other hand, they had the diary, the murdered man speaking up from beyond the grave. It could contain the corroboration necessary to support Leona's testimony. The situation was too complex for her to figure it out on the run, and descending once again into the details of building a case after weeks of life in what now seemed a criminal phantasmagoria made her head swim. Butch would have to handle that end. She writhed as another peculiar pang rushed through her.

Focusing her energy, she waited for it to pass, picked up the diary and rose to her feet.

"Leona," she said, "you'll come with us. Mr. Doone, thank you for your public-spirited help. Harry, let's get out of here."

A flicker of something crossed Doone's face. Expectation? Satisfaction? It was too quickly gone and too recondite for Marlene to read accurately. In any case, he said nothing as they walked out, but his impenetrable stare was like a blow to their backs.

"Interesting man, Mr. D.," said Marlene when they were back in the car. Leona sat hunched in the rear seat like a pile of rags.

"Another mutt," said Bello, cranking the car and heading toward Fulton Street and Manhattan.

"More than that," objected Marlene.

"Yeah? He sells dope, he's a mutt. Look, I'll tell what's interesting. You see this shithole of a neighborhood? Bed-Stuy—what a name! It sounds like some kind of running sore. What's interesting is that maybe eighty percent of the people here get up in the morning and go to work, mostly at the shittiest jobs in town, take care of their kids, send them to school, and all the rest. Despite it all. The rest are dirtbags like your friend there. Why do they do it? How the fuck do they find the strength? It amazes me. I worked here twenty years and it still amazes me. I couldn't hack it myself. I give them all the credit in the world."

"What, black people?" asked Marlene, startled by the intensity of his expression.

"Fuckin' A, black people," said Bello. Then, after a while, more softly, "I got that from Jim." Marlene was startled even more when she saw tears welling in his eyes.

They drove in silence for half a mile, and then Marlene asked Bello to patch his car radio through to a land line so she could call Karp.

"Marlene! What the hell!" said Karp when she said hello.

"Relax, it's OK. I'm on my way home. I got the diary and the sister."

"Jesus, Marlene, I've been tearing my hair out here."

"I *said* I'm OK, maybe a labor pain or two."

"What! What!"

"It's fine, that kind of thing could go on for days. Don't you want to hear about what I found out?"

"Yeah, sure, OK, shoot," said Karp, exhibiting a heroic effort at self-control.

Marlene looked back over her shoulder at Leona, who was by now so deep into withdrawal that she would not have paid attention to the Second Coming. She quickly summarized Leona's miserable story.

362   *Robert K. Tanenbaum*

"What about the diary? Any help there?" asked Karp.

"I haven't had a chance to read it. I intend to make some tea and curl up with it as soon as I get back. What are you up to?"

"The Knicks game is tonight. I'm just about ready to go to practice."

"Do we have enough to pick up Wallace?"

"Read the diary. If it corroborates Leona's story, he's dead. But in any case, we have enough to squeeze him. Which I intend to do." His tone changed. "Listen, you're sure you're OK?"

"Yes. Labor lasts for days sometimes with the first kid. They're still very far apart."

Karp relented and signed off.

Bello dropped her in front of the loft, behind a huge truck delivering spools of wire to the factory in her building.

"You're sure you're OK by yourself?" asked Bello.

Marlene smiled. "Honestly, between you and Butch . . . I'll be fine. Don't worry. Take care of the witness."

"I don't know," said the detective doubtfully. "These guys, the shooters. What'd you say their names were?"

"Carmine Fraschetti and Joey Castello. Why?"

"We got APBs out on them, yes?"

"So I hear. Look, Harry, relax! Like you said before, it's ass-covering time. This is too far gone for threats. Those guys are back in la-la land or beyond—Palermo even."

"But watch yourself until we know for sure, hey?"

Marlene nodded and kissed his cheek and hauled herself heavily to the curb.

A man watched her enter the building and walked down to a phone booth on Canal Street and made a call. Carmine Fraschetti listened quietly for a moment, grunted acknowledgment, and hung up. His next move was clear, but he was still oppressed by a sense of fore-boding.

Don't rock the boat was Fraschetti's motto. His whole life had been devoted to insuring that when the boat ever did get rocked, the vibrations were damped as quickly and elegantly as possible. This fixing basketball games was boat rocking in a big way. It was going to rip tens of millions out of bookies and players across the country and from the people those books worked for and from big-time players who were well connected.

Fraschetti had been sent east when Chaney had called Tona in a screaming panic, to make sure the deal went through, and more important, that it was not exposed, and most important, that Jimmy Tona was in no way associated with it. Now things were completely out of hand, in all three ways.

Fraschetti got out of his chair and went to the bathroom. He washed his face and combed his hair with a wet comb. He buttoned his shirt collar and pulled up his tie, slipped into his suit jacket and then a tan poplin-lined raincoat. He cleaned his glasses and went into the bedroom to get Joey.

Jimmy Tona liked the young Castello, for reasons that Carmine had never been able to see, and the kid was connected to some heavy hitters, family people. Jimmy had said, "Take the kid, maybe he'll settle down, maybe he'll learn something." So he took the kid, which was why things were in the mess they were in.

What the plan was, they were supposed to lift the player, take him to a quiet spot and make it look like a robbery. But as soon as they got in the elevator, Joey starts in on him, riding him, not being reasonable at all. The player gave him some lip. Before Fraschetti knew what was happening, Joey had shot the player one through the chest.

So there was one thing at least he could teach him, how to clean up after a hit in the wrong place. A royal pain in the ass. Then all of a sudden it looked like everybody knew their business, on top of which there was Chaney calling every day, screaming at Jimmy that it was all going to shit, and then Jimmy yelling at him, fix it, fix it.

Joey was on the bed, watching *Jeopardy* on a small black-and-white television. "Let's go, Joey," said Carmine. "She's back and alone."

Castello groaned and heaved himself up. "This shithole! Can we do one fucking thing? Can we get a fucking decent TV in here?"

"We ain't gonna be here much longer, Joey. We just gotta clean up and then we're home."

Carmine pondered this while Joey got himself together, grumbling and cursing. Cleaning up. The Ciampi woman had to go, that was first, and pick up that goddamn diary. The people who were Fraschetti's usual clients did not keep diaries, and its existence had amazed him when he had learned of it that day. So, Ciampi, that was one; the sister, two, but she was on ice with the cops. He would have to arrange an inside job for that one. Three, Chaney had to go down. He would do that one himself. Then Wallace, four. Maybe the kid could handle that. Maybe if Wallace was set up in a barrel of cement on the deck of a boat, the kid could shove him in the water. Four, that wasn't so bad. The D.A., the big guy, they could leave. Once the others were gone, he couldn't do shit.

Joey was ready at last. Carmine cast a doubtful eye over his ensemble: razor-cut hair, leather car coat, open to show the gold chains, the gold ID bracelet, the gold

Oyster, the pointy shoes. He needed a light-up sign that said "MAFIOSO," was all. But what could you do?

They walked down the musty stairs of the building they had been sheltered in and out onto Mulberry Street. The place had no amenities, but, more to the point, neither did it have any eyes or tongues living in it. When they left, no one would have ever seen them. Carmine paused to light a Macanudo Sovereign.

"Hey, Fish—" said Joey.

"Don't call me Fish, Joey, I told you a million times. Carmine."

"OK, *Carmine*, this bitch—I get a crack at her before we do her, right?"

"Right, Joey. Jimmy says, make it look like niggers did it. But first we make sure we got the goddamn notebook. And don't take all day."

"Yo, Fi—Carmine. She gonna suck mah dick, though. That OK with you, *Carmine*?"

Carmine said nothing, but pulled up the collar of his raincoat, and chewed at his cigar, and wished for the ten-thousandth time that he was back in L.A.

Marlene's plans to sip tea and read Marion Simmons's diary were upset by the simple fact that while she had the diary, now sitting open on her desk, she was out of tea. She was by no means a great tea drinker, but when she had to have tea, nothing else would do—not coffee, not wine, not soup, gave the comfort of tea.

Comfort was needed. The pangs in her belly that she had so casually brushed off at Doone's had increased in intensity and frequency. A cold prickle of fear raced up her arms and across her scalp. Wait to be sure. Another hour at least.

OK, calm, calm, she told herself. She walked over to

the lift shaft and shouted down it, "Stu! Larry! Are you home?"

Two voices called up cheerily that they were.

That was what she would do. Walk carefully down the stairs to Larry and Stu's, where they would make much of her and feed her tea, and then Larry would tell her what was going on, and then she would borrow a full teapot and come back and read the diary.

Something to bring—she couldn't keep going down there empty-handed. That was it! Near the door lay a bundle of wire clothes hangers. Stu had sent the word out that he needed wire hangers for a big sculpture he was doing, and everyone he knew had been delivering bundles of them for days.

Marlene picked up the hangers, grabbed her key, and walked out her front door, at which point Joey Castello stepped from around a bend in the hallway, grabbed her, and clapped a hand around her astonished mouth and pulled her back into the loft.

CHAPTER

eighteen

He slammed her up against the wire screen that guarded the lift motor, twice, violently. The bundle of hangers dropped from her hand and scattered at her feet. He had one hand over her mouth and one twined painfully in the thick hair at the back of her neck.

It was the younger one who had her, she could see that plainly through the blur of tears. The older one had locked the door and was moving through the loft, checking it out.

The young one was grinning at her. His eyes were glowing with enjoyment. "You yell, bitch, I'll break your neck. You ain't gonna yell, are you? Are you?" Another yank at her hair to emphasize the question. She shook her head. His smile broadened and he took his hand away from her mouth.

The older man came back from his tour. "Save yourself some trouble, lady," he said. "Just give us the diary."

"What diary?" she said. The younger one savagely twisted her hair and she cried out involutarily. She felt a hot wetness seep down her thigh. God! she thought, I'm pissing myself.

The older man said, "Get it out of her. It'll take a fucking year to toss this place. You could hide a phone book here. I'll do the rest."

Marlene heard him stomp off and then the sounds of smashing things. Her captor was talking to her. "Where is it? Come on, you're gonna give it up sooner or later. Make it easy on yourself. Come on. What's your name, hey? What, the silent treatment? You don't like me? Hey, everybody likes Joey."

He smashed her across the face, forehand, backhand. She felt his rings cut into her cheek. "You like that?" he asked. "You wanna be a tough guy, hey? Hey, I'm a tough guy too. I got a knife here. You wanna see your baby? I'll do a delivery right here, a whachama-callit. You won't have to stretch your cunt."

As he talked, he was twisting her hair tighter, pulling her downward. She was on her knees. She could feel the wire hangers digging into her through the thin cotton of her jeans. "Oh, yeah, you're gonna talk to me. You're gonna tell me everything I want to know, but first we're gonna have some fun." He told her in some detail about the fun they were gonna have.

While this was going on, part of Marlene's mind was cranking away, under the pain and the fear. They were trashing the place, to make it look like a rob-bery, which meant they were not going to leave her alive, which meant there was no point in playing for time. She knew now without a doubt that these men had murdered Francine Del Fazio. She wondered briefly why they wanted her to tell them where the di-ary was. It was right there on her desk, open.

Then it hit her: the old purloined letter. Nobody looking for a secret, hidden, valuable diary sees a diary open on a desk. She felt the faint stirrings of hope. If she couldn't outsmart these bozos ...

He was saying, "Look at it! Open your fucking eyes, cunt!"

She focused her gaze in front of her. He had taken out his penis and it was staring her in the face, faintly twitching, erect. Her head jerked reflexively in surprise, and he tightened his grip. "I bet you never seen one like that before," he said, laughing.

It was true. She hadn't. Joey Castello had two slanted eyes tattooed in blue on the head of his penis, one on either side of the slit. "You like that, hey? Start sucking, bitch!" he said.

This was a break, thought Marlene. The other guy was down at the bedroom end of the loft, wrecking the closets. If she could break this asshole's grip, it was a clear run to the lift shaft. He would have to be distracted. Marlene imagined that having the end of one's penis bitten off would be a sufficient distraction. It would have to be one swift, devastating bite.

She licked her dry lips and opened her mouth.

At that moment the lift motor roared into life and threw its belt. The loose belt flapping at three hundred rpm filled the loft with a sound like a machine gun. Joey stiffened, screamed, "What the fuck ...!" and twisted his body to see the source of the incredible sound. Marlene felt the fierce burning in her scalp ease off as his grip relaxed. She gathered her feet under her.

Then the great alarm bell went off, eighteen inches above Joey Castello's head. They had bells like that in prison and in places where robberies have gone bad. He let go of Marlene's hair and fumbled in his waistband for his pistol.

Marlene rose to her feet. Her movements seemed slow to her, too slow, like something in a bad dream. She had a bunch of wire hangers in her hand. With all her strength she whipped the ends of the hangers across Joey's fast-fading erection, then brought them backhanded across his eyes.

Joey let out a noise like a semi-trailer full of live hogs locking its brakes on a twelve-degree grade. Carmine was at this moment up in the sleeping loft emptying Marlene's jewelery case artistically across the bed. In an instant he absorbed what had happened and dropped down the ladder in two jumps. He could move fast for a big middle-aged man. He thought he could beat the goddamn woman to the door of the loft.

To his great surprise, however, she did not head toward the door but away from it. He thought, Ah shit, she's going to throw herself down the shaft. That fucking kid! He pounded after her.

Marlene felt like she was running through water. Another spasm struck and she bent almost double as she ran, her jeans soaked to the ankles with amniotic fluid. She was no longer in any doubt as to what was happening to her.

Joey was still bellowing behind her, scrabbling, trying to get to his feet, comfort his bleeding organ, and pull a heavy automatic out of his waistband at the same time, without the benefit of clear vision. As a result he stumbled into the path of his onrushing partner, and they both went crashing down on the rough wooden floor.

Marlene grabbed the diary off her desk, shoved it into the elastic waistband of her maternity jeans and swung out onto the ladder. A pang took her midway. She bore down and panted, as she had been taught, although hanging out over a fifty-foot drop was not an approved Lamaze position.

It passed, and she completed her descent. She staggered into Stuart Franciosa's studio, swung shut the heavy steel doors to the lift shaft, shot the two securing bolts, and fell to the dusty floor, groaning.

The sculptor heard the noise of the clanging doors and hurried out from the apartment section of the loft. He stopped when he saw Marlene. "My God! What's wrong?" he cried.

"Killers! Gangsters! Lock the front door!" she gasped.

"What? What are you saying? My God, you're bleeding. And you're all wet—"

"Stuart! Lock the fucking door!" Marlene shrieked, then yelled, "Larry!"

Larry Bouchard came out of the apartment at a trot, took in the scene at a glance, and quickly knelt beside Marlene. Franciosa went to throw the locks on the loft's steel front door, also dropping a broad steel bar across thick brackets welded to the door and the metal door frame. Then he went back to where Larry was helping Marlene to her feet.

"Will somebody please tell me what's going on?" he said.

"Stuart, get the shutters," said Marlene, "the ones to the fire escape. Bar them. And call 911. Burglary in progress."

Franciosa didn't move. "The windows? I'm sorry, but will you—"

Bouchard broke into this dithering in a tone of voice that Stuart had never heard him use: "Stuart! Do what she says! Move! I mean *stat*!"

Stunned, Stuart raced off to draw and bolt the steel shutters giving on the fire escape. The loft was now as physically secure as any place in Manhattan that was not owned by a major bank. He rang 911, waited long enough to have been murdered, raped, and pillaged half a dozen times, gave his message, and dashed back to the apartment section.

Larry had moved Marlene to his bedroom and laid her on his antique four-poster, on which she now

writhed and groaned. With the exception of some small
sculptures of Stuart's, Larry Bouchard's bedchamber
was a reasonable imitation of Scarlett O'Hara's.

"What happened to her?" Stuart asked.

Larry was working Marlene's jeans and underwear
off her legs. "Well, Stuart," he said, "that's a long
story. You see, first the little boy bee goes to the
flower . . ."

"She's having a baby? Here?"

"It's a possibility."

"I'll call an ambulance," cried Stuart.

Marlene uttered a louder hoot. Her face was con-
torted and damp with sweat mixed with blood from the
cut on her cheek. She said weakly, "It's really labor,
isn't it?"

Larry rolled his eyes. "No, baby, it's just a little acid
indigestion."

"Christ! How long do I have?"

"Hard to tell yet, sugar," said the nurse. He turned to
his friend. "I need some help here," he said, his voice
unstressed and workmanlike.

"You want me to boil water? I can't believe this is
happening."

"Yes, boil water, as a matter of fact. Life follows art,
don't y'know? I need that vaginal speculum I gave
you, and the O.B. forceps, and some big hemostats.
You know what they look like? Good. Get the clay off
them and throw them in the spaghetti pot with water to
cover. Put the lid on and weight it with something
heavy, like a brick. Turn the flame on high. When the
cover starts to jump around, it's done."

Marlene yelled again and Larry looked at his wrist-
watch. "My, my, my!" he said. "Pant, honey, pant your
precious heart out. That's so good!" He washed the
cuts on Marlene's face and swabbed her brow and
slipped out.

Stuart went to do his companion's bidding. As he picked the instruments from his worktable, he heard a heavy weight being thrown at his door, then the sound of violent cursing. He tried to ignore it and went into the kitchen.

Labor was a surprise to Marlene, as it always is, even to women who have had a number of children. She had heard that the pain of labor was not really pain but something unique, and she found it so. She indeed saw wonders, which she would never tell anyone about, nor would she remember them herself. Sirens sounded, far off.

Larry returned with a steaming pot, which he placed on the floor. He placed a cloth-wrapped suture set on a cherrywood sideboard, broke the seals, snapped on rubber gloves, and used the large hemostat in the set to pull hot instruments from their sterile bath. He laid these on the suture set's sterile green cloth to cool.

"OK, sugar, let's take a peekie, shall we?" Marlene felt the warm instrument slide into her. "Christ on a crutch!" exclaimed Larry.

Marlene felt a pang of pure terror. "What's wrong?"

"Not a thing, sweetness. We're just movin' *molto rapido* heah." He removed the speculum. "We're lookin at full dilation. You're in second stage. Would you tell me what the *hell* y'all were doin' durin' the first stage of this heah labor?"

"I was interviewing a witness."

"And weren't you having contractions?"

"I guess, but they were no big ... aaagh!"

"OK, honey, let it through, just pant, just pant."

Carmine cursed and picked himself off the floor and raced down to the lift shaft. He descended the ladder, pushed against the steel door unavailingly, and climbed back up to the loft. Joey was doubled over, clutching his crotch and moaning an unimaginative string of obscenities, which were nearly lost in the continuing sound of the bell.

"Get up!" commanded the older man.

"I got a splinter in my dick, Fish," whined Joey. "I'm all cut up. My eye hurts, it's all blurry."

Fraschetti said, "It's Carmine, not Fish. OK, get up, stop crying!" He heaved Joey to his feet. "Stand up! C'mon, be a man, goddammit! Put yourself away there. The silly bitch took the diary. We got to get into that loft downstairs."

But this was easier said than done. When they arrived at the door of the loft below, Joey cursed and heaved his body against it, and kicked it, and yelled. He drew his gun and would have shot at the locks had Carmine not restrained him. "Joey, it's a steel door, in a steel frame. We got a brick hallway here. You can't shoot the locks off a steel door. You'll get yourself a ricochet in the head. Besides, the building's full of people."

"I don't give a flying fuck—" began Joey, and stopped when they heard the sound of pounding footsteps. Two Latino men in greasy blue overalls came up the stairs. They stared at the two gangsters curiously. Joey was about to brandish his gun at them and ask them what they were looking at when he felt his gun arm gripped with ferocious strength by the older man.

Carmine smiled and gestured to the locked door. He said, "Repo."

The word was familiar. The workmen grinned and went upstairs to fix their hoist. The sound of sirens penetrated the building. Fraschetti said, "Come on, we're out of here."

"But, fuck! What about—"

"We'll do her later," said Carmine. "We know where she lives."

* * *

"Alert Guinness," said Larry Bouchard. He was crouched at the foot of his bed, looking at Marlene Ciampi's vulva and the crowning head of her nearly born child.

"What's the matter?" asked Stuart, hovering nervously in the background.

"Nothing, just fast is all. This child wants out. Bear down now, babe. Good, once more. Good, we have rotation. Stuart, be a darlin' and go fill the blue dishpan with three inches of tepid water—skin warm, mind—and get my old Black Watch plaid flannel from my closet. Oh, and drop an alligator clip in a cup of rubbin' alcohol and bring it heah."

Franciosa had barely returned with these items when there was renewed pounding on the door and shouts of "Police!"

"Would you deal with that, sweet thing?" said Larry. "Ah am otherwise engaged." Stuart hurried away. Marlene was red as a Coke sign, breathing through clenched teeth. She heard Larry say, "Push, push!" and she found breath to say, "I *am* pushing, goddammit!"

Larry said, "One more, good! One more, head, and one more, one more, here's the little shoulders. Get yo catcher's mitt, Bouchard! One more, and, well, it's a girl!"

Carmine and Joey made it around the corner of Crosby and Broome before the blue-and-white arrived, but not that much before. It had been many a year since Carmine had literally run from the cops, and he did not like it at all. He regarded his companion with unconcealed distaste.

"Oooh, shit!" said Joey, "I gotta see a doctor. The bitch ruined me."

"In a while," said Carmine. "Look, here's what we

got to do. I'll hang around here and see what goes down. You go get the car and bring it back here and pick me up."

"What? Hey, how come I gotta go get the car? I can hardly fuckin' walk here."

At this, Carmine turned on the younger man a look of cold malice, a gaze as inhuman and terrifying as that of a mako shark. *That's* why they call him the Fish, thought Joey vaguely, and before he really knew it, he was halfway to Lafayette Street.

Carmine watched him go with relief. He turned and walked in the opposite direction, toward Broadway. Carmine's other motto was: *When in doubt, get the fuck out.* This whole operation had been under some *maledizione* from the beginning, and he had stayed with it against his better judgment.

Something else would have to be arranged to cover Jimmy Tona. As he walked, the germ of an idea began to grow. A subordinate would have to be sacrificed. Carmine could think of several candidates. Whack him out, and saddle him postmortem with the point-shaving mess. Of course, Chaney would have to be whacked too, but he could arrange that by phone. He began filling in the details. It could work, and the beauty part was, he would never have to come back here, and never have to screw around with that goddamn woman again, the witch. As for Joey, he would have to fend for himself.

He hailed a cab on Broadway and got in. "La Guardia Airport," said Freshie the Fish.

The Chevy was parked on Lafayette. Never park where you live when you're on a job, was what the Fish said. Joey was sore and tired and resentful, and as he walked, his limited brain power was entirely occupied with thinking about what he was going to do to that cunt when he got hold of her again. Fuckin' go in with the fuckin' knife right away, he thought, get her in the fuckin' gut and twist. Let's see her fuckin' try something then.

These pleasant musings were interrupted by the sight of the blue Chevy, sitting where they had left it at Lafayette off Prince, but additionally decorated with several parking tickets under the wipers, and on the hood, a young black man in a long coat and a red-green-black knitted tam.

Joey bristled and moved toward the car. "Hey, fuckhead! Off the fuckin' car!" he shouted.

The young man did not move. Joey approached more closely. The youth just stared at him, expressing nothing. "Hey! You fuckin' deaf? I said get your ass off of my car!"

At that, the young man slid off the hood, opened his coat and shoved the barrel of an Uzi submachine gun into Joey's belly. A large yellow man who had been leaning against a building hustled forward, gave Joey a swift and expert pat-down, yanked his automatic pistol away, took his car keys, opened the door of the Chevy, and threw Joey face forward into the backseat, like a duffel bag.

"So, am Ah to be introduced to the new person?" asked Larry Bouchard. He was tucking in the bottom of the fresh sheets he had laid on the bed. Marlene was lying back on crisp, newly cased pillows with her eyes closed. Her daughter, wrapped in a soft flannel shirt, sucked noisily at her breast. On her face was the traditional tired but blissful smile.

"Lucy Dora Maria Theresa Karp. Is that a mouthful or what?"

"Ah *love* Lucy, so to speak. A nice old-fashioned name. Why did you pick it?"

"Personal reasons at first. But also, as it turned out, today is St. Lucy's day. The winter solstice, the shortest day. And, of course, St. Lucy was Sicilian too. A beautiful virgin. Her violator complimented her on the beauty of her eyes, so she plucked them out and had them sent to him. My kind of girl—her intercession is asked for ailments of the eye. Get it? Dora is for Butch's mom and Maria Theresa is my dad's mom."

"Charming," said Larry. "You'll be wanting to tell Butch. Where is he?"

"Playing basketball. The son of a bitch," said Marlene and drifted off again.

This was not true, the basketball-playing part. Butch Karp was in fact in an interrogation room at the offices of Manhattan North homicide on West 57th. In the room also were Harry Bello, Sonny Dunbar, Roland Hrcany, a police stenographer, and the man the two officers had just brought in, Doobie Wallace.

Wallace smiled when he saw Karp, and walked across the room toward him, not swaggering exactly, but at ease, with a loose-jointed stride, bouncing off his toes, with the toes turned outward.

"My man!" he said and was at the point of extending his hand for a high-five when the expression on Karp's face registered. It was not a high-five expression. Wallace converted the gesture to a wave.

"Hey, Butch, what's this about? We got a game starting soon."

"Sit down, Doobie," said Karp.

Wallace pulled out a slatted wooden armchair and sat in it, crossing both his legs and his arms. Karp looked at him intently, as if trying to psyche out which way he was going to break for the basket.

"So? What's this about? They said you all had some questions."

"Yes. Look, Doobie, first let's forget about the game. You're not playing pro ball anymore."

Wallace smiled, as if at humor. "What're you, joking? What is this, man?"

"We know about the point shaving, Doobie," said Karp. "All about it."

Wallace's smile stayed on his mouth, but Karp observed something else creep into his eyes. He was game, though: "What do you mean, point shaving? You think *I'm* shaving points? Me?"

Karp sighed. He said, "I wish we could avoid this for once. You're going to deny what we know perfectly well. You know we know or we wouldn't have brought you in. Then we show you how we know. You make up lies. We catch you in the lies. You admit to a piece of it. We break your story down some more. It's such a tedious pain in the ass—"

"What the fuck are you talking about, Karp?" asked Wallace, still smiling. "Hey, now I get it: that's how come you got to play on the team. You were investigating! Hot damn! We knew it wasn't 'cause you could play any."

Karp rubbed his face. "OK, we'll do it the hard way. Let me say one thing first, though. You've never done this before. I've done it a lot. As you point out, I'm not the basketball player that you are. Maybe I could have been once, but that's neither here nor there. You have the talent, and you've put in a lot of work.

"But I'm the same way at this, what we're doing now. Let's say you're one of the ten best pro basketball players in the country. OK, I'm one of the ten best homicide prosecuting attorneys in the country. I say that not to blow my own horn, but just to let you understand what you're getting into, and let you judge your chances of coming out ahead. You still want to go one on one?"

Wallace was staring at Karp evenly, but he was not smiling anymore.

Karp waited a full minute in silence, and then he began.

"This is what we know. Sometime in early November Howard Chaney came to Marion Simmons to solicit his cooperation in a point-shaving scheme. Chaney had agreed to the scheme in return for funds from a California mobster named Jimmy Tona, which he needed to pay off a Philadelphia mobster named Dom Scarfi, who had been feeding him money to keep his enterprises alive, especially a scheme to sell land to the city for a new stadium. That's been the point of confusion in this whole case. Who could have believed that there were two entirely separate Mafia scams involved, connected only by Howard Chaney?

"In any case, Simmons refused. Then Chaney went to you. You agreed—"

"You can't prove that!" snapped Wallace.

"Please let me finish," said Karp. "You'll have your chance. I only note that you say, 'You can't prove that' instead of 'I didn't.' It's as good as an admission of guilt. And I *can* prove it, of course.

"As I said, you agreed. You began to shave points. Simmons found out. How couldn't he have known, given what he knew about Chaney and what he understood about basketball? Shaving is hard to detect unless you know it's going on; then it's as obvious as daylight. When *I* knew you had to be shaving, it hit me right in the face.

"Simmons confronted you and said he was going to expose the scam. You went to Chaney in a panic, and he called Tona in a panic, and Tona sent a pair of killers to clean things up.

"The only problem you had was that Simmons kept a diary. You had to snatch that when you killed him.

Luckily you had one advantage. You were involved with Leona Simmons. She told you where Simmons was going to be and when. You got the word to the killers, through Chaney. And she took the diary.

"Leona gave you up, Doobie. We got all that from her."

Wallace snorted derisively. "You gonna believe that bitch? She's a junkie anyway, and she's trying to get back at me. I blew her off, man."

"And we've got the diary, *man,*" said Karp. "It's all down there in black and white, the whole story, in Marion Simmons's own hand." He was guessing, but it was a reasonable shot and it went home.

"Bullshit! You got nothing! She burned it."

Karp allowed a moment of silence for the implications of this outburst to work on Wallace's mind. Then he asked softly, "When did you find that out, Doobie? Did she tell you? Did you tell her to burn it?"

Wallace opened his mouth to say something, then closed it, then licked his lips. He said, "Um, no, I never told her to. She, ah, happened to mention it."

"Oh? You spoke to her after the murder? And she told you she had burnt her brother's diary? Why would she say that? Did she also mention that she had seen him shot and that she could identify the killer?"

"Ah ... no! It wasn't like that," said Wallace. He was sweating now, and his knees under the table were wagging and bouncing.

"What was it like?" asked Karp. "Take your time. A good plausible lie takes awhile to figure out. We have all day."

"I got to get over to the Garden," said Wallace weakly.

"Uh-uh, Doobie," said Karp. "That's finished. You're out of basketball at the very least. No game. No career. No salary. No endorsements. No autographs.

Your life has become real simple. All you have to think about is how much jail time you're going to do. Cooperate with me, and it's likely to be less. Give me a hard time, and keep telling these stupid lies, and it's likely to be more."

Time for a change of pace. Karp said conversationally, "You know, we were getting along real well when I was with the team. Filling me in about Marion and all. You said he didn't use dope and I believed you. You could have lied. You could have said that he lived on coke and sold it on playgrounds. I'd have believed you. Maybe it was because you didn't want me to follow the dope trail to Leona. You thought she might crack, right?"

Wallace shrugged and gestured assent.

"Does that mean yes?"

"Yeah, right!" Wallace snapped.

"Great! See, it's easy to tell the truth. And it comes out anyway, you know. You've already made one damaging admission when you admitted that you told her to burn the diary—"

"I didn't *tell* her," cried Wallace, his voice unsteady. "It was just a suggestion, like, there might be embarrassing stuff in it that might hurt his family. . . ."

He faded off. Karp said, "Yes, we know how much you were concerned about his family. And, by the way, *you* never said you told her to burn it. I said that, and you just confirmed it. Swish. Two points. I told you I was good at this. Want to play some more?"

Wallace was making trapped animal moves, the twitching, the darting eyes. Karp had seen it all before. He's going to ask for his lawyer in a second, he thought.

"I don't want to talk to you anymore. I want to see my lawyer."

"Always an excellent decision," Karp said, rising

from his chair. "This interview is over." He turned to Bello. "Harry, book him. Second-degree murder is the top count. I'll draw up the rest of the charges later."

"Hey, wait . . ." said Wallace. They ignored him and began to talk about assembling the various witnesses and physical evidence in the case.

"Hey, wait!" said Wallace with more volume. "I didn't kill anybody. What is this murder stuff."

Karp turned back to him. "I'm sorry? Oh, the top count. It's murder in the second degree. Your lawyer will explain the charges and what they mean. OK, get him out of here."

Bello grabbed Wallace's arm, but he jerked it away. "I didn't kill anybody. I didn't even know they were gonna kill him. Howard said they were just gonna talk to him, maybe rough him up. Just so he wouldn't tell about the shaving. I swear, that's the truth."

"Then why did you tell Leona to take his diary?" Karp shot back.

"Because I wanted to see what he was saying. What he knew and all."

"And maybe find something incriminating, some indiscretions you could use to pressure him not to talk?"

"Yeah, yeah, that was it!" said Wallace enthusiastically. And then he sobered considerably, as he realized that every single thing that he had told himself he would not give away, he had given away, and hadn't gotten anything in return. He looked at Karp and realized that Karp knew that too, that Karp could read it in his eyes.

Karp made a little hook-shot movement and said, "Swish. Game's over."

Later, after Wallace had been taken away for booking, Karp and Hrcany were sitting in the squad room, Roland because he liked hanging around cops, and Karp because there was a phone there, which he was using to call the loft every five minutes. There was no answer and he was getting increasingly worried.

"Why do you think he did it?" Hrcany asked.

"Who?"

"Who do you think? Wallace. I can see it, a college kid gets a new car, a few bucks, but what did he need?"

"He didn't do it for need. I think he did it because Chaney told him to, one, and because it was a way of getting over on Marion. He thought of himself as a hired entertainer. The boss says throw games, so he throws games. Marion took the game seriously, and it made Doobie feel like a clown.

"What does it matter? As for the hit, it was no skin off his ass if Marion got it. Guys like Doobie like to get away with stuff. An intelligent man with no morals. You want to know the bottom line? Pro athletes shouldn't be cynics. They're paid good money to be kids forever, playing games; they should keep their bargain."

Karp dialed again, waited until the machine kicked on, and slammed the phone down with a curse.

"What's the problem? Marlene?" Hrcany asked.

"Yeah, she said something about labor pains this afternoon, and now I can't get her. Shit! Maybe she had to go to the hospital."

"Is there somebody she would call?"

"Damn it, you're right! Stu and Larry would know."

He dialed another number and heard Stu's voice.

"Stu? Did Marlene leave a message or anything? I can't get her at home."

"That's because she's here."

"Oh, great! She's OK, right?"

"Fine. Congratulations, by the way."

Karp thought he was referring to cracking the case

and had a moment of confusion. "Huh! How did you find out?"

"Find out? It happened right here." A pause. "Nobody told you?"

"Told me what?"

"You have a daughter," said Stuart. "Stu and Larry's place: we deliver."

"What! You couldn't get her to the hospital?"

"It was a complex situation. If I were you, I'd get over here right now. And bring flowers."

CHAPTER
nineteen

Two weeks later, Harry Bello stood by the baptismal font of St. Joseph's Church in Queens, and promised to help bring up Lucy Karp in the Catholic faith, and on her behalf renounced Satan and all the spiritual forces of wickedness that rebel against God, as did Marlene herself. Karp, while no friend of the spiritual forces of wickedness, was not asked to so affirm. He had known at some level for months that his daughter was not going to be a Jewish princess, but at the sacred moment, the wages of his exogamy rested heavily upon him, a real and unpleasant surprise to this generally unbelieving man.

At the reception afterward, Karp drank more than he was used to of his father-in-law's strong home-made red, and engaged in a long and intricate conversation with a muster of ancient Ciampis about the doings of the Carpa family of Sheepshead Bay and Valledolmo, of which he was a supposed scion.

Marlene rescued him with a plate of delicacies.

"How're you doing?" she asked.

"I'm beat. God has that effect on me. I notice Stupenagel showed. She's forgiven you, I presume."

"Oh, yeah. The Stupe doesn't hold a grudge. Also, my statue impressed her. She called to rave over it."

"Statue? What statue?"

"Oh, nothing. I modeled for Stu, and the bronze showed up in a window of a chichi gallery on Prince."

"Yeah? What kind of statue?"

"Oh, just a little study," said Marlene hurriedly. "Yes, we're buddies again. She sent a little porringer from Tiffany's. Besides, I forgave *her* when I came out on the terrace at our freshman ball and she was sucking off my date in the bushes. She owes me."

"I guess. She's spending a lot of time with Guma."

"Oh, they're apparently an item. They had a quickie on our stairs the day Guma ID'd Frankie Mack."

"Jesus! They look like a bull terrier leashed to the Chrysler Building."

Marlene giggled. "Yes, cute. But I'm afraid the Goom is in for heartbreak. She's been pumping him for inside stuff on this case. That's why her stories have been front-page stuff. 'A source in the D.A.'s office.' When it's over, she be gone."

"I want to go home," said Karp.

They took a cab back to the city. The baby was good as gold. As Marlene said, she was Friday's child, loving and giving.

"Harry stood up, that was good," mused Marlene sleepily. She was still not a hundred percent, and the cab was one of those cozy big ones.

"Did you think he wouldn't?"

"I don't know; he seems so sad and empty. Like the City in the wintertime. 'Tis the year's midnight and it is the day's," said Marlene, "Lucy's, who scarce seven hours herself unmasks; the sun is spent and now his flasks send forth light squibs, no constant rays. The world's whole sap is sunk—damn, something something something, *drunk*; whither, as to the bed's-feet, life is shrunk, dead and interr'd; yet all these seem to laugh, compar'd with me, who am their Epitaph."

"What's that?" asked Karp.

" 'A Nocturnal upon St. Lucy's Day, Being the Shortest Day.' By John Donne."

"The joint artist? He writes poetry too?"

"No, that's *Doone*. John Donne is dead, of natural causes as far as I know. You know—he wrote, 'And therefore never send to know for whom the bell tolls, it tolls for thee.' "

"Uh-uh, that was Hemingway. I saw the movie."

Marlene looked long at him, and then laughed and hugged his arm. "My Renaissance man!" she said. "Sports. The law. Literature. He bestrides them all." Then she sobered and went back to her previous theme. "These last weeks have been very strange, have you noticed that? We've both been out of our normal element, in the grip of weird forces. I'm gestating a child—full—and everybody in the case is empty in some way.

"Some fill it by suffering, like Harry. You filled it by being heroic. Some fill it with evil, like Chaney, or Wallace, or the killers. They can't stand it, the completeness. Harmony. And then the business about Lucy here, and St. Lucy . . . I'm not saying this right, but there's a fabric to it, some invisible machinery behind our lives. Don't you ever have that feeling?"

"When I do," said Karp, "it gives me a pounding headache and I take two aspirin and go to bed."

Marlene laughed. "Anyway, that poem . . . I thought of it when I first met Harry—the zero person. But life renews itself, also as in the poem, by love. He bottomed out around St. Lucy's Day, and now he's a godfather and Lucy's born, and the bad guys are . . . are the bad guys defeated? Has Chaney showed up yet?"

"No," said Karp. "I'm not looking to see him soon.

He's either living cheap and far away under an assumed name, or playing a long, slow game of two-
handed pinochle with Jimmy Hoffa under a highway."

"With little Francine Ciccolino too," said Marlene
sadly.

"You think they got her?"

"I have a bad feeling about it. I'm fighting the guilt.
On the other hand, if I hadn't had her on my mind, I
probably wouldn't have pushed it so far on the Leona
Simmons thing, which was the key to the whole mess.
Part of the invisible fabric. But what about the other
bad guys?"

"The grand jury will indict Logan and D'Amalia on
the real estate thing," said Karp. "They're finished politically. Frank Mackey'll probably beat an obstruction
charge. Jimmy Tona, I understand, is in a lot of trouble
with the Feds and with some of his own people. He
was named in the diary, and that's public knowledge
now thanks to our victim. Tona had some guy popped
and blamed this whole point-shaving mess on him, but
it didn't sell. Those guys in L.A. watch too many movies. Doobie'll do a lot of time. So will Leona. Not
much, but some.

"Closer to home, I guess I didn't tell you, Shelly's
out on his ass, canned from the D.A. When I showed
him our evidence, he literally cried—the whole works,
blubbering, with snot bubbles and all. When he calmed
down, he bitched that 'Sandy' made him do it. I explained to him that if he wanted to implicate the D.A.,
he was welcome to do so, but it would mean disbarment at best, and probably a stretch inside. He got the
point."

"You covered for Bloom?" asked Marlene incredulously.

"Of course. He's a scumbag, but he's our scumbag.
I got a signed statement from Shelly, though. Sandy

was just doing a power-boy favor for some friends, the ass!"

"Did you go see him?"

"No. But he knows I know."

"Good. That means you'll get the bureau chief job back."

"Assuming I want it. I'm tired of running a half-assed homicide bureau out of a petty-crime operation. There should be a real bureau again."

"That could be arranged."

"It could, if I wanted to turn blackmailer. What a pain in the butt this is!"

Marlene quickly changed the subject. "What about the hit men?"

Karp shrugged. "Who knows? They haven't turned up. Maybe Tona iced them. So, in all respects, a very unsatisfactory conclusion."

"Wasn't justice served, though?"

" 'A lawyer has no business with justice'!" replied Karp with some heat. "Samuel Johnson, since we're being literary, quoted by an old criminal law professor of mine. He used to say, 'We follow the law, bring cases, and let justice fall from heaven, if it will.' I agree. We get into shitloads of trouble if we presume to dispense justice."

The cab disgorged them at the loft. Marlene grabbed the mail from the floor of the entryway and flew up the stairs like a mountain goat, still delighting in her regained mobility. Karp trudged behind, holding the baby in the plastic carapace that is the modern equivalent of the papoose.

"What's in the package?" he asked when their lamb was put away and they were sitting under the skylight at the big oak table.

"I don't know. Probably a baby present from some relative. Maybe one of yours for a change."

"Don't count on it," said Karp.

He sorted his mail and was thumbing through a new magazine when Marlene let out a shrill yelp and leaped up, knocking over her chair. Her face had gone chalk white and her hand was pressed over her mouth.

"What's wrong?" he cried in alarm.

She made a retching noise and ran to the toilet. He heard her violently dumping hors d'oeuvres.

He grabbed the package and looked into it, and it took him an uncomprehending moment to realize what he was looking at. The box contained, on a neat bed of bloody newspaper, the severed genitals of a male human being. Karp's stomach bounced a little too, and he felt giddy, but he did not fail to notice that tattooed on the shriveled penis's tip were two slanted blue eyes.

Marlene came out of the toilet with a cold washcloth on her head and collapsed on the couch.

"You OK?" Nod. "This is from Doone, right? It's the shooter."

"Yeah, the guy who grabbed me. Goddamn Doone, I knew I saw something cross his face when I took that diary. He set me up, the motherfucker! He wanted those guys and he knew they would follow the diary. He probably *told* them I had it. Why didn't I think of it before? How else could they have known?" She looked toward the box again and was seized with a long, flapping shudder.

"I want to go far away from people who send me body parts," she said with her eyes closed. "I want to teach literature and art to scrubbed schoolgirls, and I want to take Lucy to play groups at houses with lawns."

"It could be arranged," said Karp happily.

She shot him a sharp look. "We'll see. Meanwhile, what are we going to do with *it*?"

"We could have it bronzed," he said. "A conversation piece?"

"Stop! Be serious! I mean really."

"Really?" he mused. "Really, I think we should re-pack it and send it to Jerry Thelmann."

"Is that legal?"

"Of course. Isn't it a part, so to speak, of the case we've been kanoodling with? And hasn't Jerry announced to everybody that he's in complete charge of the case? What could be more fitting? And, anyway, it's a fucking Queens case."

Marlene thought about this for a while, and then began to giggle, thoughts of scrubbed schoolgirls flying from her mind. "That's great," she said. "Christ, I'd like to be there when he opens it. Do you think he'll like it?"

"I don't know," said Karp. "But in any case, it's the thought that counts."

We invite you to preview the new
Butch Karp novel . . .

JUSTICE DENIED

by Robert K. Tanenbaum

now available from Dutton

A fat man with a jaunty air and five minutes left to live walked out of the Izmir Restaurant on Third Avenue and 46th Street on the island of Manhattan and turned east. He moved with the twinkle-footed gait adopted by many of the stout, but his progress would have been faster had he not, at nearly every convenient window, slowed to check his image in the reflecting glass. He saw a bland and moonlike face, neatly mustached in the manner of the late King Farouk, a face that demanded topping with a fez, but which at the moment supported (almost as archaic) a smoke-colored homburg hat. Below the man's several chins there was a heavy silk rolled collar, a large-knotted Sulka tie in burgundy, and a dark double-breasted pinstripe suit of a beautiful, if antique, cut. Small oxblood cordovan shoes were on his feet, kid gloves were on his hands, and he had a fawn cashmere topcoat resting on his shoulders, in the manner of Italian filmmakers of the fifties.

It was a Sunday morning, and if few of the other strollers were as formally dressed as the fat man, he did not draw unusual attention, not in that neighborhood. The United Nations, whose headquarters stands on First Avenue between 48th and 42nd streets, employs thousands of diplomats, most of whom live in the immediate area, and many of whom are peculiar in their dress. The fat man was, in fact, one of these, a diplomat, although his mission this morning, as every Sunday morning, was personal.

He was a man of fixed habits. Each morning, save for the holy day of Friday, he arrived at the Izmir at eight and ate Turkish pastries and drank thick, sweet coffee, while he perused the *New York Times* and *Washington Post,* together with the previous day's editions of an Istanbul and an Ankara newspaper that had come by air. This occupied no more than ninety minutes.

Thereafter, on the four weekdays and Saturday, he would walk down 46th Street to the tall slab of One U.N. Plaza, where he had his office. On Sunday, he would instead turn south on First to the Tudor City apartment block, where he had his mistress.

He had reached the intersection of Second and 46th. Traffic was light, but there were a number of pedestrians about, enjoying the late winter sunshine. A young woman in a stocking cap walked a blond afghan hound. A couple in Norwegian sweaters pushed a stroller containing a well-bundled toddler. A blue-black man in a Burberry loden coat and an African cap spoke in French to a like-colored woman wearing a turban. Across the street, the proprietor of a northern Italian restaurant unrolled his awning. It was a peaceful Sunday in one of the more peaceful and pleasant of

New York's neighborhoods, a district that was exotic without any of the danger usually associated with that characteristic, and policed like the Kremlin because of all the diplomats.

The light changed, and the fat man twinkled across the broad avenue, casting an interested glance at the girl with the afghan. As he mounted the curb, he heard a car door open, and a figure moved into his path. The morning sun pouring eastward formed a corona around the shape of a man. The fat man smiled and politely moved to his right, but the shape moved to block his way. The fat man looked more closely at the person before him, squinting hard against the light. There was something wrong about the man's head: it was bright blue—he was wearing a ski mask.

The fat man turned sharply, alarm now flooding his body, and saw that there was another man blocking his path to the west. He had no difficulty seeing that this man wore a ski mask and a blue parka, and that there was an automatic pistol in his hand.

The fat man was frightened, but he was not a coward. He was a Turk, and Turks are tenacious in defense. He grabbed the lapel of his slung topcoat, whipped it out at the face of the man in front of him, and took three rapid steps toward Second Avenue. He heard a woman scream, and shots, many shots, and felt them strike his body, and saw the white, distorted face of the girl with the afghan whirling across the sky as he fell.

The police were there in four minutes, a sergeant and a patrolman from the permanent mobile post set up at the U.N. to control the almost perpetual demonstrations. They secured the crime scene, rounded up a group of stunned witnesses, and made the necessary calls. They prevailed on the proprietor of the Villa d'Este Restaurant to make a room available for processing these.

Shortly thereafter came the meat wagon from the medical examiner and the car from the crime scene unit and an unmarked Plymouth Fury containing two homicide detectives out of Midtown South. The two detectives were a Mutt and Jeff act: one tall, angular, watery-eyed, with a lugubrious tan fringe hanging below his boney nose—Barney Wayne; the other, shorter, younger by a dozen years, stockier, darker, a feisty man and a cigar chomper—Joe Frangi.

Both of them bore the rank of detective second grade. Wayne thought that being a detective second grade was pretty good going. He was not the sort of Wayne who gets called "Duke" in the NYPD. Frangi thought the same but also thought that he himself was good enough for the gold hat and meant to get one. Frangi thought Wayne was a good guy but a little too cautious. Wayne thought Frangi was a good guy but a little too reckless. They were a reasonably good team: neither the flawless heroes of the TV shows nor the corrupt villains of the hard-hitting investigative reports. Like most NYPD detectives, they were somewhat heroic and somewhat corrupt.

Wayne and Frangi introduced themselves to the sergeant. He was glad to see them, and to turn over possession of the crime scene. The sergeant was a detective from Brooklyn who had been placed back in uniform on a series of crummy details, of which this U.N. thing was one. Placing detectives "back in the bag," as the saying went, usually for crowd-control duties, is a means of petty discipline and harassment in the NYPD, and is one reason why crowd control in the city is often unpleasant for the crowd.

"What do we got, Sarge?" asked Frangi.

The sergeant gestured at the prostrate corpse. "They hit him at ten past eleven. It's a fresh one. The owner of that Italian restaurant called it in."

Frangi said, " 'They'? We have witnesses?"

The sergeant nodded. "Yeah, at least a half a dozen. I put them over in the restaurant. Two guys in ski masks did it and got out in a blue car." He pointed to where crime-scene technicians were photographing the tire marks left by the putative blue car.

"They hauled ass down Forty-sixth. They must have come right by me."

"You didn't spot the car?"

The sergeant shrugged, then laughed. "Hey, I got my hands full with the fuckin' Palestinians or Pakistanis or whatever the fuck they are."

The sergeant was about to get himself in trouble trying to think of a way to explain how a blue car with two assassins in it driving like a bat out of hell away from a place where moments before at least ten shots had been fired, that place being not a hundred yards from the sergeant's own command post, had escaped all notice. Embarrassed for the man, Frangi forestalled any further lies by asking the sergeant to show him the witnesses. They walked off toward the restaurant.

Wayne approached the corpse. As usual at such moments, he let his mind go blank, so as to convert it into a receptive sponge for any clues that might be invisible to the willing intellect. As usual, his mind remained blank, except for a vague sadness about the finality of death. The murdered man was not wearing two different shoes or unmatched socks. He did not have in his mouth, which was open and full of congealing blood, a mysterious signet ring, and Wayne, sighing, did not believe that he would find in the man's pocket a torn matchbook with the killer's name written on it.

Wayne moved away to let the crime-scene man put plastic bags over the victim's hands, a routine procedure, and then, stepping carefully to avoid soaking his shoes in the thick blood, he went through pockets.

Frangi, meanwhile, was getting names and addresses of the eyewitnesses and writing down where they had been at the time and place of the crime and whether they had seen anything. He decided to start with the young dog walker, who was apparently the witness closest to the crime. She had by this time recovered from her hysterics and was sipping coffee. Her afghan was quivering at her feet, chewing on a beef knuckle supplied by the proprietor.

He established the basic facts: two shooters, both had shot. There was no talking from either the shooters or the victim. The victim had tried to get away by flinging his coat. The shooters had not taken anything from the victim. They had re-entered their car and driven off.

No, she hadn't taken down the license number. No, she hadn't recognized the make of the car. Yes, she would be able to look at different pictures of cars. No, she didn't notice anything peculiar about the shooters. They were average. She couldn't tell their race because they were wearing ski masks and gloves.

The other witnesses added little to this except that, by a miracle, the restaurant proprietor had spotted the car for a '77 or '78 Ford Fairlane two-door. His sister had one just like it.

Wayne watched the body being bagged and loaded into the waiting M.E. wagon, and he then put the evidence bags with the pocket contents into a cheap plastic briefcase and walked over to the restaurant.

The press had picked up the scent already, and the sergeant had called in a few troops to handle the growing crowd of journalists and photographers. People shouted questions at Wayne and poked microphone tubes at him and held up recorders in the din to catch some marketable vibrations from his lips. He waved them off and pushed past into the restaurant along a path kept clear by the uniformed men.

Wayne put his briefcase on the table where Frangi was sitting and sat down himself.

"Have some coffee," Frangi said. "It's the first time I ever got good coffee on a crime scene. Probably the last too. I hear the jackals make it for a terrorist attack."

Wayne raised an eyebrow. "We're always the last to know. The target's right, anyway." He removed a clear plastic evidence bag from his briefcase. It had in it a long European–style notecase that had once been tan but was now almost entirely covered with red-brown stains. It had a rough half-inch hole punched through it.

"Got one right through the passport. The vic's name is Mehmet Ersoy. He's the cultural attaché at the Turkish embassy to the U.N."

"Holy Christ! Ah, crap! The slicks'll be all over us on this one."

"Yep. I'm surprised they're not here already. Uh-oh, I spoke too soon. They're playing our song."

The sound of sirens coming closer could be heard. "Hey, I just remembered," said Wayne. "Did you call D.A. Homicide?"

This was new. An instruction had been passed down from the chief of detectives that the detective in charge of a crime scene in a suspected homicide was to call the newly reconstituted homicide bureau of the New York D.A.'s office immediately upon arrival at the crime scene.

Frangi said, "Yeah, I made the call. Our luck, we'll get a fourteen-year-old girl just out of law school."

Now the little restaurant's window reflected the beams of half a dozen red lights as the slicks arrived, in increasing order of rank, for it would never do for a superior officer to arrive on a scene without his inferiors stacked up to show that they too were on top of things, and there was an elaborate system of delays and phone calls built into the vitals of the NYPD that insured that such would ever be the case.

Thus Wayne and Frangi had to tell their story to the lieutenant in charge of their precinct squad, who told it to the duty captain, who informed the deputy chief in charge of Manhattan, who told the deputy commissioner, who told the deputy mayor. It was somewhat unusual to have a deputy mayor on a slick, but the mayor knew that the U.N. brought forty thousand jobs to New York, and he was determined to let the world know that whether or not lesser New Yorkers fell like flies, the flesh of the international community was as sacred to him as that of his sainted mom.

After the word had gone down, and the deputy mayor had posed gravely before the cameras to ritually renew the city's marriage to the World Body and its every minion; and after the man from the P.C.'s office had come out strongly against terrorism in general and especially in New York (not forgetting to boast about the matchless anti-terrorism capacity of the NYPD); and after each level of command had left in decreasing order of rank, each one telling the next one down that there better not be a fuck-up on this one, they wanted clearance *yesterday,* and whosoever got the blame if there were to be a fuck-up (and it would certainly not be *himself*) would spend the rest of their career in a blue bag guarding a motor pool in the South Bronx; after all that, when there was no one left in the restaurant but the lieutenant, the two detectives, half a dozen irritable witnesses, a restaurateur wondering whether a story he would tell for years was worth losing a Sunday lunch hour, and a dog who had to pee, Wayne said, "Hey, Lou, could you tell us one thing? What's all this horseshit about terrorists? We don't know zip yet. The guy's old lady could've had him whacked for the insurance or something."

The lieutenant stared at him. He motioned the two detectives to follow him into the restaurant's small bar.

"Nobody told you?"

"Nah," said Frangi. "I mean, what the fuck, we're just the detectives on the case, why give us any information? It'd be like cheating . . ."

"A guy called the *Post* and CBS. He gave the time and place and the name of the vic and said that he was the Armenian Secret Army, and then a lot of political horseshit. We got a transcript back at the house."

"Armenians, huh?" said Wayne. "You think it's legit, Lou?"

The lieutenant rolled his eyes. "The fuck I know. The brass wants a terrorist. If it turns out the guy was dorking some big *gaucho*'s kid sister, well, we'll have to work around it. But, guys—I need speed on this one. Whatever your need—cars, radios, stealers up the ying-yang, whatever. Red ball, all right?"

Wayne and Frangi exchanged a look. Wayne said, "We'll toss his place, see if he's into anything naughty. His office too, maybe . . ."

"Uh-uh, the office is out. It's foreign territory," said the lieutenant. "The guy's a dip; we're gonna move like silk around most of the people he knows. You understand the drill."

"It's like parking tickets," said Wayne.

The lieutenant shaped his face into a false smile. "You got it. No leaning. Please, thank you, yessir, nosir. Any intrusion on U.N. mission property, and that includes motor vehicles, has to be cleared up the chain to the P.C. After you've made your calls and figured out who you need to talk to at the mission, if anyone, I need to clear it in writing. There's a form." The lieutenant paused and lit a cigarette from the butt of his old one. He asked, "You run the car yet? No? Well, get on it, and when you get the printout, check it for Armenian names."

"Armenian names?" asked Frangi wonderingly. "You think these big-time terrorists used their own car on a hit?"

"It shows movement, dammit," snapped the lieutenant. "And call B.S.S.I. too. There's a guy there, Flanagan, he's waiting for your call."

Frangi made a sour face. The Bureau of Strategic Services and Intelligence, the former Red Squad, was not popular with street detectives, who considered politically motivated crime of such trivial concern that it was not worth the time and money expended on it. Besides that, B.S.S.I. did not put people on the pavement, which meant they were kibitzers rather than helpers. The lieutenant caught the look. "Just do it!" he said. "Okay, you got the word. I want to be kept up on this on a daily basis, follow?"

Frangi let his head loll and dangled his arms at shoulder height, miming a marionette. In a squeaky voice he said, "Hi, kids! I'm a detective. Want to play with me?"

The lieutenant shook his head and allowed himself a sour grin as he left.

Wayne said, "Movement, huh? Tell me, you think this case is gonna be a serious pain in the ass, or what?"

"Well, the first movement I'm gonna make is my bowels," replied his partner. "And after that, I think we should movement the witnesses out of here before they all starve to death."

"Yeah," Wayne agreed, "and speaking of which, we could make a movement toward getting some lunch. Maybe the guy here could give us some veal scallopini on the arm, seeing how we brightened up his day so much. Hello, Roland."

This last was directed toward a man who had just entered the restaurant. Both detectives smiled and greeted him warmly, because he was evidence that they would not, amid their other troubles, have to put up with a fourteen-year-old girl assistant D.A.

"You on this case, Roland? You poor bastard!" said Frangi with feeling.

Roland Hrcany, assistant D.A. in the homicide bureau, sat deliberately down on a chair and regarded the two detectives balefully. "You know what I was doing when you guys' call came in? Do you know? I was in my bed and I was chewing on a buttock the size and firmness of a ripe cantaloupe melon and letting the juice drip into my mouth."

"Not a voter, hey, Roland?" said Wayne.

"Correct in your surmise, Detective," said Hrcany. "Twenty is plenty. OK, what do we have on this abortion?"

They discussed the case, easily and humorously. They were all pros and had worked together many times before. Besides that, Roland was the most popular with all of the police of all the A.D.A.'s in Manhattan. It was his stock in trade and he worked at it. He was arrogantly male in the way that most cops conceived maleness: profane, violent, and a tremendous drinker. He knew hundreds of available women and had made dates for hundreds of cops, not that cops needed any help in that area, but the thought counted. He would also do favors for cops in the line of duty, save them from embarrassment in court when they had screwed up the evidence, or make a cop look particularly good, or help cops stack up overtime for court appearances around the holidays when they needed extra cash.

But most of all, there was the body. Roland Hrcany was a committed bodybuilder and weightlifter. He had twenty-seven-inch arms and a fifty-four-inch chest and a nineteen-inch neck. Cops are physical people. They believe they have to dominate physically to survive. Roland was physically dominating. That he was also a very smart, aggressive lawyer, capable of grinding mutts and their candy-ass lawyers to powder in court, was just the cherry on top.

They laid out the case, respectfully, knowing that Roland would understand the fix they were in with the slicks and sympathize, and he did. Roland interviewed the witnesses and dismissed them. Frangi went to the bathroom. The patrolmen stopped guarding the entrance, and the Villa D'Este opened for business.

Frangi came back. The proprietor walked over and, smiling, offered lunch, which they accepted. His place was going to be on television, and he was happy with the world. When they had been given a huge bread basket and a round of drinks, Wayne said, "So, Roland, what do you think? A ball breaker, right?"

"Not really, Barney. I got a good feeling about this one. I think it's gonna play right for us." The two detectives made skeptical noises, but Roland advanced his case with undiminished confidence. "No, look: they were waiting for the guy, this Ersoy. They were parked where they knew he was going to pass at that particular time. So they knew him . . ."

"Not necessarily," Frangi interrupted. "They could've been pros, casing him for weeks."

"Okay, or they know his habits, but no way they were pros. A pro who knew as much about the vic as these guys did would've waited by his apartment and given him three in the head from a small caliber gun."

"How can you say that, Roland? It's on TV all the time: the terrorists in Europe and the Middle East hit these politicians like a fucking army—machine guns, rockets . . ."

"Yeah, but those people are covered by heavy security. You can't get to them unless you blast your way through. Our guy was naked. He didn't feel threatened at all. So, of all the times to hit someone, why pick broad daylight on a Sunday, with your car pointed down a one-way street whose only outlet is through U.N. Plaza, which practically every other weekend is loaded with cops and demonstrators? It doesn't make sense, unless it's amateur hour."

"He's got a point, Joe," said Wayne.

Frangi replied, "Okay, fine—say I buy that, what does that give us?"

"It means," said Roland, "that either the killing comes out of his life, as usual, and the Armenian Army thing is horseshit, a dodge, or that you're looking for a bunch of Armenian assholes sitting around a kitchen table in Brooklyn. I mean, it's not gonna be Carlos the Jackal."

Wayne sighed. "Yeah, well, nothing against the Armenians, but that would suit me fine. We have to start tracing through this dude's life, we're talking weeks, swimming upstream against this diplomat shit all the way. So I guess we have to start with the blue car and the printouts and the Armenian names. And if you're right, they *might* have used their own car."

"They might have," Roland agreed. "But we still have to check out the vic. Did I see a safety deposit key on that case you took off him? Yeah? People with boxes usually have more interesting lives than most. You're going to toss his place today?"

The detectives looked nervously at each other. "Well, that's what I mean about swimming upstream; we got a lecture about being diplomatic," said Wayne. "The

brass wants us to go through the embassy on everything."

"Yeah, well, that's fine for the embassy personnel
and the office, but his personal place is our meat. It's
a felony investigation, not a parking ticket. If you get
any heat there, call me. I'll take it all the way up the
line, if I have to, and—"

He looked up, aware of a presence looming over
him. It was a very tall, very black man wearing a Burberry over a gray suit and a brightly colored pillbox
hat on his head. He had gold-rimmed spectacles. They
all stared. The man smiled and reached into his coat.
They all tensed, but he brought out only a leather card
case.

"Excuse me," the man said. "I understand you are of
the police?"

"Yeah," said Frangi. "Who're you?"

The man passed each a large, stiff engraved card declaring him to be M. Etienne Mbor Sekoué of the Sen-
egalese mission to the U.N. He said, "I extremely
regret not coming before this, but I felt it proper to escort my sister home. She was entirely devastated by
the lamentable events of this morning. It is her first
visit to New York and ..."

"Wait a minute, you're a *witness*?" Frangi exclaimed.

"Yes, I approached one of the officers on the street
and they directed me here."

"Please sit down, Mr. Sekoué," said Roland. "Tell us
what you saw." Wayne brought out his notebook and
said, "Where were you when the shooting took place?"

The African settled himself at the table's fourth seat.
"I ... we, that is, my sister and myself, were on point
of crossing the street when we heard the shots
commence—a fusillade."

Wayne frowned. The man had been farther away

from the action than some of the other witnesses. He asked a few more questions about the movements of the killers and their victim, but this merely confirmed what they already had. "Anything else, Mr. Sekoué? Did you notice anything unusual about the killers? Or their car?"

"Of the assassins? No, no one could see anything of them. Their masks, their gloves. As to the car," he smiled self-deprecatingly, "it was a large American car, new, of the color dark blue. I am not familiar with the American marques." He paused. "Surely, however, you will be able to search it, having the license number, no?"

Frangi said, "Sure, if we had the number, but we don't."

M. Sekoué's spectacles glittered when he smiled. "Ah, but I have written it down, you see."

And he had. Before their amazed faces he produced a tiny leather address book with a gold pencil attached. A license number had been neatly written inside the back cover. Wayne wrote it down in his notebook. The three men thanked the diplomat profusely, and he departed.

"That's the kind of brother we need more of in this town," said Frangi with feeling. "Now, five bucks says it's ripped off and we're back to zero. You want to make the call, Barney?"

Wayne nodded and walked over to the pay phone in the bar. He dialed and had a brief conversation. Roland and Frangi sat waiting, not speaking. Wayne came back to the table and sat down. "It's not on the latest hot sheet. The next one's not due for a couple of hours, so it could have been boosted this morning and the guy hasn't missed it yet . . ."

"Barney, for chrissake, *who owns the fucking vehicle*?" cried Frangi.

Wayne smiled broadly. "How do you like Aram Tomasian? A local boy. Lives on Murray Hill."

Roland Hrcany laughed out loud. Frangi raised his eyes to the ceiling and said, "Thank you, Jesus!"

ROBERT K. TANENBAUM

Praised by authors from Ann Rule and William Caunitz to Vincent Bugliosi and Joseph Wambaugh, and by newspapers from the *New York Times* and *New York Daily News* to the *Los Angeles Times*, ex-New York Assistant District Attorney Robert K. Tanenbaum delivers courtroom drama, suspense, and crime fiction of the highest order.

Years on the front line of Manhattan's criminal justice system serving as chief of the Homicide Division afford Tanenbaum a unique perspective into the seamy core of the Big Apple. Only rarely does an author emerge with Tanenbaum's hard-won experience and natural storytelling gifts. And even more rarely does such an author write the intelligent and gut-wrenching kind of suspense that Tanenbaum has provided in spades with his five bestselling Butch Karp novels.

NO LESSER PLEA

"A fast moving, no-nonsense, insider's tale of crime and punishment. . . . Highly recommended!"
—*Los Angeles Times*

"A powerful, exciting tale of a young D.A.'s dogged pursuit of a mass murderer . . . bristles with authenticity." —*Kirkus Reviews*

The novel that started it all. Roger "Butch" Karp is a handsome young D.A. with an insatiable lust for justice. And he won't rest until he gets no lesser plea than "guilty of murder" out of a vicious assassin. Mandeville Louis had just killed two people in cold blood, then cleverly threw a phony crazy fit in court and walked away from his trial. Now, laying in wait in a psychiatric ward until the heat is off, Louis may slip through the system again. But Karp refuses to let go of the man who laughs at the law while he kills and kills again. For even in the relative security of a mental hospital, Louis's killing spree is not over, as Karp's beautiful colleague, Marlene Ciampi, becomes an unwitting pawn in the two men's deadly battle of minds . . . and murder.

No Lesser Plea is a breathtakingly gritty novel of the intricacies of big-city crime and the crumbling rule of law. Here, Tanenbaum lays bare the political truths that govern the pursuit of criminals and confirms the opinion that our system of criminal justice is neither systematic nor just — only criminal. If you wonder why the streets aren't safe, *No Lesser Plea* will tell you, and if you think they are, this powerful thriller will set you straight.

DEPRAVED INDIFFERENCE

Depraved Indifference brings Butch Karp face to face with his dirtiest job yet, as he confronts a master terrorist whose latest hijacking results in the death of a New York cop. The prosecution of Croat nationalist Djordje Karavitch and his band of murderers looks to be an open-and-shut case. But the trial takes on astounding proportions when Karp learns that organizations from the FBI and the NYPD to organized crime and Israeli intelligence all seem to be trying to protect the terrorists and hamstring the D.A's investigation. Karp's renowned prosecution skills and his nose for high-level corruption may have met their match as the conspiratorial web widens to include a defense team financed by the Archdiocese, Cuban guns, and a bomb that turns out to be a fiendishly clever Nazi relic. Without even the support of his own boss, Karp turns to his fellow attorney and lover, Marlene Ciampi. Together they must determine who wants to protect a band of terrorists and why, and then prove the cop killers guilty of taking human life with a depraved indifference.

IMMORAL CERTAINTY

"Convincing . . . shocking . . . begins in high gear and remains there!"   —*Dallas Times Herald*

"A bladed look at that nasty game called criminal justice. Tanenbaum is a writer whose perceptions you can trust, and the heroine of the book, Marlene Ciampi, is a passionate woman you could easily fall in love with. Tanenbaum's world, in and out the courtroom, may seem brutal and byzantine—unfortunately, it's all too real."—Clifford Irving, author of *Final Argument* and *Trial*

Immoral Certainty pits Butch Karp, an attorney who cares, against a killer who doesn't. The result is a multilayered thriller that reunites Karp and his tough-but-sweet colleague/girlfriend Marlene Ciampi in a monumental struggle through New York's darkest alleys and City Hall's red tape, as they race against time to unravel three savage murders that are bound in one deadly knot.

Heading their list of suspects is a handsome, charming, and vicious psychopath whose looks and manners make women his prey and the law his dupe. But he is only the first link in a twisted human chain that includes atrocities at a child daycare center, a deadly Mafia connection that takes Karp to California to cut an intricate deal with the mob, a showdown with a master defense attorney, and, casting a lengthening shadow, the monstrous figure that child victims call "the Boogeyman," whose unmasking is as startling as it is shattering. As Karp and Marlene are caught in the eddies and swirls of their investigations, their own relationship also becomes increasingly complex, until a shocking kidnapping occurs that threatens everything Butch Karp holds dear. . . .

With edge-of-the-seat suspense and authenticity, Tanenbaum offers a terrifying insight into the mind of a criminal who kills with the "immoral certainty" that he'll never pay for his crime.

REVERSIBLE ERROR

"A legal thriller that flies along with the breath of life ... this is the real stuff ... Tanenbaum knows his territory.... *Reversible Error* grabs and propels us." —*Rocky Mountain News*

"Excellent ... a revealing portrayal of crime ... a tense, exciting read." —*St. Louis Post-Dispatch*

Major drug dealers are being gunned down in the mean streets of Harlem, and a twisted rapist is victimizing women throughout the city. Butch Karp and his feisty lover, Marlene Ciampi, are faced with a pair of challenges that will take them dead center into New York's urban jungle. Butch and Marlene find their most solid allies are three renegade cops, known as the King Cole Trio, whose rough methods mock the law Karp is sworn to uphold. Already the three loose cannons are bending rules beyond the breaking point to find the murderer and the serial rapist.

As legal glitches threaten to make the rapist untouchable, Karp finds that cracking the drug-killings case may be more difficult than anything he's ever faced, for he discovers that old friends in the police department may actually have had their fingers on the triggers. The pressure builds as a cabal of fat cats woos Karp to run for the post of district attorney while his orders coming from the halls of power are to suppress evidence! Who in city government or on the police force can Butch Karp trust? Whom should he suspect? Whom would he be wise to fear? And how can he protect Marlene as she goes underground to catch the elusive pattern rapist? This is Robert K. Tanenbaum's home turf, a place where fiction is as hard and unrelenting as fact. *Reversible Error* is a razor-sharp legal thriller you can't afford to miss.

OFFICIAL **MUSIC TO YOUR EARS** COUPON

Enclosed please find _____ proof-of-purchase coupons from my Penguin USA purchase.

I would like to apply these coupons towards the purchase of the following Mercury artist(s): (Please write in artist selection and title)

_____   _____

_____   _____

_____   _____

I understand that my coupons will be applied towards my purchase at these discounted prices. *

Two book coupons	CD $13.99	CT $8.99
Four book coupons	CD $12.99	CT $7.99
Six book coupons	CD $11.99	CT $6.99

(* Once coupons are sent, there is no limit to the titles ordered at this reduced rate)

Please check one:

___Enclosed is my check/money order made out to: **Sound Delivery**

___Please charge my purchases to:

Amex#	_____	exp. date_____
MC#	_____	exp. date_____
Visa#	_____	exp. date_____
Discover#	_____	exp. date_____
Diners#	_____	exp. date_____

Please send coupons to: **Sound Delivery**
P.O. Box 2213
Davis, CA 95617-2213

NAME_____

ADDRESS_____

CITY_____STATE_____ZIP_____

All orders shipped 2-Day UPS mail from time of receipt.
Offer expires December 31, 1994 • Printed in the USA

And everyone who redeems a coupon is automatically entered into the **MUSIC TO YOUR EARS SWEEPSTAKES!** The Grand Prize Winner will win a trip to see a Mercury Records artist in concert anywhere in the continental United States.

For complete sweepstakes rules, send a stamped, self-addressed envelope to: Rules, MUSIC TO YOUR EARS SWEEPSTAKES, Penguin USA/Mass Market, Department KB, 375 Hudson St., New York, NY 10014. Offer good in U.S., its territories and Canada (if sending check or money order, Canadian residents must convert to U.S. currency).